a thriller novel

Also by Danielle Morris

Birds of a Feather
The Mistletoe Feud
In All My Dreams
Out of the Woods
Live, Laugh, Murder

LIVE, LAUGH, muRDeR

a thriller novel

DANIELLE MORRIS

Paperback ISBN 979-8-9876836-3-7

Cover Design by Katie Jaspersen @ K. Jaspersen Designs

Chapter headings & interior formatting made with Canva & Atticus

Edited by Rebecca McDermott

OFFICIAL PLAYLIST

"Manchild" - Sabrina Carpenter
"Sorry I'm Here For Someone Else" - Benson Boone
"Love Song" - The Cure
"Ivy" - Taylor Swift
"Taste" - Sabrina Carpenter
"Stargazing" - Myles Smith
"Mad Woman" - Taylor Swift
"Watch Me" - The Phantoms
"Spitting Off the Edge of the World" - Yeah Yeah Yeahs
"Dirty Little Secret" - The All-American Rejects
"Don't Turn Around" - Ace of Base
"You asked for this" - Halsey
"no body, no crime" - Taylor Swift
"Tear You Apart" - She Wants Revenge
"CANCELLED" - Taylor Swift
"Burn" Billy Burke
"I am not a woman, I'm a god" - Halsey

courtesy of Madeleine @berges_books

Author's Note

Dear Reader,

Thank you so much for picking up LIVE, LAUGH, MURDER. I hope you find something that resonates with you as you read. That said, this book addresses some heavier topics that may be triggering for some of you. There's only one of you in this world, and I firmly believe in taking care of yourself first—forever and always.

I've listed some content warnings below for those who might need them:

Graphic death + gore
Mentions of sexual assault - recounted in flashbacks
Mentions of pregnancy loss/abortion - recounted in flashbacks
Mentions Pro-Choice/Pro-Life
Death of parents/orphaned adult child
Adult alcohol usage
Adult language
Cheating
Thoughts of self-harm/suicide ideation (not acted upon)

I hope you find some of yourself scattered throughout this story of mine—it's definitely my wildest one to date. My whole heart has been poured onto these pages, and it means the world to me that you've picked this book up and are giving it a chance.

Love always,
Danielle

Prologue

We shouldn't have come here.

We fell for this twisted trap like mice lured in with the promise of cheese.

We weren't supposed to end up like this.

But I guess that's what happens when you reach for the stars when you were only meant to admire them from afar.

They burn you.

Scald you.

Searing you into nothing but a flame of regret.

Much like the flame alight in the roaring fireplace before us.

Our captor walks back into the room with a duffel bag slung over his muscled shoulder.

His mouth turns into a wicked smile as he takes the three of us in with his dark, amused eyes. The duffel bag drops to the ground with a loud thunk, and he winks at me as he kneels to open it. The sound of the zipper reverberates through the large study, making my insides quiver in fear. A fear like one I've never known before.

One by one, he takes three items and places them at our feet.

A dagger.

A butcher knife.

And a pair of metal handcuffs.

"Come on, Teagan," he says with a sneer. "Which one of your friends gets to live?" He sweeps his arm toward Lexi and Capri like this is some game.

But this isn't a game to any of us.

This is *our* lives. And possibly, *our* deaths.

I look at my two best friends in the world and tell them with my eyes how sorry I am for dragging us into this. My mouth is gagged, and my body bound by tape to the plush velvet teal chair.

They both glance back at me, tears trailing down their beautiful faces as they shake their heads at me.

We know this is how we die—together until the very end.

We shouldn't have come here.

PART ONE:
THE INVITATION

CHAPTER ONE

TeaGan

TWO WEEKS EARLIER

"Alright, my thriller-loving queens—and kings, that's it for this week's episode of *Live, Laugh, Murder*," Capri says into her pink microphone. "Catch us next week for another deep dive on how to survive a thriller novel—because you know there's always a way to have more than one final girl—or guy!"

"Until then, our dearest listeners," Lexi purrs before the three of us yell, "Live, Laugh, and Murder your little hearts out!"

Shouting our podcast slogan has always been my favorite part of recording sessions.

I hit stop on our recorder and grin at my two best friends in the world. "Another fantastic episode, if I do say so myself."

Capri yanks her headset off, tossing it onto the sofa next to her, and pulls out her hair tie. She shakes her teal and pink braids loose and lets out a huff of air. "That might have been our best episode. I don't know how we'll top that one."

"I do feel a little bad about how harsh we were about this particular author's books," Lexi chimes in as she stares down at her notes.

I roll my eyes at her—not that she's paying attention. "I would feel bad because A. M. Pierce is our all-time favorite thriller author," I say. "But they're a recluse. They don't even have social media, so it's not like they'll ever listen to our silly little podcast on how shitty their character's survival skills are."

Capri gives me a slow clap from her end of the couch. Capri has always been our biggest hype girl. She never misses an opportunity to make each of us feel seen and be heard.

"Did you guys see this comment on our last video?" Lexi says loud enough to tear me out of my thoughts. "We've been dubbed 'The Thriller Queens'! How freaking cool does that sound?"

"I think we should make stickers with that on them," Capri muses as we both lean toward Lexi to see the comments. "Or maybe hats! We could take some disgustingly cute selfies in them for the website!"

My front door opens, and we all turn to see my boyfriend Josh walking in with a bouquet of pink flowers. Peonies, my favorite.

"Oh," he says wide-eyed when he enters the living room. "I didn't realize the girls would be here today." The tips of his ears turn red along with the blush that creeps up his neck and over his cheeks as he sets the flowers on my entryway table with his keys. "I'll, um, go somewhere else?"

Capri is the first to stand, and she grabs her bag from the floor. "We are on our way out, Romeo. Lee was expecting me home an hour ago." She winks at me, grabs Lexi's purse from the table, and shoves it at her. "Let's go, Lex. It's date night for these two lovebirds."

Lexi looks up from her phone and blinks. "Oh, hi Josh," she mumbles as she takes her bright green purse from Capri. "Bye, Josh."

They both wave at me as Josh opens the door for them.

"See you later, Teagan. We still on for books and coffee Sunday?" Lexi asks hesitantly.

Something has seemed a bit off with her lately, and I make a mental note to text her later to see what's up. She goes through spells like this occasionally, and I know she'll tell me once Capri isn't around.

Capri may be the one who lights up my world on the darkest days. But Lex will always be my person, and I can read her like a book.

I grin at Lexi and throw a pair of finger guns her way. "Of course I'll be there. It's not like it hasn't been a permanent date on our calendars for the last three years." I wink. "You girls get home safe. Love you."

"Love you!" they say in unison.

Josh locks the door behind them after they leave, and I jump over the back of the couch and wrap my arms around him from behind.

"Hi, babe," I say as he turns in my arms to face me. "I've missed you today."

Josh reaches up, cups my face with both hands, and stares into my eyes. His own dark eyes sparkle whenever he does this, making me smile from ear to ear.

It's one of those private moments between couples that feels immensely intimate.

"I've missed you, too," he whispers before he kisses my forehead.

I could die of happiness every time he does that. Forehead kisses are every girl's secret Achilles heel, and any girl who says otherwise is a damn liar.

Josh releases me, grabs the flowers he left on the table, and hands them to me. "Happy anniversary, Teagan."

I bring the peonies to my face and inhale deeply as I take in what he said.

Oh crap.

I forgot our anniversary.

Our *first* anniversary.

I look up at him and give him my most convincing smile. "Thank you for the flowers, they're beautiful. You'll get your gift later tonight," I tease. "If you know what I mean."

Josh's smile slowly fades as he looks down at me, and I know that I'm screwed. He can smell a lie from my lips quicker than a bloodhound.

"You forgot, didn't you? You spent all day with your friends and forgot about our anniversary?" Josh stares at me, and I see the tick in his jaw—the one tell he has that shows he's angry. "Our *first* anniversary? The one I've been reminding you of for weeks now!"

"I might have forgotten, but I'll make up for it!" I promise as he scoffs and rubs a hand through his dark hair. "I'm sorry! Today was a super important episode! We needed to get it done so we can spend Sunday editing it! You know how much I love talking about A. M. Pierce's books! This is my career, Josh."

"Career...right." He rolls his eyes at me and doesn't elaborate.

"And what exactly do you mean by that?" I glare up at him.

He shakes his head and rubs his temples. "What I mean is that this podcast isn't a real career. You know that, right? You're supposed to be working on becoming an author yourself, and instead, you dedicate your whole life to playing this influencer crap with your friends. You put them above everything, including your own dreams! Even your friends manage to have real careers. Lexi works at the architecture firm with me, and Capri is studying to be a nurse! All you've managed to do is gain followers by talking shit about *real*, published writers."

His emphasis on *real* makes me see red. "You can leave now," I say through gritted teeth. It's taking everything in me not to throw these flowers at him and chase him out of my life.

He may have been my partner for the last year, but he knows nothing about what I really want in my life.

Josh glares at me and shakes his head. "Then you should spend our anniversary with your favorite author and friends. I can't keep being second place to everyone else."

He grabs the door handle and squeezes it tight enough to make the veins in his hands bulge.

"I said you can leave. I'm not going to force you to be with me if you so clearly look down on my life choices," I feel a warm tear escape and roll down my cheek as I clench my fist around these flowers. I hate that I'm an angry crier.

Josh turns toward me, and the look in his eyes makes me step back. I've never seen him this angry before. "I don't want this to be the end of us. You know I love you. But the only way I stay is if you start to put me—*us*—before your friends and before your stupid podcast. Can you do that, Teagan? Do you even know how to breathe without them holding your hand through life?" he shouts.

I open my mouth to respond, to tell him I love him, too. To promise him that I'll start putting him above the girls and my career as soon as he agrees to look at me like someone he's proud of, but nothing comes out.

Because deep down, even though I know I love him, I can't put him above my friendships. Those girls saved me in a way I didn't think I needed. They have my whole heart.

Josh lets out another hideous scoff. "That's what I thought. I'm not going to compete with your friends anymore. I deserve better than half a girlfriend, Teagan."

And just like that, the first guy I ever loved walks out of my life, and I'm left with nothing but crushed flowers and a slammed door in my face.

But, he's right. He does deserve a better girlfriend. I take a deep breath to ground myself. If the tables were turned, I'd be hurt too. I adore my friends, but I love him and want to build a life with him. I've prioritized my friends and our podcast. Anytime Josh wanted to see me for lunch or dinner, I had to check to make sure I wasn't scheduled to see the girls first. I don't think I meant to do it, but somehow I've thrown him and his needs aside whenever Lexi or Capri wanted to see me.

I really messed up this time.

My heart races as I rush to the door and throw it open. "Josh! Wait!" I yell into the deserted hallway.

My feet hit the carpeted flooring faster than I've ever run as I chase after him, praying that he hasn't left yet.

I can fix this.

I have to fix this.

Josh may not be the most supportive of my career and friendships, but he's the love of my life, and I'm not ready to give up on us yet. I can't lose him because of my ego. I reach the end of the hallway and slam my hand onto the elevator button, pressing it repeatedly until the light above shows it's on my floor. The doors start to slide open following a loud ding, and I rush through the small gap, almost hitting the metal. The flowers fall from my hand as my body slams into someone. Their arms wrap around me as I catch my balance.

"Teagan?"

I look up, and the whole world falls back into place as my eyes meet Josh's. His jaw twitches, so I know he's still upset at me. He has every reason to be, though.

"Josh, you're still here!" I finally say.

"Forgot my keys in your apartment," he tells me through gritted teeth.

"I'm so sorry. You were right. About all of it." Tears slide down my cheeks, and I wipe them away quickly. Josh has never been one for crying, so I don't need to make this any worse than it already is. "I love you, and I'm not ready to lose you."

His eyes give away nothing as he continues to stare down at me. The elevator closes behind us, trapping us in this uncertain air.

Finally, after what feels like an entire lifetime, his mouth twists into the smallest of smiles as he reaches up and caresses my cheek softly. "You know I can't stay mad at you."

I have to force myself to keep the tears at bay.

"Promise me things will be different from now on?" he asks. "You can't keep putting me last, Teagan. I love you so much, but I deserve better than being an afterthought in your life."

I nod my head at him because I know if I try to talk right now, I'll turn into a sobbing mess and ruin this whole moment.

"Well then." He reaches down and picks up the few surviving flowers. "Happy anniversary, Teagan. I can't wait to spend many more together."

My smile feels bigger than my face as I take them from him and bring them to my nose, inhaling deeply.

"I love you," I promise him.

Josh's lips graze mine softly before his teeth nip at my lower lip more forcefully. "Now about that anniversary gift..." he mumbles through our tangled mouths just before he pushes me into the elevator wall.

I'm breathless as I reach out to push the button to open the doors. The two of us barely make it through the front door to my apartment before Josh rips at my clothes. His hands are rough and relentless as he takes what he needs from me.

It feels like an appropriate punishment after I almost let him walk away tonight.

CHAPTER TWO

Lexi

I'm soaking in a much-needed bath surrounded by bubbles and lavender-scented bath beads. This week has been tough on my soul, especially knowing what's coming up.

I need to stop. I need to be a better friend.

But I'm not, and I won't. I physically can't.

I've looked forward to this long soak of pity and self-loathing all week, and nothing can disrupt my self-imposed me time. That is, until I hear my phone ping and, based on the text tone, I know it's the group chat.

I really hope that it means something went excitingly wrong tonight instead of horribly right.

I'm the worst type of person.

I stand, grab my phone from the vanity, and settle back into the warm suds before tapping my message app.

THE THRILLER QUEENS

Teagan

> So Josh and I almost broke up tonight. He was seriously pissed at me.

Capri

Oh shit! Are you okay? Do you want me to slash his tires? Because you know I will.

Lexi

Let's not get arrested.

But seriously. Are you okay, T?

Teagan

I'm great, actually. Literally so great. I just feel like the worst girlfriend ever and he deserves so much better than me.

Capri

First off, you deserve the world so I don't want to hear any of that 'he deserves better' crap. OKAY? But what happened?

Teagan

I'm sort of embarrassed to tell you guys…

Capri

Spill it!!!

Teagan

We listen and we don't judge, right?

Lexi

Of course

Capri

What's said in the thriller queens, stays in the thriller queens! Now SPILL!

Teagan

I forgot about our anniversary.

Lexi

Wow. Even I knew that it was today…

Capri

HEY WE LISTEN AND DON'T JUDGE LEX

Lexi

Okay, okay. I'm sorry. And you guys didn't break up because of that??

Teagan

It was pretty touch and go there for a minute and I didn't think I'd be able to fix it. He told me he was done if I didn't start putting him first.

Capri

Well…I hate to be the adult here, but that sounds reasonable.

Teagan

I know! Which is why I said he deserves better than me. I might need to start putting less time into the podcast until things really simmer down. He hates that I spend so much time on it.

Capri

But you guys made up, right?

Teagan

Yeah, after I had to chase him down and literally crashed into him on the elevator. I promised him I'd do better and he forgave in the best way possible…if you know what I mean LOL.

Teagan

We've also made plans to go to Hawaii in two weeks to really celebrate. He's taking time off from work and everything!

Capri

TEAGAN! I am so here for it. Show that boy what he'll be missing if he leaves you, you little minx.

Lexi

What about the podcast? We can't record if you're in Hawaii for two weeks…

Capri

Don't rain on her parade, Lex! We can pre-record everything before she leaves. It's no biggie! You guys would do the same for me if I needed it!

Teagan

Good point, Lex! I'll plan the next two episodes out and we can get them done before I leave. All you ladies have to do is show up and talk trash with me LOL. Plus, Josh might kill me if I worked during our anniversary trip so let's get it done early!

Oops, gtg! Tall, dark, and epically handsome just turned the shower off! Want to meet up for lunch tomorrow and we can discuss the details?

Capri

You had me at food.

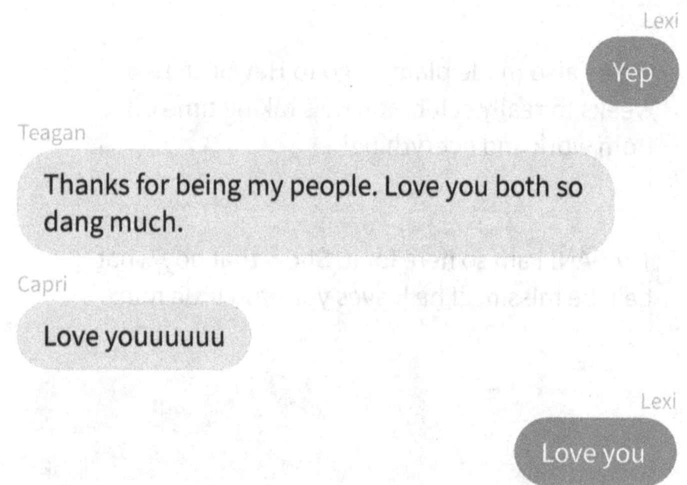

I toss my phone onto the plush pink rug and sink back into the warm embrace of lavender with a smile plastered on my face.

I truly am the worst friend in the world.

The plan was to sit in this bath and mope about my broken heart, but now I can't help but feel this rush of excitement flood my veins. I hurry through the motions of scrubbing my body and meticulously shaving everywhere.

He didn't propose to her.

But he did stay with her.

As soon as I step out of the draining tub and don my silk robe, the wave of emotions I feel about all of this makes me dizzy, and I grab onto the marble sink to catch myself.

What does she have that I don't?

I stare into the oval mirror and really look at myself. My blonde hair is limp around my face, dripping water from the ends down the bare skin of my cleavage. My lips twist into a scowl before I quickly run a brush through the damp strands, before twisting it into a bun.

Teagan has gorgeous, thick, dark brunette hair that is the envy of our friend group. She doesn't have to spend an hour each morning to get the frizz tamed and perfectly curled into soft waves like I do. Her hair is naturally just perfect. I swear she once told me she hardly even brushes it, yet it still looks like she walked straight out of a Vogue magazine.

I open my vanity drawer, pull out my face cream, and dab it around my eyes before gently rubbing it in, applying it where the wrinkles are more defined around my bright blue eyes. They are the one thing I have on Teagan. Her eyes are the darkest shade of brown, with absolutely no sparkle, unlike mine. Someone told me I had Disney princess eyes when I was a kid.

I never expected to grow up and fill the villain's shoes.

Before continuing down that rabbit hole of comparison, I hear a soft knock at my front door.

Could it really be him?

I quickly apply a mist of my favorite jasmine perfume before I head into the living room to answer. My heart is pounding with excitement, tinged with an ounce of regret as I place my hand on the knob. I shouldn't do this. I told myself the last time was the last time. But I've never been one to listen to reason.

Twisting the door handle, I pull my lips into a playful smirk as I pull it open. The person on the other side is not who I was expecting, though, and I gasp in surprise as I'm met with a bouquet of red roses in the hands of a stranger.

I hastily pull my robe closer to my chest to cover myself. "Umm, who are you?"

"Are you Lexi Casburn?"

I nod my head at the man.

"Well then, these are for you." He thrusts the bouquet into my hands. "Enjoy the rest of your night, Miss."

I'm confused and unsettled as I watch him leave down the steps and into his small hatchback car parked in my driveway. It isn't until he's turned off the street and completely out of sight that I finally go back inside and lock the door behind me.

Who sent me flowers?

Turning the bouquet in circles, I search for a card, but there isn't one. I inhale their familiar aroma as I head to my kitchen with the flowers cradled carefully in my arms in search of a vase for them.

I don't know who sent them or why, but I've never been one to let something beautiful go to waste.

Too bad I'm not something more beautiful.

He would have never seen me as a second choice if I were. He would have picked me.

I find a vase in the back of my overly cluttered cabinets and stick the roses in before adding water. I slide them to the middle of my kitchen island and then pour myself a large glass of Pinot.

I stare at the roses as I sip at my wine. They really are perfect. Each bud is close to blooming, but hasn't quite opened yet. It's been so long since I've received flowers—since I've received a gift from a man.

The men in my life only leave me broken.

I glance up at the photographs sitting above my fireplace.

There are so many of Teagan, Capri, and me. All happy, smiling, being silly in love with each other's friendship. My gaze lingers on a photo with our whole group at my birthday last month, and I walk over and pick it up. Capri and Lee are on one side of me, and Teagan and Josh are on the other as they hold up a giant chocolate cake covered in pink frosting. My name is spelled out with those cute letter candles, and we all have huge smiles.

It shouldn't hurt this much to see them together.

The frame comes apart easily from the back, allowing me to slip the photo free and bring it closer to my face. I look so happy here. You'd never guess I was burning with jealousy from the inside out.

Teagan and Josh only have eyes for each other in the photo. She has a giant smile as she looks at him, and he is caught mid-laugh at whatever she says to him.

The photo rips easily under my fingers as I tear it apart into neat strips. I place the piece of Capri and Lee back on the mantle and carry the rest to the couch.

I stare at the piece of Teagan and Josh. I should be happy for them, for the love she finally found for herself.

But I'm not.

I take a large gulp of my wine before I rip them away from each other and ball one half of the photo into my fist before tossing it towards the kitchen. I'll throw it away later.

Forcing the only two pieces of the photograph I left together, I can't help but smile. Instead of Josh laughing at something Teagan said, he's standing with me.

He only has eyes for me now.

The way it *should* be.

He said he was going to propose tonight. The fact that he didn't causes a blossom of hope to bloom inside me.

Maybe like my new roses, he'll make me bloom in time, too.

I'm a horrible person and an even worse friend—I really am. But the heart wants what the heart wants, and all I want is Teagan out of the way so I can finally have Josh the way I deserve him.

CHAPTER THREE

Capri

"**G**ood morning, sweetheart," Lee says with a smile as he cuddles me from behind.

I can't see his smile, but I know it's there. That happens when you've been married to the love of your life for years. You know them without having to ask.

I'm so incredibly thankful that Lee isn't like Josh. I can't imagine how much Teagan must force herself to smile while enduring Josh's selfishness.

"I don't want to turn and dragon breath you," I tell him with a snort. "But I do want to thank you for being so supportive of the podcast and my friends. Even when I don't make it home for dinner on time most nights."

Lee rubs his nose against my ear before squeezing me tighter to him. "I love how passionate you are about your work and the way you glow when you talk about it. I'd never want to stomp that light out of you," he whispers. "But what brought this topic on?"

This is what I love most about my husband. He sees me for who I am and loves all my bad habits as much as my good ones.

"Josh and Teagan almost broke up last night," I sigh. "He got upset that she forgot their anniversary, and he practically dumped her because he said she spends too much time with us, and on the podcast." Lee raises an eyebrow, but doesn't interrupt. "They didn't actually break up, though. Teagan promised him she'd start spending less time on the podcast and with us, and I don't know. It makes me so happy that you've never given me an ultimatum like that. It makes me love you more."

Lee lets out a low whistle. "Wow," he says. "I really thought they were in it for the long haul." He pinches his lips and shakes his head. "I don't know if any of you ladies would give up on each other the way he's expecting. He asked me for advice on picking out an engagement ring last month."

Dragon breath be damned. I roll over and stare into my husband's hazel eyes.

"He did WHAT?" I gasp. "You never told me that!"

The deep rumble of Lee's laugh loosens the tension in my chest as I stare at him in shock.

His fingers skate across my cheek, and he tucks my hair behind my ear with a soft smile. "I didn't tell you because it was supposed to be a secret." Lee lifts an eyebrow as I narrow my eyes at him. "And I knew if I told you, then Teagan would know within five minutes. You're the worst secret keeper on the planet, babe."

I can't help the grin that creeps over my face. "Dammit, I hate it when you're right."

"Yeah, but you love me."

I lean in and kiss him softly. "I sure freaking do. Now let's go brush our teeth so you can apologize for keeping such juicy gossip from me." I wink at him and slap his scrumptious behind before I hop out of bed as quickly as I can and race into the bathroom.

Lee chases me into the bathroom. I squeal as I try to shut the door behind me.

"Capri, you know that never works." Lee laughs as he pushes himself into the room with me.

He presses me against the bathroom sink and reaches to grab our brushes and the toothpaste with the most devilish smirk on his lips.

We stare at each other as we brush our teeth, taunting and teasing each other with a silent agreement not to touch. As soon as I rinse and dry my mouth, Lee's lips are on mine, and his hands tug my sleep shorts off.

We never make it back to bed.

"Hey, babe," Lee calls from the kitchen. "Did you happen to grab the mail last night? You know I'm still waiting on my official offer from the hospital."

Lee was just offered a position as the lead pediatric surgeon at the children's hospital in town. It means more on-call hours, but he's worked so hard to get here that I won't complain. Hopefully, I'll be working alongside him at the hospital soon. He's on paid leave until the official offer letter arrives, which is a significant perk since we hardly see each other with all our obligations. I have the podcast with the girls as I tackle the next step of nursing school, and Lee is about to start his dream job. Our marriage stays solid as long as he comes home to me at night.

"No, I didn't grab it last night!" I shout back from the bedroom. "Let me get some pants on, and I'll hop out and fetch it!"

Lee saunters back into the room, carrying a plate of my favorite breakfast: scrambled eggs, extra-crispy bacon, and buttered toast. He hands it to me and places a chaste kiss on my forehead. "You eat, I'll grab the mail. Your coffee is on the table."

This man is something special.

I'm munching on a slice of bacon as I make my way down the hall. Lee rushes back into the house with the biggest, dorkiest grin on his face.

"Is it your offer?" I ask with a mouth full.

Lee rolls his eyes like he always does when I talk while chewing. "No Baconator. It's actually something for you."

"For me?" I furrow my brows in confusion. "I didn't apply for any-thing."

"No, you didn't," Lee says hesitantly. "Now don't be mad, okay?" I narrow my eyes at him and wait for him to elaborate. "So you know how you and the girls are always talking about that thriller author? The recluse one?"

"Mhmm. A. M. Pierce."

"Well, a friend of mine heard about this once-in-a-lifetime meet and greet that the author is hosting," Lee explains as he hands me a dark, heavy envelope.

"They're inviting journalists, influencers, readers, anyone who knows anything about their books. Basically, anyone who can help document this unique experience—and I might have entered you girls with the help of a friend."

I look down at the envelope in my hands and gasp when I see the sender. Holy crap, it's A. M. Pierce.

"Lee," I say shakily. "Is this real?"

"Why don't we open it up and find out?" His words are soft as he comes to stand beside me. "I can't imagine they'd be cruel enough to send a rejection letter. An email would have sufficed."

I shove my thumb under the lip of the envelope and tug it open, giving myself a rather nasty papercut in my haste. I gently pull the letter out and sigh when I see that my finger is bleeding all over it.

"Can you grab me a napkin?" I ask Lee, unable to look away from the letter in my hands. The paper is some type of thick cardstock, and my heart feels like it's going to rip out of my chest as I unfold it.

Dear Lee Kim,

Thank you for your interest in this special event hosted by Author A. M. Pierce!

We are happy to announce that you and your party are officially invited to this once-in-a-lifetime meet-and-greet. As stated in your entry form, the host will cover all expenses. We ask that you and your party help document Pierce's special event.

The event will take place in two weeks, at Pierce's estate off the coast of Scotland.

Our travel agent will contact you shortly to help you and your party prepare.

Please let us know if you can come, and how many plus-one tickets you require. Each member is allowed one complimentary companion ticket.

We look forward to hosting you here in Scotland.

Safe travels,

Patricia Willis

Assistant to A. M. Pierce

Lee returns with our first-aid kit and tends to my finger as I read the letter from start to finish again.

I can't believe this is happening. We are going to meet the author who brought our friend group together. Besides Lee, Pierce is responsible for all the happiness in my life.

"All fixed," Lee muses. "What does it say?"

Hugging the letter to my chest, I turn and flash Lee the biggest smile. "It says that I have the world's greatest husband, and I think he might just get lucky with a round two this morning."

Lee's laugh echoes throughout our living room as he wraps me in his arms.

"Thank you, babe. This is amazing. I can't wait to tell the girls. You make all my dreams come true, you know that?"

His eyes twinkle as he stares down into mine. "You are my dream, Capri. Only you."

I kiss him softly as he strokes my cheek.

"I'll miss you while you're gone, though. The house will be so empty without you blasting your saucy audiobooks all the time," he says with a laugh.

"The term is *spicy*, not saucy, you dork," I tease. "And you won't have to worry about the house being silent," I smirk at him.

Lee raises an eyebrow at me.

"This invitation says we all get to bring a plus one. So get ready, babe. We're going to Scotland in two weeks!"

LIVE, LAUGH, MURDER
Episode 16

Teagan:

Welcome back to Live, Laugh, Murder, friends!
Teagan Shepherd here with my co-hosts, Capri
Hayes and Lexi Casburn! We're keeping this
episode short and sweet because our nearest
and dearest thriller girlie, Capri Hayes, will
become Capri KIM today! That's right, our
little final girl is getting MARRIED!

Lexi:

And they say romance doesn't belong in thriller
novels! I beg to differ. I love nothing more
than a love story mixed with a hefty dose of
trauma and murder!

Capri:

Thank you, thank you! I agree, Lex! There's
nothing I love more than an HEA at the end

of an emotionally devastating thriller! I'm
beyond ready to marry the love of my life. Hi,
Lee! I can't wait to kiss the crap out of you
at the end of that aisle today.

Lexi:
IT'S WEDDING DAY!!!!! IT'S WEDDING DAY!!!!!

Teagan:
Scream it louder for the listeners in the back,
Lex! Capri, you and Lee are the cutest, and
may we all find the happiness and love you
share for ourselves one day! But let's return
to our short and sweet episode before I have
to reapply my makeup for a third time. I'm a
weepy mess, guys! Today, we are talking about
our favorite author, A. M. Pierce!

Lexi:
I beg you guys, please bury me with my fully
charged Kindle, and all of Pierce's books
downloaded onto it when I die so I can reread
them throughout my afterlife.

Capri:
You can add that request to my death wishlist
as well, since you all know I have a TBR longer
than my life expectancy.

Teagan:

> Okay, well, that got dark!

Capri:
You know we live in the dark and twisty.
kisses

Lexi:
Okay, okay. Enough of the doom and gloom, you weirdos. Now, ladies, real question. Do we think Pierce is a man or a woman? We truly have nothing on them. No socials, no Goodreads bio. Those little flaps on the dust jackets that are supposed to have little tidbits about the author? Nada. Zip. ZILTCH.

Teagan:
Oh, Pierce totally has to be a man. Women don't write the type of dark and twisted stuff Pierce writes. Have you read the one about the guy who murders his entire family with a pickaxe? It's straight up insanity. No woman could write that.

Capri:
I'm offended! I would write something like that if I had the patience to hallucinate for hours while bringing a story to life!

Lexi:

I'm with Capri. Women are way more unhinged.
Wait, are you talking about the book where the
guy goes on and makes a whole new family for
a decade, just to murder them all again?

Teagan:
Yes! It's so sick. I had to keep putting it
down because I was traumatized by some of the
scenes with the kids. I can't handle kids being
harmed.

Capri:
And that's why I love books. Murder of any kind
is forgivable if it's fictional.

Lexi:
I 100% agree with you, Capri! I loved that book
so much that I've reread it about five times.
Something about serial killers just gets me
going, if you know what I mean. I also vote
that Pierce can 100% be a woman because we
ladies have darker thoughts than men do.

Teagan:
I suppose we will have to agree to disagree
here. Let's see what our listeners think! Do
you think A. M. Pierce is a man or a woman?
Make sure you leave your vote in the comments!

Lexi:

Don't forget to subscribe to our channel and tell us what books you want to hear about next!

Capri:
Alright, my thriller-loving queens—and kings, that's it for this week's episode of *Live, Laugh, Murder*. It's time for me to strut my stuff down an aisle lined with magnolia flowers and take a seriously hot pediatric surgeon off the market for the rest of our lives together!

Lexi:
Until then, our dearest listeners…

Teagan/Lexi/Capri:
Live, Laugh, and Murder your little hearts out!

Chapter Four

TeaGan

I reach across my bed in search of Josh, but his spot is cold and empty. I wake up alone most mornings since Josh lives on the other side of town and has to get up much earlier than I do for work. A weight settles in my chest that feels closely related to disappointment. Josh promised me before we went to bed that he'd be here when I woke up.

Sitting up, I shake the lingering drowsiness off. My white duvet has been kicked to the end of the bed as usual. I scan the room, hoping to find a clue that Josh is still here, but everything is in its usual place.

I swallow hard, steeling myself to make it through the morning without crying. Not that crying isn't totally valid right now, but I know crying will leave me feeling worse in the long haul. Nothing like giving yourself a migraine because you emotionally and physically dehydrated yourself.

Maybe he didn't believe me last night when I apologized for forgetting our anniversary? I grab my phone from my nightstand, yank the charger out, and toss it to the floor, hoping to see a text from Josh. There's a text from Capri asking if Josh and I enjoyed the rest of our night together after our almost breakup. What if he saw that, looked at my texts to the girls, and got angry that I shared our fight? It wouldn't be the first time he read something I wrote to my friends and got upset. Josh likes his private life to stay private, including what happens in our relationship.

Look at that, Teagan. You've gone and messed everything up again.

Or, what if he just went out to grab us breakfast, and I'm overreacting like he says I always do?

Nope. No text from him. The only unread text waiting for me is another message from Capri in our group chat, telling us we can't be late for our coffee date today because she has "big news" to share.

Whatever—like I'm ever late.

I toss my phone back onto the bed and smash my palms into my face with a loud groan. I shouldn't be this upset that Josh left. It's not like I remembered our anniversary, so tit for tat or whatever that stupid saying is.

It was foolish of me to get my hopes up in the first place.

There's a soft knock on my door. "Teagan? You okay in there?" Josh's voice hits me like a slap to the face as he opens the bedroom door.

I must look distraught because his brows furrow. He closes the small gap from the door to my side within seconds.

"Hey, hey, baby. What's the matter?" Josh sits next to me on the bed and rubs soft circles on my back while I burst into tears. I told myself I wouldn't let myself cry, but I can't stop the onslaught of emotions that invade my senses when I realize that he didn't leave.

He never left me. He kept his promise this time.

I throw myself into his arms and inhale the scent of him. I've never been able to place the exact smell—something woodsy and masculine—but his familiar cologne has always been comforting, safe, and soothing to fall into after a stressful day.

"What's the matter?" Josh repeats as his arms tighten around me.

I sniffle loudly and wrap my arms around his waist, burying my face into his amazingly toned chest. I swear his body was made for mine because I fit perfectly in his arms. "Nothing. I'm sorry," I say between breaths. "I just thought you had left me after how horrible I was last night."

His laugh shakes my entire body as I snuggle into him. "No, baby. No. I just couldn't sleep, so I figured I'd start planning our make-up anniversary trip while you slept in."

Finally, I release him and pull myself together before facing him. "Make-up anniversary?"

Josh brings a hand to my face and tucks a stray hair behind my ear. "Yeah, to make up for how crappy last night turned out to be."

My cheeks turn scarlet, and I tug my lower lip with my teeth. "I'm so sorry, Josh. I can't believe I got so wrapped up in my own world that I forgot about our anniversary yesterday. I promise I'll try harder."

He lets out a loud sigh and shakes his head. "I won't lie and say that isn't nice to hear, finally."

My stomach twists in knots at his confession.

"I know your friends are important to you. But I need to know that I'll always come first, Teagan. How are we supposed to plan a life together when I'm always left feeling like I'm in last place?"

I shrug my shoulders in response because I can't speak right now. I know if I open my mouth, the only thing that will come out is another sob.

Will this always be an issue for us?

Will my friendships be the downfall of my relationship?

Will I have to choose between them—for good?

Josh slaps his hands loudly on his thighs and gets to his feet. "Enough of this. I didn't stay here to fight with you again." He reaches his hand out for me, and I place mine in his on autopilot. "Let's go plan something amazing for our make-up anniversary."

When Josh said he wanted to plan a trip for us, I didn't expect it to involve his mother.

I don't *not* like her, per se, but I could do without the constant butting in she loves to do when it comes to her "baby boy's" life.

"Oh, you don't want to go to Hawaii," Cara states over our FaceTime call. Josh doesn't have many of her features, but when he scowls, he gets a bulging vein in his forehead that matches the one Cara is sporting right now.

Heaven forbid her baby boy get to pick our vacation spot without his mother's approval and input.

"What's wrong with Hawaii?" Josh interjects as Cara starts naming other destination spots.

The annoyed tsk she lets out before crossing her arms over her chest like a petulant child makes my skin crawl. "It'll be too crowded during this time of year. All the best resorts will have been booked months ago! You don't want to stay at one of those chain hotels. Do you, Joshy?"

Did I say I didn't *not* like this woman? That was a lie. She is the actual Mother-In-Law from Hell, not that Josh has asked me to marry him. But who calls a grown man Joshy? I bite my tongue to keep my retort to myself. I have always been cordial with Cara, and I'm not looking to ruin that since I hope to marry her son one day. But keeping my opinions to myself around her isn't easy.

Josh and I have been dating for a year, and I still don't understand how someone so loving and kind could have come from this woman's womb. His father must have been a saint to put up with her long enough to create a child together.

"Well then, Mother," Josh groans out with a grin. "Where do you suggest we go?" He grabs my hand, bringing it to his lips and kissing it softly. His eyes are alight with mischief, and I wonder if he's regretting filling his mother in on our plans. "I want this to be special. Teagan and I will only have one first anniversary, after all." Josh winks at me, making me blush furiously.

Cara rolls her eyes at us both over the screen before bringing her hands together in what looks like a prayer. Maybe she's praying that we don't have a second anniversary together.

"What about a cruise?" she suggests. "You can always book one of the nice rooms. You know the bigger ones with actual breathing room, unlike the closets they advertise as rooms for the rest of the population? The nice rooms never fill up because they are just a bit pricier than the others." Cara's voice gets higher as the idea takes flight in her mind. "A Mediterranean cruise would be magical, and you'll be glad you did at least once in your life."

Josh looks at me. I can tell he's taken with the idea—even though he knows that I am absolutely terrified of the ocean and that a cruise would be the furthest idea of a magical memory for me.

"Well, Teagan," Cara coos. "What do you think? Just say yes, and I'll sort out all the details for you! You know I love travel planning!"

Josh gives my hand an authoritative squeeze from under the table. "Just say yes, babe."

I look from him to Cara and finally see the resemblance between them. They remind me of snakes about to pounce on an unsuspecting mouse. Their posture is intimidating, and their eyes glisten with an unnamed emotion...urging me to give in to their wishes.

This is a fight I'm not going to win, and I know if I remind Josh that I'm scared of the ocean, it'll just turn into another fight. He'll find a way to throw my friends in my face again, and I'm not ready to choose between him and them.

So I nod my head at Josh before turning to Cara. "Yes," I say. My voice sounds weak and pathetically miserable, but they don't notice as their mouths twist into winning smirks.

CHAPTER FIVE

Lexi

Apparently, I drank a little too much wine because I woke up with a raging headache. My forehead feels like it's being split in two from the inside out. I should be getting ready for my coffee date with the girls, but instead I'm cleaning up the mess I left in my living room last night.

When I finally rolled out of bed this morning to hunt down something for my head, I found my living room in shambles. For a moment, I thought someone had broken in and trashed my house while I was in my wine-induced coma. I was seconds away from running back into my room to grab my cell phone and call the cops.

That thought lasted about another two seconds before I saw a ripped-up photo of my own face at my feet in a pile of dozens of other images. All torn to pieces and thrown haphazardly in my living room.

The night slowly returns to me as I drink my morning coffee silently while staring into the beautiful red roses on my kitchen island across from me.

The flowers. The wine. The photo on the mantle.

Sure enough, the frame that once held a photo of my entire friend group is now the proud home of a poorly taped-up photo of Josh and me.

I really need to quit drinking.

Rolling my eyes at myself, I grab a plastic trash bag from under the sink and start tossing all the ripped-up photographs inside. One by one, I cringe at how feral I let myself get last night.

My brain is running a looped montage of me searching through all my photo albums, then ripping apart every single photo that contained Teagan. This obsession needs to stop before someone gets hurt. What if she had stopped by out of the blue and saw all our photos torn to shreds like this? She's my best friend. I can't keep doing this to her.

What would have happened to me if my friends had seen this?

I shove the last of the evidence from last night's episode into the bag, tie it in a knot, and push it to the bottom of my trash bin so nobody can stumble upon it.

I'm startled by the loud knock at my front door. I wasn't expecting anyone, and the girls usually call rather than show up unannounced. This is the second uninvited visitor at my door in the last twelve hours, and I'm not amused.

My eyes scan the room to make sure I got every single photo. Everything looks back to normal here after my cleaning sprint. I check my reflection in the mirror by my front door and like what I see enough to let the world take a peek.

I open the door slowly, then fling it all the way once I see who's waiting on the other side.

"They forgot to send this with the roses," he says with a smirk while he twists a little white envelope in his hands. I see my name written in dark, bold ink on the front.

I grab the card from his hands and open it in a rush.

Lexi,
I would give you the world if I could.
But I hope you'll settle for my silent affection.

I smile at him and hold the small card to my heart. "I'll take whatever you're willing to share with me."

His answering smile weakens my knees as he tosses his dark hair back. "So are you going to invite me in or…"

Instead of answering him, I grab him by the collar of his charcoal grey button-up and pull his lips to mine, relishing in his warmth and the familiar taste of him.

I pull away and look into his dark eyes.

"Hi, Josh."

He pushes past me, stepping into my home like he owns the place, and throws his jacket onto the back of my white leather couch before making his way to the small kitchen.

Rationally, I know I should be annoyed that a man dismissed me so easily. But when Josh does it, I find it endearing, like he's comfortable enough here to call it his own one day.

I follow him, perch on one of the three barstools lined up against the island, and watch him silently move around my kitchen. Something about it feels deliciously sinful. My best friend's boyfriend shouldn't know where my favorite wine glasses are, and he most definitely shouldn't know what drawer I keep the wine opener in.

But Josh does. He knows almost everything about my place and even more about my heart.

Because Josh should have been mine, and he would have been in another life.

Until Teagan stole him from right under my nose. Not that she knew I had feelings for him. At the time, I was his interim secretary at the architectural design firm where he worked, and I made it very clear that he was off limits to me. Before the firm hired me full-time, I wouldn't risk sleeping with my boss.

I didn't think I had to specify to my best friend that he was also off-limits to her.

I foolishly invited her to the office for lunch one afternoon and asked her to wait in the lobby for me since the taco truck I loved was just around the corner. Unfortunately, Josh decided he also wanted tacos that day and was already waiting in line when we walked up.

I finally knew what that whole 'love at first sight' thing was when they first laid eyes on each other.

I just wish it had happened to me instead.

Not that it matters. I have him now. All it took was Teagan choosing her friends over him, over and over again, to drive him straight into my waiting arms.

"Do you want red or white?" Josh asks, bringing me back to the present as he holds up two bottles.

"Isn't it a little early for wine?"

Josh sighs with annoyance, and I know I've screwed up. "But, it's your engagement celebration, you pick," I say with a playful smirk, hoping to ease the tension I caused. I know he didn't propose.

"Last night didn't exactly go as planned. I didn't propose to her," he tells me. His face flushes quickly before his features return to their normal stoic state. "But I don't want to talk about that. I want to enjoy the next hour of free time with you."

He sighs and looks down at each bottle before putting the white back in the fridge. The sleeves on his shirt are rolled up to his forearms, and I watch the muscles bulge and flex as he twists the wine opener into the cork.

The cork comes loose with a muted pop, and he pours us each a generous glass of Merlot. Josh hands me my glass, and that electric current pulses through my body the moment our fingers graze.

I should tell him I don't want the wine because I'm supposed to meet the girls in an hour and a half. But I don't say anything because I'd rather drink him up in every way I can now that he's here with me. Plus, nothing quite cures a hangover like drinking again.

He taps his glass to mine. "Cheers to..." His eyebrows furrow for just a moment as a flash of hurt skates across his handsome features.

"No cheers, just drink," I tell him softly as I lift my glass to my lips and sip. The bold flavors of the wine erupt in my mouth, making me moan in response. "Then maybe you can fill me in on what happened last night?

He shakes his head. "I said I don't want to talk about it. I just needed a place to go and unwind in private." His eyes flash to mine as he sips his wine. "Teagan is driving me nuts with all this anniversary vacation shit. I finally got her to agree to the cruise I'm so lovingly paying for. I told her I got called into the office just to get some space away from her. I'm not ready to go back to Teagan's—" He pauses when he says her name for the second time. His eyes flick to mine with a silent apology.

The one rule is that he is not allowed to speak her name while we're together.

I purse my lips and put my glass back on the countertop harder than I meant to. Red liquid sloshes over the sides and onto the marble.

When I look back up, Josh is staring at my lips. His eyes graze down my neck and stop at the cleavage peeking out of my silk robe. His hand reaches out, grasps my belt, and tugs me closer to him before he takes a large drink of his wine.

And just like that, I know how we'll spend the rest of the morning. The girls won't mind that I'm a little late.

My lips meet his in a frantic frenzy as his mouth savagely claims mine.

"Don't tell her," I moan. I remind him of this every time we meet in secret. "She can never know about us."

Josh's lips leave mine as he grabs me from under my thighs and pulls me to him. "Never. She'll never know."

I sigh with contentment before tugging my robe off and surrendering entirely to him.

Our affair is my most coveted secret—a secret I think I might just kill to keep.

CHAPTER SIX

Capri

I look at my phone for the billionth time in the last twenty-four hours. I'm jittery and wired after my cup of espresso. Every particle in my body is screaming at me to text the girls the big news, but as Lee keeps reminding me, this type of news is much better delivered in person. His patient wisdom is the only thing that stops me every time my hand itches to text the group chat. I guess that's a perk when you marry a man a few years older than yourself.

I still can't believe this is real life. *My life.* It's more than I could have ever hoped for. Never once did I think I'd be this happy, especially when I was eighteen and going through the worst era of my young life.

Back then, I'd have laughed in your face if you told me I'd be living this dream that I'd have this wonderfully beautiful life. Thirty years old, and loving every year even more than the last. I am advancing in my chosen career in medical administration while training to become a registered nurse, all because the man I fell in love with inspired me to push myself as far as I could. I am now married to that same wise man who is the epic love of my life, while cherishing the most incredible friendships a girl could ask for.

It's not something I ever thought possible. And it's a life I'll do any-thing to keep—even if that means lying to my husband and friends for the rest of it.

I should tell Lee the truth about my past. He would understand my choices and wouldn't judge me for them. But I'm scared that if he finds out, it'll change the course of our future together.

If he knew I had a daughter out there when, for the entirety of our relationship, I've been adamant about never wanting to have children, what would he think? How would our relationship change? Would he ever forgive me?

It's not something I can risk. Ever. My life is perfect the way it is, and I believe with my whole heart that I made the right choice for that child. I wasn't ready to be a mom. My daughter deserved better than the broken shell of a person I was left with after conceiving her.

I knew giving her up would be the best way to keep her safe from the man who shares the other half of her DNA.

I lied to everyone and told them that I lost the baby in the first trimester. I had to come up with something because the case made the local news, and everyone in my hometown knew I ended up pregnant because of what happened to me.

I had just turned eighteen. I was the cheer squad captain and was dat-ing the star quarterback. My boyfriend was supposed to drive me home after the championship game, but he never showed up, which made me angry. Angry enough that I thought I'd be safe from the predators of the world, and chose to walk home instead of calling my parents for a ride. It was almost midnight, and I didn't want to bother them—especially since they hated my boyfriend. I didn't want to give them more reasons to think ill of him.

During that short walk home, I was attacked in the worst way a woman can be. He came out of nowhere and grabbed me from behind, holding me down and tightening his grip on my throat the harder I fought back. So I just lay there praying for it to be over.

He left me bleeding and broken. I couldn't breathe or move. All I could do was stare into the night sky and wonder why this had happened to me. I was a nice girl. I went to church. I kissed my parents and reminded them I loved them whenever I left the house.

Why me?

When my phone rang as I was lying there, I answered it, just going through the motions. Hearing my mother's panicked voice on the other end asking where I was broke what was left of me. She and my father came and picked me up immediately and took me to the police station to file a report before I was sent to the hospital to get checked out.

What we didn't know at the time was that this monster had assaulted other girls in our area. Raping them and leaving them broken just like he did to me.

But I was the only one left with more than a broken soul. It was a small town, and within a week of finding out, the news had spread like wildfire that I had gotten pregnant by my rapist. I naively confided in a friend, and she told her parents, who were members of the same church as my family. I didn't know how to face the people in my town. And I wasn't sure how the aftermath of having my rapist's child would affect my child or me. I knew in my soul that I couldn't handle getting an abortion. Not because I saw it as something wrong, I didn't—I don't. I would never judge a woman for making that choice for herself.

It just wasn't my choice; I had already fallen in love with this little soul growing inside of me.

My parents acted like the baby didn't exist. I think they expected me to feel the same way, that it was something wicked taking residence in my womb, so I let them believe that. I dropped out of school and finished online so that I could hide my *shameful* secret from the world for my parents' sake. However, I didn't find my pregnancy shameful.

I was ashamed of myself, but never her.

I hated myself. I hated how weak I was and that this baby would have to grow up without me because I wasn't strong enough to keep her safe from the monster that gave her to me.

Giving her up for adoption was the hardest thing I've ever done, but I knew she would be safe from *him* if he ever came back. She deserved better than to be known only by what her monster of a father did. I made her a promise before I had to hand her over to the social worker. A promise to keep the secret of her creation to myself until the day I die. It's the one thing I *can* give her—to keep her safe.

Lying about her existence is my biggest and most shameful secret. It festers in my soul like a slow-burning fire just waiting to engulf me from the inside out.

It's why I can't let myself become a mother—I already failed one child in this lifetime. I don't deserve a do-over.

Nobody in my life knows that she exists outside of my parents. And they passed away in a car crash right after I left for college. Now I'm the only one left to carry the secret of my daughter's existence, and it's heavier than I could have ever imagined.

After that, I was entirely alone for the first time. I had just started school here in North Carolina. I had no friends, no parents, no baby. No one.

It was the darkest time of my life, and I struggled to survive every moment of the day. I thought about ending my suffering myself countless times. That is, until I stumbled into this same cafe I'm sitting in now and saw two random strangers sitting outside at my go-to table, reading and talking about my favorite thriller books. It may have been a touch creepy to watch them from afar for a couple of weeks, but I was too nervous to approach them. Until one day, while ordering my favorite chocolate croissant, Taylor and Madeleine, the cafe owners, asked if I wanted the last three for free since they were closing soon.

Those three chocolatey desserts gave me the courage to approach Teagan and Lexi.

I'd like to credit fate for putting them in my path when I needed them most, but I also credit Taylor and Madeleine and their superior baking skills.

Teagan and Lexi happily let me into their little book club duo with a finesse and ease that felt like I was sent by a higher power to find them. Someone who knew I needed help saving myself.

After that, the three of us were inseparable, and a few years later, we decided to start our own podcast. Now, *Live, Laugh, Murder* has over 500,000 subscribers, and we've recently started selling our own merchandise on the website Lexi made for us.

I grab my phone to check the time for what feels like the hundredth time and roll my eyes because the girls are late. Teagan is typically on time, but Lexi is notoriously late by a few minutes. Usually, these little quirks are endearing, but not today. Not when I'm seconds away from exploding with earth-shattering news and excitement. I knew I should have just texted them and told them in the group chat!

My phone vibrates in my hand. A text from Lexi says she's looking for parking now.

Lexi is never this late, so whatever or whoever kept her up all night must be worth it. She's been the only one in our friend group not to settle down in the last few years. She says it's because she's keeping her options open, but that doesn't stop her from having a wickedly fun time *after hours*.

Sometimes I'm envious that she is so confident and sure of herself that she can let herself have fun like that with no attachments. But then I look at Lee and me and fall in love with love and commitment all over again.

"Sorry, I'm late," Teagan says as she sits next to me on one of the wrought-iron chairs the cafe has outside. "I was dealing with Cara, aka, the worst future-mother-in-law on the entire planet, by myself after Josh got called into the office."

I roll my eyes. "And what type of architect emergency could there be?" I wince and flash her a strained smile, knowing how upset she gets when she has to deal with Cara alone. "It's fine. I just have the best news that I'm dying to share with you and Lexi," I tell her as I hand her one of the three coffees on the table. "But sorry about Cara. She sucks." Teagan nods before grabbing her drink of choice.

Teagan is a solid mocha-latte girl, and Lexi would murder someone for a pink dragonfruit tea. I prefer my coffee black with a splash of milk and honey.

"Cara does suck. But tell this news of yours!" she exclaims before looking around. "Wait, where's Lex?" Teagan asks as she brings her cup to her mouth and blows gently.

I shrug my shoulders and take a sip of my coffee. "I'm guessing she was up late last night entertaining a hot, bearded lumberjack of a man. You know, her usual."

"First off, he only had a bit of scruff," Lexi says, appearing in the seat next to me. "Secondly, he was a fantastic lay and even offered me seconds this morning. If you know what I mean." Lexi wags her eyebrows and tosses her blonde hair behind her before she grabs her pink drink and takes a long swig. "Urg, this is delicious and exactly what I needed. Thanks, Capri."

I give her a nod and a mock salute. "Always. Anyone we know?"

Lexi shakes her head and looks over at Teagan. "Nope, just another one-nighter with a stranger. Well, I guess, a morning-er, too?"

We all laugh. This is the part where the three of us would typically sit in comfortable silence, sipping our drinks and people watching. But this isn't a typical day, and I'm nearly leaping out of my skin to share my big news with them. "Okay, so I know today is supposed to be your day to explain everything that happened with Josh, Teagan," I say after a few seconds. "But I have like, really, really, big news."

Lexi gasps and spits pink juice all over the table before diving into a coughing fit. I grab napkins and wipe up the mess as best as possible while Teagan repeatedly pats Lexi on the back.

"Oh. My. God. CAPRI!" Lexi shouts. "Are you pregnant?!"

My eyes nearly pop out as I look at my friends. They're both waiting anxiously for confirmation. I shake my head and laugh into my hand to keep myself from screaming. I hate this topic. I hate that the second you get married, people just assume it's okay to ask such personal questions. They are my best friends, so they get a little more leeway, but I still hate it.

"No. Sorry guys. You both know that's not something I want, so that's a big fat negative."

Both of their shoulders slump in disappointment before giving me reassuring smiles. I hope they can't see the lie on my face. On the inside, my heart races like quicksand trying to swallow me whole.

"Sorry to disappoint, but you both know how I feel about kids," I joke with a mock shudder. "And anyway, this news is much better than a baby. I promise."

Lexi and Teagan glance at each other across the small table and wait for me to explain. I take another sip of my coffee before pulling out the dark envelope from my purse. I hold it close to my chest as I explain its meaning. "You guys, Lee did something amazing for us. Like really, really amazing. If I weren't married to the man already, I'd marry him all over again because of this."

I hand the envelope to Lexi and watch her eyes skim over the letter. They widen, and her jaw goes slack before she jumps up and grabs me by the straps of my yellow overalls. "Tell me this isn't a joke? CAPRI! If this is some sort of joke, I might kill you!"

"Can someone please tell me what's going on?" Teagan pouts from the other side of the table.

Lexi releases my overalls and slams her body into mine, hugging me tightly. "If you weren't married to the man, I'd probably snatch him up and marry him myself!" We both giggle and untangle ourselves. Lexi retakes her seat, looks at Teagan with the biggest smile, and hands her the letter.

I watch Teagan's face scan the letter and can't contain my joy and excitement as I look at Lexi. She winks at me when Teagan finishes reading it.

"Get the hell out. Are you serious?" Teagan looks down at the letter again in shock. "Are we really going to Scotland in two weeks to meet our all-time favorite author?"

I nod frantically while Lexi jumps up and down in her chair. Teagan stares at the letter again, her face erupting into a pained smile.

"What's wrong?" Lexi asks, looking over to me. Our brows knit in confusion.

Teagan hands the letter back and crosses her arms. "Josh and I just booked a cruise...and it's also in two weeks."

Lexi lets out a low whistle and tosses her hair back. "Josh will just have to understand. It's not every day you get invited to meet your favorite author for an all-expenses-paid trip. Right?"

My heart aches when I see the hesitation flit across her face, followed by a flash of fear on Teagan's face. I know she loves Josh, but I've always thought she deserved better than him. She can't see it because she's too wrapped up in his spell, but he's no good for her. My eyes flick to Lexi's, and I see her jaw tensing as she picks at her nails.

Teagan deserves better than both of them, but it's not my place to tell her.

I reach over and squeeze Teagan's arm. "Hey, just talk to him, okay? We can bring a plus one, so maybe he'll join us in Scotland? Lee's coming too, so he'll have another dude to hang out with as the three of us fangirl over Pierce."

Lexi scoffs loudly before her lips slide into a wicked smile. "I guess I'll just have to find myself a hot Scottish guy, while the four of you are off gazing into the Scottish sunsets or whatever. More cute men for me, right?"

I roll my eyes as Teagan shakes herself out of her stupor.

"You're right. I'll just talk to Josh about it. There's no way I'm missing this trip," Teagan says with the fakest enthusiasm I've ever heard spew from her lips.

We all sit in silence as we finish our drinks. Only this silence isn't comfortable at all. For some reason, all my excitement about this trip turned into dread in my stomach.

LIVE, LAUGH, MURDER
Episode 21

Lexi:

Welcome back to Live, Laugh, Murder, my favorite murderous friends! Lexi Casburn here! I'm with co-hosts, Teagan Shepherd and Capri Kim, to talk about A. M. Pierce's newest novel, *Escaping the Lighthouse!*

Capri:

Before we start, I'll warn you all that there will be spoilers in our chat ahead, so if you haven't read *Escaping the Lighthouse*, we suggest tuning out of this episode until you have!

Teagan:

Or maybe you should save yourself the headache and disappointment by taking it off your

shelves and tossing it into a blazing fire
instead.

Lexi:
Teagan! You can't just tell our listeners to
go around burning books!

Teagan:
Trust me, guys, you'll want to burn this one.

Capri:
Clearly, our girl Teagan has some serious
complaints about this book. Would you like to
fill us all in?

Lexi:
scoffs

Teagan:
The entire book was just ridiculous! It's like
Pierce was obligated to give up another book,
but that doesn't mean Pierce gave us a good
book! First off, how, as a woman, do you let
yourself get lured to an island in the middle
of nowhere with a group consisting of ONLY MEN?
MEN!

Lexi:
I don't know, but that sounds like a grand ol'
time.

Capri:
Down, Lex. Keep the daydreaming in your
pants—please and thanks.

Teagan:
Anyways, the whole premise of this story is
just so unrealistic. There's no way a woman
would let herself get put into a situation
where she has to rely on four strange men
to save her. A real final girl would find a
way to save herself—no man required. Instead,
our FMC lusts after the hot guy who becomes
the villain! It's by far the stupidest book
Pierce has given us. And you all know I live
and breathe for Pierce's novels. This one just
fell flat. So I say again to our listeners, go
ahead and toss your copy into a fire and save
yourselves from this epically bad novel. If I
could give negative stars, I would.

Capri:
Well then, don't sugarcoat it, T.

Lexi:
It's not like Pierce would waste crucial
writing time by listening to our silly podcast.
Don't get me wrong, that was pretty harsh. But
I do like it when Teagan shows us her teeth.

Teagan:
Okay, okay. I'll play nice. I just really hated
that book.

57

Chapter Seven

TeaGan

I'm an idiot through and through. But hell if I'm not a stubborn idiot. I promised Josh I would be better about putting him and his needs first. Yet here I am standing in front of his house, trying to come up with a plausible reason that Scotland will be better for an anniversary trip than the cruise he and his mother have planned.

Even my subconscious knows that this is foolish because my stomach has been twisting itself into knots since Capri dropped this life-changing bomb on us. How can I live with myself if I give in to his wants over something like this? How do I make him understand that even though it's a trip with my friends, I'm not *choosing* my friends over him?

This time I'm putting myself first. I'm choosing me.

I take a deep, anxious breath and ring the doorbell. Josh answers it with an excited smile, but I don't miss how quickly it falls from his face once he realizes it's me. Was he expecting company?

"Teagan," he says, strained as he opens the door wider for me to enter. "What are you doing here?"

I step into his house and set my purse on the entry table before heading toward his leather sofa and sitting in my go-to spot. My nerves are on fire with anxiety by the time Josh sits next to me and puts one hand on my thigh, squeezing it reassuringly like he always does. I keep my hands clasped on my lap. "We need to postpone our cruise," I blurt out. My voice is shaking right along with my hands.

Josh releases a long sigh. I tense up, waiting for the screaming to start. Instead, he asks, "And why exactly do we need to do that?"

I finally risk meeting his eyes and nearly wince when I see the anger building behind his baby blues. "I have to go to Scotland," I tell him. "Well, I mean, you can come too. No wait—this is coming out all wrong. I meant to say I want you to come with me to Scotland."

He brushes a hand down his face, and the hand resting on my thigh squeezes again, but it's more painful this time. I squirm and try to move my leg from under his grasp, but he refuses to move.

I swallow hard. "The girls and I have been invited to meet A. M. Pierce for an all-expenses-paid trip to Scotland. It's a once-in-a-lifetime opportunity, and I can't miss it," I explain calmly. "It's the same week as the cruise. I was hoping we could reschedule, and that you'd come with me as my plus one."

Josh shakes his head in fury. "So you just thought you'd go ahead and choose your friends over me again, and that I'd be okay with it? Teagan, you forgot our damn anniversary! And I found it in my heart to forgive you and plan an expensive cruise. In case you forgot–again–, this is *also* an all-expenses-paid trip for you because you don't have to contribute a dime!" he shouts.

I blink and wipe away the hot tears that have started trailing down my face. I take a deep breath. "I'm sorry, Josh. I know it's horrible timing, trust me, I wish this didn't have to be during the same week as our cruise, but I won't pass up this opportunity!" I shout back. "I'm not choosing my friends this time, I'm choosing *me*. You expect me to choose you over everyone, including myself!"

I'm not letting him bully me into giving in to him *again*. Not this time. This is too important for my career. All I want is to be a writer who is taken seriously. What better way to ensure I get off to the best start than getting advice from my favorite author?

I'm unsure where our relationship is going if he won't come with me to Scotland. I've let him down too many times, I know that. But he's also asking me to make a choice that I don't know how to make.

A choice I don't ever want to make.

Him. My friendships. And most importantly, myself.

I can't live with these ultimatums just to keep a man.

We stare at each other. His eyes are cold as his grip tightens on my thigh. I know we are at another stalemate. Neither of us is willing to compromise. We are in the same place we were last night.

Josh finally releases my leg, gets to his feet, and heads back towards the front door, beckoning me to follow him. The knots in my stomach come back in full force as I do as I'm told.

He stops in the entryway and surprises me when he tugs me into his arms, hugging me tightly. "I don't want to lose you, Teagan."

I hold him back and bury my face into his chest. "I don't want to lose you either."

"Look at me," he says softly. I look up, and he bends down and places a tender kiss against my forehead. Just for a moment, I think everything is going to be okay. That we can make this work. I love him, and he loves me. Isn't love about making sacrifices for the other person? After this trip, I promise to put him first, even before my own needs. We can make this work.

"Then you need to tell them you can't go." His jaw tenses as my eyes widen in shock. "I'm not going to Scotland to watch you prance and parade around with your stupid friends, Teagan. I'm sorry, but I can't keep having this argument with you. So you need to choose, right now. Me, or them."

I pull myself out of his arms as another warm tear streaks down my face. I no longer care that he hates it when I cry. "If this is your ultimatum, then I choose me," I tell him, my voice rising with resolve.

Josh closes his eyes like he's in pain before turning and opening the door. "Wrong answer. I won't keep handing my heart to you for you to use and abuse. I deserve someone who will always put me first. You have proven over and over again that you are too selfish to do that. So I'm done, Teagan. For good this time."

I step through his door and leave without another word.

"There goes an entire year of my life," I mumble into the glass of tequila before tipping it into my mouth and swallowing the contents in one gulp. Lexi rubs my back and hands me another lime to suck on.

After I left Josh's house, I sent an SOS text to the girls asking them to take me to the seediest bar in town and get me drunk off my ass. Capri said she was working at the hospital, so she couldn't make it. Lexi, though, always comes through for me. She's been my person since the day I ruined her favorite shoes.

Lexi and I met during our first year at the University of North Carolina in Wilmington after I saw a flyer for a book club posted on the communal dorm bulletin board. I found the book club's Facebook group and saw that they had already read many of the books on my shelves. I was thrilled to discover a group of readers who shared my taste.

Thriller books are typically consumed by a unique group of individuals. We tend to appreciate the macabre and the emotional trauma that come with a well-written, disturbing story.

I remember walking into the small coffee shop, full of nerves, with a tote bag filled with books I loved and wanted to share my thoughts on. Imagine my shock when I was directed to the reserved room at the back of the joint and saw it was full of men. Not that there's anything wrong with a book club full of men, but showing up as the only female? I immediately felt out of place and extremely uncomfortable, especially when many of them grazed my body up and down with something other than mutual interest in books in their glazed-over eyes.

I ran out as fast as I could, and ran straight into a gorgeous, tall blonde, knocking her iced coffee all over us. Her white blouse was ruined, along with my tote bag full of my favorite books.

I apologized profusely, turning as red as a cherry tomato while she *laughed*. She told me her name was Lexi and asked me what books were dripping coffee onto her no longer white Toms. We sat outside the coffee shop and chatted about books for over two hours while meticulously dabbing each page of my annotated books with napkins.

That became our weekly thing—minus the spilled coffee—for the next month. Until one day, this stunningly beautiful stranger with long teal and pink braids that reached her hips came and sat down at our table with three chocolate croissants and a book by A. M. Pierce tucked under her arm and introduced herself as Capri.

They are my family.

I could never choose a man over them, even if that man is Josh. I'm still stupidly in love with him, and I might regret my choice in the morning.

Lexi nudges me with her elbow, pulling me out of my gloomy thoughts. "Don't you dare text him," she says as she takes her next shot easily.

I roll my eyes and flash her an annoyed smile. "I'm not going to. But it's not like I can just turn my heart off that fast, Lex," I tell her as I hand her a new lime. "We only broke up," I look down at my watch, "less than four hours ago."

Lexi hands me the salt shaker. "Maybe this is a sign that you and Josh aren't meant to be."

My heart feels shredded by her words.

"Sorry, T. That came out harsher than I intended," she quickly amends with an apologetic smile. "I just meant that you two have had this same issue since you got together. One of you needed to give in to make it work, and neither of you did. You deserve better."

I shrug. "You're right. I know you are. I just can't believe it's really over. Josh was my first real relationship. I loved him. You know? It's hard to get my heart in line with my head."

Lexi hands me another shot, and I down it quickly, relishing in the burn as the alcohol slides down my throat.

"How about we put a pin in the sad-girl talk and go dancing?" Lexi suggests. "No more Josh talk. Just the two of us enjoying that single life while we're hot and young." Her enthusiasm is infectious, and before I know it, she's pulling me out the door, and we're walking with our arms linked down to our old favorite dance club. This might be the perfect way to overcome a self-inflicted broken heart.

Chapter Eight

Lexi

It's no easy feat to listen to Teagan bitch and moan about her relationship with Josh being over, especially because I can't let her know how thrilled I am about it or how anxious I am to text him.

I've managed to keep our affair a secret for the last three months; no need to ruin it now. Even though I'm the worst friend in the universe for what I've been doing with Josh behind her back, she's also my best friend, and I genuinely hate seeing her in this much pain.

I take a sip of my water, twisting my blonde ponytail in my fingers. I need to sober up a little before I fall into the trap of drunk texting my best friend's ex. We've been dancing for what feels like hours, and I'm finally starting to feel my age. Thirty is nowhere near as fun as my twenties when it comes to clubbing. The club is full of college kids, and Teagan and I have both giggled over how out of place we feel.

"Hey!" Teagan shouts over the music. "Are you ready to head out of here? I think I'd rather just go home and keep drinking. This music is starting to give me a migraine."

I nod and book an Uber. "The car should be here in five minutes, so let's go wait outside!" She gives me a thumbs up and almost falls off her stool. "Good call, because you are way drunker than I anticipated!" I grab her by the waist and sling her arm over my shoulder to help her to the door.

The cool air sobers me up instantly. The same thing cannot be said for my little drunk friend. Teagan steps out of my arms and stumbles into the brick wall on the side of the club. She slides down and plops herself on the sidewalk. I slide down next to her while we wait for our car to get here.

"What if we just go to Scotland together?" Teagan says, her voice taking on that happy-drunk quality that I've always been so fond of.

"You want me to be your date?" I raise my eyebrows and smirk over at her. "You gonna wine and dine me while we're there?"

"No, you ass. I just meant that it might be better if you and I go solo. We can gal-pal it up while Capri and Lee bask in all the romantic scenery that the Scottish countryside has to offer. Plus, I know you don't want to watch them be all adorable and coupley. You're just too nice to admit it," she slurs out. "But I know you, Lex. And I know you're a hopeless romantic at heart just like me. You pretend to have this whole 'I don't need no man' thing going until you catch the right one. So let's say screw it and be each other's dates. What do you say?"

I roll my eyes and smile. "I'll always be your date, T."

"Maybe we'll meet a couple of hot guys while we are there! Didn't Capri say that the submission was for all sorts of influencers, journalists, and whatnot?" Teagan asks as she rubs her hands together for warmth.

"What the hell," I say, shrugging. "Let's go meet some gorgeous Scottish men and have our way with them."

We both erupt into laughter just as my phone vibrates in my back pocket. Our car has arrived, so I help Teagan up. My phone dings again as I get into the backseat. I feel like I've been dunked in ice water as I read the text.

Josh wants to meet up in half an hour. He left so quickly this morning after we finished that I assumed that he might be sick of me. I glance over at Teagan before texting him back, promising to be there as soon as I can. The drive to Teagan's apartment is quick. I ask our driver to wait as I help her get upstairs.

"Want to stay over?" Teagan asks once we step out of the elevator. "I have pizza."

"I'd love that, but I have to get up early for work, so raincheck?" I hope she can't hear the lie in my voice. Sober Teagan knows I don't work on the weekends, so I'm hoping she's drunk enough right now to forget that little fact.

"Absolutely. I'll just inhale a whole pizza by myself," she jokes. Her voice still has that happy drunk slur to it. I tell her bye and head back towards the elevator. "Get home safe, Lex!" Teagan shouts after me.

I flash her a thumbs-up and continue to walk down the hallway. I wonder if she can tell that my heart feels like it's being ripped to shreds on the inside.

I really am the worst thing to ever happen to her.

Teagan and Capri are the first true friends I've ever had. They've both been there for me through all the highs and lows of growing into myself as an adult. They still love me when I'm rude, blunt, and judgmental. And here I am, betraying one of them so deeply for my own selfish needs. I hate myself for it, but I can't seem to find the willpower to stop myself. As soon as Josh flashes me that wicked grin, I'm a goner.

Josh's lips skate across my body in the most delicate and delicious way.

I could literally die from this.

Him.

His lips on my skin.

The way his fingers dance across my body in the most tantalizing way makes me see fireworks behind my eyelids.

I shouldn't enjoy this. I shouldn't let myself continue this secret, dangerous affair. But I can't get enough of him.

I would drown myself in him if that were humanly possible.

Josh has never called me for a last-minute...well, whatever this is. Calling it a booty call makes it feel cheap, and my feelings for this man are anything but.

He pulled me inside his house before I could even knock, and within moments our clothes were off, and he had me lying bare on his living room floor as he devoured me. My nails dig into the plush taupe rug as he brings me to the edge over and over again. Teasing me—taunting me.

"I want you." I moan. "Now." I run my hands through his hair, tugging roughly just the way he likes it, until he finally releases his invisible restraints and unleashes himself fully onto me. Slamming to the hilt over and over again with a ferocity that has me screaming his name.

We finish, drenched in sweat and a tangle of limbs, while we both struggle to catch our breath. Something about this time felt different, but I can't quite put my finger on why. Maybe it's because I know he and Teagan are finally over.

My smile couldn't get any bigger than it is now. I place soft kisses on Josh's chest as he wraps his arms around me, holding me tight to his body. I should hate myself for this, for enjoying this so much. I know it would destroy Teagan if she ever found out. But when Josh kisses me, I can't feel anything but overwhelming gratitude that they are over now.

It's one thing to sleep with your best friend's ex. It's another thing to have an affair with the man. I've never been brave enough to ask Josh if sex with me is different from sex with Teagan. For some reason, having that knowledge would make me feel dirtier than I already do.

If Teagan wanted me to know about her sex life, she would share it. Instead, we've always been reserved when it comes to the intimate details of each other's relationships—not that I've had an actual real relationship since I met Josh. I make up stories about fake men that I pick up at fake bars while she tells me how happy she is with Josh. Capri shows us both up by having the most wholesome and enviable marriage in the world.

It's just how the three of us roll.

"What are we doing?" Josh says in a hushed whisper, almost as if he's still scared to be caught with me.

I look up at him and take in how marvelous this man is. His eyes are closed, making him look like a statue sculpted by the hands of Michelangelo. He has a strong brow and nose, along with cheekbones that look like they were made for the runway. The stubble on his face is new; usually, he keeps a clean shave, but it looks incredibly sexy on his sun-kissed skin.

I reach up and run my fingers through his hair; he hums with approval. His hair is a little damp after our escapades, which makes it curl slightly on the ends. I love this look on him. Messy, gorgeous, and so damn intoxicating.

Josh opens his eyes as I shift to kiss his lips, and the look he gives me stops me cold.

Why does he look—unsettled? Upset? Regretful?

I instantly sit up and cover myself with the burgundy throw blanket perched on the arm of his leather couch next to us.

"What's wrong?" I hate the sound of my voice right now. It sounds pitiful and nervous—a far cry from my usual confident self.

He sits up and scoffs loudly. I don't miss that he can't seem to meet my eyes.

"I'm in love with Teagan," Josh admits after a beat of silence. "Even after she hurt me again by choosing you and Capri, I can't help but still love her. To want her back." Her name coming out of his mouth makes me flinch. "How can I win her back when I'm still sleeping with her best friend? What kind of people are we, Lex?"

I open my mouth to defend our actions, but when his eyes finally meet mine, all I can see is the pain and regret glaring back at me.

"I—this," I stutter. "I thought we both wanted this. I know I did. I do. I've wanted you since the moment I laid eyes on you, Josh. You know that. It's not my fault that she got in the way. You two are finished now. She made it clear tonight that she wants to look for someone else while we're in Scotland. She doesn't deserve you." I scramble to get closer to him and place my palm softly against his cheek, wishing I could grab hold of his heart through his chest instead and claim it as mine. "I know what we've done isn't ideal. I wish we had found a better way. I do. But, Josh, I love you. I don't regret us for a second."

Josh remains still, his breathing strong and steady, entirely unlike mine, which pounds with a ferocity that makes me feel empowered. I love this man, and I've finally admitted it.

I slide my hand through his messy hair. "We obviously can't rush into a relationship right away. I couldn't do that to Teagan. But I'm hoping that after a few months, maybe longer, I don't know, we could finally be together in the open. We could talk to her, tell her that it just happened, explain that we love each other, and beg for her blessing. It'll be awkward and painful at first, but I know after some time she'll be okay with us."

I lean in and place a kiss on his cheek. "I *know* she'll be okay with us. We just have to give it some time."

Josh blows out a long breath before he finally looks into my eyes. I smile softly at him, waiting for his response. I've never told him that I loved him before, but he needs to know. He deserves to know how I feel so he can stop worrying about Teagan's feelings.

What we have between us is *real*.

"The thing is," Josh says as he reaches up while cupping the hand I have on his cheek. "I care about you, Lexi. But I don't love you. I love her. And I think we need to put a stop to this finally." He pulls my hand gently away from him and places it in my lap. "I'm sorry. You've done nothing wrong, I promise. But now I realize that letting Teagan walk away today and asking you to come here so soon after was a mistake. I can't use you to heal what she broke. I need to find a way to fix things with her. Whatever this is between us, it's over." His blue eyes harden. "I think you should leave."

My mouth falls open, somehow forgetting how to form a single word. Every atom in my body goes numb. Josh stands and disappears into the hallway. A door shuts moments later, and it feels like it's the final nail in my heart.

He's still choosing her over me?

CHAPTER NINE

Capri

I'm practically dancing around Karyme's, my favorite local department store, while Lee and I shop for the trip to Scotland. I swear, the last two weeks have flown by ever since telling the girls about the invite. Thank goodness the girls and I have passports from our vacation to Canada a few years ago. That would have been a nightmare to navigate on such short time.

We leave in just a few days, and I'm nowhere near ready. I hate packing. I'm the type of woman to leave it until the very last minute. Luckily, I have a husband who knows this about me, and I've caught him secretly packing away outfits for us both over the previous week.

I look up at Lee, and my heart grows tenfold. I still can't believe this wonderful, amazing, beautiful man of mine made this happen.

"What's that look for?" Lee asks with a slight grin.

I scrunch my nose and wrap my arms around his neck, kissing him hard on the lips. "I just really love you. That's all."

"And I really love you," he replies before smacking my butt. "Now let's find you a dress so I can get you home and show you just how much."

He nips playfully at my lower lip. I wish we were back at home so that I could have my way with him. But...shopping. I reluctantly pull out of his arms and continue my search for the perfect dress to meet A. M. Pierce in.

"Happiness looks adorable on you, babe," Lee whispers into my ear as I flip through the racks.

"You make me the happiest woman in the world. If happiness looks cute on me, you can go ahead and give yourself full credit for that."

We go back to searching the racks as my mind drifts to what it'll be like meeting A. M. Pierce. We know nothing about her—or him. Literally, the 'about me' portion on the inside flap of all of their books just says that they reside in Scotland and have been writing thriller novels for almost a decade now. A. M. Pierce could be anybody, and none of us would be any the wiser.

I'd like to assume that Pierce is a woman, primarily because all their novels are written from a female perspective. But there are plenty of male writers who write incredible thriller novels using a woman's point of view.

"You should get that red one." Lee points at the most stunning dress hanging on one of the mannequins. "You always look beautiful in red."

I can't help but roll my eyes playfully at him before I hunt down the rack with said dress on it. I find my size and throw it into the cart along with a handful of other options.

"Okay, I think it's time to try them all on. If I hate them, maybe we can hit the mall next?" I ask Lee while we make our way to the dressing rooms located at the back of the store.

"You know you'll love them all." Lee winks at me.

"We'll see about that." I grab the clothes from him and disappear into the dressing room.

I slip the sequined green ensemble on and gaze into the full-length mirror. I like it, but I don't love it. It's definitely more Lexi's style. I snap a photo of myself in it to send to her later, in case she needs one for our exciting meet-and-greet.

Next, I try on this gorgeous velvet navy ensemble. It's got a deep V-neck plunge and hugs my dark russet skin like a glove, making my ass look fantastic. I'm naturally a tiny person, so anything to help give me some curves always goes into the 'yes' pile.

Last, I pull on the red dress that Lee picked out. I'm not sure of the material, but it's got lacy long sleeves with small floral stitching over a darker red slip. The pattern gives off a bohemian vibe, while still being classy. It stops just above my knee and hugs my body like a second skin.

It's perfect, of course. I'm not surprised, Lee always knows what looks best on me.

I carefully pull the dress off and tug my skinny jeans back on, along with my Nirvana crop top, before slipping my feet back into my white and red checkered Vans. As much as I enjoy these gorgeous dresses, I'm naturally a jeans and t-shirt type of gal. I adjust the claw clip, keeping my heavy braids in place, and head back out to meet Lee to tell him that his dress won over my own choices.

I'm not surprised to see that he's nowhere to be found. He's the type of man who will tolerate my shopping, but the moment I have to try clothing on, he finds something else to get distracted by. I head towards the book section first—nine times out of ten, that's where he'll be.

I circle the book aisles twice before deeming that Lee isn't there. Odd, but also not concerning. I make my way over to the video games. He's still nowhere to be seen. I guess I'll have to resort to calling him to see where he wandered off to.

Punching his name on my phone, I head back towards the front while the line rings, since I still need to grab a few toiletries. The phone rings loudly in my ear as I cut through most of the clothing aisles while my eyes tear across the store in search of my missing husband.

My phone falls out of my hand once I finally spot Lee in an aisle we typically avoid at all costs. He's holding up a pink little onesie with florals splayed all over it.

Why is he in the baby section?

And why does he have the most wistful smile on his lips as he stares at the tiniest of outfits?

I watch as he hangs the onesie back on the rack and grabs his phone from his pocket.

"Shit," I mumble and dive to the ground to fetch my phone before he answers. My insides feel like lead. "Hey," I say quietly from my position on the floor.

"Hi, gorgeous. You done trying everything on?" Lee asks, his voice calm like always. Like, he's not standing in the aisle he knows I hate most. "I bet that red one was the winner, right?"

I feel as though I've been stabbed in the heart. He knows how I feel about not wanting children of my own after what happened to me. I've never hidden the attack from him, and he's read all the news articles about the case. He's held me during the nightmares that used to plague me years ago, and knows that my attacker is still out there somewhere. I've never held any of those truths from him.

But I can never tell him that I lied about losing the baby to give my daughter a better life. All he needs to know is that I don't want to risk ever getting pregnant again because I'm too scared to lose another one. Half-truths and half-lies keep my daughter safe.

"Baby? You there?"

From my angle, I can see him walking away. I wait until his shoes disappear before I risk standing. "Umm, yeah. Sorry, I was getting distracted by more clothes. The red one was great," I choke out. "Where did you go?"

"I'm in the book aisle, naturally."

I clear my throat. "Oh, I looked over there but didn't see you."

Lee chuckles over the line. "I've been here the whole time, so you must not have looked very thoroughly, my dear."

"I must have missed you. I'll be right there," I force out.

Why is my husband lying to me?

I pick at my Caesar salad from Lucene's pizzeria, moving the lettuce and croutons around my plate in listless waves. I'm too upset to eat after seeing Lee holding that stupid onesie.

Not only am I upset, but I'm also confused as to why he lied to me about it. When did our marriage turn into one where we can't be open and honest?

When we met, he was just as adamant as I was about not wanting children. We agreed that there is absolutely nothing wrong with being childless by choice, especially with the careers we were pursuing. Because that has always been *my* choice, and I loved him for agreeing with that choice. He told me he didn't see himself having children, since working in a hospital is such a taxing, time-consuming career.

I don't know how to ask Lee if he regrets that now. I'm even more unsure if I want to know his answer.

"You're being extra quiet tonight," Lee says with furrowed brows as he stares at me from across the cherry wood table. "Are you nervous about the trip?"

I shrug my shoulders. "No, not really. I'm more nervous about fitting all my clothes into my suitcase than I am about the trip."

Lee reaches across the table and takes my hand in his, caressing my knuckles gently with his thumb. "Then what is it? You've seemed off since we left the store."

Sometimes I hate that he knows me so well because it's impossible to lie to him.

Here goes my happy marriage bubble.

"I saw you holding that baby onesie," I say through clenched teeth while struggling to meet his eyes. His thumb immediately ceases its soft swipes over my knuckles.

Lee sighs and yanks his hand away, making me flinch both outwardly and inwardly as I wait with bated breath to hear whatever lies are about to spill out of his mouth.

"Well?" I ask when he refuses to look at me.

He runs his hands through his dark hair, his cheeks flushing with embarrassment. "I don't know what you want me to say, Capri," he finally responds.

My hand forms a fist on my lap as a new wave of anger and disbelief washes over me. We don't ignore the elephant in the room. And this is a particularly large damn elephant.

"I just want to know what you were thinking when you sought out that aisle. You had this hopeful smirk on your face, like some proud papa or something," I hiss. My cheeks redden as my voice rises an octave or two. "I just thought we were on the same page, and seeing you today with that stupid flowery pink outfit just shattered my entire image of our marriage. I guess I just don't know how to feel about you right now. About us." The stupid, traitorous tears spill down my cheek and make me feel even angrier.

Angrier at myself.

Angrier at Lee.

Angrier because the lies of my past are most certainly going to ruin my marriage, because I can't ever tell Lee what really happened back then.

The *real* reason why I can never be a mother.

He would never look at me the same.

Lee rushes to my side of the table, pulls me up from my seat, and hugs me tight around the waist. One arm wraps around my body, and the other cradles my head against his chest.

"Baby, baby, baby," he whispers into my hair. "Nothing has changed. I promise you. I wasn't looking at that outfit in any kind of wishful or hopeful way. Trust me."

The sob that leaves me is disgustingly guttural as he holds me, utterly unfazed by the others in the restaurant sitting around us. "Then why did you lie to me about where you were in the store?"

His laugh vibrates through his chest and my body. "Oh, you silly woman," he chuckles, "This reaction right here is why I lied. Because I know you, and I know that you would have ended up spiraling." Lee grabs my face and tugs my chin up gently so we are looking at each other. He wipes away my tears before he continues. "Sort of like the spiral you're on right now. You know I don't like to see you upset."

I roll my eyes and lean my cheek into his palm. "Okay, fine. That's true. But then why were you in that aisle?"

Another laugh escapes his lips before he reaches into his back pocket and pulls his wallet out. "Because I know you absolutely abhor that aisle, and I didn't want to upset you."

I raise an eyebrow at him and wait for him to continue.

"Anyways, Mariah, Aaron's wife, is expecting another baby. Aaron's convinced that this one will finally be his boy. You remember they have three girls already, right?"

I nod.

"Well, Mariah stopped by the hospital and handed me this envelope before they went to lunch earlier today. She asked me to surprise him tomorrow with the correct outfit before we leave for our trip."

Lee pulls a small black envelope from his wallet and hands it to me. I open it carefully, and when I see what's inside, I can't stop the hideous cackle that leaves my body. I look up at my wonderful, amazingly patient husband, and all the stress and anger leave my body in an instant.

"Another girl, huh?" I say with a smirk.

Lee sighs and smiles. "I would say 'poor Aaron,' but that man was made to be a girl dad, and he knows it."

I pull him down and place my lips against his. "I love you, you know that?"

"You love me as much as I love you, my dear." He kisses me senseless again before pulling away. "Now...how do you feel about going shopping with me again for a ridiculously pink and insanely frilled outfit?"

"Only if we can get ice cream on the way home."

Shopping for baby things for someone else doesn't hurt nearly as much as thinking my husband regrets the decision never to have children of our own.

LIVE, LAUGH, MURDER
Episode 37

Capri:
Welcome back to Live, Laugh, Murder! I'm here with co-hosts, Teagan Shepherd and Lexi Casburn, to talk about A. M. Pierce's novel, *An Axe to Grind!*

Lexi:
This is by far the most gruesome book Pierce has published!

Teagan:
Yeah, I may or may not have DNFed this one because the gore was just too much.

Lexi:
You can be such a baby sometimes, T. I loved it. Ate it UP.

Capri:
I enjoyed it! But I am with Teagan; the descriptions were nauseating. Listening to it on audio just made it even worse. It's one thing to read an overly bloody scene, but to have it read to you? It was horrific.

Lexi:
If a person with an axe were chasing me, I'd just turn and tackle them to the ground. An axe is heavy. It's hard to swing quickly. I'd snatch it up and chop him to bits, then lick the axe clean.

Teagan:
Respectfully, what is wrong with you?

Capri:
HAHAHAHA. Lexi is a woman, hear her roar!

Lexi:
Ain't no damn man swinging a stupid axe taking me down.

Teagan:
I'm glad you have a plan because if someone ever ran at me with a freaking axe, I think I'd faint and give up on the spot.

Capri:

That's why our men will take care of us while
Lexi goes all final girl.

Lexi:
Maybe I'll make the axe murderer fall in love
with me instead.

Teagan:
That'd definitely be an epic plot twist.

CHAPTER TEN

TeaGan

My nose is pressed up against the glass as close as I can get without leaving unsightly impressions of my nostrils on the plane window while I gaze out at the beautiful greenery that Scotland has to offer. I can't believe we are really here. We are in Scotland. And only hours away from meeting our favorite author in the world.

My stomach feels like a volcano that isn't quite dormant anymore, bubbling with nerves just waiting to explode.

Gosh, that sounds disgusting when I think of it like that.

But I haven't been able to eat properly for the last few days because I've been so excited and nervous for this trip.

I still can't believe that we are being treated to an all-inclusive stay—including travel arrangements that got us into first class!

This type of stuff doesn't happen to little nobodies like me. Sure, I work as an assistant to our local library in Wilmington while also making pretty decent royalties from the podcast. I make pennies compared to most people, and I sure as hell am not the type of girl who would splurge for a first-class ticket like this.

I don't think any of us are used to this type of treatment.

I shift my gaze from the window and stare across the row at my friends. Lexi is asleep next to me with her Kindle on her lap. Her chair is reclined, and the fluffy cow-print blanket she brought is draped over her. She took a sleeping pill and knocked out shortly after the flight attendant served us dinner that consisted of a caprese pasta salad and a red velvet cake muffin for dessert. I would give my life to have another one of those muffins.

Capri and Lee are in the row just across from us and are cuddled up together. Yes, over the vast and spacious armrest. They are watching a movie and keep giving each other looks that only people who know each other inside out could decipher.

Seeing them so happy in love makes me want to scream.

Don't get me wrong, I love how much love they have for each other. I just can't help that my traitorous heart misses Josh. He's texted me several times since he called it quits on us. I was finally forced to mute his notifications because he kept calling me every ten minutes yesterday.

Part of me wants to reach out and try again, because I do care about him. On one hand, I wish that my heart hadn't been ripped out and stomped all over by him. I might still even love him. On the other hand, I'm also excited to be single and free here in Scotland without worrying about being judged by a man for putting myself first.

There's another part of me that is angry that he expects me to push my friends and myself aside for him and his needs. I can't get on board with that.

My heart is in tatters over the entire thing. I can't talk to Josh until I figure out what I really want in life. If I don't, then I'll just end up having the same argument with him.

We both deserve better than that.

Lexi yawns loudly next to me and stretches her arms out, accidentally punching me in the face.

"Oh, T," she says through another loud yawn. "I'm so sorry!"

I rub at my jaw and flash her a fake look of betrayal before leaning on her shoulder. "I missed you while you were sleeping, you know," I tell her. "Maybe that's weird, but I would have rather hung out with you than be stuck looking at the adorably disgusting little love birds over there," I say just loud enough for Capri and Lee to hear me. They look over and grin as if they have zero cares in the world that the rest of us are still hunting for our happily ever after.

"How much longer until we land?" Lexi asks me through another lengthy and impressive yawn.

"You'd better stop yawning like that, or you're going to make me finally fall asleep," I tease, stifling my own yawn from escaping. "But we should be landing in about forty-five minutes."

Lexi gives me a thumbs up, then puts her eye mask back on. "Good, wake me when we land. I need all the beauty sleep if I'm competing with your gorgeous ass for hot single guys on this trip."

"Riiiight," I respond under my breath. Lexi has nothing to worry about. Definitely not about little ol' me stealing any men from her.

Lexi has always been the prettiest of us. Her long blonde hair, natural tan, and legs for days beat out my pale complexion and dark hair any day of the week. She's a freaking supermodel compared to me. There is zero competition. Besides, I would never choose a man over our friendship. If she finds someone here in Scotland, it's all hands off for me.

Girl code and all that.

The rest of the plane ride is uneventful. Beautiful, but uneventful, and before I know it, we have landed and are all exiting the aircraft.

The airport in Scotland surprises me because it looks just like every airport in America. The only difference is that it's not bustling with angry business people trying to fight the crowds to make their last-minute flights. That, and the fact that the overhead speaker speaks several different languages, including English, French, and what I think is German, based on my two years of German in high school a billion years ago. I wish I had paid more attention in that class instead of gossiping with my friend Beate about hot boys, who sat next to me for both years.

Lee, Capri, Lexi, and I make our way down to baggage claim and quickly find our luggage.

"What did the email say about traveling to the estate?" I ask Capri once we get outside. She and Lee coordinated with Pierce's assistant and handled all the travel arrangements for our group.

Capri takes out her phone and scrolls for a minute before telling us there should be a car waiting for us outside the airport.

"Oh, I bet that's him!" Lexi exclaims as she points to an older man with graying hair in a dark navy suit standing in front of a stretch limo. He's holding a large white sign with our names in fancy cursive.

Lee walks up to the man and introduces himself and the rest of us.

"You may call me Henry," the older man tells us with a thick and animated Scottish accent. "It's nice to meet such a fine-looking group! You four are the last of the guests to arrive, so we must hurry along now. We don't want to keep the rest of them waiting."

We all shuffle into the limo as Henry insists on loading our bags without help. As soon as we get on the road, Henry lowers the privacy screen and tells us that a popped champagne bottle is waiting in the icebox for us, along with glasses. I'm still feeling the effects of the hangover I gave myself the night before last as I cried over Josh yet again. But before I can decline his offer, he tells us that it's bad luck to deny the host's kind gesture and that we must toast to our safe travels.

"I guess we are day drinking, my friends," Lexi says as she lifts the bottle and pours us each a small glass. "Can't risk Madame Pierce hating us before we even leave the airport!"

I'm glad to see that Lexi got all the sleep she needed because I feel like I'm moments away from passing out. I refused to let the world pass me by without watching from my window seat, and I'm definitely paying for that now.

The four of us hold our glasses up as Lee gets the honors. "Cheers to a happy wife, happy life!" he says, placing a soft kiss on Capri's cheek. "And of course, to the rest of you, who make my dear wife happy daily!"

"Yeah, I'll drink to that." I grin.

Lexi rolls her eyes at me before saying, "Screw that happy married life nonsense. Not that you two aren't adorable." She motions to Lee and Capri, the liquid in her glass swirling. "We are always cheering for your happiness and marriage. But T and I want to enjoy that happy, single, and very ready-to-mingle life while we are here. Am I right?"

I tap my glass to hers before raising it to my lips. "Couldn't have said it better myself."

We clink our glasses with the group.

I was surprised to learn that Pierce owns a private island off the coast of Scotland. After driving up the coast and taking the ferry to the secluded island, Henry ushered us into another limousine to get to Pierce's home on the island. We pull into the gates of the estate about fifteen minutes later, although estate is most definitely the wrong word for the massive brick towers looming above me. There's a sign hung above the wrought-iron gate that says *Windermere Castle.*

Are we going to sleep in a freaking castle? I sit up straighter in my seat as we drive closer and take in the scene before me. Deep green Ivy clings to nearly every outer wall and archway. The castle reminds me of something on the cover of a horror novel, but without all the dark gargoyles waiting to snatch you up for their tormented masters.

There are probably more than fifty windows in this place. They are intricately designed, each with the same pattern: a black cross surrounded by hues of amber and yellow stained glass.

I wonder which window belongs to Pierce's room.

The arched doorway at its entrance hosts two suits of armor. I shiver at the thought of one of them housing a living, breathing person, hiding and watching from behind the mask, ready to hunt us down for trespassing onto their land. Clearly, I've watched a few too many horror movies.

The rest of the outside is bright and exceptionally maintained, other than the ivy that climbs the walls with no abandon. The towering brick walls are all shades of tan and taupe.

When I finally exit the limo, I swear I can taste the salt from the sea nearby on my tongue. When my eyes land on the garden, my feet move like they have a mind of their own. I can't stop myself from walking over and taking a closer peek. The apartment I live in has a small balcony, but the only plants I tend to keep alive are cacti. If the suits of armor are from a horror movie, then this garden must be one from a fairytale. It's full of lush green bushes and flowers of all colors. It looks like it wraps around the entire estate.

I'm in awe of the breathtaking landscape. It looks even more vibrant with the overcast sky above us.

Some things tend to shine with natural beauty when a little darkness touches them.

"Care to take a stroll later?" A deep, husky, male voice greets me from behind, making me jump. I turn and nearly gasp when my eyes land on his face.

Now, I'm not one of those women who believe in that whole love at first sight thing. But I could be convinced to believe in *lust* at first sight because this man might just be the most attractive man I've ever laid eyes on.

A blush creeps over my cheeks when I realize I'm just staring at him as he waits for me to say something.

"Is that a yes?"

"I—um. What?" I run a hand over my messy, traveling bun and wish that I had thought to put just a touch of makeup on before I got here. I planned on getting ready before the big dinner party. I most definitely didn't expect to meet the modern age Adonis before I unloaded my suitcase.

He grins and runs his fingers across his lips as he stares down at me. I didn't realize that he stepped closer. My heart may or may not skip a beat in my chest while I grapple for coherent words. He's looking down at me with the most intense blue eyes I've ever gazed into. Something about them feels familiar, but I know I would have remembered if I had seen this guy before. His hair is a dark mess of waves atop his head. I wonder what it would feel like beneath my own fingers.

"Hey, Teagan! Are you coming or what?" Lexi shouts from the entrance to the castle, making me jump like a fool. "We've got to get ready for the dinner party, so hurry it up!"

I curse her silently under my breath. "Yeah, I'll be right there," I yell back.

The modern-day Adonis turns and walks deeper into the garden.

"Wait." I step towards him.

He turns on his heel before those blue eyes meet mine again. "Yes?"

"What's your name?" I ask.

A sly smirk paints his lips. "Well, *Teagan*." He steps closer to me and shoves his hands into the pockets of his dark slacks. The white button-up shirt pulls taut against the obvious muscles painting his arms and chest as he stares down at me. "I guess you'll just have to find out at dinner tonight."

He winks at me, then turns on his heel and strolls back into the garden, leaving me wondering if I conjured him up entirely with my sleep-deprived mind.

CHAPTER ELEVEN

Lexi

"**I**'m telling you, Lex. This man was the hottest man I've ever seen in my entire life. Like a full-on male main character from one of those fairy smut novels that people rave about. I'm a goner." Teagan hugs her shoulders and throws herself onto my bed.

I shouldn't be jealous.

I shouldn't be jealous.

I shouldn't be jealous.

I chant this to myself on repeat, hoping that I can wish it into existence. But the acidic taste on my tongue as I watch Teagan kick her feet in the air like a love-sick child is proving how unsuccessful I am at this task.

I sit on the edge of my bed with my back to her. I can't swallow the overwhelming feelings of anger.

See, Josh, she doesn't want you like I do.

She doesn't really love you.

The four-poster canopy surrounded by white sheer curtains is the type of bed I always wished I'd had as a child. This whole place feels like a dream come true, and I need to keep reminding myself that this is a once-in-a-lifetime opportunity. I can't let Teagan's happiness dampen my excitement. Even if I am wholly and utterly devastated that Josh hasn't reached out since he told me he was choosing her.

I know he has both texted and called her because she told me while we were waiting to board our flight. That knowledge makes me hate my best friend in a way I didn't think possible. I quickly shut that conversation down by telling her she should mute him and ignore him for the duration of the trip. What I really wanted to say was that she should forget about him forever and let me have him.

What does she have that I don't?

What makes her so special compared to everything I have to offer someone?

Teagan's hand on my shoulder comes out of nowhere and makes me flinch. "Hey," she says in an almost motherly tone. "Is everything okay? You seem off lately. You know me, and you know I won't pry until you're ready to open up about it, but I'm here for you, Lex." She rests her head on my shoulder, grabbing my hand in hers. "Whatever it is. I'm here. Always."

I wish she were a worse friend. Because then it wouldn't make everything I've done to her feel as gut-wrenching as it does right this minute. Obviously, I can't tell her I'm grieving the loss of *her* ex. So instead, I pat her hand with my other one and flash her my most convincing smile. "I'm okay. Promise." I reassure her. "I'm just really freaking nervous to meet our favorite author. My stomach is all twisted into knots and whatnot. That's all."

There, not a complete lie, but not the whole truth either.

Teagan gets to her feet and pulls me up with her. "Well, that makes two of us. So how about we spend the next hour getting dolled up and dancing to some overly loud music? That's always our happy place. Right?"

I flash her a grin and nod my head. "Right."

I hadn't planned on buying this emerald green dress when Capri sent me a photo of herself in it. But as I run my hands down the delicate sequins and dainty beads that adorn the dress, I'm so glad that I did.

It's perfect. It makes my usually tan skin look eerily pale and my blonde hair almost white in its high ponytail. I feel like one of those seductive vampires from a fantasy novel as I stride down the hallway in my leopard print Louis Vuitton's with Teagan by my side.

"Where's Capri and Lee's room?" Teagan asks. Her lips are painted a deep burgundy, while the rest of her makeup is more toned down. She looks as stunning as I feel, with her dark hair curled perfectly to one side in an off-the-shoulder burnt orange dress that hugs each of her curves.

I hear the distinct sound of another set of heels on the hardwood floor behind me and turn as Capri and Lee appear from one of the other many hallways. She looks beautiful in her red lace dress, with half her hair pulled into a golden claw clip resembling a butterfly. Lee looks handsome as always in his black suit and gives us a kind smile in greeting.

"I never thought we'd find you!" Capri cheers as she catches up to us. "I swear Lee took us in circles for a good ten minutes before I finally noticed we were passing the same painting over and over again."

It would be so easy to get lost in this place. I was shocked when we pulled through the gates and saw that we would be staying in a literal castle. When in Scotland, I suppose.

Henry informed us on the long drive here that there are over a dozen of us staying for the week. The only ones sharing a room are Capri and Lee. It appears no one else wanted to bring a plus-one.

Or maybe they were dumped on their asses like the side piece I am.

"I need a drink," I mutter as we walk through yet another set of giant double doors.

"I think I can help with that, lassie," says a man's voice with a thick Scottish accent.

We watch as a man with copper-red hair walks up to us with a bottle of what I assume is liquor in his hand. He's cute in a nerdy sort of way—if lean and muscular can be described as nerdy at all. He's wearing a deep red suit with a black button-up shirt underneath. His shoes look like they're made of some type of animal skin. They instantly make my skin crawl. Something about this man sets off every single red flag in my body.

Teagan smiles politely at the man and introduces herself. "I'm Teagan. Thanks for the offer, but I think we should all wait until we have some food in us. We had a pretty long day of traveling," she explains. "Do you know where the dining room is? We're supposed to meet with our host in about five minutes."

The man stares at each of us before his chapped lips twist into a sly smile. "Ahh, Teagan," he says excitedly. Maybe he's been hitting the bottle too hard. "It's nice to meet you, and your beautiful friends."

Lee clears his throat loudly.

"Ah, I meant no offense. You are just as beautiful as the ladies," he says with a wink to Lee, causing Capri to snort. "My name is Lochlan. I'm here as a guest as well, so I suppose we will all be feasting together soon. Come, come. Follow me. They're expecting us this way."

We all follow in silence as Lochlan leads us down another hallway before taking a sharp left, disappearing down a set of stairs without another word or glance back at us.

"Is this guy leading us to the basement to skin us?" I ask. Partially joking, partially worried. "He sort of has crazy eyes and weird lizard shoes."

Lee chuckles and gently pushes his way to the front. He and Capri stare down the dark stairs before taking slow steps down them together. Teagan and I follow right behind. The air surrounding us gets colder with each step into the darkness. The only noise is the clack of our heels on the floor and our fast, nervous breaths. As soon as we hit the last step, we are met with a closed door.

"Huh," Lee says, puzzled. "I don't think I heard a door after Lochlan disappeared down the stairs."

Capri steps forward and reaches around for something. "I can hardly see a thing down here," she whines while searching for the doorknob. The only light we have is coming from the door at the top of the stairs. "It's locked," Capri says before she knocks hard three times.

"I'll head back upstairs and see if we somehow missed Lochlan and took a wrong turn," Lee finally says once we realize nobody is going to answer. "Be right back." He kisses Capri on the side of her head before he disappears. The door at the top of the stairs slams shut behind him as soon as he reaches the top, plunging us into complete darkness.

Teagan slips her arm through mine as we both scream into the pitch-black room.

"Lee?" Capri's voice is full of fear. "Lee!" Capri shouts louder, stepping on my foot, then tripping over Teagan and me. "Sorry! Sorry! I'm freaking out here, guys," Capri whispers into the deafening silence surrounding us as her small body clings tightly to us. "Lee! Can you hear me?"

A small, bright red light appears above us, illuminating the space in ominous hues of red. While I hated the darkness, I might hate how twisted and terrifying my best friends look right now even more. Their features take on strange, blood-red shadows as we all look around the room in panic.

"What's going on here?" I ask. "This isn't some sort of game!" I shout at the red light. "Let us out of here!"

The crackle of a speaker makes the three of us jump.

"Hello, ladies," says a voice from the speaker. It's distorted, almost like they are using one of those voice apps to change how they sound to cover up their true identity.

"Before we get started, I just wanted to tell you all what a huge fan I am of your little podcast. Listening to *Live, Laugh, Murder* is a guilty pleasure of mine. It seems like you ladies sure know your stuff."

Teagan's voice is small, but fierce as she yells up at the ceiling, "Who are you? Let us out of here!"

The mutated voice lets out an ugly, awful sound, which might be some twisted version of a laugh. "Why, I'm the person you've been dying to meet," the voice answers. "But, to meet me, you have to prove you're worthy."

"What—," Capri starts, her voice shaking like a leaf in the wind. "What does that mean? Is this a joke?"

"It means, Mrs. Kim," the voice continues, "You must survive this first test if you ever want to see that handsome husband of yours alive again."

A digital clock appears on the wall across from the red light. It's counting down from 10:00. The three of us stare at each other, sharing the same horrified expression as we realize this isn't a game. The author we've been dying to meet might just be the one responsible for this confusing and horrifying situation.

"Clock's ticking, ladies."

CHAPTER TWELVE

Capri

N*o, no, no.*

We have to get out of here.

I have to get to Lee. I have to save him.

Rationally, I know this is probably just some prank, but what if it's not?

What if it's not?

My thriller girlie brain can't help but immediately think the worst, though. I have to save him from whatever twisted form of torture our captors have planned for him.

My palms are sweating like crazy, and I hastily wipe them on my dress as I spin in circles to see if there's another way out of this tiny, red prison.

My late father's words come back to me as I feel myself start to spiral.

Stop. Breathe. Assess the situation.

I take a deep, shuddering breath to calm my nerves before I jump into action. Someone has to take charge here, and it might as well be me since I have the most to lose if this isn't just some twisted game. "Teagan, go up the stairs and check to see if that door is locked," I snap a bit more forcefully than I should. "Lexi, start feeling around the wall with the clock. Maybe there is an escape hatch somewhere."

Lexi scoffs loudly while shaking her head at me. Teagan nods and takes off running up the stairs, disappearing out of sight just like Lee did only minutes ago.

"No, I'm not entertaining this," Lexi spits back at me. "This is stupid. I didn't come all the way to Scotland just to be accosted by a man who thinks he can use and abuse us for his own pleasure. I don't care how famous he is."

"Fine!" I shout at her. "Then get the hell out of my way so I can check. I don't care if you think it's a game. I will *not* risk my husband's life over your stubbornness, Lexi." My tone is as sharp as knives as I lecture my best friend. "Also, we don't know that Pierce is a man. Now do we?"

"I assure you, ladies. I'm a man," the voice coos from above.

"Whatever. Man! Woman! Does it really matter? This isn't some sort of escape room, Capri! It's a sick, twisted game that our *host* finds funny, and I'm not playing." Lexi leans against the wall and crosses her arms over her chest, causing the green sequins on her dress to glitter in the muted light like the rage boiling inside me.

Defiant as always when she doesn't get her way. Usually, I find this trait of hers endearing, but right now I want to punch her square in the face, especially when my husband's life might be on the line.

We are alone in a foreign country. We don't know a single soul here. Even worse, nobody knows precisely where we are because the travel plans didn't have an official address. All it said was that we'd be collected at the airport in Glasgow.

This might just be a game, but it also might be real.

I ignore the panic clawing up my throat and start searching the walls surrounding us. What am I looking for? I'm not even sure. But I know that there has to be a way out of here, and I'll stop at nothing to get back to Lee and make sure he's okay. I'm pushing and pulling on every inch of the stone walls as Teagan reappears on the staircase.

"Holy hell, T!" Lexi shouts. "I didn't hear you coming down the stairs!"

Teagan's face comes to life in the red lights above us, and a small kernel of hope blooms when I see that she looks excited.

"Sorry, I took my heels off," she explains. "But look! This was hiding on one of the steps!"

She hands me a glass bottle. As soon as I bring it to my face, I realize that it's the same bottle of liquor that Lochlan was holding when we ran into him. I also notice the bottle is empty, but when I shake it, I hear something moving inside.

"So that creepy man with the lizard shoes is in on this?" Lexi scoffs. "I freaking knew it. Nobody trustworthy wears hideously disgusting shoes like that."

"Shut up, Lexi!" Teagan snaps.

My jaw drops open in surprise as I look at her.

Teagan's never talked to Lexi that way. The two of them have always been closer and shared a much closer bond than I have with either of them. I've always tried my best not to let that closeness flare up that small kernel of jealousy that resides in my heart over it. But hearing the venom in Teagan's voice and seeing the anger radiating from her eyes toward Lexi shocks me to my core—it almost feels like she's choosing me this time.

I glance at Lexi and see a flash of hurt and possibly regret in her expression.

As much as I want to ease the tension between us, I also know we don't have time to waste, so I return my attention to the bottle.

The red light above us doesn't do much for me as I try to peek through the glass. "I think it might be a piece of paper."

Teagan reaches out and gently takes the bottle from my shaking hands. The room is freezing, and my dress is made up of useless scraps of fabric, letting the bone-chilling air seep through my skin.

"I know this is about to sound so stupid, but does anyone have a wine opener?" Teagan asks. "I don't want to break it unless I have to."

Lexi steps away from her spot on the wall and pulls her necklace off. "It's not a wine opener, but maybe we can use it to pry the cork out?" Teagan brings the necklace to her face and inspects it. It's gold and features a relatively large dragonfly pendant. I'm surprised I didn't notice it right away, but Lexi's natural beauty tends to distract from the minute details of her fashion choices.

"The tail is thick and long and curved just enough that it might actually work," Teagan says in a rush before she turns and sets the bottle on the steps behind us. "Here, you two hold the bottle still while I work on prying the cork out."

Lexi shrugs and sits next to me on the steps. Her hands are above mine on the bottle as we work to keep it steady so Teagan can do her part.

It's a slow, agonizing task. The only sounds in the room are the sounds of us breathing and the dragonfly pendant hitting the glass lip of the bottle while Teagan uses it to break the cork apart. After what feels like hours, she gets the cork shredded enough and uses her thumb to push the rest of the broken cork into the bottle.

"There! We did it!" Teagan's eyes are alight with excitement as we all stand. She flips the bottle upside down and gives it a good shake.

Lexi puts her hands under the bottle as Teagan tries to shake out whatever is waiting for us inside.

I glance up at the clock. My stomach turns leaden. "Guys, we only have six minutes left. We need to hurry this up!"

"We got it!" Lexi shouts. She unrolls the paper, and we all squint to see the words.

TRUTH OR DARE?

"What is this?" Lexi says incredulously. "Truth or dare? Are you serious?" She walks over to the door and bangs on it several times with her fist. "Let us out of here, you damn psychopath!"

The speaker crackles above us again, and the distorted voice greets us. "Truth or dare? Clock's ticking, ladies."

"This is bullshit! Let us out!" Lexi screams again.

Teagan meets my gaze and looks back at the clock. We now have five minutes left. Who knows what will happen to us, or to my husband, if we don't play along.

I can't risk it. I won't risk Lee.

"TRUTH!" I shout to the ceiling. "Truth! Truth! Truth!"

The crackle of the speaker starts again before that same demented, sinister laugh booms out. "Good girl, Capri."

Teagan reaches over and grabs my hand, squeezing it tightly as we wait for the speaker to continue. Lexi crosses her arms and scoffs, but thankfully stays quiet this time.

"If you answer this honestly, Capri. You and your friends will be free to go," the voice explains. "If you lie, you stay—and you don't want to know what happens then."

My heart races in my chest as I wait to hear what could be the question to gain my husband's freedom.

I can do this, I can do this.

"What dark truth have you been hiding from your friends?"

Lexi and Teagan look at me, both confusion and curiosity alight in their eyes. I feel my face getting hot. My hands are sweating again as I race through what this stranger might know about me. There's no way they know about my past? Right? Nobody knows the truth about what I did all those years ago. Do they?

No. There's absolutely no way this person knows about my daughter.

But then what truth are they talking about?

I glance at Teagan and then at Lexi and swallow hard.

Because I do know one truth, but it's not my truth.

Lexi's eyes are wide as she looks at me, almost as if she knows I'm about to blow her entire world up for the sake of keeping mine whole.

"Lexi," I say, my voice breaking entirely as my eyes shift to Teagan's. "I'm so sorry."

I look up at the clock again. Three minutes left. The guilt I feel nearly swallows me whole as I open my mouth again. "My dark truth is—" I swallow hard again as tears slip down my face. "My dark truth is that I know that Lexi is having an affair with Josh."

The speaker says, "Thank you for your honesty, Capri." Then we hear a click of a lock.

I risk a glance over at Lexi and Teagan, knowing I've just ruined everything. But I can't help the slight rush of relief I feel when I realize that my own, true dark secret is still safe. My child is safe.

I've broken my best friends to keep myself whole.

What kind of person does that make me?

The door before us opens, and we are met with a round of applause and bright lights.

Lochlan and Lee stand at the doorway with sheepish smiles as they offer us glasses of champagne.

I rush forward, my body full of fury, and slap Lee hard across the face. The sound reverberates through the entire room, causing all our onlookers to go silent.

"What the hell was that, Lee?!" I scream at him before I bury myself into his chest and break down. "I thought they were going to kill you. I was so scared!" I pull away as the fire in my veins flares. "And this whole time you were out here, what? Just playing with your new friends instead of trying to help us?"

Lee rubs at his cheek after handing Lochlan his glass. "Baby, no. I didn't know what was happening until the door opened. I got locked out as soon as I walked through the door to the hallway. Lochlan found me wandering the halls like a lost lamb. He invited me for drinks and said we would go around and meet you here. We walked in a second ago."

His voice sounds so sincere that I believe him. I fall back into his arms and cry into his chest. "I'm sorry. I'm so sorry." I cling to him as hard as I can and let myself breathe in the fact that he's okay. He's actually okay, and this was all just a twisted joke like Lexi guessed as soon as we got locked in.

The soft muttering of voices around us finally pulls my focus. I realize that we're not as alone as I assumed we were when we came out of the dark room behind us. We have an audience of about a dozen people who are dressed to impress, just like the rest of us. These must be Pierce's other guests.

"You ladies did amazing!" a woman wearing a tight-fitted dress tells me.

"The dragonfly necklace was genius!" Another guest chimes in from somewhere in the back.

I flush as I take in everyone's eyes on us.

"How did they see us?" Lexi asks through tear-stained cheeks.

Lee grabs my hand and points to the giant television behind us. "I only saw the last bit," he admits. "But I'm guessing everyone was able to watch the entire thing on that."

Everyone just watched me turn on my best friends for their own amusement. What kind of twisted place is this?

LIVE, LAUGH, MURDER
Episode 46

Teagan:

Welcome back to Live, Laugh, Murder, your go-to spot for all your thriller needs! I'm here with co-hosts Lexi Casburn and Capri Kim to talk about the thriller book, *Running With Children*, by our favorite A. M. Pierce.

Capri:

Content warning disclaimer! We are going to discuss how the use of children in thriller novels can affect the outcomes of certain stories, specifically A. M. Pierce's novel *Running With Children*. Spoilers ahead!

Lexi:

We want to know, do you think you'd fight harder to survive if a child were in your care

during one of these twisted scenarios we find
in almost every thriller novel?

Teagan:
Would you push yourself to the brink of death
if you knew a child's life was in danger?

Capri:
Could you put a stranger's child's safety
before your own?

Lexi:
In *Running With Children*, we know the FMC
is taken hostage while on vacation on a
cruise ship. She finds that her cabin neigh-
bors have been brutally murdered, and their
five-year-old son is missing.

Teagan:
And keep in mind, our FMC has never met this
child, but she still spends the duration of
the novel searching in vain for him. By the
end of the story, she has to choose: her life,
or his. I won't give away the ending to those
who haven't finished, but I will tell you that
it's one of those books that haunt you forever.

Capri:
Would you choose a child's life over your own?

Lexi:

I don't know if I could answer this without
getting myself cancelled.

Teagan:

That's because you're a woman, and as a woman,
we are born to be responsible for the safety
of children. If we were men, then your answer
would be totally forgivable.

Lexi:

What would you do?

Capri:

I would without a doubt sacrifice myself to
save a child. Kids are supposed to be protected
at all costs. Children are the only pure
goodness left in this world.

Teagan:

For someone who doesn't want children, you sure
have the heart of a Mama Bear, Capri.

Capri:

Whether you're a parent or not, hurting a child
is unforgivable.

Lexi:

Remind me to give Capri godmother rights if
I ever decide to take that terrifying plunge
into motherhood.

Chapter Thirteen

TeaGan

I need to get out of here before my rage and grief fully consume me in front of these strangers surrounding us. My breathing comes in strangled gasps as I push my way through the small crowd.

I need to get out of here.

I hate that I'm doing it, but I scan the crowded room without really taking in any of my surroundings. My heart is still pounding with both anger and hurt after such an emotionally tolling start to the evening.

I know exactly who I'm looking for. Did he watch me on the screen? I want to ask him if he had to go through the escape room to enter this massive hall, too. Or was that horror just reserved for my friends?

Though, after what I just learned, I don't think I have any friends left.

Like a moth to a flame, Lexi appears on my left and whispers into my ear, "Can we talk somewhere private? Please, T? I really need to explain." Her voice sounds pathetically desperate. I can't stop wondering how Josh and she got away with sleeping together behind my back.

No. I don't want to know.

"Teagan, please?" Lexi asks again, her voice straining with the pressure to keep her secrets between us.

Screw that, and screw her.

I turn and raise an eyebrow at her before saying firmly and loudly, "Why? Are you going to try to lie your way out of the fact that you were fucking the man I loved?" Lexi winces. I watch with satisfaction when her eyes dart around the room. "Oh, are you worried that the rest of these fine people are going to hear that you're not only a horrible friend, but also a whore? News flash, Lexi, they saw everything!" I point to the giant television. "You don't have to pretend to be a decent person anymore. These people all know your secret now, too." My voice is stoic and cold. I know it's like a dagger straight to Lexi's heart. I've never once in my life spoken to another person this way.

And of all people, I never thought I would speak to my best friend like this.

She deserves nothing but my contempt and hatred after what I learned about her tonight.

"Teagan, please," she sobs and tries to grab my arm. I jerk away from her touch as if I've been burnt.

"Stay away from me, Lexi. I want nothing to do with you ever again," I seethe, not caring that our audience is on pins and needles as they soak up the drama between us. "You might as well be dead to me."

Lexi brings her hand to her mouth and gasps loudly, nearly falling to her knees before Capri catches her from behind.

"Teagan," Capri pleads. "Don't be like this. Let her explain."

I scoff loudly as her betrayal cuts me deep to my core. "You're just as guilty as she is, Capri. You knew what she was doing with Josh, and you kept it to yourself! How could you do that to me?" I ask her. Her face fills with hurt. "You can bury yourself right next to her because you're both dead to me."

My eyes sweep the room again, only this time I notice that I'm in a large, overly decorated sort of parlor room. There are paintings of every medium hanging on the deep burgundy paneled walls. Dark leather furniture is clustered in little sitting pods around the room. The windows are shut, but the cream velvet drapes have been pulled to the side with a thick gold cord. I make my way to the closest one and stare out into the night sky, taking deep, calming breaths as I try to ground myself and my overwhelming emotions. The moonlight illuminates the garden below. I feel it calling to me.

Beckoning me.

Screaming my name.

Maybe that's just the first sign that I've finally been truly and utterly broken by three of the people I trusted the most with my heart.

"Care to take that stroll now?" His voice is velvety and smooth, like a whisper on the wind, sending a chill up my spine.

I turn and see a hand, outstretched and waiting for me. I look up into those same tantalizing eyes that dazzled me earlier today. They are the deepest shade of blue, like the ocean's waves during a brutal storm. There is mirth, joy, and mischief in them as they gaze into mine.

I'm hesitant to trust him, but when I see Lexi and Capri coming up behind him, I give that hesitancy no more room in my chest and place my hand in his. "Just take me away from here. Please."

He turns and sees Lexi and Capri heading this way and raises his eyebrow in question.

"I need to get away from them," I tell him.

"Of course," he says, then brings my hand to his lips and places a soft, but intimate kiss on my knuckles before flashing me the most wicked smile I've ever seen. "Well then, Teagan. Let's get out of here before your friends ambush you. Or worse—our host."

My eyes widen as I take in his words before I glance around the room nervously. I forgot the strange voice in the escape room claimed to be the author himself. I'm not sure if I care to meet the person who thinks it's appropriate to throw that kind of thing at strangers he invited here.

"Don't worry, I'll make sure we get back in time for the real party to start. Now follow me," the stranger insists as he pulls me behind him with a quick pace.

We leave the main room and bob and weave through hallways, leaving the gawking faces, noise, and chatter behind us, but most importantly, losing *them* in the process.

The stranger pulls us to a pair of double doors and opens them with a flourish. The cool, crisp air caresses my skin like a phantom kiss. The sweet floral air impregnates my senses in the most calming way, leaving me breathless as the rage I felt just moments ago dissipates around me. My toes are greeted with plush green grass, and I realize that I left my shoes on the dark staircase in the room that destroyed everything I've ever counted on.

No, I don't want the memory of that to follow me out here. I take a deep breath, and I let my mind empty. There's something about fresh, unmasked air that has always had that effect on me. I stand in the garden with my eyes closed, just taking in the serenity of it all.

A loud pop from a champagne bottle nearly startles me out of my skin. I bring my hand to my chest as I spin around towards the assaulting noise.

"Sorry," the handsome stranger says with a shrug that makes me feel as though his disruption was purposeful. I narrow my eyes at him as he pours the bubbly into two flutes that have magically appeared out of nowhere. "I snagged these during our getaway."

I cross my arms as the breeze skates across my bare skin. This dress might be gorgeous, but it does nothing to protect me from the natural elements. I feel stupid for not bringing something warmer to wear. Then again, I wasn't supposed to be out here in the garden. I'm supposed to be inside with my best friends, meeting our favorite author.

The blue-eyed Adonis saunters over with two glasses in his hands. "I know you probably have nothing to celebrate at the moment," he says with a sigh. "But how about we forget everything that happened inside and get drunk while exploring the garden," he suggests, handing me one of the flutes. "Unless you want to talk about it? I'm not much for advice, but I'm sure I can whip up an inspirational quote or two to get you through the night."

I don't know what I expected him to say, but that was definitely not it. A small chuckle escapes my lips as I tip my glass to his. "No inspirational quotes necessary. A punching bag would be nice, though," I confess before taking a sip of the champagne. It's crisp, sweet, and pleasantly chilled as it slides down my throat. "But I have some questions before I abandon all my common sense and disappear into a poorly lit garden with a strange man I only met hours ago." I look him up and down and feel a strange thrill of excitement as I watch him take a sip of his own drink. His lips are very distracting with their perfect fullness and pointed cupid's bow.

Those same lips flip upward into a playful smirk as he steps closer to me. "What would you like to know?"

I gaze up into those haunting blue eyes again and swallow hard as they flick down to my lips. "What's your name?"

"Ah," he says, one of his brows arching in jest. "I told you I'd tell you my name at dinner. Did I not?"

"And what if this is my dinner?" I hold up the champagne flute before taking another sip. I don't know if I can go back into that room after the humiliating scene I just made.

He must read my thoughts because his expression shifts into something softer. "Then I guess I would be honor-bound to fulfill my oath," he says playfully while he holds out his arm for me. "My name is Quinn Gibson."

I thread my arm through his and relish the warmth of him. "Well then, I guess I have to let you give me a tour through the gardens. Now don't I, Quinn Gibson."

"My friends typically just call me Quinn."

I raise an eyebrow at him as we walk deeper into the blooming garden. The moonlight illuminates it just enough that I don't feel like we are in any real danger, while still being dark enough to enjoy the company of this strange and mysterious man.

"Are we friends now?"

Quinn stops and faces me, his free hand taking mine. "I'd like to be."

Maybe it's the champagne. Or perhaps it's the fact that I not only lost Josh, but also Lexi and Capri. But right now, all that drama and pain fades away as I stare into Quinn's eyes. Something about him feels right. Safe, even. And I know how foolish that makes me after everything I've learned tonight.

Those things don't seem to matter anymore, at least not in this second. All that matters is the burning desire and rush of excitement as I yearn to place my lips against his.

Maybe I don't need my friends to enjoy this trip after all. Maybe what I really need—what I deserve—is to let go of my heartache and throw all my inhibitions out the window and let this tall, gorgeously mysterious man have his way with me out here in this beautiful garden.

I scoff at my own thoughts and earn another raised eyebrow from Quinn. "Care to share what's going on in that head of yours?"

"Oh, nothing much," I tell him as a blush storms across my cheeks. I tip the remainder of the champagne into my mouth and swallow it slowly as I savor the last few drops. "I'm just thinking that I've never been one to let myself swoon over a mysteriously handsome man in the middle of a fantasy-esque garden." I quickly glance at his lips again, wishing I were exactly that type of girl. The one who was brazenly confident enough to lean in and press my lips to his and let the troubles of tonight flow away.

But I can't look at Quinn and let myself feel these types of urges for him without thinking of Josh. The revelation that he's been having an affair with my best friend has punctured me too deeply to ignore.

So, instead, tears start crashing down like a tidal wave, and there is no escaping them. My body spasms and convulses as the reality of what happened tonight finally hits. There's no drug to get over a broken heart. You can stave it off temporarily by immersing yourself in a new friend, a beautiful garden, or even a glass of bubbly champagne. But there is nothing that can stop the full magnitude of your brain catching up with your heart after a momentous betrayal like this.

Quinn grabs the empty glass from my hand and leads me to a stone bench sitting at the base of a small pond while I struggle to catch my breath.

How could I have missed this? How long were they sneaking behind my back? Was I too blissfully unaware and ignorant to catch on?

Quinn sits a respectful distance away from me on the concrete bench, but he places his hand on my back and rubs it in soft, comforting circles. "Well, like I said earlier," he says quietly as he gazes towards the pond. "I'm here if you want to talk about it. But if you don't, I'm also completely fine with sitting here and keeping you company until you're ready to brave the world again."

I flash him a weak smile. "I just don't know how to face them knowing they all lied to me. How stupid I must have looked to them this entire time? I'm mortified and angry," I confess as I wipe the evidence of my breakdown off my face. "But mostly, I hate feeling this weak. I hate them for making me feel this small."

Quinn closes the space between us and cups my face gently with his hands. His expression surprises me. It's not the same cocky and arrogant one that he's shown me until now. He looks...angry? Bothered, even.

"You are not small, Teagan. Don't give them the power to make you feel like you are. They are beneath you and don't deserve to breathe the same air as you. You walk with your head held high, as if none of this has affected you. That's how you go back into that house and face them," he tells me as his soul-piercing eyes slowly start chipping away at my armor. "You are strong. Strong enough to beat them at their own game. Don't let them see you fall."

The way he's so fiercely adamant makes me wonder who in his life made him feel this way, because you don't talk like this without having firsthand experience.

"Who made you feel small?" I whisper.

Quinn's eyebrows knit together, his mouth dropping open in surprise before he pulls his hands away from my face and drops them in his lap. "My family. They aren't very nice people." His voice is soft and vulnerable. Something about it tugs at my foolish, overly trusting heartstrings.

I'm about to ask him to elaborate when a frog croaks from somewhere in the garden, making me jump out of my goose pebbled skin. "I guess we should probably go back," I suggest, getting to my feet while looking into the dark garden. I hear something bigger moving along the path, which makes the hair on my neck stand up. The air seems to have dropped in temperature because I'm suddenly freezing.

Quinn stands and offers me his jacket. Typically, I would say no, but it really is freezing out here, so I slide my arms in and wrap his coat tightly around me. It's still warm from his body, and it feels heavenly.

"Walk back with me?" He holds his hand out for me. I slip mine into his as we head back to the house. It feels right and wrong all at the same time.

I can do this. I'll walk in there with my head held high. I won't let them ruin this trip for me.

"Wait." Quinn stops. He tugs my hand and pulls me towards a large tree. My back hits the bark as he boxes me in with his hands.

"What?" I ask, my voice trembling slightly as he looks down at my lips. "Quinn?"

He lets out a strangled groan. "I have to do this. Just once," he proclaims before his lips are on mine.

The kiss almost ruins me. I could drown in the taste of him and the feeling of his body pressed up against mine.

Quinn pulls away just as quickly as it began and paces back and forth in front of me. "I'm sorry," he gasps out. "I shouldn't have done that. I promised myself I would stay away from you, Teagan. Especially since I know this won't end well. But there's something about you I just can't shake."

His admission startles me, and I'm mixed with both confusion and desire. I don't care if this will end badly. All I care about is this moment, with him.

A loud bell rings from the direction of the house. I feel myself losing him. Our stolen time together is coming to an end with each ring of that bell.

Quinn steps back towards me. "You've been saved by the bell. Now let's head back before I do something stupid like that again and end up getting thrown into the pond."

Instead of answering him, I grab the collar of his shirt and slam my lips back to his.

Chapter Fourteen

Lexi

My heels echo like rapid gunshots as I search desperately for Teagan. The abstract paintings hung throughout the many hallways of Windermere Castle flash by in a blur of color while I race to find her.

I need to fix this.

I've ruined everything, and I have no one to blame except myself. I knew I'd have to tell Teagan about Josh and me one day. I knew that day would hurt her, possibly destroy her. I just didn't expect that day to be today. I thought I had more time. I thought Josh and I would finally be able to be together in the open and that I'd have his calming strength standing beside me when we finally told her about us.

How the hell did Capri even know?

She's never said anything to me about Josh. We've been so careful to make sure that we kept our affair hidden from everyone.

I reach the end of the hallway. Left or right? Where would Teagan's mysterious knight in shining armor have taken her?

"Lexi! Wait!"

I spin around and see Capri running towards me. Her heels are in one hand, and her phone is in the other. She must have gone back to her room to fetch it instead of looking for Teagan like the traitorous two-faced bitch she is.

"Haven't you done enough?" I snap at her, causing her to stop short just a few feet away. I don't miss the flash of hurt that flits across her face, but right now I couldn't care less about her feelings. Not after the bomb she just detonated.

She wipes at her cheeks. "I'm so sorry, Lex," she cries out. "I thought they were going to hurt Lee. I panicked and—"

"I DON'T CARE!" My voice cracks as I scream at her. "I don't care why you did it! I just care that you did it! That you could even do such a thing to me! To Teagan!"

Capri flinches at my harsh words. "That's not fair. I'm not the bad guy here, and you know it."

The broken laugh that escapes my lungs makes me even more furious with her. "You don't get it. You never have to suffer like the rest of us. You have the perfect life. The perfect job. The perfect husband. You have no idea what it feels like to claw your way up from the bottom to get the things you want in life. It's all just been handed to you."

I'm shaking as I step closer to her, the adrenaline in my veins pulsing with anger and rage. "You have everything! You just destroyed Teagan because you were too selfish to give up one of your own coveted secrets. And yet you're the one who still has everything! But I'm the one being unfair? I'm not the only villain in this game, Capri."

The expression on her face and the tick of her jaw make me take an involuntary step back. I don't think I've ever seen Capri angry before, and if I'm being frank...it scares me.

Capri's eyes bore into my soul. "You know nothing about what I've been through," she hisses through clenched teeth. Her body shakes with fury as she closes the distance between us again. "You can blame me all you want for the mess you've put yourself into. But don't for a second stand there and assume you know a damn thing about me or my life. You wouldn't last a day in my shoes, Lexi."

Her hazel eyes are filled with a blazing fire that I've never seen in her before. I swallow hard and take another shaky step backwards to put some distance between me and that barely restrained anger pointed wholly at me.

"You're right," I say just as Lee comes running down the hallway towards us. "I'm sorry."

Lee finally reaches us and wraps his arm around Capri's shoulder. "You okay?" he asks her. His eyes meet mine, and he raises an eyebrow at me.

Capri's face transforms before me. You'd never have guessed that she looked like she was moments away from possibly murdering me. She smiles up at her husband and shakes her head. "Perfectly fine. I've tried calling Teagan several times, but her phone must still be in her room." Her voice is calm and collected again. So unlike the rage it was laced with just moments ago.

"And you?" Lee nods towards me. "Are you okay?"

I brush a hand through my ponytail, trying to appear as unaffected as Capri. But my entire body is on edge because my best friend is actually pretty terrifying when she's mad. "I just really need to find Teagan and fix this. After that, I'll be golden."

"I think I can help you with that," Lee says. "Henry said dinner is being served shortly and was looking for everyone. He thought he saw her head into the garden not long ago. That's why I came looking for you two. I know the three of you can work whatever this is out. You're best friends, and that kind of thing doesn't just get erased after one mistake."

My chest tightens with regret at his words. "Thanks, Lee. I'm going to grab my jacket and phone from upstairs before I look for her. Capri, do you want to come?"

She shakes her head. "No, I think this is something that you and Teagan need to talk about first. My being there might just make her even angrier." Capri steps out of Lee's embrace and places a hand on my shoulder, squeezing softly. "But you need to fix this, Lex. I don't know where any of us will stand if you can't."

She doesn't need to say it, but I know she's telling me that she's on Teagan's side.

Why does everyone choose her over me?

The temperature here in Scotland is nothing like the hot, humid nights back home in the south. The air here has that bone-chilling quality to it, frigid enough that I can see my own breath as I exhale.

I wrap my brown peacoat tighter around me as I head into the garden with nothing but a heart full of regrets and my phone to use as a flashlight. The moonlight helps illuminate the area, but it's still dark enough out here to make me jump at every slight noise.

I wonder what our host must think of us. We got out of his twisted game and still haven't met the man. Not that I plan on giving him the time of day after this stunt he pulled on us. If it were up to me, I'd be on the first flight out of here because I have zero intentions of meeting and swooning over my ex-favorite author after what he put us through. As if locking three grown women in a dark room and threatening to kill someone is just some sort of fun hobby for him? He's a freaking psychopath! Pierce and that stupid lizard shoes man are both on my hit list tonight. I don't know how, but I'll make them pay for what they've done to us.

A frog croaks loudly from deeper in the garden. I clench my teeth together to keep from screaming. I'm already having enough trouble finding Teagan in this maze of roses; the extra tidbits of sound thrown in from Mother Nature are wholly unnecessary. I strain to listen, hoping to hear my best friend's voice.

There!

I creep around a perfectly trimmed square hedge and follow the faint sound of laughter. I can't tell if it's Teagan, but I know I hear someone in this fortress of floral doom. I've never been much of an outdoorsy girl, so as gorgeous as this estate is, I prefer to stay indoors. Even if that means being caged in the same walls as a crazy pants author.

I swat at what I hope are imaginary bugs and continue down the trail—thankful that the owner didn't decide to turn this garden into an actual maze. So far, it's been a pretty straight path. It would be hard to get lost in here.

My heels sink into the plush grass as I stop short. I hear a man's voice just beyond me, "I have to do this. Just once."

I quickly turn the flashlight off on my phone and sneak around the bend as quietly as I can. It's Teagan and her mysterious acquaintance. He has her pressed up against a large oak tree and has his hands pressed against the trunk just above her shoulders, boxing her in entirely as he whispers something to her.

Usually, this would be a cause for concern, and I'd be the first one in line to kick this man between the thighs for accosting my best friend. But the way Teagan is looking at him stops me. She's completely and utterly smitten with the man as he snares her like a prized mare.

How can she be over Josh this fast? They just broke up, and she's already throwing herself at the first man to give her an ounce of attention? I know we both agreed to a solo-trip together, and even joked that we'd find our own hot Scottish men here—but I would have never actually gone through with that. Not with how shattered I feel about Josh ending things with me. He's the only one I want.

How can he want her back when his side of the bed isn't even cold yet before she's hooking up with someone new?

Teagan lets out a breathy moan of pleasure as her new friend kisses her thoroughly.

I can't watch this. I'm so disgusted by her right now. How can she do this to Josh when he wants her back so badly?

Josh wants *her* back.

An inferno of fury alights under my skin as I continue to watch. I should go. I should look away. But my mind and my hatred for her at this moment can't be reasoned with.

A bell rings from somewhere, and I know my time is almost up.

I check my phone to make sure my flash is off, then do something I know will truly be the end of us. I take photos of her being mauled by this man. Then I switch it to video mode and hit record as she grabs him and pulls his lips back to hers.

This will do just nicely. I hit stop on my phone and hold it to my chest before I turn and walk out of the garden.

The loud bell rings again near the front of the estate. I quicken my pace so Teagan doesn't catch me out here. I don't need to talk to her anymore. There is really no point in fixing this friendship when I'm so close to finally having everything I want.

When I exit the garden, I see Henry standing at the bottom step to the entrance, ringing a small silver bell.

"Hey, Henry," I greet him with a smile.

He returns the smile and ushers me up the steps. "Ms. Lexi! I've been looking all over for you and Ms. Teagan! Dinner is about to be served, and Mr. Pierce would like you all in attendance."

I roll my eyes and open my mouth to tell him that I have no interest in being Pierce's guest just as Teagan and her new beau stroll out of the garden hand in hand. Teagan sees me and immediately drops his hand and pulls away from him. Her expression turns to stone as she sheds his jacket and hands it back to him. He takes it from her with a smirk, throwing it back over his shoulder like some sort of male model. He looks proud of her as he holds his arm out for her. She takes it without argument. That pride turns to undiluted anger as he looks up at me. I glare right back at him.

Teagan was right about one thing: this man is obscenely gorgeous. He has that Disney villain vibe about him. Tall, dark hair, great body, and the most intense eyes I've ever seen. He's the type of guy who could flay you alive with a single glance. If I weren't entirely committed to Josh, he'd be exactly my type.

I can't help but relish in the small kernel of victory that flares up inside of me, knowing that I have this type of effect on Teagan. To see that she still cares about my opinion enough to use this tall, dark, and handsome man as a crutch instead of facing me.

And here I was, just moments away from grovelling at her feet to forgive me. I don't need her forgiveness. I need her out of my life so I can have Josh. Clearly, she doesn't care about him the way I do, and this little video will show him that. This is just another game I'll make sure to win.

"Oh! Ms. Teagan and Mr. Quinn! It's time for dinner with Mr. Pierce. I will escort you both, along with Ms. Lexi, to the dining hall. Come, come! We mustn't be late!"

I personally have no desire to meet this illustrious Mr. Pierce. Still, I find myself following right behind Henry, Teagan, and Quinn as we navigate through the crimson halls of Windermere.

Nothing this crazy author does to us will be worse than what I'm about to do to Teagan. I can't stop the smile that snakes across my lips as I press send on the video message to Josh. There's no way he'll want her back once he sees this. Soon, I'll have him all to myself.

CHAPTER FIFTEEN

Capri

The dining hall we've been led to is immaculate. It's like something out of a Victorian novel. The vast ceiling looks hand-painted. Little cherubs dance amongst fluffy white clouds and laugh across the sky-blue mural.

It's the only bright spot in the room.

A long, but skinny, massive hardwood table spans nearly the entire room with a forest green table runner placed perfectly in the middle. Brass candelabras stand every couple of feet with three candles each, flames casting shadows on the walls around us as Lee and I search for our seats.

Each place setting has handwritten cards atop golden-lined china with swirls of deep red patterns. My stomach starts to turn when I realize that they remind me of blood splatters.

Earlier, after Lexi left to hunt Teagan down, Lee and I returned to the sitting room we found ourselves in after the mock escape room. We spoke to a few of the other guests, all of whom had undergone their own trials before being allowed entry. As much as I hate the drama that unfolded in our little friend group, I'm glad that we weren't the only ones tested.

He might be insane, but I'm still anxiously excited to meet A. M. Pierce. He is the reason why we're here, after all, and I'm not letting

Teagan and Lexi ruin that for me. Even if I'm partially responsible for them being at each other's throats right now.

There are green velvet chairs on each side of the table, with one chair sitting alone at the head of the grand table. We find our cards toward the middle and sit. Lexi's name is written on a card between Lochlan and Lee. Teagan's spot is right next to me. It's probably best that they have Lee and me as a buffer.

"Where do you think they are?" I whisper to Lee as I glance nervously about the table. Almost everyone has found their seats and is whispering amongst themselves. But there are still five empty seats. Two for Lexi and Teagan, the one on the end that I assume is reserved for Mr. Pierce, and two more that haven't yet been claimed directly across from us.

"Maybe they decided not to come?" Lee answers just as the double doors at the head of the table open. Henry strolls in, flashing a polite smile to each of us.

Teagan walks in a moment later with a new man on her arm. They both look like they're ready to burn the whole place down. I can't help but shudder when I notice that her eyes are trained on mine. She and her new friend walk down the length of the table, looking at each guest card. They stop short when they get to Lee and me.

"Well, this won't do," the strange man says as he picks up her name card. He grasps Teagan's hand, and they walk to the other side of the table. He must find his card because he smirks over at Teagan and swaps her card with whoever was supposed to sit next to him before pulling her new seat out for her.

He glances up at us from across the table. "Mind putting this one there?" he asks Lee while handing the card out to him.

Lee stands and grabs the card, his eyebrows narrow as he reads the name. Lee introduces himself to the stranger before nodding at me. "This is my wife, Capri."

Teagan's friend shakes my husband's hand with a grin. "Quinn Gibson. Pleasure to meet you both."

Teagan stays quiet and refuses to meet my eyes. I don't blame her, not after the secret I kept. However, I am surprised to see her trusting this strange man so quickly. Teagan has never been one for making rash decisions. Both Lee and Quinn sit back in their seats before the muted conversations start up again around us.

"Babe, did you see this?" Lee hands me the card that Quinn gave him. My eyes widen when I read it.

Josh Marshall.

"What the hell is he doing here?" I hiss at Lee. "Do you think Teagan and Lexi know?"

Lee takes the card from me and puts it in the empty spot. "I have no idea. But I have a feeling this is going to end in bloodshed. Let's make sure to lock our doors once this dinner is over."

I stifle a giggle and remind myself that whatever happens between my friends, I still have the most fantastic man on my team. "Hey," I whisper to Lee. "I love you. And I'm so sorry about earlier. I don't know what came over me when I saw you standing there, safe and laughing. I'm just mortified."

Lee brushes a kiss against my cheek. "And I love you. Always, my darling. The slap was just a little extra zest that our marriage was missing. Let's agree to save that for the bedroom next time, yeah?"

If I didn't love the man enough already, then he goes and says things like that. Things that make me swoon over him even more. I grab his thigh from under the table and give him a playful squeeze. "I can't wait to have you all to myself later."

Lexi takes her seat next to Lee before he can respond. "I'm starving. I hope they serve this crap quickly," Lexi says as she glares over at Teagan and Quinn. "I can't wait to be back in my room and far away from *her.*

Not too thrilled to be next to this one, though." She nods at Lochlan, who flashes her a lopsided grin.

"Lexi!" I berate her, giving Lochlan a quick apology for her rudeness. "You don't get to play the victim here! What happened to trying to fix things with Teagan?"

Her smile is nothing short of pure evil. "I've decided I don't want to fix things."

Before I can question her further, the color drains from her face. I shift my gaze to where she's looking, and my eyes stop on Josh. He's standing in the doorway, hands balled tightly into fists at his sides as he stares across the room at Teagan and Quinn. They're laughing at some shared whisper between the two of them. I'm not sure Teagan knows that he's here or if she's playing up the fact that she's happy to spite him and Lexi.

I grab Lee's hand and squeeze hard in anticipation of the full-blown war we're all about to experience. Someone taps their knife on a glass to silence us.

"Mr. Marshall. Please find your seat so we can get started," Henry commands loudly over the now silent dining room.

Teagan's head snaps up at the mention of Josh's name. She pales as her jaw drops open. It's clear she had no idea he was coming, either. Quinn looks back and forth between them before placing his hand over Teagan's. I can't tell if he's being protective or staking his claim. Josh's eyes blaze with fury as he watches them, then he stomps to his seat, throwing it back angrily and sitting down with a loud scoff.

"Mr. Pierce will be joining us momentarily," Henry continues, flashing Josh a look of annoyance after he finally settles in his chair.

As if summoned, the doors on the opposite side of the room open with a flourish. "Hello, my dearest friends, I'm so honored to have you here in my home."

Pierce isn't exactly what I was expecting. He's all smiles as he waves at the lot of us. I guess I didn't expect the writer of my all-time favorite thriller novels to be this buoyant and approachable. I expected him to be creepier, I think. More serial killerish? Especially after subjecting the lot of us to cruel and unusual mind games before being allowed to sit at this table with him. I guess he *is* giving off a bit of Patrick Bateman vibes with that megawatt smile and those subtle, crazy eyes he seems to have going on.

We're all waiting with bated breath as he makes his way to the head of the table. Henry hands him a glass of red wine just as the rest of us are served plates of appetizers from the kitchen staff. It's almost like a dance, how each staff member balances the silver trays and places one in front of each of us without making a sound.

"Please, eat! Don't worry, I'm not going anywhere. We can all get to know each other over the next few days. Trust me, you all will get very much acquainted soon. So eat, my friends!" Pierce insists with a sly grin. He looks to be in his mid-forties. His dark hair is combed back neatly and complements his closely trimmed beard well. He has a distinguished look with sharp features and stunning blue eyes that don't seem to miss a thing. Something about him looks familiar, but I can't quite place it.

The room erupts with the sounds of utensils as we all dive into the first course. Henry announces that it's a traditional Scottish summer salad, consisting of fresh greens picked straight from the garden, juicy tomatoes, and crunchy cucumbers, topped with feta cheese and served over roasted potatoes with thyme. It's absolutely delicious, and I make a mental note to write down the recipe later if Henry is willing to share it.

Josh finishes his plate in record time before turning to me. "When did this happen?" he asks under his breath while glaring over at Teagan and Quinn.

I take another sip of the red wine and nearly choke on it when I notice Mr. Pierce looking right at me. "Mrs. Kim, isn't it?" he asks me. The rest of the table turns eerily quiet.

Clearing my throat, I nod. "Yes, Mr. Pierce. You can call me Capri, though. Thank you for inviting us to your beautiful home." My cheeks redden as he narrows his eyes at me, almost as if he's enjoying a secret laugh to himself.

"Then I guess you can call me Atlas, since we're to be good friends after this week is over," he says with a teasing tone before turning to the rest of the guests. "Let's all say our preferred names. No more of all this formality!" Atlas nods at the person to his left. "You can start."

We all go around the table, saying our names and professions.

There are sixteen of us, not including Mr. Pierce, or I guess, Atlas. It's odd to think that he has a normal, regular person name after all the personal details of his life have stayed under lock and key over the last decade or so. I don't think I'll ever be able to refer to him as Atlas. It feels intimately wrong.

I breathe a small sigh of relief when I realize that all of us are basically in the same line of work. Some are journalists. Others are influencers. We have a couple of book reviewers and photographers mixed in. And then there are the three of us podcasters. All of which revolve around all things books, writing, and authors. I was nervous when we left the escape room and saw that so many more people had been invited here to meet Mr. Pierce. It made me feel inadequate up until this moment. Because now I know we are all here for the same thing: to get the major story on A. M. Pierce's life.

Lee and Josh are the only two who are plus ones, and I'm still not entirely sure who Josh is here with.

Henry floats in again with more staff following behind him. They swap out our appetizers with another traditional Scottish meal: Haggis with neeps and tatties.

Lochlan claps with glee and savagely digs into his meal the moment it hits the table. "Oh, this is the best haggis I've ever tasted!" he says through a mouthful as juices slide down his chin.

Lexi looks disgusted and slides her chair closer to Lee.

I'm hesitant to dive in since I'm not entirely sure what's on my plate. The only food I recognize is the potatoes, or tatties. I scoop a little of each item onto my fork and bring it to my mouth. The rich flavors are exquisite, and I moan loudly, inciting some genuine laughter at the table.

"I'm pleased to hear you like your meal, Capri," Pierce muses. "We had the haggis brought in from a local butcher who only raises his livestock on organic feed. The neeps, or turnips to you American folks, are from the garden outside."

I finish chewing before taking a sip of wine. "It's all delicious, Mr. Pierce. Thank you again for having us."

Pierce's eyes darken as he stares at me. "Atlas, please."

I nod, blushing, before turning my attention back to my meal. Something about him unsettles me.

The rest of the meal is uneventful. Mr. Pierce asks us random questions, but nothing of real substance. Definitely nothing about his books. It's almost as if he's waiting to give up any personal details about himself or his writing life until dinner is finished. He mostly talks to his staff, giving them orders to bring more wine to the table and to take empty plates. It's nothing as I expected. He invited us here, and now I can't help but wonder what the catch is.

None of us is brave enough to ask Mr. Pierce any questions. Instead, we all eat in silence and laugh at the appropriate times when Mr. Pierce has said something entertaining.

When Lee raises his hand, the entire room goes silent as Mr. Pierce smiles at him. "You don't need to raise your hand here, Lee. Please, think of us as a giant family," Mr. Pierce responds.

"Sorry, I may have had a few too many glasses of wine, Mr—Atlas," Lee states, embarrassedly. I know he only drank one glass because he doesn't typically drink with strangers. "But I'm wondering what the point of your little task...or game was for?"

Mr. Pierce raises a perfectly manicured eyebrow at my husband as the room ceases to move. "You mean the game I played on your dear wife and her friends?"

Lee nods, grabbing my hand under the table. "Yes, I just wonder why not everyone had to play it to have a seat at this *family* table with you. Specifically, why didn't I have to play?"

I stare daggers at my husband. I cannot believe he just called out our host like that, even if I've been wondering the same thing myself. Maybe Lee's glass of wine was stronger than the rest of us, or perhaps he drank more with Lochlan than I initially thought.

Mr. Pierce folds his hands in front of him and rests his elbows on the table. "Didn't you want to know your wife's darkest secret? Didn't you want to know if there was anything she was keeping from you? It's not very often that a husband gets to hear those intimately dark details of his lady's life without having to get his hands dirty. You're saying you didn't enjoy it?"

Lee chuckles curtly. "No. I can't say that I did. I wouldn't want to learn anything if it meant putting her through that type of distress. I trust my wife to tell me her secrets when she's ready to share them, not because she's forced to."

"Well then," Mr. Pierce muses before he gets to his feet, leaving the rest of us sitting around this table like puppets hung on his every word. "You're going to have a hell of a time once you find out what I have in store for the rest of you lucky ducks. Now let's call it a night. I have more fun tasks for you all tomorrow, and I promise you'll want your beauty sleep if you're going to play. The staff will deliver dessert to each of your rooms in about half an hour."

Lexi scoffs loudly, and I hold my breath as Mr. Pierce narrows his eyes at her. "Don't worry, dear Lexi. You'll enjoy the next game on my little list of horrors as we get to know each other better." He glances at Teagan and Quinn and tosses an unsettling wink their way before exiting the room.

Lee and I make our way back to our room in silence as we unwrap the events of tonight. The trip so far has gone nothing as I expected. Lee must be feeling the same way because as soon as we close the door behind us, he locks it and shoves the chair from the small secretary desk under the handle.

He holds his finger to his lips and sneaks into the bathroom, beckoning me to follow. Once inside, he turns the sink on and closes the door behind me as I perch on the countertop.

"What's with all the cloak-and-dagger behavior?" I whisper to him.

Lee looks towards the door, a flash of anxiety clouding his features briefly. "I think we need to get off this island as soon as possible."

My eyebrows knit together in confusion. "Why?"

He runs his hands through his dark hair several times and paces the small bathroom, clearly frustrated. "I can't put a finger on it, exactly. I just feel like something isn't right here. Something about Pierce and this place makes me feel like I'm walking into a surgery I know won't have a good outcome," Lee admits.

"Come here," I beckon Lee towards me and wrap my arms around his shoulders once he's flush against me. Sitting on the countertop gives me a slight height advantage that I usually never have, and I rub my nose against my husband's. "Hey. If you don't feel comfortable here, then I trust you," I tell Lee. "Something about Pierce unsettles me, too."

Lee looks at me in a way I never thought another person would. Like I'm truly his entire world. But he's my whole universe, and I won't let anything break him.

"We can talk to Henry tomorrow and ask if he can arrange a car and ferry ride back to the airport. We'll get on the earliest flight that we can."

Lee shudders against me, and I wrap my body around him tighter. "Thank you," he whispers. "I'm sorry I'm ruining your trip."

"This trip was ruined the moment Mr. Pierce locked my friends and me in that room and twisted my arm into thinking you were in real danger," I reassure him. "As long as I have you, then my life is perfect."

Lee pulls back and kisses me, wrapping his hands in my hair and pulling me closer to him. "What if we just stay in Scotland until our flight out? We can find a hotel and rent a car when Henry takes us back to the airport. Then maybe we can explore some of the country outside of this twisted castle and its creepy owner."

I grin as I reach for the zipper on his pants. "I think that's a wonderful idea. For tomorrow, I mean. Right now, I think I have a better idea. Let me take your mind off of the creepy castle and secluded island..."

He moans and continues to kiss me as I grasp him in my hands, pumping him slowly. I love having the power to undo him completely. I nip playfully at his bottom lip with my teeth. "I love you," I tell him, quickening my pace as he hardens even more in my fist.

"I love you, too," he says, groaning against my lips. "Fuck, Capri." His breath comes in labored pants as he finishes in an explosive wave of pleasure.

I giggle and head to our bed as he cleans himself up. If I know my husband, I know he's about to unleash himself on me here momentarily. I'm already salivating with anticipation.

There's a soft knock at the door just as Lee comes out of the bathroom in a deep navy robe. He gives me a puzzled look, and I shrug. "Maybe it's the dessert?"

"Ahh, that must be it." He tightens the robe around him and slides the chair away from the door before turning the handle. "Come right in," Lee tells whoever is on the other side.

There's a loud bang, almost like an explosion. Thick, white smoke fills our room, choking me where I sit. The last thing I see before I succumb to darkness is the look of pure panic and confusion on Lee's face as he reaches for me.

PART TWO:
THE TRIALS

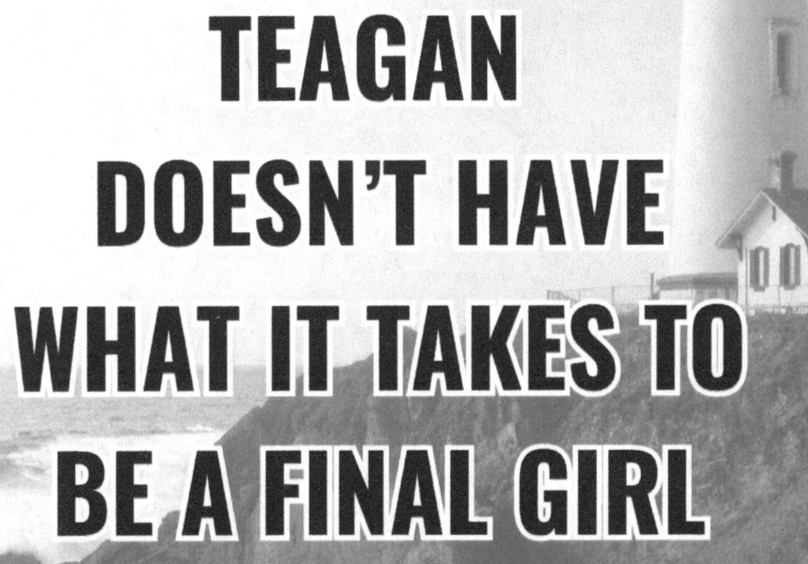

TEAGAN
DOESN'T HAVE
WHAT IT TAKES TO
BE A FINAL GIRL

Chapter Sixteen

Teagan

Everything is immensely peaceful, except for the chill permeating through the air and settling into my bones. The subtle sounds of the ocean waves breaking along the nearby coast are soothing, lulling me to sleep yet again.

"Teagan!" Someone shouts my name, I think. But they seem so far away. I drift back into my peaceful slumber.

"Teagan! Wake up!"

I jerk awake with a painful jolt. I'm lying on a concrete floor, surrounded by hay and the smell of mildew. My entire body hurts as I struggle to take in the unfamiliar surroundings. Someone *is* shouting my name. My brain is in a haze of confusion. I'm disoriented and nauseous as I gaze up at the slanted ceiling and bars above me.

Where am I? How long have I been asleep?

The last thing I remember is leaving the most awkward and uncomfortable dinner of my entire life. Josh was sitting there next to *my* friends like he owned the place. At least he wasn't sitting with Lexi. I don't know if I could have kept my mask of indifference up if they were here together. There's no way Lexi invited him. So why is he here?

Mr. Pierce wasn't what I expected. He left in such a rush and didn't really tell us anything about himself. He told us dessert would come to our rooms.

Oh no.

It starts coming back to me in flashes—the knock on my bedroom door and the smoke that filled the room moments later, rendering me unconscious before I could do anything.

"Teagan!"

I sit up quickly, causing my head to pound painfully. It feels like I'm taking an ice pick straight to my eye socket as I fight against the brightly lit room to search for the voice. The sound of waves nearby still lingers, and the air smells like the ocean back home. The sun is peeking through the small circular windows lining the walls above. At least it's daytime. I wrestle the fog in my brain to take in my surroundings.

The first thing I notice is that I'm in a cage. It's about four feet by four feet and surrounded by thick metal bars. The second thing I notice is that I'm not alone.

Directly across from me is Quinn. He's locked in his own matching cage about six feet from mine. He looks rough. His hair is in disarray atop his head, and the white shirt he was wearing when I last saw him is torn on one sleeve and dirty.

I look down at myself and see that I'm also wearing the same dress I was in last night. Except I'm not lucky enough to have shoes on because I stupidly showed up to dinner without my heels. They're still in that damn escape room in the castle.

"What's going on?" I ask Quinn, my voice cracking as I realize how parched I am. Something about these cages tugs on a buried memory.

There's a noise on the other side of me. I turn and see Amber, the woman from dinner who was sitting next to me. She's crying and locked in a cage of her own. I don't know much about her other than she's another one of Mr. Pierce's guests and an influencer invited to document this event. Her thick, curly blonde hair is sticking out in every direction, and she's in the same ivy green dress that she was wearing at dinner.

I stand on shaky legs and take in the rest of the room. There are six of us locked in six separate cages. None of the cages are close enough to touch. Quinn, Amber, and I are the only ones awake so far. I breathe a small sigh of relief when I don't see Capri, Lee, Lexi, or Josh. I may be angry at most of them, but I wouldn't want them waking up to this confusing nightmare. I also know I can count on them to find me once they realize I'm missing.

They have to notice at some point, right?

"I don't know what's going on here," Quinn says, his gruff voice momentarily startling me. I turn back towards him. He's leaning against the metal bars of his cage, facing my own. "But I'm going to figure out how to get us out of here."

My veins flood with fear as I come to grips with the reality of our precarious situation. I feel momentarily paralyzed before I remember Mr. Pierce likes to play games. Didn't he say we were in store for more?

"I'm sure this is just another one of Pierce's mind games," I say. Flashbacks of the horrible faux-escape room play like a broken film in my mind. "Have you looked for clues or anything in your cage?" I ask Quinn as I start sifting through the dirty, damp hay on the floor of my cage.

Quinn shakes his head. "There's nothing in mine. Trust me, I've looked from top to bottom while waiting for someone other than her to wake up." He points at Amber, who has wrapped herself in a ball and is sobbing into her hands.

There has to be a catch or escape button in here somewhere. I tug on each bar forcefully while trying to calm the wave of panic rising in my chest. "Maybe we—"

A loud, blaring alarm goes off above us. Quinn and I cover our ears while the other three guests finally wake in their cages.

"Good morning, ladies and gentlemen. Welcome to the next level of the game."

That voice. It's the same voice that taunted us in the escape room.

"I do hope you're all well rested. Because I guarantee you won't be getting a lick of sleep after today." The distorted voice lets out a hideous cackle. "Now, Teagan, my dear. I give you a choice."

Me? Why am I being singled out? I cross my arms across my chest and look nervously at Quinn. He's staring up at the camera mounted on the ceiling above with such hatred and anger in his eyes.

I clear my throat. "And what choice is that?" I ask hesitantly.

The speaker crackles before the voice returns. "You—and only you—may allow one of your teammates to be released. One teammate. You cannot choose yourself, for I have more plans for you in our near future."

I look to the rest of the group and see that David, Travis, and Ahmed are now wide awake. Their eyes are wild with fear as they stare at me. Waiting for me to decide their fate.

"I DON'T WANT TO PLAY YOUR STUPID GAMES ANY-MORE!" Amber screams. "I JUST WANT TO GO HOME!" She's completely hysterical as she slams her hands onto the bars of her cage. I stare at her in horror as she starts biting and kicking them, tears stream down her flushed face as she shouts at the ceiling. "JUST LET ME LEAVE!"

"You really don't want to play, Amber?" the voice asks.

Amber's hazel eyes bore into mine as she sobs harder against the bars. "No," she pleads as she shakes her head. "Please just let me go."

I wish I could wrap her in a hug. Instead, I'm stuck watching her unravel before me.

"What happens to the person I choose?" I finally ask.

The voice's laugh echoes throughout the room. "I won't make them play with the rest of us."

Amber's eyes are pleading as she gazes at me. I look at Quinn, and he gives me what I hope is an understanding nod. I can't let Amber fall apart like this when, for some unknown reason, I have the power to end her suffering.

"It's going to be okay, Amber." I force a smile at her before I look back at the camera. "Okay, then I choose Amber." She cries harder as she smiles, her mouth twisted wide in panic, showing off all her teeth between her wobbling lips. I'm too nervous to look at the rest of the group. I know they must hate me right now for not giving them a second thought.

"Wish granted," the speaker's voice booms out.

Shots are fired in rapid succession from somewhere outside. Amber is shot three times before I can even scream. Hot, red blood splatters me as she falls to the ground.

"Don't make a sound," the voice orders. "Now that I have your attention, I'd like to tell you the rules of the game. Raise your hand if you're ready to listen. If not, you'll end up like poor, sweet, dead Amber."

Quinn raises his hand. Travis is next. Then David. Ahmed stares at Amber's body as he raises his hand.

I can't take my eyes off Amber. Her lifeless body is twisted at an unnatural angle. I can't help but stare into those beautiful hazel eyes. Eyes that will never see life in color again. Because I—I just killed her.

I killed her. I only wanted to help her. I didn't want this to happen. My body goes numb all over, and I fall to the ground. The hay pokes and prods into my bare legs.

"Must you make me repeat myself, Teagan?" the voice sarcastically drones on from above.

"Teagan, raise your damn hand," Quinn pleads.

I meet his eyes and raise my hand weakly into the air. I think I might be in shock. My body is shaking against my will as tears stream endlessly down my face.

The cages all make a clicking sound, and the doors slowly open.

"Thank you for your cooperation. Isn't this fun! You'll find instructions outside the door to your left. Don't disappoint me again. I hope to see you on the other side." The speaker's distinct hum goes quiet, and just like that, the reality of my situation sets in.

This isn't a game.

Amber has just been murdered in front of us....because of me.

This is life or death for all of us.

Quinn is the first to step out of his cage. He reaches mine in several strides before yanking the door open. He grabs my arm, pulling me out of my cage and into his arms. "This isn't your fault, Teagan. None of this is your fault," he whispers into my ear. "I'll get us out of here. We *will* get through this. Whatever this is. Now take a deep breath. Then let's see what our next step is."

I nod silently against him, unable to speak.

Travis and David are whispering to each other as they stand over Amber's body. I nearly hurl when I see Travis bend down and inspect her even closer. He touches her bullet wounds and pokes her before sliding his hands down to her face and closing her eyes forever.

"Do you think this is fake? There's no way they just murdered one of us, like for real? Right?" David asks as he chews his fingernails. His red Hawaiian shirt is crumpled and dirty against his pale skin as he paces around the room.

Could this just be another prank on us? I touch the blood on my dress and bring my hand to my nose. It's definitely real blood. My knees wobble as the pungent, coppery-iron scent overwhelms me. Quinn's arms wrap tighter around me while I take deep breaths through my mouth, trying my best not to puke. Now isn't the time for romantic feelings, but he's the only thing keeping me from losing myself entirely.

"Umm, you guys. You need to see this." Ahmed's voice jerks me out of my shocked stupor, and I pull away from Quinn in search of him. He's standing by the door that holds whatever comes next in this twisted game of Pierce's mind. As we get closer, I see that he's already opened the door. My heart starts racing in my chest. I wonder what horror awaits us behind it.

Quinn's presence next to me is like a reassuring security blanket as I stop in front of Ahmed.

Ahmed looks directly at me. His dark eyes penetrate mine with a look of disdain. "Why does all of this seem to be because of you?"

"What?" I risk looking into the next room. My brows knit in confusion when I see what's waiting on the other side.

There's a small round table sitting at the bottom of a staircase. On the table is a black typewriter, and on it sits a letter with my name written on it.

But the most disturbing thing is the vase of pink flowers sitting next to it. They are the same flowers Josh gave me for our anniversary. The *exact* same flowers. Wilting in the yellow vase I put them in—*my yellow vase.*

How is this possible? Has Pierce been following me—stalking me? Is Josh a part of this plan? No. I refuse to believe that Josh would put me through this even if he's angry at me. Plus, how would they have met? Josh doesn't know a phone book from a thriller novel.

"Teagan," Quinn whispers low enough so only I can hear him. I look into his impossibly stormy blue eyes and see a hint of doubt hiding in them as he reaches past me to grab the letter, thrusting it into my hands. "What did you do?"

"I don't know. I don't know why this is happening. I'm just as clueless as the rest of you." I look at the group and see three pairs of angry male eyes boring into my soul.

"Open the damn letter already before you get the rest of us killed!" Travis yells. His bald head does nothing to stop the sweat from dripping down his angry, red face.

Grasping the letter with shaky hands, I see it's the same thick card-stock that the invitation to this place was written on. I tear it open and pull the letter out. The guys step closer so they can read it over my shoulder as I read the typed words myself.

Teagan,

Does this all seem familiar to you yet?

Four men, one woman. Locked in cages at the bottom of an abandoned lighthouse?

Well, it should, since you released the harshest, most condescending podcast review of this book—my very own book —three years ago.

Don't remember how the story goes?

Let me refresh your memory, Teagan.

You said, and I quote, "There's no way a woman would let herself get put into a situation where she has to rely on four strange men to save her. A 'real final girl' would find a way to save herself. No man required."

Well, my dear. Here is your task: Prove me wrong.

Survive the night and find your way back to Windermere with these four men hunting you down.

But here's the catch: if they kill you, they get to go back home.

If they don't, I'll kill all four of them.

Prove me wrong by following the rules I've laid out for you, and I give you my word that your friends will remain safe.

Fail, and you'll all be dead by the end of the day.

Good luck, Teagan. And don't forget to Live, Laugh, and Murder your little heart out.

A. M. Pierce

P.S. And don't trouble your pretty little head about Amber's fate. It was painted in the stars the moment you and your friends set foot into my home. After all, how can there be a true Final Girl if there are two of you?

No, no, no.

Now I know why this all felt so familiar to me. It's one of A. M. Pierce's stories come to life.

Quinn shifts next to me as the three men standing behind me all stop breathing. I swear I can feel their undiluted hatred and need for survival permeating through the air around us, suffocating me. The hair on the back of my neck stands up, sensing that I'm now in danger.

I suddenly wish I were locked back in the cage again for my own protection.

CHAPTER SEVENTEEN

TeaGan

S econds tick past in slow motion.

I turn on my bare heel and face four domineering men. Three of whom are staring daggers at me.

Travis is clenching both his fists, bouncing on the balls of his feet. He's the one I'm the most scared of. Something is unnerving about the man, and that's without adding in his massive size and unforgiving features. Travis told us he's a photographer and was invited here to document Pierce's life. Still, I'm starting to think he has a darker and more sinister portfolio than those perfectly curated author headshots he talked about at dinner. He looks *excited* about the challenge. It's almost as if he's been waiting for an opportunity to hurt a woman physically.

Ahmed at least has the grace to look conflicted. He's tall, but wiry. He doesn't look like much of a fighter, and the way he's standing makes me think that he might be the only one second-guessing the task laid before him. The anger and fear he had written on his features just moments ago have been replaced with confusion. I can't let that go to waste. He's a journalist, not a fighter.

My eyes land on David and his ridiculously cheery Hawaiian shirt. It seems inappropriate in this situation with its mock humor. Nothing about this is worth cheering about. He is looking back and forth between Travis, Ahmed, and me, clearly waiting to see who makes the first move—whatever that move will be. Like Ahmed, David looks uneasy about the prospect of murdering me. He doesn't seem like the type of person who would kill to survive, even if he boasted about writing some cutthroat reviews during dinner.

I can't be sure of anything anymore.

I force myself to look at Quinn and find that he isn't looking at me like the other three are. Instead, he's taken a small step towards me. It's almost as if he's twisting his body towards the other men. Just slightly. I want to believe he's shifted to protect me, but I know it's foolish to trust anything right now.

Not when all four of these men have been tasked with killing me.

The five of us are at a standstill, waiting with bated breath to see who will be brave enough to blink first.

Travis takes a heavy step towards me, his veins bulging menacingly on his overly muscled arms. "Don't take this personally, Teagan," he says with a chillingly calm voice. "But if it's between you and the four of us, then you might as well lie down and give in to your death now."

I instinctively take a step back, hitting the small table at the bottom of the steps. The vase rattles behind me, but doesn't tip over. Good. This is precisely what I need. I wrap my hands around the thin neck of the vase, praying to whoever is listening that this stupid idea will work. I just need a moment of distraction so I can put some distance between myself and them.

Travis lunges toward me, and I slam it into the side of his head as hard as possible. The glass vase shatters against his temple, and he falls to his knees, clutching at the side of his bloody face. "You bitch," he moans. "I'll kill you for this!"

Ahmed and David both reach for Travis in a poor attempt to help him. Travis is enraged and throws them off of him before clutching his bleeding face again and sliding face-first onto the floor. David stumbles and trips over the uneven wooden floor, falling backwards. The back of his head hits the bars on the metal cages with a sickening crunch.

Everyone stops and stares at him as he falls to the ground with a pained moan.

Now. I need to go now.

I turn and race up the stairs behind me, praying the rest of them are too distracted with the chaos before anyone has a chance to notice me slip away.

The staircase leads to a small hallway with two closed doors, one on each side, and a small circular window between them. I can see the ocean waves and overcast sky, but nothing to indicate where I might be. We must be on the island, but we could be miles from Windermere.

"GET HER!" Travis screams from the floor below. I hear another loud noise. Something heavy hits the floor, then everything goes silent again. I wonder where Quinn is. I don't remember seeing him after Travis lunged for me. Not that I'm stupid enough to trust him. Just because Quinn and I shared a moment last night doesn't mean he won't fight just as hard to make it out of this alive, same as the rest of us.

Mr. Pierce made the rules simple: them or me.

I hear heavy footsteps stomping up the stairs behind me, accompanied by heavy breathing.

Which door? Right or left?

My bare feet throb in sync with my pounding heart as I whisper a silent prayer that the door I choose is unlocked. I throw myself at the door on the left. I enter quickly, just as Ahmed hits the top of the stairs with Quinn right on his heels. Quinn is holding the small table over his head. I let out a strangled scream when he brings it down on Ahmed's head.

"Teagan!" Quinn shouts as I slam the door behind me. The door has a thick beam of wood, like something you'd find in a castle dungeon. I quickly fling it down. It fits into a metal latch on the opposite side of the door, locking me inside and Quinn out.

I lean against the door as the pounding starts. "Let me in, Teagan! We can figure this out together! I'm not going to hurt you! I swear on my own life, I won't hurt you!"

My breathing is erratic, and my chest burns with fire as I struggle to calm myself down. This door won't open unless I open it. Nobody can get me if I stay here.

I'm momentarily safe, but I need a plan.

Quinn pounds on the door again. "Please. I won't hurt you." His voice sounds as broken and betrayed as I feel. I want more than anything to believe that he's telling the truth, but even if he is, only one of us will make it to the finish line.

And it has to be me. I have to save my friends at whatever cost.

I hear what I assume is Quinn sliding down the door and to the floor. I step away from my side as quietly as I can, wincing when the top of my foot blazes in pain. Blood pours out of it at an alarming rate. I must have cut it on a shard of glass after I hit Travis with the vase.

I've basically left a trail of breadcrumbs right to me. If I have any chance of hiding from the rest of them, I need to staunch the bleeding. Looking around the room, I see I'm in a small bedroom. There's another window sitting above an old wooden dresser on the wall across from me, with a twin-size bed next to it. Dust clings to every inch of surface here, so I don't think anyone has stayed here in some time, wherever *this* is.

I start opening the drawers at random, hunting for anything I can use to wrap my foot. It looks like mainly men's clothing, but beggars can't be choosers. I find a few pairs of long socks and do my best to clean the wound on my foot. It isn't deep, so I don't think it'll need stitches, but I wish I had a first-aid kit with some clean bandages and antibiotic cream.

Instead, I use one of the socks, wrap it around my foot to cover the cut, and slip on two more pairs of socks.

Once that's handled, I pull out a pair of pants that look about five times my size, a black t-shirt, and a green and blue thick flannel. I shed my dirty dress and put them on. The black pants are huge on me, but I pull a shoestring out of one of the discarded pairs of shoes thrown at the end of the bed and use it as a makeshift belt before putting on a pair of tan hiking boots. Again, they are much too big, but the doubled-up socks fill in some of the space.

Now, if only I were lucky enough to find a weapon and some food in this abandoned room. I search under the bed, find a small duffel bag, and throw some extra clothing into it. One more sweep around the room tells me that there is nothing else of use in here.

A door slams loudly from the hallway, and I throw my hand over my mouth to mute the scream snaking up my throat. I need to get the hell out of here before they find a way to break the door open.

Travis's voice slips into the room. I cease to breathe. "Where is she? Did you find her?"

"She went through there," Quinn answers after a beat of silence.

The handle shakes viciously as Travis tries to open the room I'm in.

"That door is locked, clearly," Quinn says, his voice oozing with arrogance. "That's why I said she went this way. And I'm assuming she took off down the steps and ran into the forest. If she's smart, she'll be long gone by now."

Steps? What is he talking about?

Travis scoffs loudly. "And what happened to Ahmed?"

"He was gone by the time I got up the stairs. He probably chased her into the forest. We need to hurry so we can help him. Nobody else needs to die if we kill her first."

Loud, heavy footsteps pace in the hallway. I'm too scared to even breathe. I don't know why Quinn is lying to Travis, but I can't screw up this opportunity. He's pretty much told me where Travis is going and how to get out of here.

"Where's David?" Quinn asks.

Travis stops pacing and lets out a boisterous laugh. "The fool knocked himself unconscious. I tried to wake him, but it was pointless. I snapped his neck instead. One less idiot to screw things up. Now let's go find our little princess and end this thing."

I hear movement again; this time, it sounds like Travis's steps are moving farther away. I finally let out a small, painful breath just as there is a quiet tap on the door. Goosebumps prick my skin as I press my ear against the wood separating us.

"There's a broken table leg sitting in the hallway out here. Use it. And be safe. I'll keep him away from you for as long as I can," Quinn whispers. "Whatever you do, don't go into the woods."

Can I actually trust Quinn? Or is this another trick that ends up with him leading me right into my own grave?

A long, torturous half hour or so passes by with no noise from the other side of my chosen prison before I risk opening the door. I hold my breath and tug the wooden barricade up, pausing to listen for sounds. I hear nothing except the lull of the ocean waves. I set the wooden plank on the bed since it's too heavy for me to use as a weapon anyway. I finally open the door.

My eyes instantly spot the wooden table leg Quinn left for me. I grab it, holding it tightly to my chest. I feel more in control of my own fate with it as I step further into the hallway.

There was definitely some type of fight out here. Dark, crimson blood coats the floor and a few sprays on the wall near the top of the staircase. This isn't just from the cut on my foot. The table the typewriter was on is in pieces around me. Quinn had to have used it to knock Ahmed unconscious. But where is Ahmed? He obviously didn't chase me down the stairs.

The stairs!

I throw open the second door in the hallway and see that it leads to a small balcony with a winding set of iron stairs leading up and down. If I go down, I'll reach a rocky shore. The forest sits just yards away. I don't relish the idea of being anywhere close to Travis.

Maybe if I go up, I'll be able to scope out the area better and find a place to hide.

The iron steps creak ominously under my weight. I quicken my pace to reach the top. There is yet another door waiting, but this one is being propped open with a large cinder block. I tighten my grip around the table leg and tiptoe into the small space, letting out a sigh of relief when I realize I'm alone in here. It's a small circular room with large open windows lining the walls and a giant light at its core.

It's a lighthouse! It must be the one we passed on the ferry to Windermere from the mainland. I can see everything from where I'm standing. This is the perfect place to figure out where I am without being seen by anyone.

I crouch and crawl around the circular room, peering out of each window while trying my best not to get spotted.

On one side of the lighthouse lies the ocean. On the other lies a large, vast forest full of trees so thick I can't see anything through the canopy.

But what I can see in the distance, only about a mile or so away from the looks of it, nestled into the heart of the woods, is Windermere. The exact place I need to go.

My blood boils under my skin as I think of the man dwelling safely behind the stone fortress. Pierce is the reason I'm here and the reason why my friends are now in danger. They may have broken pieces of me, but they still hold a sacred place in my heart that I can't quite release their hold on. At the end of the day, I'd choose them every time. They're my heart and soul, and I won't let this ruin us.

I want to ruin him the way he's trying to ruin us.

Maybe it's time to turn this game of cat and mouse around and send him running for the hills. After all, it really is every man—or woman for themselves now as we fight to survive.

CHAPTER EIGHTEEN
Teagan

First things first, I need a plan.

Quinn warned me not to go into the forest, but if I'm going to reach the estate before they find me, then the forest is precisely where I have to go.

I need food, water, and a real freaking plan before I decide to go full-blown Xena the Warrior Princess to save my friends. There have to be some supplies stored in this lighthouse somewhere. I risk one more glance into the woods before heading back downstairs. I've already searched the small bedroom, but none of us really checked out the surroundings of the room we woke up in. My whole body is on edge as I tiptoe down the last set of stairs before I reach the main room. Travis said he killed David, and I know Amber is dead, but I'm still hesitant to make my presence known since I don't know where Ahmed is hiding.

Who else might be creeping around this lighthouse? Somebody shot Amber, so it's safe to assume someone has to be nearby. I enter the room filled with our cages and gag. I've always hated the smell of blood. The coppery, tangy scent of Amber's blood is overwhelming, making me dizzy and nauseated as I search the room. David's limp body is hunched over next to one of the cages, his neck twisted at an unnatural angle.

Travis really did kill him.

But why? You'd think he would want the extra set of eyes and ears as they hunted me down.

Instead, Travis has partnered with Quinn, who is busy keeping him engaged far away from me. At least I hope he is. I'm still unsure how I feel about Quinn's help. He was being truthful about the table leg, and he must have done something to Ahmed to get him out of the way. While helpful, it doesn't erase the kernel of doubt and suspicion nestled right there next to my heart.

There isn't time to debate his motives right now. I need to hurry up and get out of here before someone finds me. Travis will only hunt in the woods for so long before making his way back.

The large room has two more doors lining the walls, in addition to the door leading to the staircase. Raising the table leg, I make my way quickly to the first door while scanning the room for hidden danger.

Please have something in here I can use.

I twist the handle, and the door opens with a loud, thunderous creak. Turning back towards the cages, I pause to make sure the area is still clear before slipping through.

I want to scream in frustration when I see that it's a small bathroom. There isn't even a shower curtain to use. Just a small sink, toilet, and standing shower. All of which are covered in rust and grime. The room smells like urine, making my stomach roll all over again.

I hurry out and toward the last door. I'm surprised to find that this door is also unlocked. The handle turns like butter on a hot day and opens quietly, almost as if begging me to enter. I take a hesitant step into the room, my eyes darting in every direction. The room is about the size of a walk-in closet, though instead of clothing, there's a large, black trunk sitting in the middle of the floor.

And sitting on top of the closed trunk is another bouquet of pink flowers. These are very much alive, unlike the dead ones left for me earlier. Sitting next to them is another note with my name written on it.

My hands shake as I reach for the note, pulling the letter out slowly.

My dearest, Teagan,

If you've found this, then you've exceeded my expectations.

You just might have the heart of a true final girl if you were able to escape your new friends, or should I say foes?

Now, do you have the guts to do whatever it takes to get back to the estate and rescue your fellow thriller queens before time runs out?

Inside this trunk are the supplies you desperately need. But you have to earn them. To get them, you'll have to be willing to get your hands dirty.

Are you ready for your next task, Teagan?

You'll find what you need in the pocket of Amber's dress.

Good luck, my dear. And don't forget to Live, Laugh, and Murder your little heart out.

A. M. Pierce

I already know he has something sinister planned for me. My nerves feel like they are flaying me alive from the inside as I force myself to walk over to where Amber's body rests.

I don't want to do whatever Pierce has planned for me. I can't risk the lives of my friends, though.

Amber's body is sprawled across the floor, sitting in a giant pool of her own blood. You wouldn't think that a person would have this much blood in their body. I gag again as the coppery scent hits my nostrils.

I'm glad her eyes are closed so she can't watch me dry heave over her corpse. I find myself strangely grateful to Travis for this one kind gesture because I don't think I could go through with this if she were staring right up at me with her lifeless eyes. Eyes that were staring at me with such gratitude only an hour earlier. Tears pour down my cheeks as I whisper an apology to her, wishing I had gotten to know her better before her life was stolen away because of me.

I wish Pierce had killed me instead.

It takes me a moment to get control of my emotions. I'm pouring sweat, snot, and tears. I use the flannel sleeve to wipe my face.

I can do this, I can do this.

Reaching into the pocket of her dress, I rummage around for whatever Pierce has waiting for me. I expect it to be a key to the chest, but instead, my hand wraps around something hard and metal. When I pull my hand out, I see that it's a pocket knife. I open it and look at the blade. The top part of the blade is sharp and smooth, while the bottom half is serrated.

The crackle of the speaker above makes me scream. I slam my hand over my mouth as the creepy voice floods back into the room.

"Good girl, Teagan. You found my gift. But you know that won't get you into the chest."

I gaze into the camera on the ceiling and cross my arms over my chest. "Then what do you want me to do?"

The voice lets out a shrill laugh. "I want you to find the key."

"And where is this key at?" I ask. Surprising myself when my voice comes off strong and confident, even if my insides are quaking with fear. I know whatever he wants next won't be pretty.

"The key is located inside one of your fallen comrades, of course."

"Inside?" I look to Amber and then to David, both dead at my feet, and feel faint again. I grab the bars of Amber's cage and gulp down deep breaths of air. It tastes like salt and iron.

"I'll give you a hint," the voice says. "It's in the place that's responsible for your unfortunate circumstances. Good luck."

The hum of the speaker goes silent. I'm left with nothing but two dead bodies and a pocket knife to carve them up with.

What does he mean by the place that's responsible for my circumstances?

My brain? For having my own thoughts and feelings about his novel?

My mouth? For speaking those thoughts aloud?

I've never been good at riddles, so I try a different route of thinking. If there is a key hidden inside of David or Amber, surely there'll be an incision, right?

I shove the knife in my pocket and delicately lift Amber's head to check for any evidence of a post-mortem surgery. It's covered in blood, so I have to feel my way around her blonde locks. I don't feel anything but matted up tangles. I check her hands next, which are just as bloody, but much easier to inspect. I find nothing except torn fingernails and more blood.

Using the flannel to wipe away my tears again, I head over to David's body to search the same places. His hair is nearly shaved to his scalp, so I'm able to rule that out quickly before checking his hands. Again, nothing.

What does he mean by the place that got me into this mess?

I look back down at David and notice there's a darker red patch staining the chest of his Hawaiian shirt. I yank the shirt open while whispering my apologies to him for having to do this. I didn't know him well, but he deserves better than having his body mutilated for Pierce's amusement.

There! Right above his heart are newly placed stitches that spell out T.K.S...my initials...Teagan Kaitlyn Shepherd.

Everything around me blurs as I fall to my knees.

"How the hell did my heart get me into this mess?" I shout, shoving my hands into my hair. I can't do this. I can't rip him open.

The speaker crackles again above me. "Are you not doing this because you love your friends? How does that not prove that your silly little heart led you right into my grasp?" the voice says. "I expect it won't be the last time your little heart gets you into trouble while you're my guest."

The hum of the speaker goes silent again, leaving me alone to wrestle with my torn emotions.

I'm doing this to save my friends—but also to save myself.

"I'm so sorry, David," I whisper as I crawl towards his body and pull the knife out of my pocket. "Please forgive me."

Using the tip of the knife, I pluck at the stitches, loosening his flesh, giving myself ample space to fit my fingers into. Though he's been dead for about an hour now, blood still runs freely out of his body as I dig around for a key. I'm sobbing now in earnest, my tears mixing with his blood as it pours out of him.

I've been searching for so long that I start to wonder if Pierce is playing with me, that maybe there isn't even a key, and this is just another pointless task to show that he's in complete control here. I'm just about to give up when my fingers finally brush against something hard. I know before I pull it out of David's chest that it's the key.

As soon as I have it safely in my palm, I rush back to the dirty bathroom and hurl my guts out in the toilet, leaving a trail of David's blood dripping behind me. My body shakes uncontrollably as I empty the contents of my stomach. When the heaving subsides, I get to my feet and rinse my hands in the sink, watching the blood on my hands disappear down the drain. Thank goodness for working plumbing in this decrepit lighthouse. Too bad the water can't rinse away my sins.

I'm the reason Amber and David are dead.

I need to get to Windermere before I'm forced to do something even worse. I rush back to the room with the chest as soon as the violent aftershocks of the adrenaline coursing through my veins stop. My hands are shaking, making it difficult to insert the key. Once I do, I turn the latch and throw the chest open to see what I've just sold a fraction of my soul for.

Inside are several boxes of water, foil packs of tuna, granola bars, some fresh fruit, and a large bag of trail mix. It's not the medium-rare steak I was hoping for, but it's better than nothing. I grab an apple and nearly choke as I inhale it. Juice drip down my chin, and I hastily wipe them away before chugging down one of the boxes of water. The granola bar goes down just as painfully. I'm not sure how long it's been since I last ate. The more I consume, the less hollow my stomach feels.

Now that I've got some supplies, I need to get out of here before Travis circles back looking for me. I grab the duffel bag I found upstairs and shove all the food and water into it until there is nothing left in the chest but a long, black velvet bag. Lifting the bag carefully to inspect it, I find a machete inside and smile for the first time in what feels like days. I tuck the table leg into the bag with my provisions, pat the pocket knife in my pants to make sure it's still there, and swing the machete in the air a few times.

This will do perfectly.

It's time for me to save my friends—and hunt down my prey.

CHAPTER NINETEEN

TeaGan

The ocean breeze hits my face the moment I step outside. I've never been so happy to feel the sunlight on my skin. The damp mist hits my face as the air stirs around me with the breeze. The forest is fighting its own fight, its natural perfume refusing to be ignored, as the strong scent of the forest nearby weaves and bobs against the pungent aroma of the sea.

I take a deep, steadying breath as I recenter myself and my surroundings. It's the first real breath of air I've had in hours that doesn't have the underlying scent of death tinged in it. The air smells like a mix of salt and brine, making me homesick for the comfort and safety of my everyday life back in North Carolina.

Not that I can ever expect to have a normal life after this.

I grip the machete tightly in my hand, and I take a quick lap around the lighthouse in case there's something else out here I can use. It's just your run-of-the-mill lighthouse, though. Dead plants and overgrown weeds line the outside, further confirming that this place hasn't been used in months, possibly years. Something catches my eye in the dirt under my foot. I bend down to inspect it. It looks like blood. Fresh blood.

Raising my machete, I follow the trail back around the lighthouse. It leads me to a dumpster tucked into the corner that I somehow missed before.

Teagan, you have got to pay better attention to your surroundings if you're going to get out of here alive.

Something in the dumpster moves when I tap the side with the handle of my machete. Like the fool I am, I risk opening the lid to take a look when I hear a muted moan. What if it's Quinn? Travis could have tried to kill him like he murdered David and thrown him in the dumpster. What if it's Travis, and Quinn attacked him first?

I have to know who's in there, and who's still out there hunting for me.

The hair on the back of my neck stands upright as I peer into the dumpster. My eyes take a moment to adjust to what I'm seeing, but once I do, I slam the top closed with a loud bang. The noise ricochets through the air. Great, another damn homing beacon to lead Travis right toward me.

Ahmed lets out a pitiful shout from inside the dumpster. I should leave him and run. But I can't. I don't think I'm capable of leaving a person to die alone, even if that person has been tasked with hunting me down and ending my life.

I open the top again. He winces when the light hits him. "Ahmed," I whisper, looking towards the forest to see if anyone is heading this way. "It's me, Teagan."

He stirs and sits up, grasping the back of his head painfully. When he pulls his hand away, we both gasp at the blood covering it. "What—what happened?" he asks.

"Umm, I'm not sure. I was hiding in the lighthouse until about half an hour ago." The lie slips off my tongue easier than I'd like to admit. I can't tell him that Quinn most likely hurt him to save me, especially when I'm not sure what angle Quinn is playing, *yet.* "Will you promise not to hurt me if I help you out of there? I mean it, Ahmed. I will shut this damn dumpster lid on you and leave you here to figure it out yourself."

Ahmed hesitantly meets my eyes and nods. "I promise. Besides, I don't think I can get out of here on my own." He shifts his position and winces. "If you really do leave me here, I think I might just lie back down and die." He lets out a strangled laugh, which makes me trust him a bit more than I probably should.

"Okay, let me see what I can find to use as a step stool," I tell him. "I promise I'll be right back."

"Don't worry, I'm not going anywhere," Ahmed sasses back.

I stifle a laugh and turn to leave him when my eyes catch more blood drips. No, not drips. They are tiny little paw prints. It looks like they're going under the dumpster. My heart pounds with irrational fear as I kneel to take a closer look. What if it's a raccoon that wants to tear my face off? It would make Pierce's day knowing I failed his game by being eaten alive by some rabies-infected, dumpster-diving rodent.

There is a flash of movement, and I hear the tiniest little meow before my eyes land on a grey tabby-striped kitten cowering in the corner near one of the rusted wheels. The poor thing is shaking fiercely and cannot be older than a couple of months. She's just a baby.

I drum my fingers on the ground, trying to entice the kitten to come to me. "Come here, you sweet thing. Where's your mama?" It lets out another tiny meow and takes a hesitant step toward me as I continue to coo softly. It sniffs my outstretched hand, and its tail vibrates as it starts purring against my palm.

After a few preciously wasted minutes, the kitten follows my dancing fingers as I coax her out from under the trash can. I pick her up gently and bring her to my face, cuddling and soothing her as she meows again.

"Is that a cat?" Ahmed's voice startles both my new tiny friend and me. I jump to my feet with the kitten held safely to my chest.

I look into the dumpster at Ahmed. He's sitting up and has some color back in his cheeks, which seems like a good sign.

"Sorry, I got distracted." I carefully lift the kitten to show him. "Do you think you can take her while I find a crate or something to help get you out of there?"

Ahmed's eager smile and joyful brown eyes are answer enough. I pass the kitten to him. Then I toss him a pack of trail mix, a box of water, and a pack of tuna before I go hunt down something to help Ahmed. He isn't a large man, but there's no way I can help him get out if I can't even get myself into the disgusting dumpster.

I circle the lighthouse again and start to wonder how heavy the chest of supplies is when I see a rusted metal ladder under the set of stairs that lead into the lighthouse. Grabbing it, I lean it against the wall and add some weight by carefully stepping on the rings. It's creaky and loud under my weight, but it'll work.

When I get back to the dumpster, Ahmed is sweet-talking the kitten. "Do you think you can stand and get onto the ladder?" I ask him as I hop from the ladder into the dumpster with him.

Ahmed hands the kitten to me, and I gently tuck her into my duffel bag before helping him to his feet. He's unsteady, but he's also on a mountain of uneven trash that has been here for lord knows how long. "Yeah," he says after a beat. "I think I can get out." He lifts himself over the lip of the can, using the ladder for balance, and lowers himself out. Then, he reaches a hand back in to help me out. "Thank you, Teagan. I know this must have been difficult for you, considering our circumstances."

It really wasn't, though. I never could have left Ahmed knowing he needed my help. I could never regret coming to the aid of someone in need, even if that kind gesture comes back to bite me in the ass.

"Don't worry about it," I tell him. "Let's just take a moment to breathe some fresh air—no offense, but you smell like death—then we can decide if killing each other is our next step or not."

He gives me a reassuring, lopsided grin before we both slide to the ground in front of the dumpster. We enjoy a quick meal as the kitten finishes the tuna.

"What did you name her?" Ahmed asks while tipping the remainder of the trail mix into his mouth.

"I haven't gotten that far yet, but Dumpster Kitty sort of has a fun ring to it," I answer, petting my new little friend softly on the head, earning contented purrs in return.

Ahmed chuckles and tosses the empty trail mix to the side. Usually, I'd lecture him on that, but right now, littering is the least of my problems.

"Well, how did you find her? You can't name her Dumpster Kitty, that's just rude. Plus, she's too cute to get saddled down with a name like that."

I look over at him, then down to the kitten before I point to the little bloody paw prints on the side of the dumpster. "I followed the trail of paw prints."

"Hmm," Ahmed contemplates as he looks from the paw prints to the kitten. "What about Paw Prints? It seems fitting enough."

"I sort of love that," I agree, laughing with him. I pick up Paw Prints and nuzzle her. "We can call you Paws for short." I turn to Ahmed. "What do you think about that?"

His whole face lights up with mirth as he smiles at me. "I think that's perfect."

"So, what did you do to get yourself invited to Windermere and this game of Hell?" I ask him, popping some of my own trail mix into my mouth.

He reaches out to pet Paws and opens his mouth to respond when an arrow pierces through his throat, showering Paws and me in a hot mist of red.

"Did you really think you'd get away?" Travis yells, running towards me with a bow in his hands.

Shit, shit, shit.

I quickly grab my machete and bag of supplies, tossing Paws inside before I take off running toward the other side of the lighthouse. Travis doesn't seem to be a fast runner, so maybe I can get around the loop and head into the trees for cover as he tries to catch up to me.

"You can run, but you can't hide!" Travis shouts. " Oh Teagaaaaan," his voice takes on a creepy sing-songy tune, making my insides quiver.

His voice bounces through the air, making it impossible to pinpoint exactly where he is. I refuse to waste time turning around to look. An arrow whizzes by, landing in the sand a few feet to my right. I keep running, holding the bag tight to my chest with one hand, and pray Paws is okay. My other hand grips the machete. The forest is so close. The darkness beckons me to run faster.

I scream as another arrow grazes me and tears my flesh. Hot, searing pain ignites in my shoulder as I enter the tree-line.

But I'm not safe yet.

I dive behind a large tree and hold my hand to my mouth, stifling another sob. My entire body convulses while my heart threatens to pound right out of my sternum. Angry tears stream down my face as I struggle to breathe evenly.

"Come out, come out, wherever you are," Travis coos from somewhere close. Much, much too close for comfort. I cease breathing when I hear the crunch of his footsteps over the fallen leaves on the forest floor. He's only yards away from me.

All the noises in the forest come to a halting stop.

"I give you props, princess. You used your little boy toy to send me on a fool's errand. He really did try to save you." More branches nearby break under his hulking weight. "But I'm not as stupid as the rest of them. I left a trail of arrows so I could find my way back to you, just in case he turned on me. He'll be lucky to survive the night in that stupid garden once I'm through with you."

Quinn.

I search the forest floor around me like I can somehow find the breadcrumbs that'll lead me to him. The garden is nowhere near here, but at least now I know where to find him.

I've gotten so many of them murdered today.

It's my fault. All of this death is because of me.

Amber.

David.

Ahmed.

I *won't* let Quinn die because of me.

Travis lets out an angry howl. "WHERE ARE YOU!"

Nobody else will die because of me.

I quietly place my bag on the ground, hoping and praying that Paws will stay quiet just a little bit longer.

Gripping the machete tightly, I pull myself to a standing position and peek around the tree.

Travis is standing about three yards away with a devilishly hateful grin on his face. "There you are, little princess."

I have to end this. End him.

Flashing my own smile right back at him, I crook my finger at him. "Come and get me then."

Travis doesn't hesitate before he runs toward me at a full sprint. I plant my foot and wait until he's only feet away from me before I swing the machete with full force at him. He runs right through it. The thunk of his head hitting the forest floor reverberates through my entire body.

CHAPTER TWENTY

TeaGan

My eyes linger on Travis's decapitated body.

I look down at him in disgust and find that I don't have a single regret. I told myself I could never kill a human, but I sure as fuck have no problem killing a monster like him.

I should be horrified with myself and my actions. I really should. But the more I stare down at him, the more I come to terms with the person this place is slowly turning me into.

Someone who won't blink twice when it comes to killing to save those I care about.

I reach down to grab the bow he shot me with, only to find it snapped under his lifeless body. A small meow comes from my duffel bag, breaking the spell that Travis's corpse has over me, and painfully reminding me I was shot with an arrow just minutes ago. Even though the arrow only grazed me, it still stings like a bitch when I move it. My arm explodes with pain when I try to lift it to get a better look. I grit my teeth and ignore it when I see it isn't as bad as it feels. My arm will heal, but the traumatic aftermath of this place will linger forever in my soul.

Paws lets out another panicked yowl. "Oh, Paws! I'm so sorry, sweet girl." I rush to the bag and open it, pulling her tiny little body out carefully, nuzzling her until she purrs. "It's okay. It's all going to be okay. No more crazy bald killers are coming for us today."

I refrain from telling her that there's still a psychotic author out there waiting to punish my friends if I fail for reasons I'm still unsure about. He can't really be doing all this because we talked shit about his books.

Then again, that fragile white male ego can make a sane man do some unthinkable things.

As much as I'm enjoying the slight reprieve of knowing there *shouldn't* be another person out there hunting me down, I still need to find Quinn, and quickly if what Travis told me was true.

And thanks to Travis, I know how. I just need to follow the trail he left behind. I look over at his body and smile. Another gift he didn't think he was leaving for me when he came to end my life.

"Come on, Miss Paw Prints. Let's save our friends," I tell her in my calmest voice, placing her back into my bag. She meows in protest before she lies down and gets comfortable on top of the tuna packets.

I walk about a hundred feet before I spot the first arrow buried into the trunk of a tree. I don't know how Quinn missed this if Travis was leaving this trail while following him. I don't know where Travis found an endless supply of arrows, either. Maybe he found them somewhere in the lighthouse before he found Quinn upstairs. I didn't stick around long after we discovered I was the target of this twisted game.

There's a second arrow just ahead, and a third. I find an arrow about every hundred feet. Even without the arrows leading the way, Travis's heavy footprints going toward the lighthouse are very noticeable on the damp earth of the forest floor.

I spot the next arrow just as a scream from nearby erupts into the air. I freeze.

It sounded like a woman. Do I risk Quinn's life to help a stranger? What if Pierce is playing games with more of his guests, and not just me?

The woman screams again, and I rip open a bag of trail mix before taking off in the direction of her panicked voice. Taking a page out of the un-dearly departed Travis's playbook, I drop bits and pieces of the trail mix behind me so I can find my way back to the last arrow.

When there's a break in the trees, I step through, finding myself in a clearing filled with six single-person tan tents. There's a fire pit in the middle of them that looks like someone dumped water on it not long ago. The earth is wet, but the coals are still smoldering.

"Hello?" I say, trying not to yell, but loud enough to let whoever is hiding in the tents know that I'm out here. "Is anyone here?"

I reach the first tent and slowly lift the flap to the entrance, and gasp at what I find waiting inside.

The tent holds the body of another guest I vaguely recognize from the dinner party—Stephanie, I think. Her orange dress is much too bright and cheery against the deadly angle of her neck. Her eyes are lifeless as they stare at the ceiling of the tent.

I stumble as I back away from the murder scene, earning another meow of protest from Paws. I look over at the next tent, already knowing whoever is inside didn't make it out either, based on the spray of blood peeking through the opening.

A loud gunshot rings through the air. I throw myself to the forest floor and cover my head. I need to get out of here. Whoever was screaming earlier is clearly long gone. Crawling across the damp earth, I hurry back toward the tree line where I left my trail. I take off running as soon as I'm deep enough into the woods to feel safe.

What the hell is happening in this place?

I need to reach Quinn and get us both to safety before we become the victims of another guest's survival game.

I quickly find the arrow I left and don't stop running until I see the tall, ominous gates of Windermere looming just ahead. The sun has almost set, which helps cover me as I sneak in. I just wish it didn't leave the grounds cast in a shadow that makes my skin crawl.

It's not safe here, but I need to help Quinn. After that, we can decide the best route to getting my friends back, since I may need his help.

I'm so glad I paid attention as Henry drove through the gates when he picked us up from the airport. I'm able to easily make my way to the entrance of the garden as quickly as possible.

The assault on my senses as the floral scents hit my nose nauseates me. I've been surrounded by so much death, blood, and decay that it feels wrong to take a breath of something so sickly sweet.

I take the same path that Quinn and I took. How long ago was that? For all I know, we could have all been knocked out cold for days before we woke up in those cages. I don't even know what day it is now. I wish I had my phone so I could check the date, but Mr. Pierce took that away, along with my former self, when he forced four men to try to murder me for his own sick form of amusement.

There is movement in the bushes just ahead. I hoist my machete up, ready to attack whatever or whoever is lurking. The blade is still stained with Travis's blood. I creep forward, quiet on the balls of my feet while holding my breath.

The first thing I see is a pair of legs sticking out from a rose bush. The second is Quinn's face, matted with blood as he tries and fails to sit up. The rose bush is nothing but thorns and roses, marring his handsome face with thin cuts and scratches.

"Quinn!" I set my bag down and hurry towards him.

His stormy blue eyes meet mine, wide with surprise. "Teagan? Is that really you?"

"No, it's your fairy Godmother," I sass, rolling my eyes at him now that I know he's okay and not dead. "Stay still. I'll get you out of there," I reassure him, using the machete to hack away at the beautifully offending flowers.

Helping him up, I bring him to the bench where we first sat together. "You okay?" I ask, looking him over for other injuries I can't see. He's sporting a rather large bruise across his right cheek, along with what looks like a busted eyebrow.

Quinn reaches out and grabs the hand I was extending toward his face before brushing a chaste kiss upon my knuckles. "Thank you for finding me. When Travis realized I was trying to lead him away from you, he knocked me out and threw me into those bushes. I'm ashamed to say that I was scared shitless when I heard you creeping about the garden. I thought it was him coming back to finish what he started," he explains, his voice shaking and his cheeks staining red as he grips my hand harder. "But I was even more terrified that his coming back meant that he had found you...and had succeeded in killing you."

I can't help the way my heart swells hearing his confession, because I feel the same way now that I've found him alive. It might be wrong to trust him, but it feels a little like fate has brought us together to keep each other alive during this. I don't think I would have made it this far without him.

"We both made it. Well, almost. I'm not sure what comes next," I say with a sigh.

Quinn's lips twist into a sad smile, like he knows that it won't be as easy as both of us walking out of this place together. "How about we find a place to hide, and then we can worry about what comes next."

"Where do you suggest?"

He gets to his feet and pulls me up with him. "Come, I know a spot."

My heart flutters in my chest with both elation and worry as he leads me further into the darkening garden. The sun has set, and the stars are starting to show themselves against the velvet sky above us.

Quinn stops when we get to a small wooden shed hidden amongst the towering trees and shrubbery. "Trust me?" he asks, his voice trembling slightly.

I nod and let him guide us into the shed. Except, once inside, I realize it's not a shed at all. It's a tiny cottage. One fully equipped with a full-size bed, a small kitchenette, and, I hope, a bathroom.

I'm about to ask him how he knows of this place when Paws makes her presence known by howling from my bag.

Quinn takes a step back and raises an eyebrow at me before pointing to the noise in question. "What the hell is that?"

Unzipping the bag, I let Paws stick her head out. "Quinn, meet Paw Prints," I tell him with a grin. "But Ahmed and I call…called her Paws." I hold my hand to my chest as too many emotions I've forced down swell to the surface. "Ahmed saved my life. Travis shot him through the throat with an arrow."

Quinn pulls me into a hug. "I'm sorry, Teagan. I'm so sorry. I tried to hide him in the dumpster, hoping it'd keep him safe while he was unconscious. Travis was busy looking through the cages to see if there was anything he could use to tie you up. I thought Ahmed deserved a chance—a chance Amber and David weren't afforded."

I pull away and wipe at a tear, resolving to let that be the last one I shed until we get out of here. "We can mourn him once we get out of this mess we're in. I just wish I knew where Travis found that bow and arrow. I feel like this game is rigged. Pierce is obviously playing with us all. I just don't understand why he's singled me out."

Quinn tenses, then nervously runs his hands through his dark hair, taking a seat on the edge of the bed. "Ahh, I know how he found the bow," he tells me as he plays with Paws, who has gotten herself free of the bag and is swatting at Quinn's fingers on the aged quilt covering the bed. "When we were heading toward Windermere, we stumbled upon a bunch of tents."

"The tan ones in the clearing? All facing each other?" I interrupt him, sitting on the bed next to him.

He gives me a questioning look before continuing. "Yeah. Did you find them too?"

I nod, twisting my fingers in my lap as I remember my own gruesome discovery. "Did they have dead people inside of them when you found them?"

"Dead people? No..." Quinn knits his eyebrows together as he looks up at me. "We didn't even think to look inside. Travis saw the bow and the quiver of arrows sitting against the fire pit, and we ran as soon as he grabbed them. I wasn't about to sit around waiting to get shot like Amber."

I close my eyes as I remember all the death I've seen today, swallowing hard against the knot forming in my throat. Travis must have finished the trail of arrows on his walk back to the lighthouse after attacking Quinn.

"I'm so sorry for everything you've gone through today, Teagan," Quinn says as he closes the distance between us. Paws hops off the bed and squeezes herself back into the duffel bag sitting on the floor at our feet. She seems to feel safer there, the same way I feel safer with Quinn by my side.

Lying my head on Quinn's broad shoulder, I look down at my hands, still covered in so much blood and grime. "It's not your fault, Quinn. You didn't bring me here. You aren't the one putting us through this nightmare."

Quinn kisses the top of my head softly. I close my eyes for the first time in what feels like days. It's the first time I've felt safe enough to lower my guard. "If you had been killed today, I never would have forgiven myself."

He sucks in a sharp breath before continuing, "Because it is partially my fault you're in this mess."

My eyes fly open as I jerk away from him, stumbling off the bed like it's made of those same burning coals I found in the fire pit. "What? What do you mean by that?"

His expression is full of self-loathing, pain, and regret. "Atlas...Mr. Pierce...is my oldest brother."

My mouth drops open. I stumble away from him, going as far as I can in this tiny cottage. "No, no, no," I gasp, my back hitting the oven in the corner of the room.

His brother? I stare at Quinn and take in his features—the dark hair, the high cheekbones, those same stormy blue eyes. I saw them all on Pierce, too. How can I be this stupid not to put two and two together? No wonder Quinn's been trying to keep me alive. They must have some sick finale waiting for me.

Quinn stands and takes a step toward me. "Wait, let me explain before you jump to conclusions. I'm just as much a pawn in this game as you are, I swear," he pleads, inching closer to me.

"How can you stand there and expect me to believe anything that comes out of your mouth?" I reach behind me, grasping for something to defend myself with when he takes another step closer, cursing myself that I left my machete on the floor near the only exit.

My fingers wrap around a metal pan, and I swing it at him without a second thought, colliding with the side of his head. Quinn hits the floor with a loud thunk just as the cottage door bursts open.

Henry and two other men step inside.

"Tsk, tsk, Ms. Teagan. We had higher hopes for you. Mr. Pierce won't be pleased to know that you broke the rules," Henry chastises, then snaps his fingers. One of his henchmen lunges forward and grabs me, dragging me out just as Quinn starts to stir.

"No! What are you talking about? I followed his rules!" I yell, fighting against the man holding me. "I followed the rules!"

Henry smiles. "You were supposed to be the only survivor. A true final girl. But would a final girl fall for the villain? I don't think so, Ms. Teagan."

"You have to let my friends go! They didn't do anything wrong!"

Quinn tries to sit up, but his head is bleeding again. "Teagan..." he groans.

Henry strides over to Quinn and kicks him in the face. "Down, you filthy dog. Your master won't be pleased to know that you broke his rules either. And when she dies, you'll only have yourself to blame!"

Something sharp pinches the side of my neck as I try to decipher the meaning of Henry's words.

Then everything fades to black.

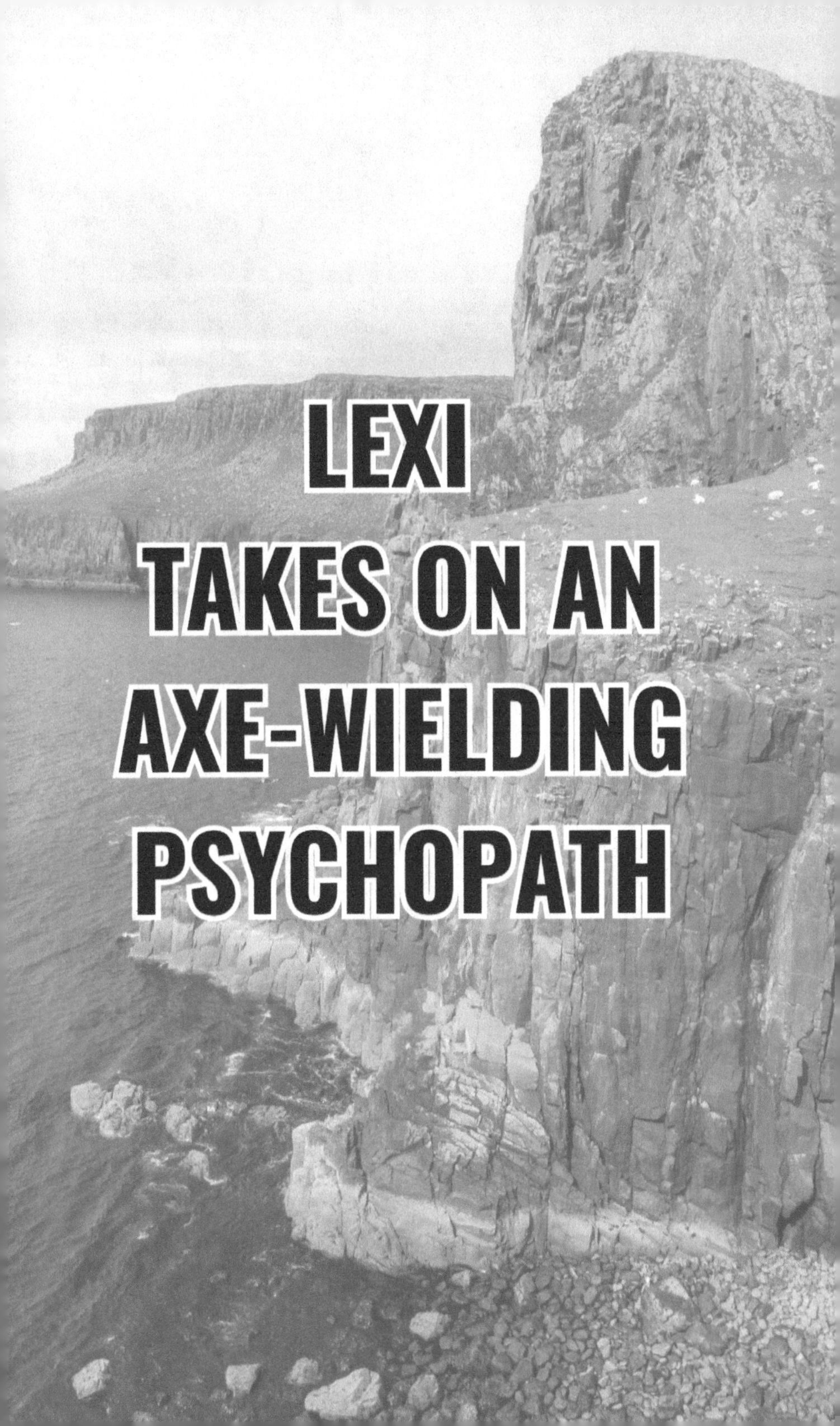

LEXI
TAKES ON AN
AXE-WIELDING
PSYCHOPATH

CHAPTER TWENTY-ONE

Lexi

"Lexi!"

"Lexi!"

"LEXI, WAKE UP!!"

My eyes fly open, and the first thing I see is my best friend's husband standing in a robe. Lee's terrified expression bores down on me, his hands gripping my shoulders as he shakes me awake.

When I don't move, he shakes me again. "Lexi! Get up, NOW!"

I struggle to take in the unfamiliar surroundings. I'm in some sort of man cave or hunting cabin. Lifeless, dead animals with black pits for eyes are mounted on every square inch of the place.

"Where the hell am I?" I sit up and face Lee, my eyes still tracing every bit of the room as quickly as I can. My head is spinning. "Where's Capri? And why are you screaming at me?!"

"I don't know where she is." His voice laced with panic as he grabs my arm and pulls me off the leather sofa. My sweat-slicked skin makes a disgustingly unladylike noise as I peel away from the leather. I cringe when I see the moisture buildup on the couch.

How *gross*.

I look down at my dress and sigh. I should have changed into my silk pajamas and out of this stupid sequined ensemble. Or at the very least, put some real shoes on. These three-inch heels won't be very kind on my feet if I need to walk further than ten steps. You'd think whoever kidnapped me would have made sure I had proper getaway gear on before placing me in this stupid mancave.

At least I'm not wearing a robe like Lee is. Why is he wearing a robe anyway?

"Where's my phone?" I ask, searching the couch cushions. "It has to be here somewhere!" Panic crawls up my throat as I frantically continue my search with no luck.

"Lexi…" Lee's voice turns stern, like he's trying to coax a stubborn child into eating their vegetables, knowing damn well those peas are only going to end up on the floor. "We have to run. Now!"

I furrow my brows at him in exasperation. "Why? What's your deal, dude?" Usually, he's so calm, collected, and utterly unfazed by the chaos of life going on around him. It's one of the few things I envy about Capri; she's got a catch of a husband who takes all her neurosis in stride.

If only the rest of us could get that lucky.

I'm startled by a loud bang behind me. I turn to see an axe—a literal axe—poking through the mahogany wooden door just feet away from us.

"*That* is my deal! Now you'd better get up and start running, or I'll be forced to explain to my wife that I left her best friend behind to die because she was too full of herself to listen!" Lee shouts the last part, spit flying out of his mouth as the vein in his forehead pulsates viciously.

I've never seen this man scared before. It just now dawns on me that I should be scared, too. That fear kicks into overdrive the minute the axe-wielding crazy person strikes the door behind me again.

"Well then!" I yell at Lee. "Lead the way since you seem to know everything!"

He grabs my arm, and we bolt toward the back of the house, or at least I think it's the back. I've obviously never been here before, and I don't know why I'm here now.

The last thing I remember is answering the knock at my door, Josh strolling into my room with a smirk...and then...smoke?

No. There was another knock on the door right after Josh said he needed to take a shower. Someone threw something into my room that gassed us.

Lee throws open another door at the end of the hall, and we plunge inside. He locks the door behind us as I quickly scan the room for whatever I can use to block the door from the axe-wielding psychopath out there.

Who gassed us earlier? And why the hell is there a person with an axe coming after us now?

"Come help me with this!" I shout, struggling to push a heavy wooden dresser toward the door. It's a solid piece of furniture, heavy and sturdy, unlike that crap particle wood they sell nowadays.

With his help, we get the door blocked and stand in silence, listening for noises outside of our heavy, panicked breathing. I'm too out of breath to speak, but I desperately want to grill Lee with questions.

Why are we here?

How did we get here?

Where are Josh, Capri, and Teagan?

What was the smoke that filled my room, and did it happen to him, too?

Lee stares at me, and I swear his mind links to mine because he finally whispers, "Do you know what's happening?"

I shake my head. "Do you?" I whisper back.

He rolls his eyes and shakes his head.

"Look, I get that you're confused. I am too. But I'm not going to put up with your crap like your wife does. You don't need to roll your eyes at me," I whisper-yell over the deafening silence.

He takes a step closer to me and opens his mouth in retort when we hear a scraping noise coming down the hall. Our eyes widen at the same moment.

"We need to get out of here," Lee says calmly, even though his whole body quivers. "*Now.*"

My eyes dart from wall to wall, looking for an escape route that doesn't involve facing the person trying to murder us with an axe on the other side of the door. I run to the only other door in the room and throw it open, praying that it isn't a closet full of dingy plaid flannels and dirt-stained Levi jeans. I nearly weep with relief when I see it's a small bathroom.

"Here!" I shout at Lee, pointing toward the small window sitting above a clawfoot tub. "Hoist me up!"

Lee doesn't hesitate before grabbing me around my waist and lifting me, his arms shaking in protest as I shimmy the window open as far as it'll let me.

The axe slams against the bedroom door, making us both jump.

"Lexi, you need to get out of here!" Lee shouts while pushing me through the small gap.

The window isn't large by any means, but it's wide enough for an adult to squeeze through. And I do just that. My dress snags and tears as I shuffle through with Lee's help. The cabin must be built into the earth because the drop from the window is only about three feet. I fall to the ground with a loud yelp, wincing when the pine needles covering the damp ground dig into my exposed flesh.

"What about you?" I scream, throwing my hands through the window as Lee backs away, tightening the sash around his robe. "Grab my hand, Lee! You can't die here! Capri will never recover from this!"

The axe hits the door again, making an even bigger hole.

Lee looks up at me, fear flooding his features. "Lexi, get out of here. You're not strong enough to pull me up, and we both know it. Find Capri and get her out of this place! Promise me!" he shouts, pleading in a way that breaks something in me.

Hot, wet tears fall from my face as I shake my head at him and throw myself back through the window, my stupid sequins getting caught again and tugging me backward. "I can't just leave you here to die! We can fight him off together!"

The door smashes to pieces as the Axeman throws himself into it, only to be held up by the large wooden dresser. Lee slams the bathroom door and locks it, but we both know it's futile. The Axeman will get through this door in no time. And then Lee will be dead.

Just as I'm about to scream at Lee one more time to at least try to escape, someone grabs me around my waist and pulls me out of the window. I fall to the ground painfully, where I'm met with the ugliest pair of damn shoes in the world. I've only seen one person wearing these shoes.

"Fancy running into you here, lassie," he says with his ridiculous accent as he holds a hand out to help me up. I smack the hand away and gape at him in disbelief.

"Lochlan!" I gasp, getting to my feet in a rush of fury. "What the hell is going on here? Is this another one of your stupid games? Because it's not funny!" I slam my hands against his chest repeatedly.

He shakes his head, pushing me away gently, even though I've been anything but gentle with him. "No, little lass. This isn't my doing. And I don't know why I'm here. The last thing I remember is finishing my scotch right before there was a loud knock on my bedroom door," he explains, rubbing at his head, his red hair shining brightly. I vaguely wonder if he's suffering from the same headache I am. I assume it's from whatever sleeping agent they gassed us with when they abducted us. "But I did find this in my pocket when I woke up." He hands me an envelope with my name scrawled across the front.

Whatever is waiting inside this handwritten bomb, I don't want any part of it.

I shove the letter back at him. "I don't have time for this," I snap before finally getting a good look at him. His suit is covered in blood, and he has a gash across his forehead that looks fresh. "What happened to you?"

Lochlan pockets the envelope again and looks down at his bloodied attire before pointing toward the window. "Oh, you know, the usual. I woke up in a strange room with dead animals looking at me from every inch of the wall. I fought off a crazy masked-bloke who seems to have a penchant for axes," he says with a flourish, waving his hands like some sort of drunken magician before pointing toward the window. "The same thing that's going to happen to your friend down there if we don't get him out. But I don't think he'll make it out as unscathed as I did. I'm wily and quick on my feet like a fox." He winks and does some stupid wannabe kung-fu move before falling on his ass.

He stumbles to his feet just before the axe smashes against the bathroom door with a deafening crack. Lee curses and takes another leaping jump toward the window.

"Then help him!" I scream, not caring that Lochlan could be the one behind all of this, even if he does seem like an annoyingly handsome, but useless, drunk, and not some astute mastermind—or that this could just be another stupid escape room type game like before. Everyone will be laughing at my overreactions for sport the moment I cross the invisible finish line.

All I can think about is saving Lee, just like he saved me. I won't let him sacrifice himself for me. We may not be close, but he's my best friend's husband. I refuse to be the reason why she loses him. Plus, it would be very unfortunate for him to die wearing nothing but a robe that's just a touch too short.

"Lee!" Lochlan yells, thrusting his whole body through the small opening of the window. "Grab my hand if you want to live to see the next hour, mate!"

The axe hits the door behind him again. Lee wastes no time debating. He gets a running start and throws himself at Lochlan, grabbing his hands with renewed determination. I throw myself onto Lochlan's legs, a loud, inhuman grunt escaping my lips so he doesn't slide through the gap under Lee's weight. Together, we pull Lee to safety just as the Axeman bursts through the bathroom door.

He runs toward us and throws the axe at the window. It implants itself into the wall with a sickening crunch. Lochlan helps Lee to his feet, and the three of us take off running into the woods, while being chased by the masked man's screams of fury.

"YOU CAN RUN, BUT YOU CAN'T HIDE!"

"YOU CAN RUN, BUT YOU CAN'T HIDE!"

"YOU CAN RUN, BUT YOU CAN'T HIDE!"

My brain replays those sinister words over and over again as we run further and further into the unknown.

What the hell have we gotten ourselves into?

CHAPTER TWENTY-TWO

Lexi

We run deeper and deeper into the woods until our lungs give out. Well, until their lungs give out. I've been running three miles a day since I was a freshman in college to stave off that dreaded freshman fifteen. I can run laps around this lot without breaking a sweat.

I do wish I wasn't trying to run in heels—even if I look great while doing it.

"Do we think we've lost him?" Lee pants, his hands clutching his side as he leans against the trunk of a large tree, gasping for breath. "Lochy, do you know a place we can hide?"

"Lochy? When did you have a chance to come up with this riveting nickname?" I cross my arms and glare at the two of them.

Lee shrugs. "We got to know each other a bit while you girls were trapped in that room. Did you know Lochy-boy grew up here in Scotland? Isn't that right?" He gestures to Lochlan.

Lochan holds up a hand in answer just before puking his guts up onto the forest floor.

I take a few steps away from him to dodge the mess and can't help the sneer that paints my lips as I watch the two of them fall apart before me. Freaking *men*.

Why couldn't I have been left with another woman? Teagan may hate me right now, but I know she'd be a killer partner in a situation like this. That girl is the definition of tenacity and quick thinking. I'd even take Capri and her dramatics because while she's quick to fall apart, she's even quicker at figuring out a plan and seeing it through to the end.

Our friendship trio may be on the rocks right now, but if push comes to shove, we will go down swinging for each other. I trust that fact with my entire soul, even if I'm probably last on their list to save.

But instead of my final girl friends, I'll have to babysit these idiots while trying to figure out how to get us out of this mess. I have one guy who would rather drink himself to death and has a horrible sense of footwear, and another who was about to willingly sacrifice himself instead of trying to find another way to escape.

This is a disaster.

"I don't even know where we are, mate," Lochlan groans out before dry-heaving again.

Again, useless freaking men.

What we need is a plan.

"First off, we need to figure out where we are so that we can get back to Windermere, where our friends should be," I tell them, looking around the forest for anything of use. It's almost a full moon, so we have a decent amount of light illuminating our surroundings. I still wish I had thought to grab some supplies and flashlights before leaving the cabin, but I wasn't in the best state of mind while being chased by a literal axe-swinging maniac.

"Can either of you climb one of these trees?" I gesture to the sky. They both look at me like I'm insane. "Look," I say, placing my hand on my hip and giving them my 'take no shit' voice. "Someone needs to climb up and search for the castle. I'm sure Mr. Douchebag Author will have the whole thing lit up like a torch, making it *visible* from higher ground.

So one of you needs to get your climbing shoes on before that psychotic Axeman finds us. Wait, scratch that," I say, rolling my eyes hard enough that I'm surprised they don't get stuck. "I'll be out of here before either of you idiots knows what hit you. And by 'hit you', I mean axe you in the face."

The guys look from me to each other, having some silent bromance fight for a solid minute before Lee pushes off the tree and reluctantly volunteers.

"You guys keep watch while I do this," Lee orders while he rolls his sleeves up. "I swear I'll howl at the moon loud enough for the Axeman to find us all if you ditch me."

Lochlan lets out a loud belch before sliding to the ground. "You got it, mate. I'll just be here, resting my eyes next to this nice-looking tree. I don't want to see the family jewels."

"Dude, how are you still drunk?" I ask, kicking his leg out of my way as I watch Lee scale the tree. *Oh.* That's what Lochlan meant about the family jewels. I quickly avert my eyes.

Good for you, Capri.

Lochlan hiccups. "I found a bottle of whiskey when I woke up. I only got about a fourth of it down before 'ol Johnny boy came at me with that axe. I broke the rest of me bottle over his head," he mumbles. "And that's how I got away."

A *Shining* reference, huh. I may have slightly misjudged this guy. I gaze down at his feet and cringe at those hideous shoes. Nope. Definitely did not misjudge him. He's an idiot through and through.

"Okay, I think I'm high enough!" Lee loudly whispers down at us. Well, me. Lochy-boy is fast asleep and drooling slightly against the tree.

"What do you see?" I ask Lee. "Any lights?"

I hear the crunch of breaking twigs and leaves on the forest floor nearby. I freeze in place. It almost sounds like someone, or something, is running toward us.

"Lochlan! Lochlan, wake up!" I plead, searching the ground around me for something to defend myself with. I can't imagine a giant fallen tree branch will do much against an axe, but it's all I've got right now.

Hoisting the branch over my head, I prepare to swing it at whatever is running through the woods at us when Lee jumps out of the tree from above and scares the soul right out of my body.

"Lee! What the hell! I could have killed you!" I stare at him indignantly before remembering why I have this tree branch gripped so tightly in my hands. "Wait!" I throw my hand over his mouth before he has a chance to respond. "Someone was running this way! I swear I heard footsteps over there." I point toward the dark forest.

Lee's eyes widen, and he nods before motioning me to stay silent. He takes the branch from me, pushing me behind him to help guard the still totally clueless Lochan. "Wave your hands when you see them get close," he whispers, then hides behind a tree just a few feet from where I'm crouched next to Lochlan.

The sounds of the forest seem even louder as we wait for whatever horror this place has in store for us. The hoots of the owls turn sinister with each passing minute. The frogs' croaks grow ominous as the seconds slowly tick by. Even the rustling breeze feels like phantom fingers caressing down my nerves, leaving trails of unease to fester under my skin.

I see a flash of white in the trees and wave my hands frantically at Lee. He gives me another nod, and I watch the muscles in his forearms flex as he grips the branch harder. Lee gears up to swing the makeshift weapon when I see a startled, but familiar face staring back at me. Kristi!

I remember her from dinner; she's a journalist or something, and she had a guy with her.

"Stop!" I shout, jumping up from my position and throwing myself at Lee before he's able to finish his swing, so he doesn't accidentally murder another one of Pierce's guests in this unwilling game of his. "It's Kristi! Lee! It's Kristi!"

Lee drops the branch just before Kristi collapses into our arms. "He's coming. He's coming!" she howls.

"Who's coming?" Lee and I both ask at the same time. She faints before she has a chance to answer.

Looking at her up close, it seems like the Axeman may have gotten hold of her. Her once-white dress is torn and filthy, and I can see that she has a massive gash on her upper thigh. She also has a bleeding cut on her cheek, which is dripping onto her bleached blonde hair, turning it a startling shade of pink. I try to wipe away as much blood as I can while trying to coax her awake.

"Kristi, hunny," I say calmly, even though my pulse is racing. "Who's coming?" Her hazel eyes flutter open, then fall shut again as she goes limp against Lee and me.

"Who the hell is Kristi?" Lochlan's body towers over us as he rubs his temples. "Oh, she's a mess, isn't she? Well, Kristi, meet the L-Team. Lochy here, Lee, and this sassy lassie is my girl Lexi."

I roll my eyes and start to snap something rude at him when my gaze snags on something in the trees.

My heart stops beating when I realize what it is.

The Axeman stares as he slowly raises his axe and saunters toward us.

It's like a taunt.

No matter what we do or how fast we run, he'll always find us.

"L-Team," Lochlan says, his voice wobbling like he's about to throw up again. "We need to run. NOW!" he shouts, grabbing and pulling me up as Lee carries Kristi's limp body.

"YOU CAN RUN, BUT YOU CAN'T HIDE!"

We all take off in the opposite direction of the Axeman, running as fast as we can, which right now isn't fast enough.

We're running for what feels like hours, exhaustion slowly eating away at us as we're forced to run uphill.

We're never going to outrun this psychopath at the pace we're moving. Lee is staggering behind Lochlan and me under Kristi's dead weight.

The Axeman is teasing us with his screams. Far enough away to fool us into thinking we are almost to safety, but close enough to remind us that we aren't.

"YOU CAN RUN, BUT YOU CAN'T HIDE!"

None of us is stupid enough to risk looking backward. That's literally how you die in a horror movie. But we can't keep this up. We need a place to hide. To rest. To figure out how to fight back.

"YOU CAN RUN, BUT YOU CAN'T HIDE!"

Maybe this is the task Pierce mentioned during dinner. Running for our lives until our bodies give out, until we die the way this crazed author wants us to under his terms.

"YOU CAN RUN, BUT YOU CAN'T HIDE!"

My legs keep pumping, my lungs struggling to expand. One foot in front of the other. Just keep going.

It feels like I've been running for hours.

The sun is starting to rise, turning the sky shades of lavender and peach.

Maybe I can take my heel off and stab the Axeman in the face for making me run in this condition. Why didn't I take them off once we regrouped before this crazy person found us again? Because I'm an idiot, that's why.

At least we are finally going downhill now.

"YOU CAN RUN, BUT YOU CAN'T HIDE!"

The shouts never stop. Never let up. Minutes trickle by, feeling like days.

The earth comes to a startling end, and I realize we've run out of time. We can't keep running.

Lochlan goes down first. His body flails like a fish out of water as he missteps and rolls over the steep incline of the hillside, tumbling to what's sure to be his death. The white envelope that's meant for me falls out of his pocket as he spins.

"YOU CAN RUN, BUT YOU CAN'T HIDE!"

Lee is next. He collapses with a pained groan from behind me. He and Kristi slide down together, like ragdolls stuck in a mudslide. Limbs sprawled in every direction as they tumble down.

I bring myself to a halt and watch my friends land at the bottom of the hillside. I hope they're alive. I hope they can get away before the Axeman is through with me.

Who would have thought I'd think of these people I got stuck with as friends? Possibly real friends. Friends, I might just sacrifice myself to save.

Taking a shuddering breath, I let the tears flow freely down my face. I'm not going to run. If the Axeman takes me, maybe he'll leave the rest of them alive.

The sunrise over the Scottish Highlands is one of the most beautiful and enchanting sights I've ever seen. I'm glad it'll be my last.

I hear footsteps. The Axeman stops right behind me.

I feel his presence gloss over me like a second skin.

The blade of the axe grazes my body like a seductive caress.

"You can run, but you can't hide."

It's a promise given to me on a whisper of a breath.

I close my eyes, waiting for it to be over.

I hear the axe fall to the ground with a thud just before two firm hands grab me and spin me around.

"But I'm not done playing with you yet."

Hard, frantic lips meet mine. I gasp in surprise, my eyes flying open as I push away from him.

The Axeman holds me firmly in place. He's wearing a black mask that hugs his face, like a ski mask made of the tightest material. The only things visible are his swollen lips, which are parted and panting like my own.

And those impossibly bright blue eyes. No, it can't be, can it?

"I sure do hope you're the one to survive, Lexi."

It's the last thing I hear before he shoves me off the hillside.

CHAPTER TWENTY-THREE

Lexi

"Come on, lassie. Wake up. Please wake up. Don't leave me here with these boring idiots to fend for me self." Lochlan's voice is low, yet still unbearably whiny as I finally come to. His Scottish accent sounds even more prominent in my haze of confusion.

My head pounds even worse than when I woke up after being gassed. I try to move and instead let out a pitiful moan before I dry-heave repeatedly.

"It's okay, lassie. I've got you."

I'm sagging against Lochlan. He rubs circles on my back with one arm and holds himself up with the other since all of my weight is on him. I try to move and apologize, but I throw up instead.

"You hit your head pretty hard, Lex." Lee's voice sounds muffled, like he's in some sort of wind tunnel. "She probably has a concussion," he says to someone else.

"We can't stay out here in the open like this," a woman says. Must be Kristi. "That masked guy might come back. I don't know why he didn't just kill us. Maybe he thought we all died from the fall? It was a pretty rough landing, but not high enough to kill us. Do you think you can move, Lexi?"

My head hurts so badly I can't be bothered to answer for myself. Instead, I lean against Lochlan's sturdy chest and let him take charge of me as I try to keep the rest of the contents in my stomach from spewing out all over the place.

"What's that over there?" Kristi says, her voice rising.

I look up and wince at the bright rays shining down on me. How long was I asleep? How did I even get here? The last thing I remember is running...then...falling.

Why can't I remember anything?

"Lee," I croak out, my throat painfully parched. He's at my side in an instant, his face kind and comforting in this new land of confusion I seem to be stuck in. "I think something is wrong. I can't—I can't remember how I got here. It's like my memories right before the fall are gone. The last thing I remember was running from the Axeman. How did we get away?"

"You guys..." Kristi repeats.

"We aren't sure how we got away. I just know that the lot of us woke up at the bottom of this rather nasty hillside," Lochlan answers, rubbing at his shoulder and wincing.

We all look worse for wear. It's almost like we just ran for our lives and collapsed at the bottom of a damn hillside.

Oh wait, that's precisely what happened...I think.

I hate it here, but I don't have time to allow the breakdown I know is looming just behind my vaulted feelings.

Pull it together, Lex.

Where are Teagan and Capri?

The Axeman is still out there, and he's still after us. I take a deep breath, staving off another rush of emotions. A lone tear slides down my cheek. Lochlan reaches down and brushes it away. "No crying allowed, lassie. You might scare me more than anyone else in my life, but seeing you cry is even more terrifying than seeing you sneer at my shoes. The L-Team has no space for tears."

"The L-Team?" I ask.

Lee sighs, an amused smile painted on his dry lips, before explaining. "Lochy boy has decided to call our original trio, sorry Kristi, the L-Team. You know, Lexi, Lee, and Lochlan. He's a weird dude, but I like him."

I give a slight nod.

"Anyways," Lee continues, "Some short-term memory loss is typically common with a concussion. It should come back sooner or later. But until then, Kristi is right. We need to find somewhere to hide and regroup while you rest."

Kristi shrieks, making the rest of us jump up in panic. I'm instantly nauseated again, but ready to run the moment someone says run. I'm not letting some crazy ass author get the last word with me, and I'm certainly not going to let him decide my fate.

Only I have that power.

Kristi lets out a loud, unabashed laugh before limping back toward the tree-line, where a lanky guy in an oversized grey suit is smiling back at her. He's another one of Pierce's guests. At least I can remember that much.

"Sammy!" Kristi screams, throwing herself into his arms. "I thought that psycho killed you after we got separated! How'd you escape?"

The two of them talk a mile a minute while the rest of us slowly make our way over to them.

"When we got out of that house of horrors, he chased you instead of me," Sammy explains, his hands gripping Kristi's arms like he's checking to make sure she's real. "I tried to taunt him into coming back for me, but by the time I followed him, you were nowhere to be found. I tried, Krissy-girl. I'm just glad you're okay." His dark, ebony skin glistens in the sunlight. He looks mostly unscathed. The grey suit he's wearing is torn, and leaves and twigs are stuck in his hair. He definitely looks worse for wear, but his smile lights up the world as he gazes down at Kristi.

I find myself jealous as I watch them. I wish someone had given me a cute nickname and looked at me that way while we navigated this nightmare together.

Instead, I'm stuck with my best friend's husband and Lochlan.

Though, and I really hate to admit it, Lochlan might be growing on me a bit.

"How do you both know each other?" Lee asks, gesturing from Kristi to Sammy.

Sammy throws his arm over Kristi's shoulder and grins. "We work together on a bookish blog back home. We were both invited by Mr. Pierce."

"I really, really wish we had ignored that invite now," Kristi adds in before they go back to talking amongst themselves.

Lee glances at me, then quickly looks away before clearing his throat loudly several times. I swear he's blushing.

I'm startled when something warm and heavy covers my shoulders. I turn to see Lochlan fixing his dress shirt, which is filthy and torn. I reach up and pull his suit jacket tighter around me.

"Thanks," I say, flashing him a grateful smile. I guess I didn't realize how frigid it is with all this adrenaline coursing through my veins.

"Lee's just too polite to tell you that your tits were hanging out," Lochlan grunts out, grinning like a madman as Lee rolls his eyes. "You were one good stretch away from a nip-slip there, lassie."

I look down and see that Lochlan is, in fact, right. My dress must have torn during my fall because it's in tatters hanging off my skin. I flush red and throw my arms into the jacket before buttoning it as high as it'll let me. It's huge on my small, yet curvy frame, but it helps me feel less exposed.

Still, at least I'm not stuck in a robe.

"I actually might have something that'll help with all that," Sammy chimes in. We all turn our attention to him and wait for him to elaborate. "I found this, like, underground bunker thing as I was running. Nearly missed the damn thing, honesty. I just happened to trip, you know I'm clumsy as all get out, Krissy." He smiles at her, and they both share a knowing laugh. "Fell right on top of the handle and chipped my tooth!" he exclaims, lifting his lip to show us the large chip on his front tooth. "Come, I'll show you. It's not far."

I stare in awe at the fully stocked supply room. This is like winning the lotto. No. It's better than winning the lotto. What could money do for me in this situation? It's not like I can go ahead and Venmo the Axeman and bargain for our lives, now can I? But food, clothing, running water, and a real pillow? That's something I can work with. It's like finding a knife slipped under your pillow in a slasher novel. It's rejuvenating when all hope feels lost.

This might just be a real slice of heaven amidst all this chaos—or at least a very well-placed miracle.

Sammy led the way and brought us to an underground bunker as promised. Only this bunker is more than just a place to hide. It locks from the inside so that nobody can get in. It's a place of safety, but it's also the perfect place to regroup, heal, and figure out what to do next so we can get out of this mess we're in.

This is how we turn the tables on the Axeman. We can use Pierce's annoyingly rich hobbies against him by using his secret bunker to get the upper hand.

But first, food and a shower take priority.

"I'll get us a meal together," Lee tells me. "You go shower before the hot water runs out."

I lift my eyebrow at him.

"You forget, Lex. I'm married to a woman. I know how feral you ladies can get once the water runs cold."

I grin and squeeze his shoulder as I pass him. "You're the best. Literally. You're my favorite of my best friends' husbands."

Lee snorts and gives me a sly smile. "I'm the only husband in the group, so it's easy to be the favorite. But I suppose you can be my favorite of Capri's friends, too. That is, until Teagan comes to save us all with her witchy magic and final girl power, or whatever it is you ladies say."

"Lee!" I gasp, trying to hold back both tears and laughter. "Since you love me so much, you won't mind if I use all the hot water." I head for the bathroom and lock the door behind me before erasing the fake smile from my face.

What I didn't tell him is that I'm not sure if I actually have any best friends left.

The water scalds my skin in the best way possible. Is there really anything better than a boiling shower after the most tiresome and adrenaline-rush-filled night of my life? No, there isn't. Being cooked alive might not be the worst way to go out.

I let the water rinse away all the grime and hard truths of the day, and finally allow myself to have that breakdown that I've been holding off on.

It's clearer than ever that I've been wrong about everything.

My tears mix with the scalding stream as I fall to my knees and cry harder than I think I've ever cried before.

What kind of friend am I?

I allowed myself to pursue a man I knew my best friend was falling in love with. I can try to rationalize all I want about how I was in the right to go after him, but at the end of the day, I'm the problem. If Josh had wanted *me*, he wouldn't have gone after Teagan. He would have chosen me.

Josh let me become the worst version of myself, and at the end of the day, I justified my actions for what I mistook as love. I can't speak for his actions in our affair, but I know what we had wasn't love. It was obsession and jealousy on my part.

Both of which I regret more than anything. And now we might all be killed because of some psycho-thriller-writer, and I may never be able to tell Teagan how sorry I am.

I might never get to right all my wrongs.

A knock on the door pulls me out of my melancholy. I stave off another sob that threatens to escape.

"Hey lassie," Lochlan says from beyond the closed door. "We're going to have a group meeting here in a bit."

Wiping my eyes and rinsing the last of the soap down the drain, along with all my emotions and regrets of my life, I shout back, "I'll be right out!"

When I get out of the shower, I find a pair of black sweatpants along with an oversized purple hoodie waiting for me. The outfit is truly horrendous, but I can't really be picky right now. At least it's not flannel.

I head out to meet the rest of the group and find them all sitting around a large oval table. There's an empty seat with what looks like a microwaved meal and two bottles of water waiting for me. I give a nod of thanks to Sammy and dig in. The food is disgusting, but I'm so hungry it doesn't even matter. I wolf it down while listening to the others speak.

"We have the element of surprise now," Lee explains. "What we should do is use one of us as bait and then take the Axeman down ourselves. It's five to one, there's no way he's walking away from an ambush like that."

Kristi crosses her arms across her chest and chews on her thumb as she stares up at Sammy. "What do you think?" she mumbles.

Sammy sighs and shrugs. "I don't know. It could work. But it's risky to whoever we use as bait. I won't force anyone to volunteer for that, and I'm sure as shit not going to. I barely escaped him the last time."

"Neither am I," Kristi agrees. "Sorry, but I don't know you guys enough to trust you."

Lochlan scoffs and slams a hand on the table, making us all jump. "We saved your life, Kristi! We risked ours to make sure you made it out alive. I don't want to hear another thing about trust. If we don't have trust, we have nothing. And I, for one, will trust these two blokes with my life." He points to Lee and me and gives us a wink.

Something in my chest tugs at his admission. I look back and forth between Lochlan and Lee and realize that somewhere between the cabin and here, we became true allies. Friends, even. And I'll go down swinging for them, too.

I get to my feet. "I'll be the bait." Lee and Lochlan immediately argue. I hold up a hand to stop them. "Look, I'm no use with a weapon, but I'm faster than the rest of you. He can't kill me if he can't catch me, right?" I ask before continuing. "But that won't happen because I'm trusting you idiots with my life. So let's kill this douchebag and get back to our people."

Lochlan gives me a salute and then hoists what I think is a crossbow over his shoulder, his green eyes shining with pride. "With these supplies, we are no longer the hunted. We are the hunters."

CHAPTER TWENTY-FOUR

Lexi

The plan is a simple one.

I'll wait at the top of the hill where we all *supposedly* fell to our deaths and scream bloody murder until the Axeman returns to finish the job. Once he's within sight, the rest of the group will come running out of the tree-line and attack him until he doesn't get back up, or until he stops breathing.

We're hoping that by doing this before the sun sets, it'll lure him out of wherever he's hiding, giving us the upper hand by seeing him before it gets dark. If that doesn't work, then we will just have to try again tomorrow.

Simple enough, right?

I can do this.

They won't let me die.

They can't let me die.

I really wish I could remember what happened before I woke up at the bottom of said hill. Something is nagging at the back of my brain, something I feel is essential, but every time I try to focus on that faded memory, it eludes me yet again.

Flashes of blue, tantalizing caresses...then nothing.

Trying to conjure up a memory I'm not sure I have anymore is futile. I stare at my haggard reflection in the bathroom mirror as I give myself one last pep talk. My blonde hair is lifeless, limp, and frizzy. My eyes are sporting bags larger than the ones I packed for Scotland. Really, the only thing I have going for me is this once-hideous outfit that's been turned cute. I cut the oversized purple hoodie into a crop top and chopped off the sleeves. If I'm going to my potential death, I refuse to be caught looking like that stupid purple dinosaur all the kids used to rave about.

Lochlan and Lee are waiting for me outside the bathroom once I finally emerge.

"Killer outfit, Lex," Lee muses with a sly smile.

Lee and Lochlan are both dressed in matching black cargo pants and fitted black V-neck t-shirts. I suppress a giggle when I realize we all have the same style of combat boots. This creepy bunker literally had everything we needed. We look like a trio that you'd find in some sort of video game. I must admit the style suits us for what we're about to endure.

"It's nice to see you out of that robe," I tease.

"Here, take this just in case." Lee hands me a large knife tucked into a black sheath. We don't acknowledge the tremble in my hands when I take it from him.

"What's this strap thing for?" I ask, inspecting the black nylon bands attached to it.

Lee shrugs before Lochlan reaches for the knife. "May I?" I nod, handing it over to him. He kneels before me and taps the outside of my thigh. "Are you a lefty or a righty?"

"Lefty," I tell him, my eyebrows furrowing in confusion. "Why?"

"Just watch," he says, wrapping the strap about my left thigh. He tugs it tight enough that it won't fall while I'm running, but not so tightly that it cuts off my circulation. He stands and flashes me a lopsided grin. "Attagirl, lass. Now you're properly prepared to take on the world."

I tug the knife out of its holder, attempt to twirl it, then slide it back in before I chop my own fingers off. It feels good to have this by my side, even if I have no clue how to use it. I guess I'll just have to stab first and ask questions later if it comes down to that.

"How'd you know how to work this contraption anyway?" I ask Lochlan. "What kind of kinky nonsense are you into, Lochy-boy?"

"Lara Croft," Lochlan says proudly with a big, stupid grin on his face. "She was my biggest crush as a wee lad."

"Mine too," I smirk, earning surprised looks from both men. Whatever. Lara Croft was hot. Anyone who denies it is a liar.

The fun mood turns serious as Lee steps forward and places a hand on my shoulder. Lochlan does the same. We form a tight-knit circle and bow our heads together. "Whatever happens today," Lee whispers, "just know that I'm glad that I got stuck with the two of you during this twisted goose chase. I'm with you both until the bitter end."

"Way to be inspirational. Clearly, Capri's epically inspiring pep talks haven't rubbed off on you yet," I respond with a weak laugh. "But, I'm also glad that you're both here with me. Just try to keep me alive." I swallow hard against the lump in my throat. "Please."

Lochlan snorts. "We got you, lassie. Now let's go give this axe-douche a taste of the L-team."

"You're such an idiot, Lochy," I tease as I wrap my arms around him and Lee. "You guys better stay safe."

"You too," they say in unison, hugging me tighter.

We join Kristi and Sammy at the entrance of the bunker. Then the five of us head out and make the trek back up the hillside.

We raided the small weapons arsenal, but there wasn't much in it. It's clear the bunker's used for hunting. I shudder as I realize that *we* might be the game now.

Is this what Pierce does when he's not busy writing novels? Promising an exclusive meet-and-greet to lure in unsuspecting victims for his twisted games doesn't seem so far-fetched now that it's happening to us.

Screw that, it's time to reverse our fate.

Lochlan has the crossbow thrown over his shoulder. Lee carries an axe, which seems oddly fitting for him. Kristi and Sammy both have knives, as I do, along with two baseball bats. We all carry extra supplies in case everything goes wrong, and we get separated or can't make it back to the bunker.

Which had better not happen because I'm much too pretty to die this young.

When we reach the top, we all split ways. I take my position as bait near the ledge and wait for Sammy's bird call to signal that the rest of them are in place and ready for me to put on the performance of a lifetime.

"Caw-caw! Caw-caw! Caw-caw!"

That's my queue. Now, here's to hoping those acting classes in college will finally pay off.

I raise my hands to the sky and scream. "COME AND GET ME YOU AXE-SLINGING DOUCHECANOE! You wanted me, you got me!"

My voice echoes through the sky as I scream and stomp my feet louder while my eyes skim the tree-line for any movement.

"COME OUT, COME OUT WHEREVER YOU ARE! Face me like a grown-up! You think you're tough with that stupid little axe? COME AND TRY ME THEN!" My lungs are on fire as I strain to yell as loudly as I can.

Just when I think this plan isn't going to work, I see movement to my left. Kristi is running out of the woods, her bat up and ready to swing. Except she's running right at *me*.

"This is all your fault, Lexi!" she screams as she approaches me. The bat makes a whooshing sound over my head, and I duck at the last minute, avoiding having my skull smashed in.

"What are you doing, Kristi!" Sammy screams, his legs pumping in rhythm with his arms as he races to catch up to the two of us.

Kristi turns on her heel, spinning to face Sammy. "You don't understand!" she howls before reaching into her back pocket. "This entire thing is HER fault!" Kristi faces me again and throws a white envelope. It floats to the ground like a feather in the wind.

"Lexi is on our side." Sammy tries to reason with her. "Why would she put herself in this situation while we all just wait to be killed off by the Axeman?"

She has her bat raised again, her arm shaking with restraint as she looks back and forth between the two of us.

Where did Lee and Lochlan disappear to? I know if they saw this crap going down, they'd be here to defend me in a heartbeat. What if the Axeman already has them? My heart starts pounding at the thought as my eyes dart from the tree-line and back to Kristi.

Sammy steps forward, his arms raised, while he pleads with Kristi to hand over the bat, just as I catch movement behind him.

"Lee!" I shout. Pure undiluted terror consumes me as I watch the Axeman and Lee fall out of the forest, tangled together. Lee's axe drops out of his grasp and rolls a couple of times before coming to a thumping stop mere feet from them. I can't tell who has the upper hand as they roll and wrestle each other to the ground. The Axeman slams the hilt of his own axe into Lee's face, knocking him out entirely.

"No!" I shout, racing past Kristi and Sammy toward where Lee lies motionless. The Axeman raises the axe above his head as he stares down at Lee. "Get away from him! Please! Take me instead, just leave him alone!" My voice cracks, and hot, wet tears stream down my cheeks as I fall to my knees next to Lee.

Blood runs freely out of the wound on his head, but his chest rises slowly. He's still breathing. He's still alive.

"Please." I look up at the Axeman. "Please let him live."

The Axeman cocks his head at me. "Choose."

The sound of his voice stirs something in me. Do I know him? "Choose what?" I ask, rubbing at my nose and face.

"Who should I kill next, Lex?"

I tug my hair with my hands as I stare at the Axeman. The mask and the sound of his voice tug at a memory, but I can't concentrate enough to pull it out of my scattered thoughts.

I won't play this game. I can't be the decider of someone else's fate—only my own.

"Me. Take me," I gasp out through my tears.

The Axeman lets out a small chuckle and stands, stepping over Lee's limp body, and stops before me.

He raises the axe above his head. "I'm not done with you yet," he responds, then lets the axe fly past me, over my head. There's a loud thunk, followed by a startled, gurgling noise behind me. I turn and see the hilt of the axe embedded in Sammy's chest. I gasp as his dark eyes meet mine, frozen in shock and fear, before he collapses.

The Axeman lets out another heartless laugh as he heads back into the darkness of the forest, disappearing.

"Sammy!" Kristi screams, skidding to a stop next to him with the bat raised over her head. It falls to the ground with a hollow thud. She looks from Sammy's dead body, then back to me, her eyes glistening with both unbelievable sadness and unrelenting rage. Her hands wrap around the handle of the axe, and she yanks it savagely out of Sammy's body before turning and stalking right toward me.

I crawl back on my hands, trying to put as much distance as I can between us. My hand hits Lee's unconscious form, making him stir slightly. "Kristi, wait. You don't need to do this!" I plead, raising my hands.

Kristi sneers and lifts the axe high above her head. "This is for Sammy!"

The axe seems to come down in slow motion. Before I can scream, it falls to the ground at my feet. I look up and see an arrow plunged into Kristi's chest, blood bubbling out of her mouth as she grips the air. She falls to the earth with a deafening thud. Her eyes stay open as she stares into mine, gasping for that last breath she can't get a hold of.

My entire body convulses. I turn and puke. Tears stream down my cheeks and mix with vomit.

How did this happen?

A hand touches my shoulder. I flinch, grasping for the knife strapped to my thigh.

"Easy, easy, Lex," Lee says with a grimace. "It's just me."

I look into his impossibly kind eyes, waiting for the judgment and hateful remarks to finally land. But they don't. Instead, Lee wraps me in a warm embrace and holds me as I fall apart.

"Is our lady okay?" Lochlan shouts from the tree-line a few yards away. Lee and I look over, and I see that Lochlan has the crossbow pointed in our direction.

He just killed Kristi...to save me.

The realization sends me into another fit of tears as I nod and wave him over. I don't think my legs will cooperate right now, but I know we need to get back to the bunker and regroup. Replan.

I look over at Sammy and Kristi. Clearly, this plan failed in the most devastating and catastrophic of ways. I collapse into Lee's arms again as the weight of our loss threatens to bury me.

A choking noise I've never heard before startles me when I realize Lochlan is screaming. The Axeman has the handle of the axe under Lochlan's throat, tugging him toward the forest.

He must have grabbed the axe Lee dropped.

"COME AND GET ME, LEX!" the Axeman teases.

Lee and I jump up just as we watch Lochlan get pulled into the forest by the Axeman, his arms flailing as he fights against him.

"We have to save him!" I shout, racing toward the forest. There's a strangled gasp behind me. Lee falls to his knees, clutching his ribs.

He throws his hand out as I reach his side. "No! Go after Lochlan! I'll catch up when I can. I just need a minute." His voice is strained as he takes short, stuttered breaths. "I think that asshole broke my ribs."

I kneel and wrap my arm under his and pull him to his feet as quickly as I can. He grunts in pain, but Lee also knows time is of the essence, and we have none to waste when we have to save Lochlan. "In no world would I leave you behind, Lee. We finish this together, or we don't finish it at all."

He stares down at me, grimacing, but nods in agreement. "Let's go save Lochy."

CHAPTER TWENTY-FIVE

Lexi

We can't be far behind Lochlan and the Axeman, but dragging Lee's practically limp body alongside mine is proving to be much more difficult than I initially expected. We're making almost zero progress in chasing them down. The longer it takes for us to reach them, the worse Lochlan's chances are.

I need to go faster.

"Dude, how are you this heavy!" I grunt out, stopping again to readjust my arm under his arm. "You don't look like someone who should weigh this much. No offense. You're just sort of on the slimmer side. Or so I thought."

"Shut up, Lexi." Lee winces before dropping to his knees with a painful moan. "Just leave me. You have to. This isn't about your lack of woman muscles." I start to protest, but he stops with a wave of his hand. "Trust me, I've seen you throw drunk men off you and the girls plenty over the last few years. But even on the slimmer side of things, I'm dead weight. We both know he's going to kill Lochlan if we don't get to him first."

I reach down and pull out the knife strapped to my thigh. "I know you're right, but I really don't want to leave you," I say, handing the knife to Lee. "Use it if you have to. The bad guys don't get to win today. I'll run back and grab the axe Kristi tried to murder me with and go save our boy."

Lee nods. "I'll follow behind you as quickly as I can. Be safe, Lex."

"You too," I call out, racing back to grab the axe. We didn't make it very far into the forest, so it's only a short jog back. I snatch the axe, and my eyes catch on the white envelope Kristi threw at me. I shove it into my pocket because right now, I need to save both Lochlan and Lee and end this once and for all.

"COME AND GET ME, LEXI!" the Axeman shouts, his voice echoing from somewhere nearby.

Again with the taunting, but at least he's telling me which direction to go in.

I might want to kill this man even if he wasn't actually trying to murder us. Nobody teases me and gets away with it.

I clutch the axe tighter in my hands and run towards his voice.

"HELP! LEE! LEX!" Lochlan's cries tie my stomach into knots as I race faster. My legs are throbbing in protest as I push them to the brink.

I'm so tired. So ready to lie down and let the earth consume my exhausted corpse of bones. I want to give up. My breathing comes out faster, labored as I resist the urge to cry.

But I won't fail my friends.

I spot Lee leaning against a tree and give him a pained smile as I pass him. I can't worry about him right now. Lochlan needs me more.

The tree-line opens before me, and I skid to a grinding halt as the cliff's edge looms ahead. The same edge that we all fell over earlier.

Flashes of memory ignite behind my eyes, but I shake my head, clearing them away as I take in the sight before me.

The Axeman is standing there waiting for me. Alone.

"Where's Lochlan?" I ask, my voice shaking as I struggle to catch my breath.

He holds his axe up and looks behind him, where the cliff's edge sits menacingly behind him, before taking a step closer to me.

"No," I gasp. Understanding crashes through my veins. "You pushed him. You killed him."

The Axeman says nothing. He only raises his axe again.

"WHY?" I scream. "WHY? Lochlan was GOOD! He didn't deserve this! WHY ARE YOU DOING THIS TO US?"

Again, the Axeman only lifts his axe, his arm almost slightly jerking as he takes a hesitant step toward me.

The silence in my head is deafening.

Lochlan's boyish grin. His mischievous green eyes and bright red hair. His nerdy logic and unfiltered sass. His kindness and friendship amidst all of this. His stupid lizard shoes that were starting to grow on me.

He killed someone to save my life.

And I wasn't fast enough to save him.

No, no, no.

Lochlan, I'm so sorry.

My body is engulfed in flames. Tidal waves of grief and fury pour over me as I toss my axe to the ground next to me and run toward the Axeman. I let all my emotions flow out of me while I race at him with every ounce of strength I can muster, screaming, sobbing incoherently when my hands make contact with his body.

The last thing I see before he goes over the edge is the look of pure, unbridled panic and fear in his eyes.

His *green* eyes.

The sound of his body hitting the bottom resonates and echoes around me just before I hear the sound of someone clapping behind me.

I turn and see the real Axeman leaning against a tree. His blue eyes shining with mirth from behind his mask.

"Bravo, Lex," he coos. "I told you I wasn't done playing with you yet. Too bad you didn't let *him* play longer. I think he might have chipped a piece of that armor you wear around your heart so well. You would have made a good match," he muses. "Don't worry, though. We will have more fun later. May your friend rest in peace."

I watch in stunned silence as he turns and disappears into the forest.

The entire universe freezes as I take in what he's said.

No.

I rush to the edge of the cliff and dare to peek over, terrified of what I'll find.

No.

No.

No.

The axe is splayed above his head, the handle duct taped to his hands and wrists.

The mask has slipped over his face, giving me just enough to see that the person underneath wasn't the real Axeman.

He wasn't trying to kill me by raising the axe above his head before I tackled him.

He was trying to *show* me.

His mouth has tape over it, but I'd recognize those sparkling green eyes anywhere.

I sink to my knees and scream at the heavens just as Lee reaches my side.

"Lex? What's wrong?" Lee grabs me, checking my body for injuries that don't exist.

"I...I killed him."

Lee's panicked expression doesn't change. "Killed who?"

A sob so guttural it sounds like a wounded animal escapes my chest. I point down to where the fake Axeman's body is twisted at an awkward angle. Lee gasps when he finally sees him.

Lochlan.

It's all my fault.

I didn't mean to do it, but this is still entirely my fault.

I killed him. Me. My hands pushed him to his death.

My fault. My fault. My fault.

Just like Kristi said.

I reach into my pocket and pull out the white envelope while Lee silently cries beside me.

Dearest friends,

You may realize that this game is more sinister than you first assumed.

My colleague will indeed strike to kill. He has a mission of his own, after all, and he's not above a bit of bloodshed.

Now, I will give you one way out.

One way to survive his wrath.

You must kill Lexi.

You see, she believes that allies would never turn on each other, even if it means life or death.

My biggest desire is to prove that she is, in fact, wrong.

I'm sorry to say the rest of you were brought here under pretenses to help me fulfill that desire. It's a shame to involve so many sacrificial lambs in my quest to be proven right, but, alas, what must be done must be done.

There is hope for you, though.

Whoever turns on her and kills her first will be granted complete immunity from my fun little game. They will also be allowed to choose one friend to leave this island unharmed.

Kill her, and live.

Fail, and you die.

Best of luck,

A.M. Pierce

My mouth gapes open in shock as I reread the letter. What kind of monster would put something like this together because of some stupid comment I made on a pointless podcast?

Who is this Pierce guy, really, and why would anyone sign up to *help* him plan this demented shit?

How does this warrant killing people? Killing me? He really enlisted people to kill to survive.

To kill *me*.

I freeze when I feel Lee move next to me.

"Lex," Lee whispers, his hand curling tighter around the knife. I look up at him, waiting for the blow. He's read the note now, too, and he knows that he can save himself and Capri if he eliminates me.

Maybe that's what I deserve. Maybe by sacrificing myself, I can save my friends. I can do this for them. After everything I've done to hurt Teagan, I can give her this. Capri deserves a life with Lee, especially after how he's helped me today.

I love them enough to give them this.

They deserve to be happy.

I'm a murderer now. I don't deserve anything good in this world anymore.

"Just do it," I plead, hiccuping as I choke back a sob. Hot, salty tears stream down my cheeks. "Do it and save Capri. Please. Save Capri, yourself, and Teagan. Please. Get them out of here. Get them to safety."

His expression is unreadable as he raises the knife. He tosses it over the edge and pulls me into a firm embrace, hugging me tightly until we are both crying uncontrollably.

"I'm so sorry," I tell him. "I didn't know it was him. I didn't know it was Lochlan. I would never hurt him. Hurt anyone."

Lee hugs me tighter. "I know. I know. And we are going to kill Pierce. Together. We are *all* getting off this island and going home."

A branch snaps behind us. We break apart quickly, and I immediately move into a fighting stance.

"I wouldn't be too sure about that if I were you."

The Axeman steps out of the forest and tosses a canister towards us. It explodes with a loud pop and gas sprays out. The smoke brings tears to my eyes, and I lose control of my senses and fall to the floor. The world turns hazy as the Axeman laughs.

The last thing I see before I pass out is him hovering over me and removing his mask.

"You," I gasp out in shock.

He smiles that tantalizing smile down at me and gently caresses my cheek. "Me."

CAPRI,
SHOW US YOUR
CLAWS, MAMA
BEAR

CHAPTER TWENTY-SIX

Capri

*N*o! No! Please stop!

I plead and scream at the monster who grabbed me in the night and pulled me into the shadows with him.

I fight. Bucking and clawing to no avail.

He's too strong, and I'm much too weak.

His meaty hands wrap around my throat, squeezing tighter every time I attempt to fight him off again.

So I quit trying. I stop fighting. Giving in to the monster as I stare up at the stars, silently begging for it to be over.

His hateful, dark eyes stare daggers down at me, beckoning me to stay quiet. His wicked lips moan in his own twisted pleasure until he's finished with me. He stands, hovering above me. The zipper to his pants is loud in the deafening silence surrounding us. I can't move. He puts himself together again, leaving me broken beyond repair on the cold, damp earth with no one but the stars as witness.

"Thanks for that. Get home safe." He winks at me before strutting back into the light of the world without a care in the world.

The last thing I see is a shooting star, falling to the earth in a heap of flames. I have no wishes left in me. Salt tears streak down my face and into my ears as raindrops cascade softly from the sky above.

Maybe they're weeping for me, too.

I jerk awake, drenched in sweat, my heart pounding with terror. I lurch up, dry heaving repeatedly while being haunted by the aftermath of my nightmare.

It's been years since this has happened.

After I gave my daughter up for adoption, that nightmare plagued me for years. I felt like it was my punishment for abandoning her, even if I still believe she's safer without me. They still haven't caught my attacker, and I won't risk him ever finding her.

My mind and body felt as if they were constantly reliving that moment every night until I told Lee what happened. Nobody in my life knew about it. I didn't want them to see me as this poor, broken girl. I've been fighting those demons for years, and I'll be damned if I let that monster define who I am.

After I confided in Lee about the attack, the nightmares stopped.

Until now.

I take a few deep breaths, reminding myself I'm not really back there. That the weight of his body, the stench of his breath, and the pressure between my legs isn't real. It's in my head. Only a memory. Repeating my mantras as my therapist taught me years ago.

I reach over, searching for Lee. His presence always seems to ground me faster than my own head does.

My heart grinds to a stop when I don't feel my husband's body next to mine. Instead of feeling the warmth and safety he brings me, my hand is met with nothing but air. Panic claws its way up my throat as I struggle to take in my surroundings.

This isn't my room, and I'm definitely not in bed at Windermere. I'm lying on a firm cot inside a tent, the fabric walls around me glowing with a flickering light.

My head pounds fiercely as I try to stand. The red lacy dress does nothing to protect me from the frigid air. I fall back onto the cot, wrapping the small, pitiful excuse for a blanket around me. A painful moan escapes my lips as my head pounds viciously. Shutting my eyes, I try in earnest to piece together what happened last night while my world spins around me.

Lee.

My eyes fly open again. I jump to my feet, swallowing the bile that still lingers in my throat. The last thing I remember is Lee's panicked expression when the smoke filled the room.

Who drugged us? Is this another one of Pierce's games? If so, I'm going to pummel that stupid grin off his face the moment I get my hands on him.

There's a plastic bag sitting on the end of the cot. I grab it and tear into it. Inside, I find a change of clothing, shoes, a flashlight, and a letter addressed to *me*. I change into the outfit and slip my feet into the sneakers, tying the laces tight before picking up the letter.

My darling Capri,

This isn't how I wanted to meet the mother of my only niece, but life rarely works out the way you wish.

Yes, that's right, my dear. We share more than just our love for the twisted and macabre.

My little brother is the one responsible for your darkest and most coveted secret—your daughter.

You see, my brother was never great at being told no. Unfortunately, you found that out the hardest of ways, and for that, I honestly do apologize. Our father was a wretched man, and his sons take after him in more ways than one.

My father was obsessed with filling in our family tree as best he could, so much so that all the children were required to submit a saliva sample to one of those genetic testing sites that are all the rage these days.

You're wondering how I know about all this, I bet.

Did you know that when a child is brought up in the foster system, they are subjected to genetic testing if potential parents request it? Color me surprised when I matched with a bouncing baby girl as her uncle years ago.

I assure you, she's been a blessing to raise here in Windermere.

Now for the really good stuff!

I'm giving you a second chance to be in your daughter's life. While we both know you don't deserve it, I'd never willingly keep a mother from her child.

You once said in one of your podcast episodes that it'd be impossible to keep a child safe if a real-life murderer were out to get you. Did you not?

Well, Capri, it's time to put that to the ultimate test.

Find your child. Keep her safe. Deliver her to Windermere alive before you're killed first by the person I've hired to hunt you down.

Easy enough, right?

Fail, and you'll lose more than just your life.

You'll lose her. You'll lose Lee. You'll lose your friends.

Everyone is relying on you, Capri. For their fate rests solely on your shoulders.

Good luck, and welcome to the family,

— A. M. Pierce

Numbness floods my body as I reread the letter. How is this possible? How does he have my daughter? And he's been raising her? Here, at Windermere?

Whatever game this man thinks he's playing, he's not going to win.

Nothing will stop me from killing him if he harms a single hair on any of their heads.

My daughter is here—and I don't even know her name.

This isn't the life I envisaged for her. She wasn't supposed to grow up like this. She was supposed to be loved and cherished by the couple I had chosen for her.

What did Pierce do to make them surrender her to him? I had never met a couple who wanted to be parents as severely as the Johnson family. Surely they wouldn't have given her up without a fight.

I thought having a closed adoption would be the easiest for us all. But what if I was wrong?

What if they tried to get a hold of me after I handed her over because Pierce was coming after them?

What if I could have stopped him from taking her?

What if he killed them?

Terror like I've never known threatens to cripple me as I shove the letter into my pocket, the lingering after effects of the drugs still filtering their way through my nervous system.

But I don't have time to be weak right now.

My heart pounds ferociously in my chest as a feeling of protectiveness seeps into my every pore. I clear my mind of everything but her—*my daughter*. I have to find her before someone else does.

Taking one last shuddering breath, I pray with everything in my soul that she's safe, while hoping Lee and my friends will understand that I have to choose her safety first, even if it jeopardizes theirs.

I unzip the tent's door and step into the wild, the air heavy with the scent of burning wood and pine.

The first thing I notice is the semi-circle of matching tents before me with a roaring fire in the pit in the center.

The second thing I see is a man dressed in a ghillie suit, perfectly blending into the forest foliage, moving on quiet feet toward the tent furthest from mine.

I watch him, mesmerized by his smooth, silent movements. He opens the zipper with deft fingers, before stepping into the tent. I'm about to follow him when I hear a guttural, horrified scream from inside the same tent he just disappeared into. All noise around me ceases until another scream of terror erupts from the woman in the tent. Only to be broken off by a loud, shattering crack of what can only be human bones.

The tent door starts to open again, and I dive behind my own tent, panting with shock. That man just killed whoever was in that tent.

And I did nothing to stop it.

Tears slip silently down my cheeks while I force myself to steady my breathing, strengthening my resolve yet again. I have to stay focused. I couldn't help the woman in the tent, but I have to help my child.

Footsteps hit the earth nearby, the leaves crunching loudly beneath them. These don't sound like the quiet, skilled steps of the man in the ghillie suit. There's a loud hiss and pop, making me flinch. Someone is mumbling under their breath, and I risk peering around my tent to find the source of the strange noise.

A man wearing a tan suit has his back to me. He's pouring water onto the fire with a metal bucket, the coals hissing and logs popping in protest.

"This isn't what I signed up for," the stranger mutters, kicking the bucket away. "It wasn't supposed to happen like this."

I slowly get to my feet, looking in all directions for the Ghillieman. My eyes stop at another tent where the tan fabric seeps crimson. Another dead person, I bet. The man in the suit is too busy having his own crisis, so I tiptoe my way over to the bloody tent.

As much as I don't want to see whatever awful thing happened to the person dwelling inside, I have to make sure it's not any of my friends or my daughter.

I peel the tent back and nearly collapse with relief when I see it's not one of my friends. It's one of Pierce's guests, Sean, I think. His throat is slit, his eyes wide open with shock. I quickly close his eyes before rushing out of the tent, tripping on my way out. The air leaves my lungs as I hit the ground. Gasping, I hear the intake of breath nearby.

Oh shit. I forgot about the man in the tan suit. Hurrying to my feet, I grab the closest thing I can find to defend myself with, the metal bucket, and throw it at the man as hard as I can.

It hits his face with a sickening crunch. He falls to his knees, grasping his nose.

"What the—Capri? Is that you?"

I look down at the man, now covered in both dirt and blood, and let out a strangled sob. "Josh? What are you doing here?"

Josh's smile is both endearing and terrifying to look at. His teeth are covered in blood, but my gosh, it's nice to see a familiar face. Josh and I have never been very close, but he's still a welcome sight, even if he's equivalent to scum with what he's done to Teagan and Lexi.

There's noise coming from the trees, and my immediate thought is that the man in the ghillie suit is back. I grab Josh's arm and bring my hand to his lips, begging him to stay silent as we slip back into my tent.

Loud footsteps clamber into the clearing. Josh and I stare at each other, both riddled with panic as we listen to every movement outside.

"Hello? Is anyone here?" the person whispers.

My heart clenches with both elation and fear. I'd know that voice anywhere. Josh's eyes go wide with recognition, too.

"Teagan?" I mouth, pointing to the door of the tent. Josh nods, then reaches for the zipper.

He almost has the tent door completely open when a loud gunshot rings through the air.

CHAPTER TWENTY-SEVEN

Capri

We hit the floor of the tent in tandem, Josh throwing his body over mine as the sound of the bullet ricochets through the air. The two of us stay frozen in place for what feels like hours before Josh finally shifts his weight off of me and stumbles to his feet.

Stifling a groan, I roll onto my back. I didn't realize how much I hated the feeling of him on me until he was gone. I know he did it to protect me, but something about it makes me shiver.

"What the hell is happening?" he asks, reaching down to help me to my feet before wrapping me into a firm embrace. "And why on earth is someone running around with a gun?

I half laugh, half cry into his suit. "I wish I knew. I just hope whoever is out there is long gone. And if it was Teagan, then I hope she was smart enough to run and hide."

Josh brushes a hand through his dark hair, nodding in agreement. "The last thing I remember was coming out of the bathroom. Lex was passed out on the floor of her room. And then, nothing." Josh releases me, pulling back until his frightened eyes meet mine. "Is she okay? Have you seen her?"

I swallow, shaking my head. "No, I woke up in this tent not long ago. When I came out, there was a man in a ghillie suit. I think he might have hurt the others. What if Lexi is in one of those tents?" I rush out of my tent, and run over to the tent where the woman was screaming and throw the flaps open. The scent of body odor hits my nostrils fiercely. I bite back a gag before finally getting a good look at the body on the cot. "It's not her," I sob out. "It's not Lexi. Teagan must have run. They're safe, still. Somewhere. They have to be."

I don't know if I'll survive if something happens to them.

Josh slides to a stop right behind me, his hand resting on my shoulder as we take in the gruesome sight before us. That feeling of wrongness floods my body at his touch. I gently shrug him off by stepping further into the tent. Something about him has always unnerved me. The way he toys with both Teagan and Lexi irritates me to no end. But I need his help, so I swallow my discomfort.

The woman is another guest, but I don't remember her name. She's wearing a gorgeous gossamer orange dress, and her neck has clearly been broken.

"He did this," I tell Josh. "That Ghillieman you saw."

We head back outside as I explain everything I know. Minus telling him about the letter. I want to trust Josh, but the letter said there would be people out there trying to kill me. Another one of Pierce's mind games, no doubt. I can't risk my daughter's life by trusting the wrong person.

"We need to get out of here then." Josh's voice hitches with panic as he scans the forest around us. "And we have to find the others."

I nod, wishing I could share the fact that I need to find my daughter as well. I just can't risk it, I can't.

"Let's gather whatever supplies we can find and get out of here," I tell him. "We need to get back to Windermere before the sun goes down, so let's hurry it up. And stay alert, the Ghillieman moves like a ghost in this place."

Josh grabs the metal bucket and then heads toward the tent with the woman in orange. "I'll take this side, you start at your tent. We'll meet in the middle."

There are six single-person tents in the clearing, so it shouldn't take us long. I give him a thumbs up before we both disappear into our respective tents. My tent doesn't have much I can use, but I roll the thin black blanket and toss it into the bag where I found my spare clothing before moving on to the next tent.

The tent next to mine smells heavily of a floral perfume. The aroma lingers in the air, almost as if it were just used by whoever was placed in here. The blankets are rumpled at the end of the cot. When I shift them around, I find a golden compact hiding under the pillow. It's about the size of my palm, with the letters REG engraved on top.

I wonder who was staying here. I should have looked in all the tents the moment I left mine. Seeing the Ghillieman was so unexpected that I didn't even think to check.

What if my daughter is in one of these tents?

I shake the thought away. I can't let the fear of losing her before I've found her again overwhelm me. I will find her. There is absolutely no other alternative.

There's a small clasp on the side of the compact. Lifting it, I open it carefully, the hinges letting out a soft squeak as I pry it open. Inside, I find a folded-up note and a black-and-white photo of a young boy glued to the circular wall of the compact. He's probably only three or four, and he's smiling from ear to ear, wearing overalls with a Christmas tree as the backdrop behind him.

I tear my eyes from the photo and unfold the note.

Rebecca,

***Do this one last thing for me, and I promise he'll be all yours
again.***

— A. M. Pierce

Rebecca must be the person who was in this tent, though I don't
remember meeting anyone by that name at dinner. I wonder what she
thought of the note when she woke up. Is Pierce holding her child
hostage, too? It seems that I'm not the only pawn in Pierce's games. If
Rebecca got a letter just like I did, does that mean Josh might have gotten
one too?

"Umm, Capri?" Josh calls out. "You need to see this."

I stuff the compact into my pocket where my own letter hides and
hurry out of the tent.

Josh is waiting at the opening to the tent next to me, his face showing
an alarmed expression. He doesn't say anything when I approach him.
Instead, he points into the tent.

"What is it?" I ask, my voice quivering in fear. Fear for what I might
find once I find the courage to look.

"Just look." He motions toward the opening with his hand, his eyes
wide with an emotion I can't quite place.

My eyes reluctantly leave him as I slowly step into the tent. My entire
body is tense with anxiety at what might be waiting for me on the other
side.

Oh.

The inside of the tent doesn't look anything like the others. The
others have had nothing but a dingy cot with paper-thin bedding waiting
behind the zippered flaps.

This tent looks like it was put together with love.

The cot in this tent is awash in pastel pink and turquoise bedding.
There's a thick taupe rug with white daisies plastered all over it on the

floor. A pair of hot pink Converse is strewn haphazardly onto it, almost as if someone tossed them off before jumping into bed for the night.

It's the perfect setup for a ten-year-old girl.

I step further into the room, taking it all in. Could this be where she was? Could my child have been here, so close, and yet ripped away from me again? There's a unicorn plush on the bed. I used to have one like this as a child, too. I pick it up and bring it to my face, inhaling the scent. It smells of lavender and vanilla.

"You okay?" Josh's voice startles me.

I quickly dab at my face with my sleeve. "Yeah, yep. Fine."

"Why would Pierce bring a child here? What kind of monster are we dealing with?" The venom in Josh's voice almost makes me smile. He never seemed very paternal, but here he is, surprising me again.

I turn back toward the tent's opening and stop in place. There's a note taped to the wall of the tent just above the opening, a note with my name on it. I quickly avoid eye contact with the wall behind Josh. I don't want him to turn and see it before I can read it in private.

"Come on, let's get out of here. There's nothing we can use," I say, following Josh out. "Oh, shoot. I should put this back in case the little girl comes looking for it." I jiggle the unicorn in my hand, inciting a chuckle from Josh.

"I have to take a piss anyway," he tells me. "I'll meet you by the firepit in a minute."

I give him a mock salute, sort of wishing I had hit him harder with that bucket for the bullshit game he's been playing with both Teagan and Lexi, but he's my only ally right now.

I wait until he disappears into the tree-line before darting back into the tent. I wrap the unicorn in the blanket and stash it back into my bag, then rip the note off the wall. I'm expecting another sinister note from Pierce, but instead I find a poorly hand-drawn map.

There are six triangles—those must be the tents.

Windermere is labeled, sitting to the east.

It looks like some type of lighthouse just south.

Cliffs lie to the west, and a giant B is written in a circle close to them.

Then there's a small house nestled right in the middle of all of them with a giant X with small handwriting smudged underneath it.

I bring the map to my face, squinting as I try to read the scribbled note.

You'll find her here.
Hurry before he finds her first.
-Rebecca

Who is the "he" this note is referring to? And how do I get to this X if I don't know which way North is? And what does this Rebecca person have to do with any of this? I want to scream in frustration, but I'll have to settle for pinching the bridge of my nose and squeezing my fist.

I wish Lee were here. He would know what to do. He's so calm in a crisis, and right now, I'm definitely falling into crisis mode.

"Capri?" Josh's voice hits me like a shot to the heart. How do I save my child and keep her safe if I don't know who to trust?

All I know is I can't let Josh see this map. Not until I know who the "he" is.

I fold the map up and shove it into my pants, my hand skimming against the cool metal of the compact. It feels like all my secrets are seconds away from burning a hole in my pocket, exposing me from the inside out.

Josh is standing by the fire pit when I finally exit the tent. "Which way do you think the castle is?" he asks, shuffling his bucket from one arm to the other. It looks like it's filled with black bedding, just like my own bag.

I shrug, breathing in the thick scent of the forest surrounding us. "Do you happen to have a compass? Because if not, then I have no idea."

Josh lets out a frustrated sigh. "Fresh out of compasses, I'm afraid."

I knew that, but the disappointment I feel is still heavy.

"Let's just head that way until we run into something, or someone," Josh suggests, pointing down one of the several paths surrounding the campsite. "I wouldn't want the Ghillieman to come back and break our necks because we took too long to leave this stupid place."

We start down the path closest to us. We've barely crossed the threshold into the tree-line when a gunshot rings through the air. The bullet hits a tree next to Josh's head, wood exploding loudly.

"Run!" he yells, grabbing my hand and pulling me back toward a different path.

Another bullet hits the tree next to us before we pivot and take off down a different path.

"We need to get out of here!" I yell, ducking low and running as fast as my short legs can.

"No shit, Sherlock!" Josh snaps back, turning us back toward another path.

Another gunshot, another bullet in another tree high above our heads.

"Wait!" I come to a stop, leaves cascading from the sky in a soft embrace around us from the last shot. We're both breathing heavily as Josh stares daggers down at me.

"Why are we stopping! Are you trying to get us killed?"

The shooter isn't trying to hit us. They are shooting near us, but only when we start down a new path. My heart beats in sync with my rapid breathing.

I think the shooter might be trying to show us the way.

"Stay here!" I shout at Josh, then I run back to the first path we took, praying that I'm right and not about to get gunned down for pure idiocy.

The next shot blares through the air, and the bullet hits above me, showering me with pine needles and twigs.

"Capri! What are you doing?"

Something not stupid, I hope.

I'll test my theory one last time before explaining it to him. I hurl myself down one of the other routes we chose. I nearly shout with glee when the bullet hits high above me *again*.

I have to be right, I have to be. This is totally the type of mind game I expect Pierce to play.

Racing back to Josh, I grab his arm and pull him along with me. I nearly cheer for joy when we reach the last open path, and run through with no gunshots to be heard.

CHAPTER TWENTY-EIGHT

Capri

"The shooter was trying to lead us to the correct path!" I shout, my legs turning to jelly beneath me as I struggle to keep up with Josh's long strides.

We've probably run at least two or three miles by now, jogging the last mile or so at a snail's pace through this never-ending forest. Neither of us wanted to risk stopping until we put some significant distance between ourselves and the shooter.

Josh finally skids to a halt a few paces ahead of me. I scream as he throws his arm out, catching me before I hit the deep slope ahead of us and fall into a creek.

"Thanks," I gasp, gripping him hard with my sweat-slicked skin before falling to my knees.

He plops down next to me, panting heavily as he runs his hands over his face. The dry blood flakes like confetti onto his suit jacket. "Explain that again."

I groan, exhaustion seeping into my soul, and lie my body on top of the damp earth. Staring up at the forest foliage, I tell him my theory again.

Josh lies next to me, his breathing rapid like my own. "I mean, I guess I could see why you'd think that," he says after a beat. "But what if the shooter wanted us to run this way so the Ghillieman could hunt us down?"

My eyes widen, and I shoot to my feet. "I didn't think of that," I say in a hushed whisper, my eyes searching the forest surrounding us.

Before I can tell Josh to get up and start running again, we hear a loud shout from somewhere.

"COME AND GET ME YOU AXE-SLINGING DOUCHECA-NOE! You wanted me, you got me!"

Josh and I look at each other in both shock and awe—because we'd recognize that voice anywhere.

"Lexi!" We shout at the same time before running in the direction of her voice.

"Wait!" Josh grinds to a halt when we reach a fork in the forest. "You go that way, I'll go this way! Eventually, we have to meet back up."

I gnaw on my lip. "I don't think we should split up. It could be another one of Pierce's ploys."

Josh's hands cup my face roughly, forcing me to look up at him. I flinch before meeting his bright eyes. "Trust me, please?" he pleads. "We can't let them get away, Capri."

I shake my head, slipping out of his grasp. "Okay. But if you die out there, I'm going to be so pissed."

"Same goes to you," he says, grinning, swinging his metal bucket back and forth. "See you on the other side!"

I take the opposite path, jogging at a quick pace. My lungs are on fire. My body has hit its breaking point. But I can't stop. Every so often, I pause and wait for Lexi to yell again. She's not as close as I initially thought, but whoever she's yelling at must have really pissed her off.

Lexi's taunting voice rings through the air again, "COME OUT, COME OUT WHEREVER YOU ARE!"

It sounds like it's coming from behind me, while also above me. I'm at the bottom of some type of hillside.

"Echoes," I mumble to myself. "Her voice is echoing off the hills." I start running deeper into the forest, hoping to find an opening so I can find a way to climb up. Being up high is always an advantage, right?

Another voice shouts from ahead. Only this time it's definitely a man's voice. "HELP! LEE! LEX!"

I stop short, my heart thumping in time with my frantic breathing. Did he just say, *Lee*?

"LEE!" My voice comes out like a strangled whisper as fear and relief engulf my senses. Choking sobs escape my throat as I propel myself forward.

I can't give up now. Not when I'm so close. I make a silent promise to tell Lee everything about my past the moment we're reunited. I'm not leaving this place without him and my daughter both safely in my arms.

My body gets a second wind as I race around the hill, searching in earnest for a spot to climb. It's useless. There are no paths that lead up, and the hillside is flat and barren, almost as if it's been made to be unclimbable just to torture us. Every time I think I have a handhold, the dirt crumbles beneath my fingers. There's no way to climb it. It's only ten feet or so, which makes my failure cut even deeper.

My people are right up there.

"I'm coming, Lee! Lexi! I'm coming!" I try to shout, my voice hoarse and dry.

I'm exhausted. Dehydrated. Nearly dead on my feet. But I can't stop. I have to find a way up. I have to help them.

There's a guttural, terrifying, and definitely female wail from somewhere above. I look to the sky and watch a person dressed in black fall from the ledge just a few yards away from where I'm standing. I can do nothing but stare and wait in horror as the person falls to their death.

Except the body doesn't hit the ground the way I expect it to. They don't hit the ground with a sickening thump. Instead, their body hits the ground, then bounces several times before coming to a complete stop, almost as if there's a trampoline hidden under the debris of the forest floor.

What is happening?

The person has an axe in their hands, making their body look abnormally twisted. They shift their head towards me, and I see that their face is covered in some sort of ski mask.

The person moves again, a strangled groan escaping their lips. The mask slips askew so that I can make out masculine features.

I can't move.

Can't breathe.

Black spots plague my vision.

No, no, no. Please don't be Lee. Please don't be Lee.

My knees buckle, and the last thing I see before my world goes dark is the axe. Why is it taped to their hand?.

There's a strange pounding in my head. It's as though someone is taking a hammer to my skull.

Thump, thump, thump.

"Wake up, lass. Please wake up."

Thump, thump, thump.

I drift in and out of consciousness, the thumping lulling me to sleep, then pulling me back to reality.

"It's official. I'm going to die out here. I didn't even get to plant a kiss on my favorite, sassy, blonde. Even after all that work I had to do with my tongue to get this tape off my mouth."

Thump, thump, thump.

Someone's voice floats through my ears, a voice with a thick Scottish accent.

"Lexi definitely would've woken up and saved me by now."

Thump, thump, thump.

"If that rat bastard had tossed Lee off the cliff, I bet you'd be awake by now."

Lee.

I open my eyes, squinting into the brightness. I'm on the forest floor. Twigs dig into my ribcage as damp leaves coat my face. The smell of pine and mud coats my nostrils.

"About bloody time! Capri, isn't it? I'm your husband's newest best friend, and I'm sure he'd be quite sad to know that you left me to wither away and die while you napped away so peacefully."

My head pounds painfully, and my throat feels like sandpaper when I try to swallow. I finally pull myself to a seated position to take in my surroundings. The man with the weird shoes is sitting next to me.

"Lochlan?" I rasp out, getting shakily to my feet.

The axe taped to his hands thumps against the ground again. Well, that explains the strange hammering noise in my head.

I kneel beside him and carefully pull the mask off his face. "What happened to you?" I ask, removing the duct tape from his hands as gently as I possibly can. He winces as it tears the skin on his hands, but grins up at me once the axe falls from his grip.

He rubs his wrists. "Thanks for that. It's hard to wake someone when you have an axe taped to your hands. I was too scared to yell and bring the Axeman down to you," he explains in a rush. "That crazy Axeman thought it'd be a real fun joke to dress me up as him and have Lex throw me off the ledge. She probably thinks she killed me." His voice cracks with emotion, and I can't help but be grateful that Lexi had him on her team during this.

"What about Lee? What happened to him? I ask, my own voice heavy with fear.

Lochlan sighs. "The last I saw of him, he was alive. Injured, but alive. The Axeman ambushed me and grabbed me from behind. I tried to fight him, but he told me that if I wanted to save Lex and Lee, I had to play dead. Some twisted bugger, that one."

Lochlan looks up at me, surprising me with a fiendish grin. "But I guess we'll show them, won't we, lass. Now help me up so we can take this axe and finish the job. I call dibs on the fancy author."

He tries to stand and groans in pain.

"Wait!" I order. "Now I don't know what the hell happened to you guys, but I have people I need to protect, too. Before we can do any of that, I need to make sure you're okay." My voice rises with hysterics as I look him over. "In case you didn't realize, you just fell from a freaking cliff, Lochlan! You could have internal injuries. You could be paralyzed!"

Lochlan scoffs, getting to his feet. "Not paralyzed, obviously. My ribs hurt a bit, but that bouncy mat thing broke my fall." He points to the spot where he fell, and I see the black nylon trampoline buried in the earth.

Another one of Pierce's mind games. I can't imagine what Lexi must be feeling right now. She may act all hardcore, but that girl loves fiercely. I know she'd never be able to live with killing someone she cared about.

Lochlan faces me, placing his hands on his hips in such a Lexi way. "I'm going after them with or without you, but Lee would kill me, for real this time, if I left you behind." His smile is adorably magnetic.

I gaze up at this man, who is basically a stranger, and find myself smiling back.

Can I trust him? What would Lee do?

There's something about Lochlan that calls to me, begging me to let my guard down. I may not know this guy, but something tugs at me, urging me to trust him.

"Okay, I'm in. But there's something else I need to do first," I agree, before pulling out the map I found in my daughter's tent. "Do you know what any of this means?"

Lochlan takes the map from me and gently opens it. Analyzing it in full. "That's gotta be the bunker," he says, pointing to the circle with the B written in it.

Bunker? What bunker?

It's as if Lochlan reads my mind because seconds later, he explains how they found a bunker in the woods filled with clothing, food, water, and most importantly, weapons.

"Well, that's convenient," I spit out harsher than I mean to. "Sorry, I'm just a little annoyed that you guys got food and weapons and all I got was Josh and this drab outfit." I gesture to the black ensemble and laugh when I notice Lochlan is wearing the exact same thing.

"Josh? Lexi's Josh?"

I grimace. "Eww, don't call him that," I say in disgust. "Crap, I should probably find him. We were supposed to meet up here after we separated to find Lexi."

Lochlan goes eerily quiet, refusing to meet my eyes.

"What is it?" My lungs struggle with each breath as I wait for whatever hammer to drop.

"He uh. He did come back," Lochlan mumbles. My brows furrow in confusion before he continues. "I thought it was the Axeman coming back to finish the job after Lex pushed me, so I pretended to stay dead a little longer." He stretches his arms above his head and winces. "But it was Josh. I was going to shout out to him, but something about his demeanor stopped me. He walked over to you, rummaged through your bag, then took off again."

What? What was he looking for?

The map.

"He must be the one Rebecca warned me about," I gasp, pointing to the note written on the map. Josh must have woken up with his own little note from Pierce, too. "We have to get there before he does."

Lochlan smirks before turning his attention back to the map. "He'll have a joy of a time catching up. He's going in the wrong direction. Plus," he says, his fingers tap the small house in the center of everything. "I know where this is. It's not far from here, I don't think. We woke up there before being chased by an axe-wielding lunatic. We can hit the bunker first since it's on the way. Grab weapons and supplies."

Hope ignites inside me.

That's where I'll find my daughter.

"Okay," I finally say. "Let's get to the bunker and arm up. After that, we have to find that cabin."

We make our way through the forest in silence for a while before Lochlan speaks. "What's so important about the cabin?"

I look over at Lochlan's kind face again as we walk side by side. I don't know what I'm searching for, but again, something inside urges me to trust him. It's nothing like the feeling I got when I thought about trusting Josh with this information. Now I know why.

Josh is the person hunting for her. She must be his ticket out of here.

"My daughter," I confess. "She's what's waiting in that cabin. And I'll kill whoever I have to with my bare hands to get her back."

Lochlan lets out a low whistle. "And I thought Lexi was cut-throat. She's got nothing on you, mama bear." He bumps my shoulder with his own, earning a small smile. "Now let's go get our girls back. All of them."

245

CHAPTER TWENTY-NINE

Capri

We make it to the hidden bunker in record time, then stuff our faces with food and water. We shove all the extra supplies we can into my duffel bag and the backpack Lochlan found in the weapons room.

Both of us are armed to the teeth with knives. Lochlan carries the axe, while I feel more confident with the bow and arrows. I never thought I'd be thankful for that mandated archery course we were forced to take in my high school gym class.

"Need a hand there, lass? This bow looks bigger than you," Lochlan teases, flipping my bow in his hands as he watches me struggle with the quiver of arrows around my shoulders.

"Shut up." I roll my eyes, tightening the strap before grabbing the bow from him. "I just really hope I'm still as decent a shot as I was a decade ago. Now let's get this show on the road. Everyone is counting on us."

Lochlan tightens the straps of his backpack, and we both head out. I follow behind him, lost in my own thoughts as he leads us to the cabin.

What if I'm too late?

What if my daughter wants nothing to do with me?

How do I introduce myself to someone who might not know I exist?

How do I convince her to trust me?

All these fears and unanswerable questions plague my mind, nearly crippling me, but I won't give up. I will save my child along with everyone else who has been forced to participate in these horrors under the controlling thumb of Pierce.

I wonder what he offered Josh to make him turn on me, if he's actually done so. Part of me is hoping that Josh saw me lying there and ran to get help. The more rational side of me knows it's a fool's wish. Josh and I aren't exactly besties, but I know in my heart that he cares for both Teagan and Lexi. Pierce must have offered him the world to get him to turn his back on their best friend. There's no way they'd forgive him after this if what I suspect is true.

"So...what's your daughter like?" Lochlan asks. "Lee never said anything about her during our romantically bloody stroll through these woods," he adds with a wink.

His question catches me off guard. It feels like ice water poured onto my heart. I trip over a fallen branch and would have completely fallen flat on my face if it weren't for his quick reflexes. I pull out of his grasp and wipe my hands on my pants, thanking him for the assist as my heart does cartwheels in my sternum.

God, I hope I can trust this man because I need to get this weight off my chest, even if it just means sharing the burden with someone to get me through this.

Because I'm a coward through and through.

I can handle being shot at, chased, and nearly killed.

But coming face to face with the child I willingly gave up?

I'm absolutely terrified.

"I, um—" My voice cracks as I swallow, trying in earnest to smash down the guilt building in my chest. "I actually don't know." He raises his brow at me, but says nothing as I continue. "I gave her up for adoption when she was born. It was a closed adoption, so I have no idea who she is. I just know that I have to save her." I pull the note Pierce left for me from my pocket and hand it to Lochlan. "This can probably explain it better than I can."

He reads the letter, then hands it back to me before wrapping me in a fierce hug. My whole body tenses, then relaxes as I lean into him. I didn't realize how much I needed this. A listening ear. Someone to share the burden of this massive secret I've had to carry myself since the death of my parents. It's like an invisible weight melts off as Lochlan holds me in a much-needed embrace. A sigh of relief escapes my lips as I take a much-needed moment of silence amongst the chaos that my life has turned into over the last couple of days.

A caring stranger turned ally. A friend, even.

Lochlan gently releases me, looking down with that mischievous up-turn of his lips. "Ready to meet your daughter?" He turns me so my back is against him, then he points toward a small overgrown path. And just past it sits a log wooden cabin.

My daughter's in there.

I don't even remember moving, but suddenly I'm rushing up the front steps and through the front door with Lochlan hot on my heels.

The most surprising aspect of the cabin is its warm, homey, and welcoming scent. It smells of apples and cinnamon spice. I hesitantly walk further into the cabin and take in my surroundings.

The faded brown couch has red and yellow throw pillows tossed onto it, with a dark green fuzzy blanket pushed to the edge. The fireplace is lit, and the mantle is covered in little wooden horses.

"What happened to all the dead heads?" Lochlan whispers from behind me. I look back at him, raising a brow in confusion. "When I woke up, there were animal trophies covering every inch of wall space. This cabin looks like the rustic Martha Stewart took over and kicked the drunk lumberjack out, along with his horrid decor. I don't know which version is worse, honestly."

"Says the man with the crazy gator shoes," I chastise, chuckling at his gasp.

"You'll be happy to know Lexi *loved* them—"

A door slams in the hallway, cutting him off. We eye each other and raise our weapons as we slowly inch down the hallway.

We haven't run into the Ghillieman or the Axeman. I'm starting to wonder if coming here was exactly what they wanted.

What if they planned this and waited until we left here with my daughter to ambush us? I shudder at the thought of the Ghillieman killing us the way he killed the other two guests in their tents.

There's a muffled noise coming from behind the door on the left. Lochlan signals me to get behind him, then he turns the doorknob and pushes the door open. He steps into the room holding the axe tightly, ready to swing at a moment's notice. I follow right behind him.

My pulse pounds loudly in my head as I scan the room. It's decorated similarly to the tent. All hues of pinks, teals, and lavenders. This room clearly belongs to a young girl, but is that girl my daughter?

There are photos strung with twine and clothespins hanging above the twin bed. I can't stop myself from getting a closer look at her life.

I don't know her name, but I'd recognize her even if I haven't seen her since the day she was born.

Before I can get a real glimpse at the photos, a noise behind me catches my attention.

Lochlan lets out a small gasp of surprise as I turn toward him, then follow his gaze to what he's locked on.

My heart stops in my chest.

There's a bright yellow bean bag tossed into the corner of the room, and sitting on it, like some type of mythical creature turned real, is a young girl.

She's got a pair of white headphones on, and she's looking down intently at a book in her hands.

I choke back a sob, bringing my hands to my mouth.

"Capri?" Lochlan steps closer to me, placing his hand on my shoulder. "Is this her?

The girl looks up before I can answer him, her bright blue eyes catching my own. Her mouth drops open in surprise as we stare at each other. She pulls her headphones off, tosses them onto the bed, and stands.

"Hi," I say, tears brimming as I take in her beauty. She has my nose and my mom's freckles. Her bronze skin makes her blue eyes pop like sapphires. She's everything I hoped she'd be, and so much more.

"You're finally here!" she exclaims, rushing toward me with a smile. "Nanny told me to hide in my room once we left the campsite. She said I wasn't allowed to take my headphones off until the woman with the colorful braids found me. And now that you're here, I'm free to roam the snack cabinet." She pushes past me and out of the room, then pops her head back in. "And you took, like, *forever*."

Lochlan chuckles from behind me. "She's definitely gotta be yours. She's already got that pep in her step and sass locked down."

A piece of me breaks all over again the moment she disappears from my sight.

I can't believe I've missed ten years of her life.

Ten years of smiles and frowns.

Ten years of laughter and tears.

Ten years of the purest, most undiluted love I've ever felt. Love, I didn't know could exist in a world filled with so much hate.

I thought I couldn't love her more than I did the moment I held her tiny body in my arms. How wrong I was. I don't know how I'm supposed to go back to a world without her in it, and that realization feels like a bullet to my heart.

"Hey, you okay?" Lochaln's hand squeezes my shoulder again, bringing me back to the present.

She may not know or care who I am. But I know who she is, and I have to keep her safe.

I quickly pull myself together, turning on my heel and facing Lochlan. "Yeah, I'm just wondering who would put a child in the middle of all this." I twirl my finger in a circle. "All this death and bloodshed? Why would he put a child at risk? His own niece! Does she know what's happening around us?"

He shrugs. "Maybe her being here is just another test."

I raise my brow at him. "Test?"

"Yeah, like the escape room nonsense, and having Lex push me off a cliff. The dude is certifiably insane. I wouldn't put it past him to use a child to harm you. He knows you're tough as nails, so he dug deep to find what would hurt you most," he states, his cheeks reddening slightly with his admission.

I don't know what to say, so I just nod and give him a weepy smile.

"Now let's get back to the castle and keep that little one safe on the way there. I'm quite looking forward to seeing Lexi's face when she realizes she didn't actually murder me," Lochlan gloats, holding the bedroom door open for me.

I step out of the room, my eyes searching like I need to see her to continue breathing. Before we reach the living room, I hold my hand up to stop Lochlan. "Just cool it with the whole 'my little' thing. She may not know who I am, and I'm not ready to scare her away," I beg Lochlan.

"You got it, mama bear," he teases, saluting me as I roll my eyes at him. "No, really, my lips are sealed from here on out."

"Somehow I doubt you can go longer than five minutes without hearing yourself talk," I tease. He answers by pretending to zip his lips up.

When we make it back to the living room, we find her sitting on the couch, eating what looks like a bowl of Fruit Loops.

"Hey, I'm, um, Capri," I introduce myself as I walk toward her. "That's my friend, Lochlan."

Her blue eyes flick up to meet mine. I wonder if anyone else can feel the earth shifting around me the way I do when I look at her.

"I'm Skye." She tips the bowl back, drinking the last of the milk, then walks her dirty bowl to the sink. "Are you going to take me home now?"

Skye. What a perfect name.

Lochlan appears from behind me before piping up again. "And where is home, little lady? Is this not where you live?"

I stifle an amused snort. He lasted about a full minute before having to speak.

Skye shrugs. "I don't know. Sometimes I live here with Nanny. But mostly I live in the castle with my uncle. He's such a bore. Always harping on about 'keeping it down' because he has to write the next best thing." She rolls her eyes dramatically.

Ten years old and already full to the brim with her own personality. I couldn't be more proud—or horrified. If my mom were here, she'd elbow me in the ribs and tell me that Skye's just like me when I was that age.

Skye washes her bowl and dries it before she continues. "My uncle did tell me that I have to behave for you. And if I did that, you'd take me back to him. Apparently, he's doing some important research for his next book and needed me out of the way, and that you'd keep me safe.

Whatever *that* means…" Her voice trails off at the end. She looks at me with confusion and fear in her eyes. I can tell she's holding back tears, using humor as a deflection so we don't see how scared she truly is.

I want to tell her I'll never let anything else happen to her.

I want to grab her, hold her, and never let her go.

I want to throw myself at her and beg her forgiveness for giving her up all those years ago.

But right now, I'll settle for being the strong adult she needs.

I step toward her, pasting a semblance of a smile on my lips, which isn't easy to do when all I actually want to do is cry. "Hey, Skye," I say, my voice breaking slightly before I set myself straight again. I kneel and gently grab her hands. "I promise I'm going to do whatever it takes to get where you feel safest." I squeeze her hands, and she squeezes mine back, sniffling loudly, trying to hold back her own tears.

The front door bursts open, the door frame exploding and showering us in wood splinters and dust. I throw Syke behind me just as a man dressed in all black and wearing a mask strolls in.

"Well, isn't this a touching sight?" The man takes another loud step into the room, making the hardwood floor of the cabin creak under us.

My jaw drops when I see the axe. I grip Skye's hand harder, pushing her further behind me before risking a glance at Lochlan. The fear and anger written all over his features are enough to confirm that this is the guy who has been toying with him since he woke up in this heinous nightmare.

Lochlan's Axeman has found us.

CHAPTER THIRTY

Capri

Skye whimpers, grabbing my waist and burying herself into me. She's holding me tight against her like she's trying to claw her way back into my womb. It's almost as if some primal part of her remembers me and knows that I was once her haven.

Lochlan has moved from his spot next to the couch and has slowly made his way to my side. His body quivers in what I think is anger, but I'm too nervous to move a muscle and check his expression. All I can focus on are Skye's terrified noises and her grip on me.

The Axeman lets out an amused, sinister laugh as his bright eyes take the three of us in before he confidently crosses the room, striding past us to the fridge tucked into the corner of the small kitchen.

I turn my body in sync with his so I can keep eyes on him, forcing Skye to step with me, and farther from him.

The Axeman says nothing as he tears open the fridge. My nerves jump with anxiety and terror as I watch him. I pull Skye closer. The Axeman grabs a water bottle, slams the fridge closed, then lifts himself onto the butcher block counter top, facing the three of us, arranging his mask slightly, before taking a large, lengthy gulp from the bottle—the plastic crackles and pops as he chugs over half of it.

Lochlan steps forward, his own axe squeezed tightly in his fists, and raises it above his head.

The Axeman pulls the bottle from his lips and glares at him. "Don't even think about it. You harm a single hair on my head," he gloats. "And they pay the price. My accomplice will make sure of that."

My stomach drops. Accomplice? What accomplice?

"Now," the Axeman says, jumping from the counter. "Give me the girl." He glowers down at me. "I won't ask twice."

Skye cries quietly at his words, clutching me tighter.

"No." Lochlan's voice is laced with pure fury. A tone so unlike his usual, chipper self. "You can't have her."

The Axeman laughs, then steps toward me menacingly. The anger in his bright blue eyes could ignite the entire forest surrounding us with just one glance.

Lochlan lunges at him, screaming. "I said NO!" His face contorts with uncontrolled rage as his fist makes contact with the Axeman's chin.

The window behind us explodes.

A loud, tortured, piercing cry of pain erupts into the air.

The world is a blur of noise and motion as someone grabs my arm and tugs me, forcing me back to my feet and out of the cabin. I hit the front steps, tripping over my own feet, falling to the ground hard. My head slams onto the wooden handrail, rendering my senses useless. The world spins as I grapple to comprehend my surroundings.

"RUN!"

I look up and see Lochlan. He's pulling on me, his face covered in blood. When I notice he's holding Skye, the terror in my chest eases. Her arms are wrapped around his neck, and he's holding her with one arm as he reaches out to me again with the other. "Get up! We need to hide from the shooter!"

I scramble to my feet and follow him into the dark safety of the forest. The shooter? It can't be, can it? I thought they were helping me earlier by making sure I was going the right way to find Skye. Maybe Josh was right, and I was just being a foolish idiot. I don't know what to believe anymore.

Lochlan comes to a stop once we are deep into the safety of the forest, carefully releasing Skye before he bends down and puts his hands on his knees as Skye runs right into my arms, hugging me tightly. "It's okay, sweetheart. I've got you," I murmur, caressing her hair softly.

"Is she okay?" Lochlan wheezes. His breathing is as rapid as my own.

Skye pulls away from me enough to turn toward him. She nods and then rushes into his waiting arms. He lifts her into a bear hug, making her giggle. "I'm okay. Thanks for protecting me." Her voice cracks in between laughs as he spins her.

The sound of her crying breaks my own heart into a billion little pieces, but her laughter fills me to the brim with so much happiness I feel like I'll explode from it. Is this what it feels like to love someone this fiercely? This entirely?

We need to get back to Windermere and end this. That's the only way to keep her, and everyone else, safe.

A branch breaks behind me. Lochlan drops Skye and throws her behind him just as the Axeman steps out of the tree-line. His mask is torn, and though it still hides almost the entirety of his face, his left ear has been mangled.

The gunshot in the cabin. The blood on Lochlan's face. The bullet must have hit the Axeman.

"Give. Her. To. Me!" he screams, raising the axe and running toward me.

Another gunshot blasts through the air, surprising us all when the bullet grazes the Axeman's shoulder. He goes down with a strangled groan.

"GET TO WINDERMERE!" Lochlan yells, grabbing Skye's hand and taking off into the forest. "This way!"

I don't have the energy to ask him how he's sure, all I can do is pray that he's right and follow after him and Skye.

We run, and run, and run. Only stopping long enough to drink water and rest for moments before jogging toward the castle again. As soon as we break through the tree-line, we see the towering gates of Windermere awaiting us.

The sun has nearly set entirely in the sky, leaving us with muted darkness, only broken by the reddish hue leftover by the stubborn slice of sun that refuses to fall wholly.

Skye is silent as she clutches my hand, her tremors of fear hitting me like an electric shock. We hide in the trees while Lochlan sneaks around the wall to check to see if there are any more nasty surprises awaiting us through the massive wrought iron gates.

There are so many things I want to tell my daughter, but I keep those thoughts to myself. They'll only confuse her, and she doesn't need any more stress on this nightmare of a day.

When I find Pierce, I'm going to slit his throat for putting her through this.

There's a soft whistle—Lochlan's signal that the coast is clear. Skye and I hurry around the gate and duck into the garden where Lochlan is waiting for us.

"Where is everyone?" I ask as we head further into Pierce's massive garden. It's gorgeous. The flowers are all in bloom, and the small pond is filled with lily pads with frogs perched on top of them. It would remind me of a Disney movie if it weren't for the fact that we're being chased by a man with an axe who's trying to steal my kid.

Skye tugs on my hand. "This way! There's a cabin back here we can hide in!"

I glance over at Lochlan. "She's got to know this place better than we do," he says with a shrug. "We can hide in there until we figure out how to sneak into the castle. It's better than sitting out here like ducks waiting to get our heads axed off."

I can't help the chuckle that leaves my body. He's got a point. We follow Skye a little further until we see a small fixture hidden behind the overgrown hedges and trees. I don't think I'd call it a cabin, per se. It's more of a shack, but beggars can't be choosers, and we need to hide from the Axeman.

Lochlan goes in first to check if it's clear when a branch breaks behind me. I turn to see the man in the ghillie suit and throw Skye toward the open door. "Go get Lochlan!"

"I swear I come in peace," the Ghillieman says in a strange robotic voice before tossing the rifle to the ground. They take a step back and raise their hands into the air.

I rush forward and grab the gun.

"Check to make sure it's loaded," Lochan instructs, coming up from behind me.

The gun is completely foreign in my hands. I've never held one before, let alone used one. "I don't know how," I admit, looking down at the rifle like it's some type of dangerous animal waiting to strike.

"Grab the handle on the bolt there," Lochlan says, stepping to my side and pointing to the metal thing on the side of the gun. Skye is hovering behind us in the doorway. "Lift it, then slide it back." An empty shell casing pops out of the rifle, hitting the ground near our feet. "Now slide the bolt back into place and put the handle back down to load it."

I do as he says, then lift the rifle as I've seen in the movies. It's heavier than I expected. I have to readjust a few times before I point it at Ghillieman. "Why are you following us?"

Ghillieman sighs. "Can I take my mask off before I explain?" The robotic voice reminds me of the voice Pierce used in the mock escape room. That feels like light-years ago, even though I think it was just yesterday. Time seems to have no power here. I reluctantly nod my head in approval at their request. I want to know who we're dealing with.

They reach back and rip the mask off, throwing it to the floor at my feet. The person standing before me isn't what I expected. It's a woman. An older woman, to be precise. Her brown eyes are wary, but kind. Her hair is mostly gray and pulled back into a long braid. Tendrils of flyaways are coated with sweat and stick to her face. The laugh lines around her lips remind me so much of my mother's. She doesn't look like the type of person who could murder two people.

"Who are you?"

The woman flashes me a melancholy smile. "I'm Rebecca. I'm the one who left you the map to find her." She points to Skye. There's a startled gasp from behind me as Skye rushes toward Rebecca.

"Nanny!" she yells, throwing herself into her arms.

Rebecca cradles Skye, and I can't help the flush of jealousy that stains my soul. She knows my daughter better than I ever will.

"Rebecca," Lochlan drawls. "Who are you and why are you here? Why are you helping us? What's in it for you?"

I couldn't have said it better myself.

"Come on, Sweet Pea," Rebecca says to Skye, taking her by the hand before facing us again. "I'll explain everything, I promise. But we need to get out of here before the Axeman finds us. I'm a perfect shot, so I know he's only slightly injured. He'll catch up to us in no time. We can't let him take my granddaughter."

I watch her for a second longer before deciding to trust her. I know that look. She's full of both rage and fear, but with a ferocity like no other to keep Skye safe.

Rebecca is just as much a pawn in this game as the rest of us are.

"Lead the way," I tell her, lowering the rifle. "But make it fast. We need to get to the rest of my friends as quickly as possible and put an end to all this bullshit."

She squares her shoulders, her gray braid swinging behind her as she pushes past Lochlan and me, disappearing with Skye into the small cabin.

"Do we trust her?" Lochlan asks, his voice low.

There's a loud commotion in the cabin. "Nanny! Look, it's a kitten!" Skye's laughter erupts through the air.

I sigh, smiling gently. "I don't think we have much of a choice. If Skye trusts her, then I do too."

We get into the cabin and take in the small space. It's definitely some type of worker's quarters. A bed sits in the middle of the room against one wall, and on the opposite side sits a smaller kitchen with a door to a bathroom on the same wall.

Skye is sitting on the bed with a small bundle of fur in her arms. Lochlan reaches over and gives the kitten a small pat on the head, inciting a small meow of protest from her. Skye looks like she's in heaven right now. All the fear of the day has vanished from her blue eyes as she snuggles the kitten close to her.

"Rebecca," I say, clearing my throat. "Can we talk outside for a bit?" She eyes me warily, but agrees and follows me out.

I need to know why she's here and what she plans to do with us now that she has Skye.

We sit together, hidden in the shadows of the trees, close enough to see the cabin door, but far enough to not be overheard. It's like she knows what I was bringing her out here for, and immediately explains everything to me.

Rebecca wasn't lying about wanting to help us. As we sit here, she explains she was told her son's life was on the line if she didn't do precisely what Pierce ordered her to do. That included killing the other two guests in the tents, along with another unnamed guest who was in Teagan's group.

My head spins at her admission.

"I broke the rules by leading you toward the correct path to find Skye," she admits. "I knew there was another person out there, waiting to find you. And I couldn't let them find Skye."

My next question burns on my tongue, but I don't know how to ask it.

She lets out a dry cough and shakes her head at me. "I'm not really her grandmother, dear. That's just what Pierce has ordered me to be since he dropped her in my arms a decade ago. My son loves her like a little sister, and I love her like she's one of my own."

Hearing that eases a fear in my heart that I didn't know was taking root. I was scared that Skye grew up with someone who saw her as a burden, but it's clear that Rebecca loves Skye.

I listen to the rest of her story without interrupting.

She tells me she's been raising Skye in the cabin, while also being Pierce's housekeeper. When she was informed of his wicked plan to invite us all here, she was roped into this mess the same way the rest of us were.

As someone who knows what it feels like to watch him toy with your child, I have no place to judge her.

"You're just another pawn in his game," I concede. "A pawn with wicked good aim." I raise my brow, and she and I share a laugh. "Thank you for keeping her safe. Thank you for loving her in the way she deserves."

Rebecca reaches over and grabs my hand, squeezing it. "She loves you, you know?"

My jaw drops. "She doesn't know who I am? Does she?" My heart pounds with both hope and fear.

The sad smile on her lips is answer enough. She shakes her head. "No, she doesn't know *you* are her mother. But she knows her mother is out there, somewhere. I couldn't let Pierce destroy that kernel of hope in her, so I lied. I told Skye that her mother was forced to go away, but one day she'd be back." She pauses, wiping at her face. "That someday her mother would come save her from this place and take her somewhere beautiful and magical." Her voice trails off, and she picks at her messy braid.

I open my mouth, then close it again. I haven't given any thought to what happens if we make it out of here. How can I become her mother after abandoning her? What would I tell Lee? I smile at the thought. Lee would do nothing but love her, I know that with my whole soul. But am I ready to do this? Will I even be allowed to? Will Skye *want* me?

My thoughts have taken on a mind of their own when Rebecca finally speaks again. "I'm sick, Capri. And Skye cannot stay here with them. You must do whatever you can to get her far from here. My son will help you. He knows of my wishes."

I choke back a sob. "I don't know what to say."

"Don't say anything. Just promise me you'll keep her safe," Rebecca urges, squeezing my hand harder until I finally nod in agreement.

Skye bursts out of the cabin, her face filled with terror. "It's him, it's him! It was in his bag!" She throws herself between Rebecca and me just as Lochlan strolls out.

A strange mask covers his face, and he's holding something oval-shaped in his hands. He tosses it toward us, then it explodes, misting us with smoke.

My senses go numb. My eyes go heavy. I slide to the ground, trying and failing to hold onto Skye.

Lochlan bends down and brushes a hand down my cheek. "I'm sorry, Capri. I'm so sorry. I didn't want to do this."

PART THREE:
THE FINAL GIRLS

CHAPTER THIRTY-ONE

TeaGan

I'm already manifesting what I know can't be true.

When I open my eyes, I'll be back in my apartment in North Carolina. I'll be safe, tucked into my bed. I won't be in Scotland. I won't be trapped in a smothering castle, surrounded by people who are trying to kill me. I won't have fallen for a man who turned out to be a villain in my story. I won't have watched people die in front of me. I won't be a murderer.

I refuse to accept those facts as true. I refuse to believe this is real. When I open my eyes, I'll be free.

I'm lying on something firm, but covered by a soft blanket. A door slams, and I pinch my eyes tighter as I hear hushed whispers close by. The sounds are all muffled and distorted, like I'm trapped underwater. The door slams again, leaving me in silence.

Please don't be locked in a cage again.

Please don't be surrounded by a bunch of men who want to murder me.

Please don't make me dig through another person's dead body to escape.

Please don't trust a man, only to be captured by the people he worked with to cause this.

After what feels like hours, I risk a glance. My eyes flutter open, then close shut against the bright overhead fluorescents of the room. My tongue feels like sandpaper in my mouth while my head pounds so hard it threatens to crush my skull.

I sit up, shielding my eyes with my hands against the lights, and take in my surroundings.

Manifestation did absolutely *nothing* to help me.

It's definitely another cage, but this one has glass walls instead of steel bars. There's a door on the opposite wall, but I won't even bother checking that because chances are, it'll be locked. Across from me, separated by a clear divider, I see another door. Next to it, there's a cot, much like the one I'm on, with what looks like a person lying in it. The blankets cover them, so I can't make out who it is. I hope it's anyone but Quinn.

I don't know how to feel about him right now.

He wiggled his way into my heart with his steel blue eyes and dangerous smile, all while lying to me about who he truly was.

He's the little brother of the monster who trapped us here.

How am I supposed to trust a thing he says after he kept such a momentous secret from me?

He did protect me from Travis, though. Quinn kept me whole and stitched me back together when all I wanted to do was fall apart at the seams.

The person on the cot shoots up, making me jump, even though I know I'm safe behind a layer of thick glass—as safe as I can be in a place filled to the brim with murderers. They throw the blanket off them, and when their frazzled, panicked eyes finally meet mine, I fall apart.

"Teagan?" Lexi chokes out, jumping up and rushing toward me. I can't contain my emotions long enough to tell her about the walls before she smashes face-first into them.

Lexi grabs her nose and looks to the sky. "Well, shit. So much for saving you."

My heart swells. I'm so unbelievably happy to see her that I can't even be bothered to care about anything that happened before. If anything, Pierce's twisted sense of humor has done nothing but light a burning fire of camaraderie for her and Capri both. Our friendship can conquer anything if it means we all get out of here alive, together.

Lexi slides to the white tiled floor on her side of the glass and gives me a wobbly smile. She looks like she's been through the wringer. Her face is scratched and matted with dried blood, while her normally sleek blonde hair is frizzy and tangled into a messy bun.

I wonder what horrors she's been through. Hopefully, they don't match my own. I stare down at the blood on my hands and shudder. What will she think of me when she learns about my own fight for survival?

"I'd never judge you," Lexi says. I open my mouth to respond, but she holds up a hand to stop me. "I can see it written all over your face. You're already knee deep in judging yourself. There's no room for that here." She sighs, placing her hand against the wall keeping us apart. "We did what we needed to do to make it out alive," she pauses, "I'm glad you're here."

I slide up next to her and put my hand on the glass over hers, wishing it would shatter so I could wrap her in a hug instead. "I'm glad you're here, too. Even if we are still locked in a cage for Pierce's amusement."

Lexi lets out a strained laugh. "Oh, he'll get what's coming to him. I promise you that. I'll make sure he pays for what he made me—" she pauses, her eyes avoiding mine as she gnaws at her lip.

I've always been able to read Lexi like a book, or at least I thought I could. She hid a lot from me over the last few months, but I know this isn't the time to bring that up. That's a conversation for a different time.

She looks up at me again, tears welling up in those gorgeous eyes of hers.

"Whatever you had to do, just know you're not alone in these feelings. Pierce turned me into a monster out there in those woods," I tell her, my own voice cracking heavily with unshed tears and guilt. "I'm sure the two of us can schedule some much-needed group therapy sessions when we get home," I tease, trying to lighten the mood before we both break entirely.

Lexi scoffs, then rubs her hands through her messy hair. "It better be the four of us, or I'm not going."

I furrow my brow at her. "Four of us?"

She shakes her head. "Yes, all four of us. You, me, Capri, and Lee. He's invited too. He helped me in more ways than one during our trial or whatever you want to call that horrific nonsense."

I sit up straighter against the cold glass. "Was Capri with you, too?"

"I freaking wish," Lexi replies. "She would have figured out how to get us out of that mess without anyone having to die." Her eyes drift to her fingers as she picks at her nails.

I wish more than anything I could reach out and comfort her with more than just my words, because I know there are no words to ease the burning hole in my own chest.

Before I can think of anything else to help her through this, a loud, blaring buzzer goes off above our heads. We both cover our ears and look at each other. Without having to ask, I know her heart is pounding in terror just like my own.

"Hello, ladies," Pierce's voice coos from a speaker mounted on the wall. "It's almost time for your next challenge. But first, we have to make sure you're presentable. You two are quite the fright to look upon."

My flannel is covered in blood and dirt. I glance over at Lexi and notice her purple crop top is torn and bloodied as well. I guess we both missed that in the chaos of being reunited. Or we both chose to ignore it because asking questions will only lead to more heartbreak for each of us.

I want to scream, yell, shout at the speaker, and the man perched somewhere on the other side like a coward. One look at Lexi tells me she's feeling the same way. She shakes her head in warning before I can open my mouth.

We have to play his game to survive. While this might just be a game to him, it's life and death for the rest of us still standing. Hopefully, that includes Capri and Lee, too.

The door in my room opens at the same time as the door on Lexi's side of the divider does. A red-haired woman enters Lexi's room as a dark-haired woman enters mine. They're both wearing the same attire as the servers wore during dinner.

"You will follow them, and do exactly what you're told," Pierce says over the speaker. "You disobey, and you will be punished. Nod your head if you understand."

I look at Lexi just as her eyes meet mine.

"Listen to everything they say, okay?" She urges me. "I love you, Teagan."

"I love you, too, Lex."

We both nod our heads and follow the servants out, going opposite ways.

I just pray whatever Pierce has planned next leaves us both breathing by the end of it.

CHAPTER THIRTY-TWO

Lexi

I follow Pierce's red-headed minion out of the room and into a long, sterile-looking hallway. The walls are the same glaring white as the room Teagan and I were just in, and the floor is the same hideous slate grey tile.

Clearly, someone with poor taste designed this.

Is this another one of Pierce's underground bunkers, or are we in another strange part of Windermere that Pierce only uses to intimidate us?

"This way," the minion says, ushering me through a set of double doors. I stare daggers at the back of her head. I could totally take her down if I needed to. She's thinner than I am. From the timid glances she keeps daring to give me, I know she's more scared of me than I could ever be of her.

There's nothing I won't do to get out of here and back to Teagan. So for now, I'll pretend to play this game, at least until I know where everyone is, including myself.

The new room we enter is nothing like the one we just left. We are definitely back at Windermere because there is no other place decorated this ostentatiously. I think I'd take the sci-fi hall of doom and gloom over this monstrosity of a castle.

Heavy maroon velvet drapes line the windows, their thick golden cords hanging limp on the sides. We pass dozens of closed rooms lining the long hallway before the minion stops at the base of a long spiral staircase.

"If you go up, you'll find your new quarters waiting for you. Mr. Pierce has requested that you shower and change into the dress he has left for you. You have one hour before I come back to collect you," she instructs rather loudly.

I roll my eyes at her and start up the stairs. No need to speak to the help, right? What am I supposed to do? Thank her for forcing me to play the puppet to her puppeteer? Absolutely not going to happen. Besides, I can't wait to take a shower and wash all this death off of me.

A hand grabs my wrist before I take my next step, and I look down to see the red-headed minion. She's giving me a look of panic, which is the only reason I don't jerk away from her touch.

"Please, do as he says. I can't stress that enough." She glances behind her, her expression full of fear.

I lower my voice. "What do you mean? Who are you? Are you trapped here like the rest of us?"

Her green eyes widen momentarily before she gives me a barely perceptible nod. She straightens and pulls back from me. "Just follow the rules. I beg you," she reiterates, turning on her heel and strolling back down the corridor we just came from.

I watch her until she disappears from my sight, wishing I could chase her down and beg her for more information. There's something she's not telling me. She's trapped here like the rest of us, but why is she doing what Pierce demands?

Is there anyone in this place who actually wants to be here? Or does Mr. Control Freak author have everyone here as unwilling participants in our torture?

Taking the steps up to my new room, I ponder this and wonder if I should have told Teagan that Josh is somehow twisted up in this, too. I was too scared to break the bubble of trust she extended, though, to speak of him.

What if I've just put her in more danger now that they've separated us again?

I get to my room and slam the door behind me. It's almost loud enough to muffle the sound of my heart pounding heavily with regret.

Without a second glance, I take off into the adjoining bathroom and tear my filthy clothing off, flinging it at my reflection in the mirror before hopping into an ice-cold shower.

I scrub myself raw as my teeth chatter hard enough to draw blood when they snap down on my tongue.

I don't deserve happiness.

I don't deserve forgiveness.

I don't deserve Teagan.

I should have told her the moment I saw her sitting on the opposite side of the glass wall, our friendship be damned. She *deserved* to know that Josh is a monster just like the rest of them.

I should have told her that *he's* the Axeman.

My entire world shattered when Josh stepped out of the woods and smiled at me right after I was tricked into pushing Lochlan to his death. He was the one who kissed me before I ended up at the bottom of the hillside. I should have known it was him. He was all I dreamed about for years, and then when he finally deigned to give me the time of day, I consumed everything about him.

How could I be so stupid? I can't believe I ever fell for him. I was ready to throw my friendship with Teagan away for nothing but lies and deceit.

He's a disgusting, pathetic excuse for a man, and I was stupid enough to fall for his trap. I should have known. If I had paid more attention, I could have saved everyone. Kristi, Sammy, and Lochlan.

Josh tricked me into murdering Lochlan.

My heart constricts painfully as I step out of the shower and dry off. I choke back my emotions. I have to. I can't let myself think of Lochlan, or I'll fall apart entirely. I don't have time to stitch myself together when I have more friends who need saving.

I walk out of the bathroom and look around the lavish room that's been prepared for me. The deep-forest-green duvet on the overly large four-poster bed makes me sick. It's the same color as the trees Lochlan, Lee, and I ran through to survive. The cream white curtains and rug only remind me how dirty my soul is now, and how I'll never be clean and pure again.

My eyes finally land on a garment bag hanging on the handle of the chestnut armoire. Unzipping the bag, I take a look at the assaulting bright color I'm supposed to wear for whatever comes next.

I rip the dress off the hanger and grab my makeup bag, blow-dryer, and jewelry holder from my suitcase, which has been moved into this room, and head back into the bathroom.

Quickly blow-drying my hair, I tease my blonde locks to the side, using one of my golden barrettes to pin them into place. Next, I apply my makeup, swiping black eyeliner along my eyelids until the points are as sharp as the knife Lochlan secured to my leg. I dust my cheeks with blush and shape my eyebrows with expert precision.

I take a step back, admiring my reflection. I don't look like someone who just murdered a man she could have seen a future with. If only there were a makeup brand to hide the stain on my soul.

The dress goes on next. The satin glides over my skin like a lover's soft caress. I tie the halter top in place and run my hands down my body.

The material is thin, but hugs my every curve, leaving nothing to the imagination. Usually, this is the type of dress I'd murder for.

Instead, the bright, vibrant red makes me want to puke. It's the color of freshly spilled blood. The kind of blood I've seen much too much of lately.

I swallow my nausea and slip my black heels on, then dig through the jewelry I brought with me. I wish I had my dragonfly necklace; it would go perfectly with this dress. I'll have to settle for a couple of gold bangles and a pair of pearl teardrop earrings that Capri got me at a vintage boutique a couple of years ago.

I miss her and Teagan so much it hurts.

There's a soft knock at the door. My hour of mock freedom must be up. I open the door and see the same redhead servant waiting for me on the other side.

"May I come in?" she asks, glancing behind her nervously again.

I give her a strained smile and wave her in, shutting the door behind us. I check my hair in the vanity mirror one last time.

She pulls something out of her pocket and hands it to me. "I was asked to pass this on to you." I take the black velvet bag from her waiting hand. "Oh, and this goes with it," she says before handing me a small, folded-up piece of paper.

I open the bag first and find my dragonfly necklace inside. My lip quivers as I run my fingers down the bent tail.

She clears her throat and holds out her hand again. "May I help you put it on?" I turn and watch her in the mirror as she moves my hair aside and secures the necklace with gentle fingers.

I turn around and face her. "Who gave this to you?"

She smiles and points at the note in my hand. "A mutual friend. Someone who wants you to survive this," she replies, reaching out and squeezing my hand hard before standing up straight again. "Now, I think you're missing one last thing. Give me one moment, and we will be ready to go meet Mr. Pierce." She disappears into the bathroom.

I open the note and nearly faint at the words written on it.

Give him hell, lassie.

Lochlan wrote this? When? My mind spins in circles with questions as the woman returns from the bathroom. How did he find my necklace? He must have returned to that stupid escape room to collect it.

"Don't ask me questions that I *cannot* answer," she whispers. The emphasis on her words rings clear as day. "But here, I think you need some of this to really pull the whole outfit together." She hands me a tube of my red lipstick.

"What's your name?" I ask as I head to the vanity to apply the lipstick. Surely she can answer that, right?

"Ashley," she responds. "Ashley Sutter. If that's all, Miss Lexi, I'll be waiting outside. You should use the lights in the bathroom so you don't smudge in this dull light." Ashley's tone is nothing but formal, but her eyes flick to the bathroom quickly before she continues. "Please do hurry. Mr. Pierce doesn't tolerate tardiness."

Why does that name sound so familiar? I nod and head into the bathroom to open the lipstick tube as she leaves the room. I stop short when I see a small piece of paper shoved inside and quickly open it.

There is a knife hidden underneath the seat of your chair in the dining room. We're all counting on you to set us free. And beware, the walls have eyes.

I reread the note, then flush it down the toilet before returning to the mirror to apply my lipstick.

If Pierce wants to play, then I'll make sure to give him a game he's going to die to win.

CHAPTER THIRTY-THREE

Capri

Salmon-smelling sandpaper chafes my cheek. Nudging and nipping at me until I finally come to.

I open my eyes and startle when I see the tiny kitten sitting on my chest. She lets out a small meow of protest when I sit up.

That's the last bit of comfort I'm afforded before I realize that I'm locked in a room that looks like something you'd find on an alien space-ship. The walls and floor are horrifically bland and sterile, muting all colors around me.

I look around the room in panic for Skye and Rebecca, but see neither. Instead, I see that guy Teagan brought to dinner, sitting on the ground a few yards from me. He's looking at his hands, tapping them against the floor.

The kitten hops off my lap and struts over toward him. She stops about midway and paws at an invisible barrier, then lets out a sad meow before coming back to me. That's when I notice the glass wall separating the two of us.

Teagan's friend waves at me. "I'm Quinn, that's Paw Prints. Paws for short." He points to the kitten at my feet. I can't quite read his mood, but he reminds me of a child who just lost his favorite toy.

I pet the cat's little head, earning some happy purrs in return. What an odd name for a kitten.

"Teagan named him," he adds with a gruff laugh, almost as if he read my thoughts.

Grabbing the kitten, I walk over to the glass so I can get a better look at Quinn. He looks like he's been through hell. His right eye is bruised, and the side of his head is covered with dried blood, matting his dark hair to his face.

Did any of us get out of those woods unscathed?

I wonder if he went through something like I did. Then I wonder if the blood on his hands is his or if it belongs to someone else.

"What did you do to get on Pierce's bad side?" I ask, hoping to break the tension between us. I don't know him, and he doesn't know me, but maybe together we can figure out a way to escape.

Quinn lets out a humorless laugh. "My biggest sin was being born." His blue eyes flick up to mine, and something about them reminds me of someone.

Who? Who has blue eyes like his?

"Is Skye okay?" Quinn asks, stopping my thoughts dead in their tracks.

His eyes look just like Skye's.

I gasp, backing away from him until my back hits the wall on the furthest side of the room. Far away from him.

It's him. He's the man who attacked me. He's Skye's...*father.*

Quinn stands, his confused eyes following my every move. I put Paws down and cover my face with my hands, dropping to the floor as I try to catch my breath.

His voice is laced with panic now. "Is Skye okay? Please tell me he didn't hurt her," he pleads for answers through the glass like he gives a damn about her. If he cared about her, he would have left her alone. He wouldn't have hurt me, which would inevitably hurt her.

Fury snakes through my veins as I get to my feet again. Crossing the space, I slam my hand onto the glass where his face is. "You have no right to ask about her! You have no right to know my daughter!" I scream, pounding on the glass repeatedly. "You attacked me! You should be DEAD!" I spit the last word out with all the venom in my body. If I could reach through this glass and kill him with my bare hands, I would.

Something flickers over his features before he blows out a long breath, wiping his hand over his face.

"Capri," he says gently. "I'm not who you think I am. I swear it to you. I wasn't the one who attacked you."

All I can do is stare at him as he scrambles to explain.

Quinn sighs, rubbing a hand through his dark locks. "Skye is my niece. My brother is the one who raped you. Not me, I swear it."

I shake my head at him in disbelief. "Wait, what?" I look down at him again, and that's when it all clicks together. "You're Rebecca's son, aren't you?"

His gaze pierces mine as he nods his head. "How do you know her?"

I slide to the floor with my back against the wall as Paws weaves through my legs. "Rebecca saved me. She left me this," I tell him, reaching into my pocket and pulling out the small compact. "This is you, isn't it?" I show him the photo of the young boy and he smiles.

"Yeah, that's me. Mum told me nobody had a dorky grin like that except me," he reminisces. "Is she okay? My mum?"

I wipe unshed tears from my eyes before I look at the photo again. "She was the last time I saw her—she *and* Skye. We were betrayed by someone I foolishly trusted. Now I'm stuck here with you and Paws. Totally useless." I gesture to the kitten, then add, "No offense."

The door opens on Quinn's side of the room. Lochlan strolls in with the rifle in his hands. "Well then, I guess it's your lucky day, lass," Lochlan says with a mocking grin. "It's almost time for your next task. But first, I have to teach my friend here a lesson in *family* secrets."

Quinn gets to his feet and stares at Lochlan like he wants to murder him, and honestly, I don't think I'd stop him if he tried. I might be tempted to murder him myself if he were on my side of this stupid wall.

Lochlan takes an angry step toward Quinn. Everything about this version of Lochlan is entirely unfamiliar. This isn't the same guy who helped me face my fears about meeting my daughter. This isn't the same man who kept us both safe as we ran from multiple dangers.

I don't want to believe that this person can be a monster like the rest of them.

Then he slams the butt of the rifle into Quinn's face, and I know the person I thought he was is gone. Blood sprays the glass as Quinn falls to the ground, coughing and choking. Lochlan kicks him in the ribs several times. "Family secrets aren't yours to share!" he shouts at him. "Next time she'll pay the price of your loose lips!"

I swear I hear pounding on the wall next to me, but I can't pry my eyes away from the horror happening in front of me. Lochlan rears his leg back again.

"No! Don't hurt him anymore! He gets it! He understands!" I scream, pleading with the man I thought was a friend. Quinn might be a stranger, but I refuse just to sit here and watch him get beaten. "Please. Please stop." My voice cracks in tune with my heart.

Lochlan straightens up and looks over at me. "I wish things were different," his voice is soft, almost apologetically so.

"Why?" I sob out. "Why did you betray us?"

Lochlan looks toward the door and takes a heavy breath. "Because that's just how things are. I'm sorry, I can't explain more." He heads to the exit without a glance back at us.

"Wait!" I shout. "Did you hurt them?"

He looks back and cocks an eyebrow at me. "Who?"

I shuffle up my side of the wall, trying to get closer to him. "Lee, Skye, Rebecca, Teagan, Lexi," I say their names in a rush. I swear he flinches when I say that last name. "Are they dead?" I whisper.

Lochlan gives me a stony look. How can this man feel nothing for us after everything we've survived together?. "Don't ask me questions I can't answer." He leaves the room, slamming the door behind him.

The glass wall lifts the moment the door shuts. I rush over to Quinn, helping him to his knees. With the beating he just took, I know there's a good chance his ribs are broken, or at the very least, painfully bruised. I take a look at his bloodied face and try to wipe it up as much as I can with the sleeve of my sweatshirt. His nose might be broken, too, but at least he's alive and breathing. I'm counting that as a win for the time being.

The speaker on the wall next to us erupts with Pierce's voice. "Hello, my darling. I do hope my friend Lochlan didn't give you too much of a fright. My youngest brother is a bit of a loose cannon when it comes to learning to keep his mouth shut."

Brother? Is Pierce the one who attacked me? No, he called Skye his niece in the note he left for me. Is there another one of them here?

Quinn sits up straighter and groans. "Fuck off, Atlas."

"See what I mean?" Pierce says, his voice laced with unrestrained anger. "I've given my brother the world, yet he does nothing but spite me. But no more free handouts, dear brother."

The door Lochlan exited opens again, and two of Pierce's servants walk in. They are pulling two people tied in heavy, thick ropes behind them.

Quinn and I both gasp.

It's Rebecca and Lee.

Both of them are wide-eyed as they return our stares. Duct tape covers their mouths, and their hands are tied.

Pierce laughs over the speaker. "Now, for your next task. One of them has to die. You have two minutes to decide who. If you don't choose, you all die. Aren't games fun!"

Quinn takes a sharp intake of breath, forcing me to look over at him. His eyes are lined with fear, matching my own.

How are we supposed to choose which of our loved ones gets to live—and which one has to die?

"Tick, tock," Pierce mockingly teases. "Tick, tock."

LIVE, LAUGH, MURDER
Episode 51

Teagan:

Welcome to Live, Laugh, Murder! I'm here with co-hosts Lexi Casburn and Capri Kim. We're back with another heated debate. So you know how in most thriller novels, there's usually a hot stranger who comes out of the woodwork? Either to assist the FMC or to betray them, right?

Capri:

We want to know, if you were in a thriller novel, would you trust the steamy, muscled-up stranger?

Lexi:

I'd trust them to distract me with some hot guy tricks and take my mind off the fact that I'm running for my life or being haunted by ghosts.

Teagan:
I don't even know how to respond to that.

Capri:
Does anyone really know how to respond to the
nonsense that spews out of Lexi's mouth?

Lexi:
Maybe the hot stranger would.

Teagan:
I'd never trust a hot stranger. That's like
horror movie 101. Don't fall for the villain!

Capri:
But what if they've been written into the story
because they're also trapped? They could be
sitting there thinking the hot girl is the
villain. Did you ever think about that? Not
all men suck.

Lexi:
All the men in my life suck.

Teagan:
Hey! Josh is perfect. And Lee is like the
greenest flag ever to walk the planet! One
day, you'll find your own prince.

Capri:
clears throat Umm, yeah. I'd trust the stranger. Definitely.

Lexi:
I'm sleeping with the hot stranger and then strangling him while he dreams about how epic our night was together before he turns the tables on me first.

Teagan:
Help us settle this debate in the comments: Would you fall for the villain?

CHAPTER THIRTY-FOUR

TeaGan

I'm ushered from the room right after Lexi leaves. She goes left, following the red-haired staff member, and I go right, following the brunette female assigned to me.

"Where are we going?" I ask, pulling my filthy flannel tighter around me to stave off the frigid breeze in the stark white hallway.

The brunette turns down another hallway, ignoring my question entirely. I haven't decided whether or not to hate her. On one hand, I understand that sometimes your job makes you do things you'd never have chosen to do. On the other hand, what kind of person just goes along with locking people up in cages and standing aside as they kill each other?

"You need to shower and get dressed. We don't have much time before dinner, so you need to hurry," she instructs as she pushes me through yet another white door. "I'll be back in half an hour to fetch you."

The room turns out to be a bathroom. It looks the same as every other room here: boring and undecorated. Lexi would have a cow if she saw this place. There's a mirror on one wall with the sink, and a standing shower on the other, next to the toilet. It reminds me too much of the bathroom in the lighthouse. Swallowing hard, I push the vision back. I can't let myself relive that right now.

I pull my disgusting clothing off and toss it into the corner before hopping into the shower. I quickly wash my hair and lather my body with the soap left for me. Vaguely, I wonder if there is poison in it. Or if cameras are watching me right now. That'd be right on track with Pierce's house of horrors, wouldn't it?

The shower runs cold much too soon, forcing me out and back into the real world. On a hook next to the sink, there's a white towel waiting for me that I swear wasn't there before. I dry off and turn to see a deep plum V-neck dress hanging on the back of the door, along with sharp heeled silver stilettos that are much more Lexi's style than mine.

My makeup bag has been left on the sink. Someone was definitely in here while I was naked in the shower. I roll my eyes and get dressed in a hurry—no need to give these creeps a longer peep show. There's not much I can do with my hair, so I guess I'm just going to have to let it air dry. I dab a bit of makeup on and finish putting on my shoes when the door opens.

The brunette looks me up and down. "You'll do. Follow me."

I narrow my eyes and follow her out. We turn down several more white hallways before she stops in front of a door at the end of the hall and holds it open for me. "Mr. Pierce has a surprise for you," she says, nodding into the open doorway for me to enter.

"What if I don't want any more gifts from him?" I spit out, gesturing at the dress.

The woman sighs. "I'm afraid you don't get a choice here, Teagan." Her following sentence comes out in a low whisper. "None of us gets a choice when it comes to his wants and demands."

"What's your name?"

Her dark eyes meet mine, and she flashes me a polite smile that doesn't quite meet her eyes. "Allison."

I step through the door, then turn on my feet back towards her. "If anything happens to me in there, *Allison,*" I say through a condescending smirk. "Just remember, I'll come find you, and you'll get exactly what you deserve for playing your part in this." I glare at her, running my eyes up and down her body, memorizing everything about her in a way that would make Lexi proud.

Her shocked expression gives me the strength to enter the room without a glance back. She shuts the door behind me, leaving me in pure darkness and silence so loud I hear the hairs that raise on the back of my neck.

I stick my hand out, taking small steps into the room. "Hello? Is anyone here?" My fingers brush something cold. I jump back, falling into someone's arms, letting out an earth-shattering scream before light fills the room from a rectangular window. That must be the cold thing I touched.

"Hello, there, Teagan. You look beautiful. That color suits your skin tone."

I jump away and turn, finding myself trapped in a small room with Mr. Pierce. He's blocking the only exit, and the smirk painted on his lips makes me see red.

I lunge at him, but he side steps and evades me much easier than I would have liked.

He purses his lips. "Now, now. There will be no more of that. You try it again, your friends pay." He points toward the window and winks.

Nausea and disgust roll through my body as I turn and see Capri and Quinn trapped in the same type of room Lexi and I were in.

Pierce presses a button on the wall, and their voices flood the room.

Capri is shouting at Quinn, calling him a monster. I stand as close to the window as I can, listening to their conversation with bated breath.

I'm both confused and shocked when Capri mentions having a daughter—and even more floored when Quinn says *her* daughter is *his* niece.

My eyes shift over to Pierce. "Are you—" I struggle to find the right words as the realization hits me.

Pierce rolls his eyes and scoffs. It's the first thing he's done that seems remotely human. "Please. I don't need to attack young women to get them into my bed, Teagan. I'm not like my father, or my brother," he seethes. "I know Quinn told you about his relation to me, but I assure you I'm not the child's father. And before you ask, neither is Quinn. His very presence may irritate me to no end, but he's not a rapist." He grimaces like he sucked on a sour lemon before he continues. "Alas, we have another brother. He's the real black sheep of the family, but that's a story for another time." He gestures toward the window, and I shift my attention back to Capri.

The rage on her face dissipates before my eyes as she walks over to the glass wall separating the two of them.

Oh, how I wish I had the power to snap my fingers and shatter glass with my mind.

Capri pulls something out of her pocket and shows Quinn. My heart pinches when I see the wistful smile he gives her. Then I notice Paws at Capri's feet and can't stop the onslaught of tears that trickle down my face.

I'm shouting their names as I bang on the window.

Pierce steps into the small space next to me, his hands behind his back. His navy blue suit makes my dress feel less ridiculous in this tiny room. "They won't hear you. It's soundproof," he explains in a bored tone before pulling a chair out from the corner. I watch his every move as he sits, folding his leg over his knee in that way men do. "There's a chair on your side, as well. Might as well get comfortable. You're in for a show." His blue eyes flicker with mirth as his lips twist into a knowing grin.

I pull the chair out and sit as far from him as I can in this small, claustrophobic room, just as Lochlan steps into Quinn's side of the room.

"Lochlan is working for you? Has he been in on this the entire time?" I gasp in shock. Pierce winks at me before turning his attention back to the window.

I can do nothing but watch and listen as he repeatedly beats Quinn. Lochlan rears back to kick Quinn once more, and something snaps in me. I stand, grab my chair, and slam it into the window.

Capri briefly looks my way, then goes back to watching Quinn and Lochlan. She screams and beats on the glass wall separating them until Lochlan finally stops.

Pierce shakes his head, then snaps his fingers at me. "Pick it up and sit down. I won't ask again." As much as I want to fight back, I'm worried for the safety of my friends if I don't do as I'm instructed. "Now for the fun part," Pierce says, pulling a small radio from his suit pocket. "You stay quiet, or they all die."

I don't need to be told twice. His presence is domineering enough to scare me into submission. I suddenly feel sorry for Allison. If I had to work for a tyrant like Pierce, I'd do anything not to have his ire turn my way. I wonder if Lochlan is being forced to do these horrible things, too.

Pierce gives instructions over the radio to Capri and Quinn. I have to forcibly hold back a gasp when Lee and an older woman are dragged into the room.

What does this monster have planned for them? I look at all my friends and the older woman, and pray with everything in me that they all stay safe. Though I know it'll be another unanswered prayer.

Pierce laughs into the radio. "Now, for your next task. One of them has to die. You have two minutes to decide who. If you don't choose, you all die. Aren't games fun!"

The radio goes silent, and Pierce turns toward me. "Who would you pick? Lee, Capri's dear husband? Or Rebecca, Quinn's mother?"

No, no, no. I'm not doing this again. My head spins, and my stomach rolls.

"Tick, tock," Pierce mockingly teases into the radio. "Tick, tock."

"Why are you doing this to us?" I ask, my voice shaking with barely restrained fear and anger.

Pierce cocks his head, bringing his hand to his chin, deep in thought. "You know, I wish I could tell you. But for now I'll just settle with..." he pauses, then gives me a creepy, overly large smile. "Because I can."

He shifts his attention back to the room, and I can do nothing but follow suit.

Capri throws herself at Lee the moment Pierce's staff leaves the room. My heart cracks as I listen to her tell him how much she loves him. It breaks even more when Lee apologizes for bringing us all here.

Rebecca walks over to Quinn, holding her head up and standing tall with her shoulders back. She whispers something in his ear, and his expression cracks before my eyes, then he falls into his mother's arms, sobbing. She kisses his cheeks and holds him tightly.

The anger I had toward Quinn's betrayal starts to dissipate slowly. He was only trying to keep his mother safe. How can I hate him for that?

"What are we going to do?" Capri finally says once Quinn straightens himself. He grabs his mother's hand, and they both turn to face Capri and Lee.

Lee steps forward, clearing his throat. "I volunteer."

Capri's answering wail rattles throughout the room, shaking me to my core. "No! You can't play the martyr here! I need you! We both need you, Lee!"

"Both of you?" Lee asks, his face contorting in confusion as he looks from Capri to Quinn.

I look at Pierce. "He doesn't know about Capri's daughter, does he? That's the big secret you wanted her to divulge in the escape room, wasn't it?"

"Look at you, Teagan, putting it all together. Bravo, my darling," Pierce answers, his voice filled with pride.

He can take that pride and shove it right up his—

There's a loud gunshot from the room. When I jerk my head back to the window, all of them are on the floor now. Lee is shielding Capri, while Quinn has thrown himself over his mother.

"Time's up, my friends," Pierce coos into the radio. "You have three seconds to choose, or you all die."

How can this man be so calm and collected while he ruins people's lives?

There's nothing I can do as Quinn gets to his feet. "Kill me. It's about time you got on with it. I can't wait to watch you *write* your own books from my grave."

Pierce mutters something under his breath. I turn to see his face twist into rage as he glares at his younger brother. He brings the radio to his lips again as my entire body vibrates with nerves. "So be it."

"No!" I shout, slamming my hand against the window at the same time Rebecca stands and screams, throwing herself in front of Quinn.

The gun goes off, and I see the front of her shirt turn the brightest shade of red before my eyes. Tears fall from Quinn's eyes as he cradles his mother until she finally slips away.

Pierce clicks his tongue. "Well, that didn't go as planned. But so be it. I was getting rather tired of looking at my father's trash every time she came into Windermere to clean." He stands and claps his hands together. "Now, Teagan. I have one more gift for you. Don't say I'm not on your side. Allison will escort you to the dining room now. I'm sure what you find there will be very...*informative.*"

He leaves the room, and my head spins in confusion, while the heartbreaking sounds of my friends crying continue behind me. My soul shatters as I look at them. Capri holds Rebecca's hand as Lee places a hand on Quinn's shaking shoulder. He has his mother's lifeless body in his arms, whispering to her, knowing she'll never hear those words.

I wish there were something I could do to take their pain away, even though I know it's pointless.

We are never getting out of here alive.

CHAPTER THIRTY-FIVE

Lexi

Ashley, Pierce's red-haired servant, silently escorts me back down the stairs. I have about a million questions I want to ask her, but I keep quiet and follow her lead.

My eyes narrow at every photo, every corner, anywhere cameras could be hiding and watching us.

She leads me to the large dining room where dinner was held on our first night here. I take in the surroundings, glad to be back in a semi-familiar place again. It feels like a lifetime ago that we were all in here, pointedly hating each other.

I trail my fingers across the ornate designs of the chairs and make my way to where I sat previously. My heart lurches when I realize the table has only been set for two.

What has he done with the rest of them?

I turn toward Ashley and find that she's no longer standing at the entrance to the dining hall. Instead, Josh is standing there. His arms are crossed over his chest as he leans against the door frame like he owns the place. His grey slacks and white button-up shirt are in pristine condition. The twinkle in his eyes is nothing short of predatory as they trail up and down my body.

This is the version of Josh that seduced his way into my heart with his forked tongue.

"Hello, Lex." His deep voice penetrates that traitorous part of me that still loves him. "You look stunning, as always."

He crosses the room in a few long strides and takes the seat next to me. I flinch when his hand reaches toward mine.

"Don't you dare," I hiss, yanking my hand back. "You don't get to put your hands on me ever again."

Josh lets out a huff of annoyance. "Lex, what can I say to make you forgive me? I'm just as much a pawn to Atlas's games as you are."

I laugh loudly. "You're on a first-name basis with him? Why am I not surprised? Like calls to like and all that. You're a power-hungry jackass like he is." I give him a look of pure hatred and grin when his eyes widen with shock.

He raises his hands in surrender. "You don't understand. I had to, Lex! I didn't have a choice! I had to follow the plan!"

I roll my eyes, crossing my arms over my chest. "And I'm sure forcing me to kill the guy that you saw as competition was a part of his plan?" The venom in my voice makes him flinch, which only makes me feel more powerful.

"I couldn't care less about that waste of space, believe me. Lochlan's not the man you think he is."

He *is*, not he *was*. So does that mean Lochlan *is* alive? I touch my dragonfly necklace and stifle the hope blooming in my chest.

Josh snaps his fingers. Ashley strolls through the door moments later, carrying a serving tray. She places two plates of salad down in front of us, then pours red wine into our glasses before hurrying off again.

I wish I could follow her out and run far from the fire in Josh's heated gaze. I want nothing more to do with him or his lies. He's tormented us. Stalked us, chased us. Murdered Sammy. The man I thought he was couldn't be further from his true self.

I stab at a tomato on my plate, wishing it were Josh's flesh instead. "You made me kill Lochlan."

His jaw ticks in anger as he shoves food into his mouth. "Firstly, I didn't make you do anything. Your actions were your own," Josh says through a mouthful of his salad.

His table manners were consistently awful, but now I only see him as a disgusting excuse for a man. In my eyes, he's nothing but a bug I need to squash under my stilettos. I pick at my salad as he continues his excuses, ones I will certainly not be entertaining.

"And secondly, I only did what I was instructed to do." He pauses, swallowing hard before looking at me with the most pleading, broken expression I've ever seen from him. "I had to follow the rules, Lex. He was going to kill you if I didn't. He was going to kill all of you."

I blanch at his admission, dropping my fork. His eyes are pleading and sincere. He's always been great at playing the game and putting on whatever face got him the furthest in life. My mind and heart wrestle for dominance as I look at him.

Josh reaches out and takes my hand. This time, I don't pull back. "Please, Lex. You have to believe me. I would never purposely hurt you. You know that. You know me," he proclaims, his voice heavy with emotion.

Ashley walks back into the dining room carrying another large tray, breaking the moment between us.

Josh sits back and glares at her. "Not now, Ashley," he snaps. The way he looks at her seems much too familiar, too intimate.

She jumps at the anger in his tone and nearly drops the tray. "Sorry, Sir. I'll come back later." She glances at him, her face full of fear. She avoids my gaze completely as she walks back out.

Ashley Sutter.

That's how I know that name! She's the woman he was dating when I first started working at his company. He told me she was insane and that she had stalked him after he dumped her. He filed a restraining order against her to get her to leave him alone.

It can't be true, can it? There's no way it's a coincidence that she's here now. I look at Josh, and my breathing quickens.

What did he do to her?

What is he going to do with me?

I don't know why, or how, but somehow Josh is involved in all of this. He shows up without an invite. He ends up being the Axeman who chased us through the woods and tormented me. He's killed people—he *might* kill me.

I have to get out of here. I need to find Teagan and tell her the truth about him. I'm such an idiot. Here I was moments away from falling for his lies again.

My eyes dart from the door Ashley exited through to Josh as a plan forms in my head.

I flash Josh what I hope is a sultry smile and trail my fingers up his arm. He's rolled his sleeves to his forearms, and his muscles flex under my fingertips. I have to hold back a gag the minute my skin touches his.

"What do you say we get Ashley to bring our meals back so we can eat?" I run my tongue along my lower lip, knowing it'll drive him wild. It always does. "Then maybe we can head back upstairs. I should thank you for doing everything you did to keep me safe."

Josh's eyes flare, and his mouth drops open as he stares at my lips. I lean forward, one hand trailing up his bicep as my other hand searches underneath my chair for the knife Ashley told me was hidden there.

He leans in, his lips only a breath from mine. "Oh, you foolish, foolish tease," he whispers, his hand gripping my chin and squeezing it hard.

"Looking for this?" His other hand moves in my peripheral vision. I gasp when I see the knife he's holding. "I can always tell when that little brain of yours is ticking. You're not just a pretty face, are you?" He slides a finger across my jaw before gripping my chin again. "Tell me? When did you figure it out?"

I furrow my brows. "Figure what out?" I say through clenched teeth.

His eyes narrow. "Don't act dumb now. Who told you about Atlas and me?"

His fingers dig into my skin, making me cry out in pain. "I don't know what you're talking about!"

He brings his face closer, his breath mixing with my own. Usually, this would have me begging for him, but I've never been less attracted to him than I am now.

"You know that Atlas is my brother. How do you think I ended up here? It's my job to procure the players in our family's favorite tradition. I don't know how you managed to figure it out, but kudos to you. You're not just a dumb blonde after all. My mother would have loved you. She always told me I needed to find a woman who had guts enough to kill for what she wanted. That's what made my father choose her. Obviously, they weren't in it for the long haul, but they've both helped shape me into the man I am today. A man who takes what he wants. That's why I brought you here, after all."

His lips crush into mine, and I jerk out of his grasp and slap him hard across the face. "*You* brought us here? Why?" I hear a door open from somewhere behind me, but I'm too enraged to give it any attention.

Josh rubs at the red mark on his cheek. "Contrary to what you think, I'm not my father's favorite son. Atlas is smart and cunning like him, his pride and joy," he grunts out. "Quinn is a solemn, melancholy child who was brought into this world by raping the help." He spits at the floor. "But me? Like most middle children, I've always been overlooked by our father. Until I threatened to ruin the family name by partaking in one of my father's favorite pastimes." He smirks up at me. "When he found out that I left behind some evidence..." He trails off, his eyes unfocused and wild. He looks lost in thought. A wistful, reminiscent smirk plays on his lips.

For a moment, I see a glimmer of danger hiding behind the face I once trusted.

Josh's gaze darts back to me, that danger still lurking behind those blue eyes. "Well, my father couldn't ignore me any longer, now could he? He finally had to bring me into the fold and gave me one job: bring him new toys to play with."

He stands and approaches me slowly. "It was just a bonus that you and your stupid friends dedicated an entire podcast to bashing Atlas's books. It was easy to convince them to let me choose you all for the next round of games once I made him listen to your episodes about him." Josh runs a finger up my thigh as he sucks in a breath. "You, though, Lexi, you were one of my favorite toys."

I jump to my feet before he can touch me again, just as Ashley is dragged into the dining room by Henry, the butler who picked us up at the airport. His hand is fisted tightly in her red hair. Her lip's busted, and she's bleeding down her chin.

"I'm sorry. I'm so sorry," she cries out, looking at me as Henry throws her into the room before us.

Henry gives Josh a look of pure loathing. "Fix this. Now!" he snaps before leaving the room and slamming the double doors behind him.

Josh lets out a long sigh. "But, you've always brought me more trouble than you're worth." He stands and cracks his neck. "Teagan was always meant to be mine. Watching her fight tooth and nail to survive was something special to behold. She takes what she wants and gives no apologies. I was a fool to not see that fire in her." He sneers at me before continuing. "You and Capri both were just disappointing distractions. Though I guess I should thank Capri for her part in all this." His expression turns dark.

My jaw drops. Capri...and Josh? Did they have an affair as well? How could she have been so judgmental about Josh and me when she was doing the same thing, only worse, because she had Lee waiting for her back home?

Josh steps behind Ashley and yanks on her hair, causing her to yelp in pain, forcing me to stay in the present.

"Leave her alone," I threaten, my eyes never leaving Ashley. "Ashley didn't do anything. Clearly, this is a case of daddy issues."

The fire in Josh's eyes makes me take a step back. "You don't want to piss me off right now." He places the knife at Ashley's throat. Blood trickles down her pale skin.

"No! Stop! I'm sorry, please don't hurt her! She hasn't done anything!"

"Oh? And you just so happened to have this waiting for you under your chair after being alone with her for a few moments? Thank goodness I decided to switch the chairs," he boasts, tugging on her harder and making her cry out again. "The walls have eyes! Did you think that didn't apply to you?" he screams into her ear.

"Stop!" I plead.

Josh flashes me a sardonic grin. "If you want me to stop, then prove to me you're on my side. Prove to me I can trust you, and you'll get to walk out of here, *alive*." He tosses Ashley to the floor. "Kill her."

"Absolutely not," I respond, rushing forward to help her. "You're insane if you think I'd ever choose you again. You're just as crazy as your twisted family is!"

I reach Ashley and grab her hands. "I'll get us out of this, I promise."

Josh's laugh echoes throughout the room before he propels himself toward us. "Just remember, you caused this, Lex." He grabs Ashley's hair, then slices her throat open as her hands slip from mine.

I fall back, staring in shock as she bleeds out before me. She reaches out for me, and I grab her hand. "I'm sorry. I'm sorry. I'm sorry," I cry, squeezing gently. Her eyes turn glassy before her chest ceases to move.

"You fucking monster!" Teagan shouts from behind me.

I turn toward her voice and sob in relief.

She's okay.

Then, I watch in complete shock and awe as she pulls one of her stilettos off, wielding one as a weapon, and tackles Josh in a blaze of purple fury.

Chapter Thirty-Six

Capri

Lee and I are quickly pulled out of the room by Lochlan, leaving Quinn behind with Rebecca's body.

I can't believe she's dead. I didn't know her well, but she saved me in more ways than one. She kept Skye safe and loved when I couldn't. I'll never be able to repay her for that kindness.

We follow Lochlan out of the cold, white-washed maze of hallways and end up back in the dark, ornate hallways of Windermere. The drastic change in appearance and climate gives me whiplash.

"Where are you taking us?" Lee demands, his voice laced with anger as he tightens his grip in my hand.

Having him back in my arms is more than I deserve after lying to him for the entirety of our marriage. I have to tell him about Skye the moment we get a second alone.

Lochlan heads up a set of spiral stairs, refusing to answer Lee's question. It still feels unreal that Lochlan has been in on this game the entire time. I know Lee must feel as betrayed as I do since they spent their whole trial together.

I'll never get Lee's expression out of my head after he realized he was alive and not dead at the bottom of a hillside.

Lochlan walked in right after Rebecca was murdered with the rifle still in his hand. At first, Lee was elated. He smiled at his friend and jumped up to hug him. Then, he saw the gun, and his expression fell apart into confusion and heartbreaking betrayal. I've never seen that type of devastation on my husband, and I never want to again.

But I might be the reason it happens again when I tell him about Skye.

I wish I had been brave enough to tell him about her before. I was a fool who thought keeping her a secret was somehow keeping her safe. Look where that got her! She's been trapped in this castle with a man who plays murderous games for fun. At least she had Rebecca. How am I going to tell her the woman she grew up believing was her grandmother is now dead?

Lochlan looks around, his expression almost anxious, before pulling a gold key from his pocket. He opens the door in front of us and ushers us both in quickly. The room is pitch black, and I hold Lee's hand harder. Lochlan flips a switch, and I take in our new surroundings with wide eyes.

Where on earth did this man bring us?

The room is filled with screens lining three walls from top to bottom. Lochlan sets the rifle on a desk in the middle of the room, then sits down in a large leather chair and presses a few buttons on a laptop. The whole room comes to life in motion pictures. Each screen shows a different room—a different part of Windermere. There are cameras in the gardens, the little cottage, the tents, and so many more places I don't recognize.

We were being filmed this entire time.

This whole time, the gruesome deaths, our heartbreak, our panic and terror, it really was just a game to these people. They used us as entertainment just because they could.

Rebecca lost her life for nothing. All so her death could be filmed and used as a theatrical reel for their immensely twisted pleasure.

Lochlan spins in his chair to face us. He looks nervous, and he should be. Lee is vibrating with tension next to me. I know my face is as murderous as it's ever looked while staring at another human being.

"I know I can't fix what I've already put you both through," Lochlan says. "But I had to show you this so you'd understand why I had to do it." He gestures to the screens. "I know you want to murder me. Especially you." His eyes flick to mine. "And honestly, you have every right to. But will you let me explain first?"

Lee looks to me before nodding his head. "I think that's the least we deserve. We want the truth. All of it."

Lochlan scratches the side of his face, his head hanging in defeat. "Three years ago, I was recruited here by Josh. I was living on the streets in Aberdeen. I had lost my job, my wife, everything. I was in a shitload of gambling debt, and I was hiding from some nasty people. One day, Josh appeared in the alleyway where I was living. I knew instantly he didn't belong. His shoes alone cost more than the entirety of my meager possessions did," he chuckles dryly.

"I was so angry that someone of his stature was just showing off. I nearly spit on him. But then he pulled out a wad of bills and offered not only to pay off my debts but also to provide room and board at his family's estate. I didn't care what the cost was; I needed the money more. Little did I know his family was partaking in their own little human trafficking ring."

My mind runs in circles as I listen.

"When I got here, I was wine and dined just like you all were. Then I was gassed, and woke up in a horror story," Lochlan continues. "It was kill or be killed."

"And clearly, you won. So why do you still choose to be here?" Lee asks, his voice full of contemplation instead of anger, as I expected. He's always been a calm man in a storm of emotions.

Lochlan sighs and points to the camera screens again. "Because it's not as simple as winning. This family wants total control. We're all stuck here because they have proof of us committing deplorable and reprehensible sins. If we try to leave, our darkest secrets and regrets get exposed to the world. It's either stay here and work for him, or go to prison for the rest of our lives. It didn't seem like much of a choice to me. All the workers you've seen are here because Josh tricked them and recruited them to his family estate, just like he recruited you."

He gives Lee a pointed look, and Lee turns ashen before turning toward me. "It was Josh. He's the one who told me about Pierce's once-in-a-lifetime meet and greet." Lee gasps and pulls me into his arms. "I'm so sorry, baby. I didn't know."

"None of us knew. This family has gotten away with this for decades. It's easy to escape the law when you have the type of money these people have. He changes his story every few years. Sometimes it's an exclusive trip to the hidden castle here in Scotland. When I came, it was a promise of room and board in exchange for helping around the gardens. This year's ploy was the closest to the truth, since Pierce has always been a reclusive writer," Lochlan confesses.

"This year, I was to pose as a guest and get Capri to Skye by any means possible. I didn't know you, so what did that matter to me? But when he threatened Skye's life, I knew I couldn't sit idle anymore. I've always had a soft spot for that girl. It's a miracle she didn't spill my cover. She's seen me around the garden now and then. But I guess kids really don't pay attention to the boring adults around them," he jokes, his lips curving into a thin smile before his expression hardens again. "I'd rather be in prison than watch that little girl suffer at his hands. And when I met you and realized who you were and that you and—" Lochlan's voice trails off as his eyes widen at me.

I gulp. My mind is stuck on one tidbit of his long, sordid tale. "*Josh's family's estate?*" My voice sounds weak and pathetic. I hate myself for already wanting to cover my ears and pretend Lochlan didn't risk his life to share this with us, because I know in my gut what's coming next.

Lochlan nods; his expression softens. "Mr. Pierce is his brother."

My world goes black as I take in what that means. I stumble back and trip, falling to the floor painfully. Lee is there in an instant, but my eyes are glued to Lochlan's. Nausea rolls in my gut.

"You knew?" I mutter out. "This whole time, you knew it was him."

Lochlan's wince is answer enough. "I didn't know how to tell you. I made a promise to Rebecca, and I couldn't risk you breaking before getting you and Skye both to safety. You are her only chance out of here now."

Lee looks back and forth at us, clearly confused, but as always, he chooses to give me space to figure out my own demons before jumping in to save me.

I love him for that, and I hope that he forgives me after the bomb I'm about to drop on him. "Baby, I have something I need to tell you. I lied about losing the bab—"

I'm cut off when an alarm roars. We throw our hands over our ears. Lochlan's looking wildly from screen to screen. Lee and I jump up to help.

"WHAT ARE YOU LOOKING FOR?" Lee shouts over the blaring sound.

Lochlan's eyes widen as he points to one of the screens on the wall. "WE'VE GOT TROUBLE! WE'VE GOT TO GO!" He takes off out of the room, and Lee follows him as I stare at the screen.

We've got to get to the dining room before Teagan murders her cheating ex-boyfriend.

But selfishly, I want to be there to watch Josh's life leave his cold, blue eyes.

The eyes I should have recognized every time he smirked at me from across the room while cuddling up next to Teagan. The eyes that haunted my dreams for a decade. The eyes that stared down at me and enjoyed milking every whimper of pain from me when he forced himself onto me.

The same eyes I saw when I looked at my daughter, triggering a memory that I couldn't quite grasp at the time.

I should have known when he wormed himself into my life through my best friends. But I refuse to punish myself for being deceived by him. He hid his monster too well. I've done everything to protect Skye from him, including ripping myself out of her life, and it still wasn't enough to keep her out of his grasp. All I can do now is make sure those monstrous eyes never see the light of day again, and that they never lay eyes on my child.

I check the screens one last time, searching desperately for Skye.

"CAPRI! WE HAVE TO GO!" Lee shouts from the doorway, waving to me to hurry up.

A weight hits my chest when I can't find Skye, but I know I can't waste any more time. Teagan and Lexi need me right now. I just have to pray that Skye is somewhere far away and safe.

I grab the rifle before I chase after the boys.

LIVE, LAUGH, MURDER
Episode 63

Capri:
Welcome back to Live, Laugh, Murder, friends!!
Capri Kim here! I'm here with co-hosts, Teagan
Shepherd and Lexi Casburn. We're coming at you
with a crucial question.

Lexi:
What if the person you loved was the person
behind the mask?

Teagan:
Can you tell we just watched the original
Scream?

Capri:
Hey, if Lee woke up and decided to become a
serial killer, who am I to stop him? Live your
dream, babe.

Lexi:

And you say I'm deranged! I could totally see
Lee running around in a clown mask, taking down
unsuspecting victims.

Teagan:

Ohhh, what weapon would Lee use?

Capri:

Let me ask him! Babe! If you woke up one day and
had to be a serial killer, what mask, weapon,
and motive would you have?

Teagan:

Is he getting on? Are we about to have our very
first guest star?

Lee:

Hello? Do I just talk into this thing?

Capri:

Yes, babe. Everyone, say hi to my husband,
Lee!

Lexi & Teagan:
Hi Lee!

Teagan:

Okay, Lee. Serious question here. If you were to become a serial killer, what mask, weapon, and motive would you have?

Lexi:
And before you start arguing with us about the moral dilemmas, just remember this is for fun!

Lee:
Well, if a gun were put to my head, and I had to choose. Then I guess I'd wear something normal. How many movies have we all seen where the killer is dressed in all black and has a mask that stands out? Too many. I'd probably pose as a doctor, just wearing my normal scrub cap and mask. How many people are going to stop a doctor?

Teagan:
Interesting, I like it. Now what weapon are you using?

Lee:
My weapon of choice would definitely be a bone saw. I could hide that baby in my sleeve and cut down anyone who came at me.

Teagan:

I don't know how a bone saw would do for long-distance murdering. You'd have to be up close and personal to your victims.

Capri:
Yeah, I'm all about you doing what makes you happy, but a bone saw? Baby, we can do better than that! I need you back home with me at the end of the night. We'll pause on figuring out a weapon for now. What about motive?

Lee:
Anyone who texts and drives. They'd be added to my hit list immediately. You pick up your phone while driving. I'm coming for you.

Lexi:
Okay, I sort of love you, Lee.

Capri:
This is my life, guys.

CHAPTER THIRTY-SEVEN

TeaGan

I rush past Lexi and tackle Josh to the ground. His eyes widen in shock as he raises his hand in surrender. But it's too late for him to beg for forgiveness.

Not after what he's done to us.

To Capri.

To Lexi.

To me.

He's just another man who thinks they can use and abuse the women of this world and get away with it because he has a famous family name with too much money to count.

I won't let him plead his way through the system and throw cash at whoever can get him acquitted.

No longer will I let him toy with us.

The point of my stiletto comes down hard in the middle of Josh's palm as we fall to the ground in a loud crash of body parts and shouts just as an alarm blares through the air. It stops almost as soon as it sounds, leaving a whining, high-pitched noise in my ears.

"Teagan!" Lexi cries, pulling at my midsection.

I glare at her.

"Don't you *dare* defend him! Not after what he just admitted!" I tug the heel out of his palm and bring it above my head so I can hit him again.

Lexi grabs my wrist, stopping me mid-swing. "Bitch, are you stupid!" She yanks the heel out of my grip and throws my body aside. "I want a stab at him too!"

"No!" Josh shrieks, pushing her off of him before scrambling to his feet. He's holding his injured hand like it's the most precious thing in the world to him. "You're both insane!"

Lexi stands next to me with my heel clutched tightly in her fist. I pull my other one off and do the same. How I tackled this man with one heel on and didn't break my ankle, I'll never know.

Maybe fate is a scorned woman, too.

I smile at the thought.

Josh sneers at me. "And what's so funny? You think because you did this," he waves his hand, "that it makes you this tough badass woman now? You're the same gullible whore who spread your legs for me the first night we met. You are so desperate to be loved, Teagan. It's pathetic."

Lexi steps forward. "Do *not* talk to her that way," she commands.

Josh's sardonic laugh echoes throughout the room. "You're just as sad and pathetic as her."

The double doors behind Josh swing open. My heart drops when I realize it's Lochlan. That means the entire security team must be coming in behind him. But to my surprise, it's Lee and Capri.

Lexi laughs and cries next to me when Lochlan flashes her a grin. "Hi, lassie. Miss me?" She sprints into his arms. I don't think I've ever seen her so happy or relieved to see a man before.

For Lexi's sake, I really hope that his being with Lee and Capri means he's actually not one of the bad guys. I might have to stab him, too, if he is.

Capri's gaze is locked on Josh. Her body is quivering with what I think is fear and barely restrained anger. Her hands grip the gun in her hand so hard that her knuckles are bone white. Her jaw clenches and unclenches in waves as she stares him down with eyes that threaten nothing but danger.

Somehow, she didn't know.

Something in me breathes a sigh of relief. I don't know how I could have lived with myself if Capri had been knowingly keeping that from me while I was sharing a bed with him.

We all fell for the mask that hid that monstrous side underneath.

Lee is looking at us all in confusion, but he's primarily focused on his wife's livid expression at Josh. He steps between them, whether it's to protect Josh from Capri's fury or to protect his wife from doing something that might destroy her, I'm not sure.

Josh refuses to break eye contact with Capri. "Hello, again." His lips turn into a devilish grin.

Capri chokes out a gasp. "I should kill you for what you did to me," she finally says, her voice shaking with every word.

Josh pulls a napkin from the table and presses it to his injured hand. "You don't have it in you to commit cold-blooded murder, Capri. If you did, you wouldn't have let me take you so easily all those years ago. You didn't even try to fight back." He starts to pace the length of the dining table as we all watch him. "And my, how I enjoyed myself with you." He winks at her and puckers his lips, blowing a kiss her way.

My stomach turns as acid creeps up my throat. How can Josh be so callous about what he's done to her? To us?

Lee looks back at Capri, his eyes full of shock and pain. "It was him?" Tears slip down her cheeks, and she silently nods.

With a confused look, Lexi asks, "What is he talking about?"

My own insecurity has me momentarily glad when I realize Capri didn't confide in Lexi about this massive secret either. But it breaks my heart to know she's carried this alone for all this time.

Josh chuckles darkly. "Oh, Capri, you wound me. You really didn't tell your friends about our little rendezvous together?"

"You raped me!" Capri screams.

"Call it what you want. We both know you enjoyed our time together." Josh grins. "Otherwise, you wouldn't have kept our daughter a secret all these years."

Lee lets out a strangled groan as he looks at his wife.

"Does it hurt to know that she wanted a child after all, just not yours?" Josh mocks, tilting his head in Lee's direction.

Everyone holds their breath when Lee walks over to Capri, and we all exhale when he places a gentle kiss against her forehead.

In that same breath, he tugs the gun from Capri's hands before turning and shooting Josh in the chest.

Josh gasps as his body hits the floor. He coughs out one last, rasping breath. "You're all dead now." Then his body goes slack, blood pooling around him in a tidal wave of scarlet on the ancient tan rug.

The room erupts in chaos. Lochlan is laughing. Capri has fallen to the ground and is sobbing as Lexi runs to her side to console her. Lee is standing over Josh's body.

He's dead. He's really dead. It can't be that easy. We need to find a way out of here before Pierce finds us. The only thing I want to do is grab my friends and run.

Lexi and Capri are both screaming and pointing at me, but I can't make out anything over the loud, piercing ringing in my skull.

"We need to get off this island," I shout to the group. Someone taps on my shoulder from behind. When I turn, I'm met with a person in a mask. They pull the pin in the metal object they're holding and throw it past me.

The room fills with gas, and I hit the floor the same way Josh's body did moments ago, before everything goes black.

When I regain consciousness again, I find myself tied to a chair. Lexi and Capri are across from me, tied to their own chairs. Their eyes bore into my soul, and I feel nothing but undiluted terror for their safety.

I don't know where Lee or Lochlan are, but I'm momentarily glad they are far from this.

We shouldn't have come here.

We fell for this twisted trap like mice lured in with the promise of cheese.

We weren't supposed to end up like this.

But I guess that's what happens when you reach for the stars when you were only meant to admire them from afar.

They burn you.

Scald you.

Seared you into nothing but a flame of regret.

Much like the flame alight in the roaring fireplace before us.

Our captor walks back into the room with a duffel bag slung over his muscled shoulder.

Pierce's mouth turns into a wicked smile as he takes the three of us in with his dark, amused eyes. The duffel bag drops to the ground with a loud thunk, and he winks at me as he kneels to open it. The sound of the zipper reverberates through the expansive study, making my insides quiver in fear. A fear like one I've never known before.

One by one, he takes three items and places them at our feet.

A dagger.

A butcher knife.

And a pair of metal handcuffs.

"Come on, Teagan," Pierce says with a sneer. "Choose which one of your friends gets to live." He sweeps his arm towards Lexi and Capri as if it's some sort of game.

But this isn't a game to any of us.

This is *our* life. And possibly, *our* death.

I look over at my two best friends in the entire world and, with my eyes, I tell them how sorry I am for dragging us into this. My mouth is gagged, and my body bound by tape to the plush velvet teal chair.

We wouldn't be here if I hadn't trusted Josh—if we all hadn't trusted him.

Tears trail down their beautiful faces as they shake their heads at me. It's like they know I'm not solely responsible for this. We all tried, and we all failed. But at least Josh is dead. He will never hurt another woman again. I take solace in that as I meet Capri's and Lexi's stares.

This is how we die—together until the very end.

We shouldn't have come here.

Pierce slaps me hard across the face, then pulls the tape from my mouth. The sticky fibers tear at my skin, leaving a stinging afterburn that matches the burn on my cheek. "Tick, tock, Teagan. We don't have all day for you to decide."

"Go to hell," I answer, looking into his eyes with as much defiance as I can muster.

He clicks his tongue and turns away from me, walking toward the stash of weapons he's brought. He picks up each one, scrutinizing it.

"Bring in the others," he commands.

Lochlan, Lee, and a young girl I've never seen before are escorted in by Henry. He's sporting a confident smile as he kicks the men to their knees before he leaves through the door they entered.

Capri instantly starts screaming through her gag, fighting against the binds, like a woman possessed. The girl starts crying, and that's when I realize who she is. She must be Capri's daughter.

Lochlan and Lee are both gagged and bound like us, but Capri's daughter is mercifully left free.

Pierce holds his arm out to her. "Come here, Skye." She looks around the room nervously before reluctantly going to his side. "Now, Skye. I have to ask you a crucial question. I need you to answer honestly."

She bites her lip and looks down at her pink Converse. "Okay," she mumbles.

"Which one of these fine people would you like to see die today?" Pierce asks, his voice full of mirth as he makes eye contact with each of us. Capri cries harder, shaking her head furiously. Lee and Lochlan are both yelling through their gags.

Skye shakes her head. "I don't want anyone to die." The tremor in her voice breaks my heart, but seeing Capri fall apart before my eyes is just as painful.

I look at my friends, and I realize I'll do anything for them, even if it kills me.

CHAPTER THIRTY-EIGHT

Lexi

"Just kill me," Teagan sobs. "Don't make her do this! She's just a child!" Her gaze meets mine as I shake my head in protest.

He can't kill Teagan, he just can't. We've barely gotten each other back. I'm not ready to lose her again. I shout obscenities through my gag at Pierce.

Pierce narrows his eyes at me before turning on his heel to face Teagan again. "And which weapon would you like me to use? Maybe I should get the rifle you lot murdered my brother with? I admit, I had my own issues with him. Yet, he was still family, and somebody needs to pay for his death. You would have *all* been welcome to stay here at Windermere as my staff, but you've gone and thrown that opportunity away with your hysterics and rash actions." He shoots a look of loathing at Lee. "What to do, what to do," Pierce muses while he paces in a circle around us, tapping his chin. "Oh! I know! Let's make this a game! You all know how I adore games."

Pierce stands behind me and taps me firmly on the top of my head before moving on to Capri, then Lee, and so on. "Duck, duck, duck, duck," he sings, bopping us each on the head while Skye stands in the center of the room watching with eyes wide with terror.

She looks so much like Capri. I've never been maternal, but I would kill to have the chance to scoop her up and get her far away from this horror.

"Goose. I choose *her*."

The psychopath that Pierce is points directly at Skye. The whole room ceases to breathe before we all start screaming through our gags. She wasn't even part of his circle of headbops! How can he willingly murder a child? Isn't she his niece? This man is more deranged than I initially thought. Somehow, he outdoes himself at every turn.

He looks at each of us. "You only have yourselves to blame for this. We need more staff to keep Windermere standing now that you've gotten so many of the others killed. I can't risk losing any more of you. Now her?" He gestures toward Skye, who is standing there shaking in place. "She'll take more effort than she's worth now that Rebecca has perished."

Noises I've never heard from another human being, or any animal for that matter, escape from my best friend next to me. Capri tries to stand in her chair, then slams it down to the ground. Repeating this over and over again, as we can do nothing but watch.

Pierce grabs Skye by the arm and tugs her along with him. "Come, my dear. But they need to be punished. I know you don't understand, and for that I am sorry." He digs through his bag and comes up with a small black case. He unzips it, and the air leaves my lungs when I see the syringes inside. "This will only sting for a moment. Then you'll go straight to sleep."

He doesn't have to say that she'll never wake up again.

Lochlan and Lee both struggle to stand, both of them fighting to yell through their gags.

All I can do is sit here frozen in shock.

They always say you find out if you have the fight or flight instinct when something truly horrible happens around you, but they never warn you that some of us have a full-on shutdown mode.

I've become completely immobilized as the adrenaline and fear fight for dominance in my system. There is no fight or flight in me; there is only numb, crippling, uselessness.

Skye fights against him—her screams of panic nearly rival Capri's. But no one in this room fights as Capri does. How someone so tiny can erupt with so much rage is almost magical to watch. She's gone completely and entirely feral, slamming her chair over and over again until it finally breaks apart under her weight. She falls to the ground next to me in a heap of wood and velvet.

I watch awestruck as she gets to her feet and untangles herself from the rope, her breathing rapid and her eyes glazed over with a primal fury unlike any I've ever known.

"What—how?" Pierce proclaims loudly. For once, he looks shocked, something I didn't know any of us could do to him and his perfect, uncrackable demeanor.

If I could smile under this tape, I would. It's not often you see a man look as terrified as he does while looking at my tiny, rage-filled best friend.

Capri savagely rips the tape from her mouth. "Don't you *dare* touch my daughter."

Pierce drops the case holding the syringes and rushes toward the wall behind Teagan, releasing his grip on Skye in the process.

Skye's eyes widen before a small, hopeful smile sneaks through her mask of terror, and then she runs to her mom. Capri scoops her into a bear-crushing hug and kisses her head. "Go help Lochlan get free, okay? I promise he's a friend." Skye nods and takes off toward Lochlan.

Capri watches her for a moment to ensure Skye's safety, then she picks up the butcher knife and inspects it the same way Pierce did. His features turn ashen as he cowers away, hitting a bookshelf as he steps further from her.

"Now, Mr. Pierce," she coos. "Which weapon would you like me to kill you with?" Capri cocks her head, looking more insane than I've ever seen her.

I've never been so proud of her, or so terrified.

Pierce runs from the room, slamming the door behind him as he lets out a tortured, high-pitched wail of terror.

Skye gets Lochlan free, as Capri rushes to get Teagan untied.

"That might have been the greatest thing I've ever seen," Teagan says before throwing her arms around Capri. "You went like, full on mama bear."

I nod my head in agreement since I'm still tied up with my mouth covered. A body blocks my view of them. I look up to see Lochlan grinning down at me like a madman.

"Fancy meeting you here, lassie." He disappears for a moment, then I feel my wrist go free before he kneels in front of me and carefully peels the tape away from my lips.

As soon as the tape is off, I throw myself at him, slamming my lips to his. His lips smile against mine before he kisses me back.

I've never been so happy to see this Scottish idiot as I am now.

Someone coughs, and we break apart, both of us blushing furiously.

Lee chuckles. I look up to see him, Capri, and Skye standing together, holding hands. They make a damn cute family. "How about we figure out how to get out of here before we start the celebratory smooching? We still have a crazy author to take down, don't we?"

Lochlan gets to his feet and pulls me up with him. "Aye. That we do, but I know where the limo keys are stashed. We can drive it to the ferry and finally get off this island of death."

"I can't leave Quinn," Teagan says, grabbing the dagger and handcuffs Pierce left behind. "Can you guys get Skye to the limo?" She points to Lee and Lochlan.

Lee looks down at Skye with so much love in his eyes already. "I'll keep her safe if Lochy-boy can show us where to go." Capri gives them both a hug, tactfully avoiding touching anyone with the butcher knife she's still holding before joining Teagan at the door.

"What am I supposed to use?" I complain.

Lochlan pinches my behind. "Your sass and good looks have gotten you this far, aye lassie?"

I smack his hand before pulling him in for another kiss. "Stay alive for me, okay? I'm not done with you yet." He winks before heading out with Lee and Skye.

"You girls ready to finish this?" Teagan says.

"Absolutely," Capri responds.

"I was born ready to take down the evil white men of the world," I chime out, flipping my hair back before noticing the case of lethal syringes on the floor. I grab it and pull one out. "Let's end this."

The three of us stare at each other for a few seconds. None of us says anything; we don't have to. I choke back the rush of emotions I have for these two women. I'm so proud to have them by my side, especially in this insane place we found ourselves in. While I never want to go through something like this again, I can't deny that it showed me what true friendship really looks like. I would happily kill anyone who hurt them, and I know they'd willingly do the same for me.

"Okay, okay. No sappy stuff or I'll start crying." I quickly wipe my eyes, careful not to stab myself with the deadly poison I'm holding.

"Where do we start?" Teagan asks.

Capri's face twists into a knowing smirk. "I know exactly how to find where that cockroach of a man is hiding. Follow me."

CHAPTER THIRTY-NINE

Capri

Why would we waste our time searching this place from top to bottom when I know there's a room full of screens monitoring every inch of it?

Lexi, Teagan, and I jog through the ominously quiet corridors of Windermere as I fill them in on the room Lochlan showed Lee and me. I also tell them about the security footage and how all the staff have been trapped here as hostages.

"We should be able to find Quinn, too," I assure Teagan. "I'm telling you, there are literally fifty or more livestreams going on at once. It shouldn't be hard to find him if we each take a wall."

"But first, we find Pierce. I cannot believe he ran out of there when you went all She-Hulk," Lexi chimes in, nudging me fondly with her elbow as we run. "That was seriously epic. If we end up getting out of here, I'm definitely dedicating an entire podcast episode to that moment alone."

I giggle and feel a blush tearing across my cheeks. "Shut up," I gasp with a smile.

My stamina isn't up to par after running nonstop for the last day or so. At least Lex and Teagan were able to change. I feel absolutely disgusting in my days-old survival clothing and feel horrible knowing they must both be politely ignoring the stench of blood and sweat permeating from my skin.

We enter the massive dining hall, and all three of us come to a halting stop while we take in the bloody scene before us.

Josh's body is still lying there, surrounded by a large pool of dark blood, and the gun Lee used to kill him is sitting on the dining table. I walk over, grab the rifle, then check to make sure it's loaded before walking over to where the girls have paused.

It's the other body that has my heart pinching painfully in my chest. The red-headed staff member that Josh killed is in the arms of another staff member. She's holding her and crying into her friend's chest. I don't know either of them, but I know now that they're both just like us. Pawns in this game, and we couldn't save one of them.

"Allison?" Teagan steps toward her, her voice soft not to startle her.

Allison looks up, her dark eyes full of tears and pain, leaving mascara streaks down her face. "She was my best friend," she whispers. "She was stuck here because of me. I talked her into joining me on this trip years ago. All because I wanted to travel the world." She looks down and places a kiss against her friend's forehead. "And now she'll be stuck here forever."

Lexi kneels and places her hand on Allison's shoulder. "Ashley tried to save my life, and I'm sorry we couldn't save hers. But Allison, you can come with us. We're getting out of here. Can you help us?"

Allison eyes the weapons we're all holding. "It was her dream to find a way to escape this place, for *all* of us trapped here," she tells us, wiping away her tears. "Tell me what I have to do."

I don't know this woman, but I'm in awe of her strength right now. Something tells me she's someone who would fight tooth and nail to keep her people safe.

"Can you find all the others trapped here?" I ask her, and she nods. "Gather everybody and meet us in the forest. We'll all head to the ferry together once Lochlan gets the limo. All of us are getting off this damn island."

Allison gives Ashley one last squeeze, then gets to her feet. "I'll get them all out of here, I promise. You girls, be safe. We won't leave without you." She walks toward a door opposite us, then turns back. "And if you can," she stutters, before her demeanor hardens. "Burn this place to the fucking ground."

Lexi salutes her. "You got it, friend. We'll leave what remains of this family here to rot among the ashes." They share a conspiratorial smile before Allison disappears through one door while the three of us take off out of the other.

I've never been so thankful for my uncanny directional skills as I am right now because I'm successfully able to get the three of us back to the security room without getting lost.

We all pause at the door when we hear a playful voice with a Scottish accent on the other side.

"No. Stop doing that, you wretched creature."

Teagan gasps and pushes her way through Lexi and me, throwing the door open before either of us can stop her.

"I knew it was you!" she shouts joyfully at Quinn and jumps into his arms. He looks both shocked and relieved to see her. "I'm so sorry for everything. I should have believed you. And I'm sorry for what happened to your mom." Her voice trails off as Quinn cocks his eyebrow at her. "Pierce made me watch everything. He's sick and demented. Honestly, I don't understand how you are related to him and Josh. They're psychotic."

Quinn sighs. "I'm just glad you're okay." He squeezes her tighter. "And just for the record, you can blame my father for those sick and demented genes." He looks over Teagan's shoulder, meeting mine and Lexi's gazes. "I'm sorry for everything you all went through because of my family. I don't claim any of them aside from Skye. She's a pretty awesome kid." He and I share a knowing smile, and I can't help but be happy that she still has him in her life.

"Not to kill the vibe, but why were you in here anyway?" Lexi points to Quinn.

Quinn runs a hand over his face. "I came here after Allison let me out of the white room. I figured this was the best place to find Skye and Teagan."

Lexi crosses her arms, her eyes scanning him up and down. "Fair enough. If Teagan trusts you, that's good enough for me."

Quinn flashes her a thankful smile. "Did you find Skye?"

I squeeze past him and Teagan, starting to look over all the screens as Lexi does the same on the other side. "Yeah, he and Lee have her. Allison is getting the rest of the staff out now." I point to one of the screens showing her in the kitchens directing the staff out.

"What in the hell are you?" Lexi screeches while dodging a grey ball of fur.

"Paws!" Teagan, Quinn, and I all say in unison before Teagan scoops her up from the floor. "I can't believe you saved her!" she gushes, giving both Paws and Quinn lovey-dovey eyes.

It would be adorably cute if we weren't all running from a man who wants to both murder and trap us here to turn us into his unwilling servants.

Lexi rolls her eyes and gives Paws a pat on her head. "I guess you're sort of cute," she says coolly. "Look at us! Capri got herself an actual child, and Teagan and I snagged ourselves some hot Scottish men. You're Scottish, right?" she asks Quinn. "I only ask because Josh definitely didn't have an accent, and Lochlan's is much more pronounced than yours seems to be."

Quinn raises an eyebrow at her before shaking his head. "Yes, I'm Scottish. My mother was also from America, which definitely played a part in my less pronounced accent, as you say. Josh's mother raised him in America, so he never really picked up on the accent. And Lochlan is the proudest Scottish man I've ever met, annoyingly so, sometimes," Quinn explains in a rush.

Lexi grins. "Then I guess we really did score those hot Scottish men, after all, T." She winks at Teagan before turning back to her wall of screens. After a second, she taps a long nail on one of the monitors and announces, "And that, my *Thriller Queens*, is where we find our next victim."

The four of us watch as Pierce and Henry shout at each other in a small, closet-type room.

Quinn chuckles dryly. "I know exactly where those two are hiding," he says with a twisted grin.

He may look like his brothers, but he doesn't exude that same sadistic aura like they do. Well, did. Rot in pieces, Josh.

My hand grips the rifle tighter as the slow burn of fury reignites in my stomach. "Where?"

Quinn takes Teagan's hand and struts to the door. "They're in the escape room."

"Wait!" Lexi stops and points to the computer. "We need to destroy the footage. We can't let this see the light of day. We owe that to everyone who came before us."

Quinn walks back in and sits in the chair Lochlan occupied earlier. His dark hair falls over his eyes while he types something. "There. All we have to do is type the password."

Lexi scoffs, raising her eyebrow at him. "And I'm guessing you know what that is?"

Quinn's answering smile is devilishly charming. I totally get what Teagan sees in him. "It's our father's name." He types in each letter slowly as we watch.

H-E-N-R-Y

"Henry? Like the butler guy? That Henry? He's your father?" Teagan chokes out, pointing to the screen where Henry and Pierce continue to fight.

Quinn nods and presses enter. The screens all go black before our eyes. A blinking bar appears, showing all the files being deleted in real time. "Done. And yes, that Henry. He made us all prove our worth to him. Atlas is his last hope of keeping the family traditions alive. He's done a great job of it all, hasn't he?"

I gnaw on my lip. "And how do you feel about us lighting this castle on fire and leaving them to die within its walls?"

He stands and faces me, his face alight with emotion. "I'll finally be free."

We follow Quinn out, weapons and Paws in hand, as he leads us to the other side of Windermere. We make a few stops to grab some supplies. I'll be damned if I don't give Allison the one thing she asked for: ashes. It doesn't take long before we are all standing in front of the door that leads to the stone stairway of the escape room.

How fitting that the place that started this all will be where it finally ends.

LIVE, LAUGH, MURDER
Episode 77

Teagan:

Welcome back to Live, Laugh, Murder! Teagan Shepherd here! I'm here with my beautiful co-hosts, Capri Kim and Lexi Casburn.

Lexi:

Alright, my little murderers! What's the absolute WORST thing that could happen in a thriller novel? The sky is the limit!

Capri:

For starters, the death of anyone who isn't the bad guy.

Teagan:

Yeah, that puts a real knife in the story, now wouldn't it?

Capri:

They could be trapped in a haunted house with
ghosts who only haunt the place at night by
dropping the top 20 hits of the '90s.

Lexi:

Or worse, elevator music.

Teagan:

Could you imagine a gaggle of ghosts just
jamming out to elevator music all night long?

Lexi:

Hey, it's better than ghosts twerking on your
face at midnight.

Capri:

Or what if you're the ghost and you constantly
have to relive stubbing your toe on the corner
of a coffee table?

Teagan:

I would definitely make it everyone's business
by haunting whoever was living a good life if
I had to live in pain for my eternal afterlife.

Lexi:

This topic got so off track.

Capri:

Oh! What if the ghost haunting you had a busted record player and the track just kept skipping in the background while they were trying to scare you out of their house?

Teagan:
You know, ghosts would get things done a lot quicker if they just inconvenienced people instead of trying to scare them to death.

Capri:
If I were a ghost, I'd be stealing all the toilet paper from the living. Nobody gets to use my toilet.

Teagan:
I would totally keep filling the dishwasher with dish soap and turning it on. Bubbles everywhere. All day, every day.

Capri:
Devious!

Lexi:
I don't even know what to say.

CHAPTER FORTY

TeaGan

We stand before the closed door, listening to Henry and Pierce shout at each other.

"This is all your fault! You had one job, you useless dog!" Henry screams out, his voice laced with unbridled anger.

My heart shreds in my chest when Quinn flinches next to me. The memory of Henry calling him something similar while beating him when we were hiding in the garden, hits me square in the chest.

How could a father treat his own children like this? I look at Quinn and see so much of Rebecca's kind-heartedness and goodness in him. I didn't know her, but watching her sacrifice herself for her son, I know without a doubt that she was good.

"I trusted you to fix this! Instead, you've gone and made things so much worse! Now these stupid women know everything! They will tell the world what we've worked so hard to keep under wraps! My family legacy is now in jeopardy because of you," Henry bellows. "You were supposed to be better than your brothers."

A moan of pain follows a loud crash. "Father, please! I tried my best! I tried my best!" Pierce wails.

The sound of his voice gives me goosebumps. It's the same voice that's tormented us. The same voice that made the command to kill his brother, instead killing Rebecca. The same voice that taunted and teased us for his own pleasure.

But it's also the voice of someone completely and utterly terrified. Is it possible for Pierce to feel fear and remorse after all the monstrous things he did to us?

Quinn takes a deep breath as the screams of pain continue from behind the thick wooden door.

My heart skips when I see how handsomely broken he is. "Are you okay?"

A flash of uncertainty flicks over his dark features. "I...I don't know if I can do this," he confesses. "Don't get me wrong, I want to see them punished as much as everyone else. I just didn't think it would be this difficult to watch it happen."

Quinn doesn't have to say it. It can't be easy to know that once Pierce and Henry are dead, he will be alone in this world aside from Skye. I can't imagine how torn up inside he must feel right now. I wish I knew what to say to get him through this unscathed, but I don't think any of us are leaving here without a few more sins tainting our souls.

"Hey, you don't have to stay here. You can find Lochlan and Lee and help them get everyone from the forest to the ferry using the limo. No judgment," Lexi interrupts gently. She's tugging on her red dress nervously. "I know how hard it is to grapple with that part of you who still loves the monster."

Capri squeezes her hand for support. I reach out and touch her shoulder.

Josh really did a number on us, hiding that dark part of himself over the last year.

Quinn sighs and drops his shoulders, releasing all the pent-up tension there. He looks over at Lexi, reaches into his back pocket, pulls out a key, and hands it to her.

"No judgment?" he asks.

Lexi smiles warmly at him and twirls the key in her fingers. "None at all, loverboy. You go on and keep my new favorite niece safe. We'll be out in a flash."

I've never loved her as much as I do now. Somehow, she knew what Quinn needed to hear at that moment when words and actions had failed me entirely.

"I'll do one more quick sweep to ensure Allison got everyone out." Quinn turns to me and brushes a soft kiss against my lips while taking Paws from me. "Be safe. I'll be waiting with our tiny furball for you outside the gates."

Now I know most women would be mad about the man they're crushing on leaving them alone to deal with his psychopathic family, but I'm not most women. I'm proud of him for knowing and respecting his limits. He may be the only one of us who still has the strength to do so.

Quinn kept my will to live intact during our trial and saved my life multiple times. Taking this hardship on and carrying this weight is the least I can do for him. I watch him disappear down the hall with a stupid smile plastered on my lips, knowing there is so much more for me to fight for still.

"You guys ready for this?" Capri asks, jarring me from my swoony thoughts. "Once that door opens, there's no going back."

"I'm ready," I say, grasping my dagger and blowing my unruly hair out of my face.

Lexi steps forward with the syringe in one hand and the key in the other. "Let's go show these assholes what *Live, Laugh, Murder* is really all about."

Capri looks to me, and we both stifle a giggle.

"What?" Lexi asks as she shoves the key in the lock and turns it with a loud creak.

"That was so lame," Capri says. "So, so lame."

Lexi rolls her eyes. "Hey, if we can't joke after everything we've been through, then I don't even know who we are anymore."

Pierce and Henry both go silent. We hear footsteps retreating moments later. They must be running down the stairs. They have another thing coming if they think they can escape us.

I use one of the gas containers we found in the shed to hold the door open. I'm not letting this door shut us in again. We are no longer mice in a cage for this family to torment.

Capri shushes us before I can respond, and the three of us head down the stairs slowly. The red light clicks on, casting us in demonic-looking shadows as we face off with Pierce and Henry.

"Fancy finding you ladies here," Henry muses, his lips twisting into a menacing grimace.

Pierce looks up at us from the fetal position on the floor, his eyes full of terror as he glances at his father. It looks like Henry gave his precious boy the same treatment he gave Quinn. Pierce's lip is busted and bleeding freely down his red-tinged skin.

"I'm sorry," Pierce mumbles. "I'm so sorry."

I don't know if he's talking to us, or to his father, but the smallest kernel of unease tangles my stomach into knots. I risk looking over at Lexi and Capri, and their expressions match mine.

None of us know what to do now.

CHAPTER FORTY-ONE

Lexi

I've never been one to mourn the loss of a man's power, but watching Pierce scurry away from his old ass father makes me sort of miss the strong, confident man Pierce was.

Sure, he tortured people and put us through literal hell. And yeah, I guess he was about to murder his niece to make a point before taking us all as working hostages.

But watching him turn into this pathetic mess of a coward?

It's the most pitiful thing I've ever witnessed.

Henry steps forward, and all three of us raise our weapons. "Don't even think about it, old man," I order. "You take one step closer, and this needle is going right into your eyeball."

"Please, please just let us go," Pierce pleads from his corner, cowering like a dog who's just been chastised. His voice is high-pitched and grating like the pathetic joke of a man he truly is. "We won't say anything. I promise. Just don't kill us."

Henry glowers at me before turning on his son and kicking him hard in the ribs. "I said shut up! You're worthless! You are no son of mine!"

Teagan uses the chaos to step behind Henry, and she places the dagger to his throat. "Don't touch him again."

Henry's laugh echoes through the small space, giving me goosebumps. He sounds insane. The red light doesn't help as it morphs his features into something sinister.

"You're really going to protect him?" Henry asks incredulously. "Are you that big of a fool? I know the three of you are obsessed with his books, but would you still defend him if you knew his darkest secret?"

Teagan's brows knit as she looks from us to Pierce, her blade still sitting against Henry's bare throat. "What are you talking about?"

"Father, please, don't." Pierce gets to his knees and pleads with his father.

Henry lets out a mocking snort. "Come on, son. Why don't you tell them about how their favorite author is a sham?"

Pierce pales and rubs his hands through his dark hair, leaving it in disarray.

"Nothing to say there, huh, boy?" Henry instigates, pushing himself close enough to the blade to draw blood. He doesn't seem to feel it, though. He's too engrossed in making his son feel small. "Well, let me fill your biggest fans in on the truth. After all, didn't you force them to share their darkest secrets to escape this little room? I do love a full circle moment."

Capri points the gun at Pierce. "Explain. Now!"

Pierce whimpers and throws himself back into his corner.

"What is he talking about?" I ask, walking closer to Pierce. I bend down so we're on the same level. A part of my heart softens when I see the genuine fear in his eyes. "It's okay. He's not going to hurt you anymore. You can tell us."

Henry scoffs loudly, then yelps when Teagan digs the blade in deeper.

Pierce looks to his father, then his bright eyes flit back to mine as his breath quickens. "I'm not a real author." He shifts back to his knees, biting at his nails while he looks at each of us. "Quinn is my ghost writer.

We forced him to write the stories so we could get a big enough fan base to lure enough of you here." He looks down at his shoes with shame.

"It was my idea, brilliant, wasn't it? Quinn was always a talented kid; he takes after his father," Henry says with pride. "But I couldn't risk letting him leave. I couldn't trust the boy to come back like Josh always did. And Atlas here was being trained to take over," he snaps at Pierce before continuing. "So we traded Quinn's mother's safety for new stories. She was allowed to stay and raise Skye while he wrote. Saying that out loud makes it seem foolishly unbelievable, but it worked. It got the lot of you here, didn't it?"

Pierce sobs loudly into his hands.

"Is that true?" Teagan asks. "Did Quinn really write all the books for you?"

"Yes," Pierce concedes. "All but the last one. He refused to write it after realizing we planned to bring more people here. He thought that if he stopped writing, nobody would want to meet him. Father had me write it instead."

Well, it makes sense why the last book was absolute trash. What kind of ridiculous idea is that? Every time I think this family can't get any crazier, they drop some crap like this on us.

"You realize how insane this is?" Capri says to Henry. "You forced all your children to do your bidding for this?" She gestures at the walls of Windermere. "Because you wanted free labor to take care of your pretentious castle? Why?"

All Henry does is shrug, before his lips twist into a sardonic grin. "Because I can."

"You're completely deranged," I quip. "It's a wonder your children didn't murder you in your sleep."

This elicits a reaction from him. The smile disappears, replaced by a grimace. He glares at me, his nostrils flaring with anger. "My children wouldn't dare. They are weak and useless." Henry spits at Pierce. "Besides, I no longer have any children. I refuse to claim this useless trash as my own kin."

Pierce lunges at me, catching me off guard and wrestles the syringe out of my hand with a grunt before hopping to his feet. I scream and wait for the enviable pierce of pain, but it never comes.

Instead, we all watch in shock as Pierce shoves the needle into Henry's eye and empties the contents with a furious shout. "YOU ARE NO FATHER OF MINE!"

Henry's body goes limp and hits the ground within seconds. Teagan moves faster than I've ever seen before and is at my side a moment later, helping me to my feet. Capri's mouth is open in shock, but she shakes it off quickly and points the rifle barrel at Pierce.

He raises his hands in surrender and falls to the floor next to his father's body. "Just make it quick." His voice is empty and emotionless.

Teagan surprises us all when she pulls the handcuffs from her bra and snaps one side onto Pierce's wrist, then closes the other around her own wrist. "How about we make you a deal?" she says, pointing the dagger's tip at him. "You come with us and tell the world everything that happened here, and you get to live. You refuse, and Capri will shoot you and leave you to die here with him." Her eyes blaze as she stares at Pierce, daring him to call her bluff. "Remember that you'll also have to tell them that Quinn is the real brilliant mind behind the novels. You'll most likely end up serving life in prison, as well. But, the choice is yours."

Pierce lets out a sigh of defeat, and he and Teagan get to their feet. "I'll do whatever you want. Just get me out of here."

"It's more than you gave us when you lured us here." I scoff and push him toward the stairs, Teagan following right behind him with the dagger still pointed at his back.

We reach the top of the stairs, and Capri grabs the gas container. The door to Henry's tomb closes loudly behind us, sealing him within his precious castle forevermore.

CHAPTER FORTY-TWO

Capri

Lexi and I take turns splashing gasoline throughout the halls of Windermere while Pierce and Teagan lead us toward the exit.

I can't believe we're actually getting out of here. I pictured this moment in my head so many times throughout this ordeal, but I never really thought it would happen. Every time I dreamt about it, I also dreamt that one of us was left behind.

We reach the front doors just as the canister runs dry.

It feels like fate.

We survived. We're about to go home.

This place may have turned me into a monster and stained the walls of my soul for eternity, but it also gave me so much more. I would have never been reunited with my daughter if I hadn't come here.

All the bad that happened doesn't outweigh that miracle.

Teagan throws the door open, and Lee, Skye, Quinn, and Lochlan are waiting on the other side. They're all huddled up near the front gate of Windermere.

We did it.

I run straight into Lee's waiting arms and scoop Skye into the hug. "We made it. We actually made it out alive." Lee kisses my head, and Skye squeezes me tighter before a tiny meow of protest breaks us apart.

"Oops," Skye says sheepishly. "I forgot I was in charge of Paws." She reaches into her hoodie pocket and pulls the kitten out to snuggle her. Quinn steps up and ruffles her hair before giving Paws some ear scratches, then makes his way over to Teagan.

"Where is everyone else?" Lexi asks from under Lochlan's arm.

Lee points to the limousine waiting on the road just past the gates. "Most of them are at the ferry waiting for us. Allison went into the garden with a few others to do one more sweep of the grounds to make sure everyone was out. Besides, we couldn't let you girls do everything yourselves, now could we?" he teases, pulling out an emergency flare from his back pocket. "Figured you'd need something to start the fire."

Lexi's jaw drops open. "How did we forget about matches? We can't start a fire without, you know, actual fire?"

"Don't worry, lassie. We got you." Lochlan chuckles and takes the flare from Lee. "Found this puppy on the ferry boat. Who wants to do the honors?"

I set the rifle down, let it rest against the fence, and face my friends and family as Pierce keeps his head bowed next to me. He's been nothing short of a model prisoner. "It doesn't matter who does it as long as this place burns to the ground."

Quinn steps up from behind Teagan, ignoring his brother's presence entirely. "May I?"

I hand him the flare just as Teagan is yanked backward. She hits the wrought iron fence with a shout, banging her head and sliding to the ground. Pierce grabs the rifle, and he tugs her arm up with him, making her cry out in pain as she stumbles to her knees.

"Nobody move!" Pierce orders, pointing the gun at us in sweeping motions. "You really thought you'd win? You don't get to come into my home and ruin my life. Windermere is mine now."

We all look to each other, knowing it's hopeless. Pierce has the gun that I stupidly discarded because I thought we were finally out of this nightmare. I was so stupid to believe it could be this simple. The only way out of this is to tackle him simultaneously, but even that leaves too much room for error.

An error right now will result in more deaths.

"You don't want to do this, Atlas," Quinn says in a low voice. "Just let us go, you can have the castle. You can have it all."

Pierce chuckles. "The only way I get everything I want is with all of you in the ground." Skye whimpers from behind me, and he turns toward us. "Skye, my dear. Come here."

"Don't you touch her," Lee says through gritted teeth, stepping sideways to help shield her. "Leave my girls alone." I interlock my fingers through his and squeeze tightly.

"You silly idiot, did you not hear me? There's no escaping this island. You're all going to die here." Pierce laughs maniacally. "Might as well start with you."

The gun goes off, and I feel Lee's body jerk beside me.

Everything is in slow motion as I look to him; his wide eyes meet mine before he looks at his shirt. Bright crimson oozes from his sternum before his body hits the ground with a muted thud.

Someone is screaming.

Hands are on his chest as hot, viscous liquid pours out of the wound.

Lee's eyes struggle to stay open as he chokes on his own blood. "I love you. I'll always love you."

It takes a moment to realize what's happening.

They are my hands.

I'm the one screaming.

And Lee is dead.

Rough hands are pulling on me, tugging me to my feet. "We have to leave! Now!" Lochlan shouts.

I look around, and I'm met with a flurry of activity.

A group of people comes running out of the garden. The only person I recognize is Allison. She sees Pierce and lets out an earth-shattering scream as she runs at him with a hammer raised over her head. She swings it down, and a spray of blood hits her face as she smiles. Someone else comes running with a pair of bolt cutters. There's a frenzy of movement as the others follow suit with various makeshift weapons of their own. They surround Pierce, pausing for what feels like hours. Then the screaming starts. That weak, pathetic wail rings through the air.

It stops moments later.

Allison steps out of the circle surrounding Pierce, and I see what's left of him. They've beaten him to a bloody pulp.

"Teagan?" I whisper, my heart pounding in fear when I remember she was handcuffed to him.

Lochlan picks me up and carries me. "She's okay. They cut the handcuffs before it started. She's with Quinn. Lexi has Skye." His voice is clipped and odd-sounding, and I look up at him. I'm met with tears that match my own.

He's crying because Lee is dead.

"I'm so sorry," Lochlan chokes as he stops in front of the limo where Quinn is waiting.

I look back at my husband's lifeless body, swallowing the grief that's come to life inside of me. "I can't leave him here."

"We'll get him," Quinn says before he opens the door for me. He's still holding the flare. "We'll bring him home."

I fall into the limo and into Lexi's and Teagan's waiting arms, letting them hold me together as I fall apart. This can't be real. It was supposed to be over. We were supposed to be safe. But now, Lee is dead, and nothing will ever be the same again.

"Capri?" Skye's voice both calms and startles me, and I sit up to face her. Her lip quivers as she tries so hard to stay strong. "Mom?" she says hesitantly. I open my arms, and she falls into them, holding me tight.

Teagan and Lexi wrap themselves around us as others file in. I can't decipher faces or think of anything but keeping myself whole for Skye. All I can feel is a weight crushing numbness as the limo starts to pull away from Windermere.

We watch the flames come to life in the safety of each other's arms as we cry for the ones we lost here. We mourn the people we were before this place laid claim to our souls, taking pieces of us we will never get back.

Epilogue

THREE MONTHS LATER

TEAGAN

"A re you ready for this?" Quinn asks, fiddling with the tie I got him last month for his birthday.

Once everything about Pierce and his family came to light, Quinn could finally take credit for the books he wrote. He's being interviewed today to discuss it on one of the local radio stations, and I couldn't be prouder of him.

I place my hands over his, stilling them. "I'm always ready. But you, my love, seem riddled with nerves," I tease. "What can I do to help?"

He blows out a long breath. "I've never been in the spotlight before. I was always fine hiding in the background. I don't know how to discuss my part in these books, knowing it's being filmed for the whole world to hear. I've never been allowed to talk freely about them before."

I grab his face and kiss him gently. "It's one interview. We'll all be there right next to you. Lexi and Capri will meet us here, then we can go to the station together."

"Yeah, but you girls do this for a living. I'm the newbie here, and it's a bit nerve-racking."

"First off, you don't need this," I tell him as I pull his tie off. "It's a podcast, no real cameras required. You could sit there in your briefs if you felt more comfortable that way."

He raises a brow at me. "Oh, don't tempt me. I may scare the radio hosts off when I decide to jump into the booth and ravish you instead of doing this interview."

"Any other day, I'd probably let you. But this is a big deal, Quinn. You should be proud of how far you've come." He rolls his eyes at me as he nips playfully at my neck. "Besides, you won't be the only newbie there. Lochy is coming too."

His lips pause as he looks up at me. "Really? He's coming?"

I nod. "Lexi's picking him up from the airport and driving straight here. It was supposed to be a surprise."

We haven't seen Lochlan since he returned to Scotland after Lee's funeral. He needed space to process everything and volunteered to ensure all the staff Pierce held hostage got home safely. He also cooperated with the police as they investigated what happened at Windermere, so he needed to stay in Scotland. Lexi has traveled back and forth a few times to visit him, but this is the first time we will all be back together in months. She told us the island is still standing, but the castle is nothing but rubble.

Good riddance.

Quinn pulls me to the bed, so I'm straddling him, and kisses my neck again. His fingers travel up my spine, making me flush. "I guess if Lochlan can brave the world, I can too," he says against my heated skin. "But first, I have other plans with you."

I laugh against his lips as Paws jumps onto the bed with us, inciting a groan from Quinn. He pushes me off his lap and grabs Paws, kissing her little nose before setting her outside the bedroom door. "You're too young to watch the things I'm about to do to your mother in here." Paws meows and walks down the hall. He closes the door quietly before diving back into bed with me.

I still can't believe this man is mine. He came back to America with me and moved in almost immediately. I know, I know. Taking things slow would have been the smart thing since both of his brothers and his father tried to murder me.

But after what we went through and watching Capri lose the love of her life, I refuse to let life pass me by.

I'm in charge of my own fate now, and all I want is him.

LEXI

I hate airports. The parking is expensive. The elevators take five million years. The crowd is too... crowded. And half the time, the coffee shop is closed for no reason other than to make my trip to the airport even worse than it already is.

But, while I hate airports, I also sort of love them.

I love watching children's faces light up when they finally spot their grandparents. And don't even get me started on military homecomings. I bawl like I'm an extra in a Hallmark movie every dang time.

My favorites, though, are when I'm people-watching and get to see the faces of those long-distance couples when they spot each other after looking nervously at each face that passes the gate. The joint excitement and reunions just bring out that sappy side of me that always wished for someone to look for me with nerves in their chest and hearts in their eyes.

And now it's my turn.

I'm standing on the tips of my toes as I search the baggage claim, desperate for the tall, burly, Scottish man of my dreams.

I've never felt this way about anyone before. I swear, this idiot lights my heart up from the inside out when he's with me.

Is this what love feels like? I can see why everyone's always yapping about it, now, because I might be helplessly in love with the guy.

There's a gentle tap on my shoulder. "Looking for me, lassie?" I jump into Lochlan's arms with a squeal before kissing him soundly. "I'd take that as a yes," he laughs against my lips.

With heavy reluctance, I release my hold on him. "Let's get your bag and get out of here. If we hurry, we'll have an hour before we meet everyone at Teagan's. You're going to surprise the hell out of Quinn."

Lochlan squeezes my hip. "Bags, lassie. I've got *bags*. And we will have loads of time together. That is, if you'll have me. And if I know you girls the way I think I do, then I know Teagan's already spilled those beans."

My eyes widen as I take in his words. "Are you serious right now? You're staying? Here, in America?"

He smiles that adorably lopsided smile at me and kisses my nose. "Only if you'll have me. My visa is good for three months as I search for a job here."

I let out an excited scream, startling a group of people waiting for their bags, and jump right back into his arms. "Yes, yes, yes, you big oaf. Stay forever." I gush, then take a glance at his shoes.

"I threw my favorite alligator shoes away just for you," Lochlan tells me with a grin.

"Miracles do happen!" I tease before my lips meet his. My heart explodes with happiness when he kisses me back with a smile.

I want him now, and forever. It's the least we deserve after surviving what we did.

We untangle, and he quickly finds his *seven* neon green bags.

"Those are absolutely hideous," I say with a sneer while he figures out how to squeeze all of them in my car.

He has to try three times to get my small trunk to close, but he grins when it finally does. "It's not my fault you fell in love with a horrible, fashion-challenged *oaf*, now is it?" He pushes me against the car and finally kisses me the way I crave. His tongue teases mine, and all my senses fly away when he grips my face to deepen the kiss.

"I do love you, you know." I gasp when we come up for air. "But you love me, too."

Lochlan grins. "I do, lassie, I sure do."

<u>CAPRI</u>

Grief is like a train that never stops running. The tracks are infinite, never derailing.

It's been three months since I lost Lee. Three months of living with a hole in my heart the size of his love. Three months of reminding myself that I'll never see his smiling face again.

Three months of an emptiness that sears itself into my very bones, flaring up anytime I forget for even one moment.

But today, I don't have the energy or time for grief. Today, I have to be strong—for myself, for my friends, but primarily for my daughter. Because today is Skye's first day of school, and the girl is nervous as all get out.

Rebecca homeschooled her at Windermere the entire time she was there, so Skye has never been in a classroom setting, let alone around children her age. I know she'll do great; she's light-years ahead of any child in her grade. Rebecca taught her well, and I thank her every day for being there for my baby girl when I wasn't.

Skye shifts her purple backpack nervously as she stares up at the doors of her new school. "I'm scared."

I bend down and brush a hair from her cheek. "I know, baby, I know. Change is scary. But I promise you'll have so much fun. You're going to meet so many new friends."

She looks around the school yard and watches the other kids with interest. "What if they don't like me?"

"Then you'll find one who does. All it takes is one friend to make you feel invincible."

She cocks an eyebrow at me. "But how did you get two best friends? You have Aunt Teagan and Aunt Lexi?"

My heart thumps happily in my chest as I remember first meeting them. It's a nice change-up from the painful pulsing it usually does these days.

"Well, I got lucky with them." I wink at her, making her laugh. "But you know how I got so lucky?" She shakes her head. "I walked right up to them with chocolate treats and a smile and introduced myself. You just have to be yourself, sweetheart. After all, you're my favorite human on the planet. And if you keep being yourself, you'll be someone else's favorite, too." The bell rings, and I stand and kiss the top of her head. "I love you."

Her blue eyes take my breath away when she looks up at me. I no longer see her father's eyes when I look at them. I only see hers. "I love you, too, Mom. Hopefully, I'll get to meet my own best friends today." She grins and salutes me before walking toward the school's double doors. They are only a few feet away from where I'm standing, but I find myself holding my breath the moment she steps away from me.

I wonder if I'll ever get used to the fact that she's mine now, and that she'll always come back.

My heart stills when two girls stop her before she can enter. "Hi, my name's Skye." She pulls two beaded bracelets we made last night off her wrist and hands them to the girls. The two girls smile at her, take the bracelets, and put them on their wrists.

"Want to be our friend?" the blonde girl asks.

Skye beams and nods her head. "Yeah."

The brunette girl fist bumps her, and all three link arms and head into the school together.

"I wish you could see our girl, Lee. You'd be so proud of how brave and strong she is," I whisper as I head back to my car. A magnolia flower falls from the tree above me and lands on my windshield.

I let out a strangled laugh as I pick it up. Lee may not be here with us, but I know he's always watching from above.

My phone goes off, and I see Teagan's name on the screen. "What's up?" I ask.

"Lexi and Lochlan just got here! Where are you?"

I can hear Lochlan laugh at something in the background and smile when Quinn and Lexi shout something.

"I'm heading that way now," I tell Teagan, putting my car into drive. "Sorry, I missed out on the surprise!"

"Teagan spilled the beans before we even got here!" Lexi shouts. "Hurry up! We miss you!"

"Can't get this show on the road without our favorite, Mama bear!" Lochlan chimes in.

Quinn laughs again. "You guys are really serious about this whole group thing, aren't you?"

"Oh, hush, you guys! She's on her way!" Teagan yells before the call drops.

I smile and turn my music up as loud as I can while singing to the lyrics to some '80s mix Lee loved because I know that somehow, someway, we're all going to be okay again one day.

This world tried to break us, and it failed.

THE END

Acknowledgements

It's surreal that I'm here again, writing the acknowledgements for yet another book. I'll keep this short and sweet since this isn't my first, second, or even third rodeo now. I'm so thankful to so many people, and with each book, that list just grows. You guys really know how to make a lady feel special.

Zach: There aren't enough words on the planet to express how much I love you and how thankful I am to have you by my side in this lifetime. Thank you for loving me on my most unlovable days, and for supporting me when I'm about to call it quits. You are my best friend, and I'm so glad I get to keep you for life.

Annabell and Cassian: You both are my whole heart and soul. I love you more than my own life. You inspire me every day to better myself and to become the best version of myself I can be. Thank you for loving me during the hard times, the late-night writing sprints, the daytime "leave me alone while I finish this scene" moments. I hope I'm your favorite author one day.

Esther: The other half of my dark and twisty soul. Thank you for being my person, through thick and thin. The Grey to my Yang. The Petty to my Betty. The Ivy to my Florence. I love you to the Moon and to Saturn. Thank you for 14 years of friendship and for helping me bring the best versions of my characters to life. I love you, always and forever.

Marisa: Thanks for always answering when I call to spiral about something you could probably care less about. I'm so thankful to have you as my built-in best friend for life. My world is so much brighter with you in it.

To my family: Thanks for believing in me and supporting this life-long dream of mine. And thank you for reading my spicy scenes and then never, ever bringing them up at family dinners. I die a little inside every time I know one of y'all will read these scenes, lol.

Rebecca Amiss: This book wouldn't exist without you. Neither would Lexi and Lochy, and I mean that with my entire soul. You helped turn this story into something wonderfully thrilling, and without you, it might not exist. I can't wait to see what our characters get into one day. I'm still SO down to write a joint series featuring Auden and Maisie.

Bex: Thanks for editing the crap out of this book. I love you. I love singing *Spice Girls,* obnoxiously loud with you while sipping—okay—chugging, champagne by your side. Thanks for turning this novel into something worth reading, and for catching all my repeated words and all that jazz. You're totally the Jackie to my Shadow, and we are basically sharing a nest now as we bring our stories into this world together.

To my early readers, Zach, Rebecca, Esther, Emma, Haley, Katherine, Bex, Kaitlyn, Mary, Beate, Amber, Taylor, Kayla, and Mads: You guys literally made me smile nonstop with your hilarious, unhinged feedback. Some of you have read for me before, and some of you are new here, but you are TRULY the best group of early readers, and I hope you know how loved and special you are to me. Sorry, I traumatized you...again.

To my wonderful street team; the Twisted Little Love Birds: You all have been so amazing and I'm forever and ever so thankful for you all. Thanks for hyping this book up when I was ready to throw her in the dumpster and light it on fire. I can't wait to add all your names into my future books. Beate helped teach Teagan german, while Taylor and Mads might own a bakery in this one, but Amber didn't get so lucky. Sorry, I might have killed you off.

To my cover designer; Katie: Thank you for bringing the cover of my dreams to life! I still cannot believe how perfect it is, and how beautiful you made it after only seeing a couple of really, really, bad mock up's I made. I'm so excited to start working on PNTT so I can show off that beauty soon!

Zelda, my favorite furry lady: Every book I write has the best feline companion because of you. But take notes, little lady. They don't meow at their people 24/7 for snacks—or keep them up all night with their zooms. But they also can't curl up on my lap as I write emotionally devastating scenes either. So I guess I can forgive you for your midnight shenanigans.

And lastly, to my readers: Let me say thank you to YOU as the reader. I am honored that you chose my book to pick up and read out of all the billions of novels out there. I hope that some part of this story resonated with you, and I hope that everyone is able to find a small piece of themselves within these characters. I couldn't do this without you. Truly. Knowing that my stories are being read is the greatest gift in the world as a writer. I am so blessed to have made such wonderful friendships online through the bookish community.

Also, if it isn't too much, please consider about leaving a review wherever you write reviews! Reviews are so incredibly important for authors, and I would truly appreciate it. You guys have literally made my dreams come true.

Love always,
Danielle

P.S. Tlktklxtklxtklxtktk - Cassian 4/23/25 (I found this little note from my five-year-old son typed into one of my chapters and told him I would add it to the acknowledgments.)

Danielle Morris

is an independent author who spends her time writing thrillers with a dash of romance and comedy. She has been dubbed the romantic thriller queen by her colleagues since publishing her debut novel, BIRDS OF A FEATHER, back in 2023. She released her second novel, IN ALL MY DREAMS, a year later, while diving into the paranormal side of the thriller genre. Danielle is a hopeless romantic at heart, with a dark and twisty soul. She enjoys late-night walks on the beautiful beaches in North Carolina with her family, extra creamer with marshmallows in her morning coffee, and loves cuddling her cat, Zelda, while coming up with new ways to off someone in her stories.

Connect with her online @daniellemorriswrites